DANTE ALIGHIERI was born in Florence, Italy, in 1265. His early poetry falls into the tradition of love poetry that passed from the Provençal to such Italian poets as Guido Cavalcanti, Dante's friend and mentor. Dante's first major work is the *Vita Nuova (New Life),* 1293–1294. This sequence of lyrics, sonnets, and prose narrative describes his love, first earthly, then spiritual, for Beatrice, whom he had first seen as a child of nine and who had died when Dante was twenty-five.

Dante married about 1285, served Florence in battle, and rose to a position of leadership in the bitter factional politics of the city-state. As one of the city's magistrates, he found it necessary to banish leaders of the so-called Black faction, and his friend Cavalcanti, who like Dante was a prominent White. But after the Blacks seized control of Florence in 1301, Dante himself was tried in absentia and was banished from the city on pain of death. He never returned to Florence.

We know little about Dante's life in exile. Legend has it that he studied in Paris, but if so, he returned to Italy, for his last years were spent in Verona and Ravenna. In exile he wrote his *Convivio,* or *Banquet,* a kind of poetic compendium of medieval philosophy, as well as a political treatise, *Monarchia.* He probably began his *Comedy* (later to be called the *Divine Comedy* and consisting of three parts, the *Inferno,* the *Purgatorio,* and the *Paradiso*) around 1307–1308. On a diplomatic mission to Venice in 1321, Dante fell ill, and returned to Ravenna, where he died.

The Divine Comedy of
DANTE ALIGHIERI

INFERNO

A Verse Translation

*with an Introduction
by Allen Mandelbaum*

Notes by Allen Mandelbaum
and Gabriel Marruzzo
with Laury Magnus

Drawings by Barry Moser

BANTAM CLASSIC

THE DIVINE COMEDY OF DANTE ALIGHIERI, translated by Allen Mandelbaum, is published in hardcover by the University of California Press: Volume I, INFERNO (1980); Volume II, PURGATORIO (1981); Volume III, PARADISO (1982). Of the three separate volumes of commentary under the general editorship of Allen Mandelbaum, Anthony Oldcorn, and Charles Ross, Volume 1: THE CALIFORNIA LECTURA DANTIS: INFERNO was published by the University of California Press in 1998. For information, please address the University of California Press, 2223 Fulton St., Berkeley, CA, 94720.

THE INFERNO
A Bantam Book

PUBLISHING HISTORY
University of California Press edition published 1980
Bantam Classic edition / February 1982
Bantam Classic reissue / August 2004
Portions of this translation, passages from Cantos XXV and XXVI, first appeared—in an earlier version—in THE DENVER QUARTERLY. The penultimate version of Canto XXVI first appeared in its entirety in THE ITALIAN QUARTERLY.

Published by
Bantam Dell
A Division of Random House, Inc.
New York, New York

ISBN 978-0-553-21339-3

Manufactured in the United States of America
Published simultaneously in Canada

BVGM 56

INFERNO

CONTENTS

INTRODUCTION

Dante is an exiled, aggressive, self-righteous, salvation-bent intellectual, humbled only to rise assured and ardent, zealously prophetic, politically messianic, indignant, nervous, muscular, theatrical, energetic—he is at once our brother and our engenderer.

We may ponder the divide between the modern and the medieval or profess our distance from Dante, but that profession only masks proximities more intimate than those that link us to antiquity. Even our recovery of the judgmental, ethical aspect of Dante, our anathemas against any Romantic falling prey to (heaven forbid) over-sympathy with Francesca, Farinata, or Ulysses, carries sanctimonious overtones only too easily available to us. Indeed, some contemporary Paraphrasts are more ready to bludgeon homiletically, to damn again the already damned, than even Dante himself—the greatest of execrators—is. And when we come to the allegorical efforts of the fourfolders, or to our frequent willingness to integrate even Dante's lateral similes into overbearing structures, we have not ventured that far from our selves. Ours, too, is an age of allegoresis; Walter Benjamin is always there, his riches ready to be ransacked or counterfeited. In sum, however more cunning he is than we are, Dante is certainly much nearer to us than is his guide, his governor, his master *(Inf.* II, 140), Virgil.

Therefore, the task of the modern translator of Dante is much more synonymic and much less metaphorical in kind than the task of the translator of Virgil. Virgil demands more de-selving of the modern translator—so much more that I was slow to hear all his demands.

For I had begun by seeing Virgil from the Dante vantage during the six years I spent translating the *Aeneid,* a work which often interrupted my translation of the *Comedy;* I was seeking in the *Aeneid* what Macrobius (in his *Saturnalia* v, i, 19) called a style "now brief, now full, now dry, now rich ... now easy, now impetuous." That style (those styles) I reached with relative ease by the third draft. Only in the later drafts did I find a music that lay far beyond what I had first been seeking: measures where the violence of silence and the violence of speech are balanced and appeased in a uniquely Virgilian equilibrium (as in the Palinurus passage at the end of Book Five of the *Aeneid).*

That equilibrium involves almost unlimited compassion and patient, unjagged breath—but, also, limited curiosity, tight verbal decorum, the most drastic lexical restraints. In my own work as a poet, the release from Virgil produced *Chelmaxioms* and the forthcoming *Savantasse of Montparnasse.* And my return, as translator, to Dante, at least in the *Inferno,* delivered me again to one who is almost wholly given to the violence of speech—even when that violence is directed to talking about the impossibility of talking about the untellable. For Dante is an Aeolus-the-Brusque, a Lord-of-*Furibundus*-Fuss, the Ur-Imam-of-Impetus. Or, for brutish Scrutinists, who reach for similes among the beasts and not among the gods, he is the lizard that, "when it darts from hedge/ to hedge beneath the dog days' giant lash,/ seems, if it cross one's path, a lightning flash" *(Inf.* xxv, 79–81). However seen, he is surely the swiftest and most successive of savants, forever rummaging in his vast and versal haversack of soughs and rasps and gusts and "harsh and scrannel rhymes" (which, in *Inf.* xxxii, 1, he claims he does not have—and then promptly produces). He is seeking those gusts that will most convince us of the credibility of his journey, the accuracy of his record, the trustworthiness of his memory. "Mistaking not" *(Inf.* ii, 6), he would offer us evidence as undeniable as that of a historian, Livy, of whom we learn, twenty-six cantos later *(Inf.* xxviii, 12), that he, too, "does not err."

Finally, he would convince us that *his* are the supreme fictions; and he would do so without contradicting his own claims

to truth, because *fictio* for Dante does not mean "pure invention" or "fantastic creation" but—as Gioacchino Paparelli has
shown—a poetic composition, constructed with the concourse
of rhetoric and music, or—we should say—prosody. And in
the construction of such fictions, he is not only a strenuous em-
ulator and intrepid pirate, but a competitor and self-announced
victor *(Inf.* XXV, 94–102):

Taccia Lucano omai là dov' e' tocca
del misero Sabello e di Nasidio,
e attenda a udir quel ch'or si scocca.
Taccia di Cadmo e d'Aretusa Ovidio,
ché se quello in serpente e quella in fonte
converte poetando, io non lo 'nvidio;
ché due nature mai a fronte a fronte
non transmutò sì ch'amendue le forme
a cambiar lor matera fosser pronte.

Let Lucan now be silent, where he sings
of sad Sabellus and Nasidius,
and wait to hear what flies off from my bow.
Let Ovid now be silent, where he tells
of Cadmus, Arethusa; if his verse
has made of one a serpent, one a fountain,
I do not envy him; he never did
transmute two natures, face to face, so that
both forms were ready to exchange their matter.

That announcement of victory over Ovid and Lucan, who
had so collegially welcomed Dante to Limbo, is strategically
abetted by Virgil's own incitement of Dante in the canto just
before, when Dante had sought brief respite from his breath-
less impetus, a sedentary truce for his *triste chair.* And Virgil's
prodding links the journey of the voyager to the journey of the
telling of the tale, in *Inf.* XXIV, 47–51:

.... seggendo in piuma,
in fama non si vien, né sotto coltre;
sanza la qual chi sua vita consuma,

cotal vestigio in terra di sé lascia,
qual fummo in aere e in acqua la schiuma.

. . . . for he who rests on down
or under covers cannot come to fame;
and he who spends his life without renown
leaves such a vestige of himself on earth
as smoke bequeaths to air or foam to water.

However, that self-announcement rings its unique changes at the very beginning of the second canto of the *Inferno:* "The day was now departing; the dark air/ released the living beings of the earth/ from work and weariness, and I myself/ alone prepared to undergo the battle/ both of the journeying and of the pity/ that memory, mistaking not, shall show./ O Muses, o high genius, help me now..." *(Inf.* II, 1–7). The canto in which Dante protests, "I am not Aeneas, am not Paul," is the same canto in which he also says *"io sol uno,"* "I myself alone," the first triple repetition of an "I" that we have in Western writing. That triplet is even more steeped in the certainty of fame than are the proclamations of either Sulmona's son, Ovidius-the-Garrulous, Amir-of-Metamorphosists and Sad-Seigneur-of-Scrutinists, at the end of the *Metamorphoses,* or Lucan in Book Nine of the *Pharsalia* (ll. 980–986), the same book in which some two hundred lines earlier, Lucan had sung of Sabellus and Nasidius. And if Dante proclaims his own victory over Lucan in Canto XXV, much later he will also appropriate the epithet "sacred" from Lucan's description of the poet's labor, twice calling his own poem a "sacred poem" in the *Paradiso* (a designation that may also echo Macrobius's term for the *Aeneid),* just as twice he calls his work a "comedy" in the *Inferno.*

Dante's "aloneness" casts a shadow, I believe, on attempts to read him as an Everyman, an exemplary pilgrim. If the first line of the *Inferno* carries with it what Leo Spitzer called the "possessive of human solidarity" in *"our* life's way," that is much more than counterbalanced by the resonances of *"io sol uno"* throughout the *Comedy.*

But the two most arduous emulations of the *Comedy* involve not Lucan or Ovid (though any Aeolus is perforce a closet Ovidian) but Virgil and Aquinas.

The first, Virgil, is involved in the most complex relation the *Comedy* presents. Dante is always with Virgil from the time he finds him "faint because of the long silence" (that strange amalgam of vision and sound, compounded by the "speechless" sun of *Inf.* I, 60) and hears him move from that silence into frequent, if not garrulous, speech, to the end of the *Inferno* and through much of the *Purgatorio,* until Virgil crowns and miters Dante over his own self *(Purg.* XXVII, 142). This finding of Virgil and this crowning of Dante are best seen against earlier way-stations in the natural history of literary affiliations.

Plato creates his relation to Socrates by annulling his own explicit voice and becoming the secret sharer and ambiguous transformer of one who had not written, devising or appropriating and developing a genre, dialogue, which has proved to be more inimitable than either tragedy or epic. Even one partial aspect of Platonic dialogue, the circumbendibus of its narrative framework—I am thinking especially of the beginning of the *Symposium,* where memory shuttles so uncertainly yet hauntingly—is so intricate, that we wait millenia before we find its match. But Dante, however much he knew of Platonism and neo-Platonism, knew no dialogue of Plato except—possibly—the Latin translation of the *Timaeus.*

Lucretius, with Dante, is the most moving exemplar of affiliation—although he was affiliated with a philosopher, Epicurus, not a poet:

> *Against the darkness you raised such bright light*
> *and first made clear the uses of this life;*
> *glory of the Greeks, I follow you*
> *and set my footsteps now on your sure way,*
> *and not as a contender but a lover*
> *who longs to imitate: how could a swallow*
> *sing against the swan, or could a young*

goat with trembling limbs outrun the strong
stallion? You are my father, finder
of things as they are, and give to us a father's
teachings: in your pages, Epicurus,
as bees in flowering fields sip every plant,
we graze on every golden saying, gold
and always worthy of unending life.

(Lucretius also shares one ancient/modern problem with Dante: the passage from the more conceptually supple Greek to Latin is not wholly unlike Dante's vying, in the vulgar, modern tongue, with Latin.) But, despite *Par.* XIV, 112–117, Dante surely shares the general medieval ignorance of all except snatches of Lucretius.

Virgil himself is often involved in tacit dialogue with Homer in the *Aeneid*. But it is tacit; and Dante, with Homer mute for him, could hardly have heard it.

Statius, at the end of the *Thebaid,* calls the *Aeneid* "divine" (an epithet that finally joins *Comedy* in the title of Dante's work in 1555), praying for his *Thebaid* to accompany—without rivaling—the *Aeneid*. That Virgil-Statius affiliation will be recuperated by Dante in the *Purgatorio*.

And, of course, we have the affiliation between two books and two sets of authors or One Author in two guises—and with many scribes—implicit, for some, in the Old and New Testaments.

However passionate these previous affiliations may have been, Dante is the first to welcome directly not only himself but his "author," "lord," "governor," "master," "father," into an epic. (Where Curtius and Auerbach reject that term, "epic," for the *Comedy,* both Hegel and Lukács accept it. For me, Dante's radical newness, one that does require the Biblical warrant of the first-person prophet, does not destroy but complements the epic intent. The journey to the underworld of Book VI of the *Aeneid* is magnified into a new whole: new wanderings and

wars, "the battle/ both of the journeying and of the pity" of *Inf.*
II, 4–5. That battle and that journey offer us both the arms and
the man—Dante himself—of whom Dante sings.) Virgil's
presence is so indispensable that when one meets the first and
only time that "father" is used with reference to him in the
Inferno, in Canto VIII (the appelation will become frequent in
the *Purgatorio),* one is tempted to gloss the unglossable lines
in that canto (VIII, 97–100), "O my dear guide, who more
than seven times/ has given back to me my confidence/ and
snatched me from deep danger that had menaced,/ do not
desert me when I'm so undone," thus: the "seven times" are the
seven cantos before this eighth. Without Virgil, those seven
cantos would not have been written. But perhaps the most paternal moment is Virgil's maternal semblance in *Inf.* XXIII,
37–42:

> *Lo duca mio di sùbito mi prese,*
> *come la madre ch'al romore è desta*
> *e vede presso a sé le fiamme accese,*
> *che prende il figlio e fugge e non s'arresta,*
> *avendo più di lui che di sé cura,*
> *tanto che solo una camiscia vesta...*

> *My guide snatched me up instantly, just as*
> *the mother who is wakened by a roar*
> *and catches sight of blazing flames beside her,*
> *will lift her son and run without a stop—*
> *she cares more for her child than for herself—*
> *not pausing even to throw on a shift...*

In prefacing the *Aeneid,* I had noted that critics' "variations
on the theme of Homer versus Virgil, using the father to club
the son," were "coupled at times with some variations on the
theme of Dante versus Virgil, using the son to club the father.
Whichever way one turned in the line of affiliation (Homer-
Virgil-Dante)—toward parricide or filicide—the middleman
Virgil lost." But Dante's own tears at Virgil's departure and his
triple invocation of Virgil's name in *Purgatorio* XXX, 49–51,
after quoting words of Dido, tell a more provocative, more

rich, and ultimately more heartening tale for readers. If one text can engender a second, perhaps the engendering need never end, and no antecedent need be forgotten.

The other text, beside the *Aeneid*, that most provokes Dante is the *Summa Theologica*, the second of Aquinas's summas, begun in the year when Dante was born and left incomplete at Aquinas's death in 1274, nine years later. Dante is not to be called an unequivocal Thomist, but Thomas's is the other epic (here used more loosely) achievement of Dante's centuries. Where Bonaventura had seen the inventions of the poets as fragile, Aquinas saw poetry as *infima doctrina*, a lesser mode of teaching (and more vulgar—and some unvulgar—theologians saw only lies). But he could call it lesser, too, because his own second *Summa* had evolved a style that Thomas Gilby limned so accurately:

> *Nevertheless St Thomas's style remains an instrument of precision once we appreciate that he was not writing a mathematical treatise or a legal document where single terms can be treated as atoms of discourse or forced into their fixed univocal sense: misapprehensions on this point brought him into false credit and discredit. He was renewing Aristotle's achievement of a synthesis beyond the static world of Parmenides and the fluid world of Heraclitus without, like Plato, finding meaning by forsaking the material world about us; he was addressing himself as a philosopher to the things first shown us through the senses and not to disembodied essences, and as a theologian to the works of God in history from which he suffered even less temptation to escape. He had to render things that were at once dark and shimmering, deep and on the surface, single and complex, firm and supple, irreducibly individual yet sharing in the common whole; and he paid them the compliment of attempting to do so without breaking into poetry.*

And even a Dante smitten with, transformed by, Beatrice, or intent on loving, affiliated inquiry with Virgil, is hard pressed to surpass the anatomy of eros in Aquinas, of which the following miscellany assembled by Gilby can offer us some indication:

> *Love is more unitive than knowledge in seeking the thing, not the thing's reason; its bent is to a real union, though this can be constituted only by knowledge. Other effects of love are enumerated: a reciprocal abiding,* mutua inhaesio, *of lover and beloved together; a transport,* extasis, *out of the self to the other; an ardent cherishing,* zelus, *of another; a melting,* liquefactio, *so that the heart is unfrozen and open to be entered; a longing in absence,* languor; *heat in pursuit,* fervor; *and enjoyment in presence,* fruitio. *In delight, too, there is an all at once wholeness and timelessness that reflects the* tota simul *of eternity; an edge of sadness similar to that of the Gift of Knowledge; an expansion of spirit; a complete fulfilment of activity without satiety,* for they that drink shall yet thirst.

To vie with Aquinas, to lift poetry from its *infima* status, Dante needs every adroit gavotte of Wholes and Parts and capriole of Part and Wholes.

He needs seeing, hearing, smelling, touching, to the point where he might well have personified Visus, Auditus, Tactus, and Odoratus. (Taste or Gustus is seldom called upon—but when summoned, it is for unforgettable purposes: the "bread of the angels" in *Par.* II, 2 and the salt taste of "others' bread," the bread we beg for in exile, in *Par.* XVII, 59). The verbs of seeing appear so often that even the most patient Scrutinist might falter in his tallies, but one—with his abacus—has told us that there are sixty-seven pairs of eyes in the *Inferno* alone, ninety-seven in the *Purgatorio,* and ninety-four in the *Paradiso.* Where others' baffled lenses may falter, Dante's never do: gazing, peering, squinting, scowling. If he has Virgil summon the "optic nerve" *(Inf.* IX, 73), we can be sure that, had his physiological manuals been more complete, he would have called on the intrepid foveae and fervid canaliculi, the everglaring glands of Moll as well as the zonules of Zinn.

He needs every tangibility he can summon from the world of the shades—but summon *personally,* crossing into that world, witnessing. He needs to begin his journey from a state *as like* to death as one can get while still alive. He needs to read his Hegel well (just as Hegel must read him) to understand that not only the Christian but the Hegelian—or the Heideggerian—poet can gather ultimate energy from only one sure fount: the fear—the absolute fear—of death, a wood "so bitter—death is hardly more severe" *(Inf.* I, 7). And to that end, it matters little whether what is feared is divine judgment or causeless nothingness, Madame Oubli and her company of Slabby-Mists, of *Nebel, Nichts, Néant,* and Dun-and-Dirty-Erebus, Unwashed-Subfusc, or more simply, just Victor Hugo's "old usherette" with her "black spectacle." Hegel's formulation of that fear couples it, of course, with service and obedience (functions Dante fulfills most immediately in relation to Virgil and Beatrice—and, ultimately, to his God):

> *Without the discipline of service and obedience, fear remains formal and does not spread over the whole known reality of existence. Without the formative activity shaping the thing, fear remains inward and mute, and consciousness does not become objective for itself. Should consciousness shape and form the thing without the initial state of absolute fear, then it has a merely vain and futile "mind of its own."* . . . *If it has endured not absolute fear, but merely some slight anxiety, negative reality has remained external to it, its substance has not been through and through infected thereby. Since the entire content of its natural consciousness has not tottered and shaken, it is still inherently a determinate mode of being; having a "mind of its own" is simply stubbornness, a type of freedom which does not get beyond the attitude of bondage. As little as the pure form can become its essential nature, so little is that form, considered as extending over particulars, a universal formative activ-*

ity, an absolute notion; it is rather a piece of cleverness
which has mastery within a certain range, but not over
the universal power nor over the entire objective reality.

For "the entire objective reality" read the Great-Gestalt-of-All-Gestalten. And if life and the living are but A-Part, then he who would sing The-All must visit The-Rest. (That Rest is, as descent to the underworld, an epic constituent of both the *Odyssey* and the *Aeneid,* but without the urgent fiction-prophecy of personal witness borne by the poet. Also, in Homer, more than in Virgil, it does not carry Orphic but de-mystifying Enlightenment elements—elements that are also present in Dante. Rescanning the way-stations of affiliation, but in some disorder, we can see that, while the Old Testament leaves its Sheol wholly lateral, an indistinct, great grey hole that *may* lie near the Musée de l'Homme, or even in unimportant, suburban precincts, the New Testament places that Rest very close to its center. As for the death of Socrates, it surely is essential to the resonance of Plato's work; but I should agree with Lukács that Plato's rejection of tragedy as the proper genre for the life of Socrates carries with it a sense of Socrates' death as an *accidental,* unessential interruption of his substance, which is speech, speech, speech—in effect, dialogue as a polemical rejection of the death-centeredness of the tragedians.)

He needs an adroit *ars poetica,* so that even when he works in plain style, he can mobilize extraordinary combinatorial precisions. Witness Canto XXXIII, 67–75:

Poscia che fummo al quarto dì venuti,
Gaddo mi si gittò disteso a' piedi,
dicendo: 'Padre mio, ché non m'aiuti?'
Quivi morì; e come tu mi vedi,
vid' io cascar li tre ad uno ad uno
tra 'l quinto dì e 'l sesto; ond' io me diedi,
già cieco, a brancolar sovra ciascuno,
e due dì li chiamai, poi che fur morti.
Poscia, più che 'l dolor, poté 'l digiuno.

But after we had reached the fourth day, Gaddo,
throwing himself, outstretched, down at my feet,
implored me: 'Father, why do you not help me?'
And there he died; and just as you see me,
I saw the other three fall one by one
between the fifth day and the sixth; at which,
now blind, I started groping over each;
and after they were dead, I called them for
two days; then fasting had more force than grief.

Salvatore Quasimodo, in one of the two essays I chose to
complement his poems in the 1960 volume of his *Selected
Writings* that I translated into English, in dealing with the first
eight lines of this passage, refers to Dante as "the greatest master" of the simple style. But neither he nor I had noted then
that, in this passage, which has so little adornment, the sequence of ordinal and cardinal numbers obeys an all-enclosing
law—no element escapes. We start with four, move to three,
one, five, six, and end with the one number needed to complete
the set: two. (Proof enough, if any were needed, that one textual variant which would have had "three days" instead of "two
days" was incorrect.) It is as if even accidental elements com-
bine to become a vise that locks Ugolino into the ineluctable.
Of course, the last line in the Italian, one which Quasimodo
omitted when he quoted the passage, is the most obviously pat-
terned of the nine, with the anaphoric closure of *"poscia"* and
very strong internal alliterative links.

Or witness the extraordinary intuition-in-labor of Dante's
tercet rhymes. For ABA exists not only on the level of interword
relations but on two other levels: 1) The hendecasyllable line itself is often accented on its sixth and central syllable. And even
when that syllable is unaccented, it may serve as a kind of center for accents on the fourth and eighth syllables, symmetri-
cally placed to its right and left. When we couple this frequent
function of the sixth syllable with what is the most frequent
Italian line-end (and, of course, the most frequent stress place-
ment in Italian words), the *piano* or feminine ending, then—
following Giuseppe Sansone's patient elaborations—we can

see that the hendecasyllable often has what I should call an internal balancing needle. Around that needle, when the obligatory stress on the tenth syllable is complemented by an initial iamb and consequent stress on the second syllable, we can generate not only homeopodic (or superimposed) symmetry but antipodic (mirror) symmetry—reinforcing ABA on the level of the line. 2) To this I should now add a reinforcement of ABA in terms of the constituents of the *single* rhyme word, a reinforcement that may seem as astonishing as the metamorphoses of Canto XXV. For the most frequent word termini in Italian are vowel-consonant-vowel termini; and that VCV echoes, on still another level, the ABA of the first two levels. English, with its even-numbered metrical positions in each line (even Milton, the most sensitive to Italian of our major poets, has little taste for feminine endings in his major work) and its paucity of vowel-consonant-vowel termini can never mime the depth of that prosodic intuition. That is *not* the reason for my forgoing tercet rhyme in this translation (which was simply dependent on my need to reach as clean and precise a rendering as possible); but it is the reason for the close phonic packing, whether in stressed or unstressed positions, which I have sought throughout this translation—with pure rhymes, pararhyme, assonances, alliterations, and consonances often called into service. (One pause is needed here: The possibility of Dante's conscious awareness of this level, the vowel, consonant, vowel trinity of the single rhyme, reinforcing the other levels, does find warrant in this: the vast majority of *piano* rhyme termini have, as we noted above, three phonemes; but two of the three phonemes are outside the stress situation. In VCV, it is the first element only that is stressed. This should lead, ideally, to heightened awareness of the poetic weight of *all* elements, tonic or not. And the ideal terminus for that ideal awareness would be the lexical independence of those two non-tonic elements, the terminal consonant and vowel. Our ideal fable finds its incarnation when Dante, in the middle of the *Purgatorio,* enjambs on the definite article, *"la,"* the first of his three such enjambments on definite articles. English will wait almost half-a-millenium for Blake to enjamb on "the"—and longer for Wallace Stevens' final "the the" in "The Man on the Dump.")

Or track Aldo Scaglione's analysis of *Inf.* III, 25–30, using the translation to heighten the detailed sense of what can and cannot be taken across a linguistic border:

> *Diverse lingue, orribili favelle,*
> *parole di dolore, accenti d'ira,*
> *voci alte e fioche, e suon di man con elle*
> *facevano un tumulto, il qual s'aggira*
> *sempre in quell' aura sanza tempo tinta,*
> *come la rena quando turbo spira.*
>
> *Strange utterances, horrible pronouncements,*
> *accents of anger, words of suffering,*
> *and voices shrill and faint, and beating hands—*
> *all went to make a tumult that will whirl*
> *forever through that turbid, timeless air,*
> *like sand that eddies when a whirlwind swirls.*

Here my English has tried to embody as much as I could of what Scaglione saw in the Italian, with the crescendo from noun and epithet in the first line, to noun and complement in the second, to noun and two epithets in the third line. Then I had to forgo the noun and two complements in that same line (with my "beating hands" for *"suon di man con elle"*) but did recoup the enjambment at the end of the fourth line and the force of sudden closure in the sixth.

The sum of Dante's needs encompasses a progression of three "words," a progression detailed in a fable that rises far from the Arno or the Tiber. (But in a climate as syncretistic as Dante's, where antiquity is appropriated by Christianity in a mode perhaps less arbitrary but no less omnivorous than the way in which a Cross surmounts an Egyptian obelisk mounted, in turn, on Bernini's elephant in the piazza of Santa Maria sopra Minerva, my calling on a Dogon fable as coda is hardly inappropriate.) According to Jean Laude, the myths of the Dogon would have us see this: "Three 'words' were revealed to humans. Each 'word' marks a stage in the order of technical invention and shows the passage from a conception of point-ed space (the point is likened to a seed) to linear space (the line is like the thread used in weaving) and, finally, to three-dimensional space (volume is likened to the hand-drum borne under the arm)." Some Scrutinists would simplify the Dogon fable, reading: Point is to Line is to Volume, as Seed is to Thread is to Drum. Dante embraces the complete progression, but it is clear that he hastens always in the direction of Volume, toward the violence of speech, away from the violence of silence. In brief, Dante is a Drummer. And this translation asks to be read aloud.

Sages, Elders, Emenders, Perpenders, Paraphrasts, Querists, Amphibolists, Nebulists, Quandarists, Rhetors, Wreckers, Embalmers, Bores, and Picadors—so many Exegetes, living and dead, from Dante's time to our own have contributed, at some point, to the understandings and misunderstandings that, over some two decades, have made this translation possible. That record of specific indebtedness will be made clear in the three companion volumes of commentary, the California Lectura Dantis, that will accompany the three *cantiche.* But in this volume of text and translation and illustration, I cannot delay voicing my gratitude: to Thomas Bergin, who had been pressed into service as Chairman of the English Department at Cornell University and, during my first year of teaching, some thirty-three years ago, benevolently shepherded a twenty-year-old through the pedagogic palestra and served as emblem for the joys that lay in the reading of Dante; to the Society of Fellows of Harvard, for my years there, 1951–1954, when Charles Singleton was still in Cambridge and Renato Poggioli was still alive; to two who paced at the Gate of Text, Giuseppe Vandelli, whose 1921 Società Dantesca critical text of the *Commedia* and later emendations through the posthumous, tenth edition of his "redoing" of Scartazzini's commentary formed the base for this translation in its earlier stages, and Giorgio Petrocchi, whose textual work anchored the later stages (the fullness of Petrocchi's apparatus and the lucidity of his decision procedures, even when one would disagree with him, are among the unequivocal gifts philology has given to the poetry of the present past); to The Graduate Center of the City University of New York, where Gian-Roberto Sarolli and Ezio Raimondi have been enthusiastic co-inquirers, Aldo Scaglione has been a precious visitor, and my students have been as able and acute as anyone who professes can merit; to dear colleagues who made my visits to Washington University in St. Louis, the University of Colorado at Boulder, the Honors Program at the University of Houston, and the University of Denver so fruitful; to Edward Cranz, whose modes of reading and detailed perception of the divide between ancients and moderns have been so uncannily close to the grit of the practical lexical problems and decisions I have encountered in translating Dante and Virgil; and to Barry Moser, for the set of plates that appear here—his arabesque of *Mens* and Lens at one with Hand and Text that, like Hell itself, is drawn to last.

The Graduate Center   Allen Mandelbaum
of the City University of New York

INFERNO

CANTO I

Nel mezzo del cammin di nostra vita
mi ritrovai per una selva oscura,
ché la diritta via era smarrita.

Ahi quanto a dir qual era è cosa dura   4
esta selva selvaggia e aspra e forte
che nel pensier rinova la paura!

Tant' è amara che poco è più morte;   7
ma per trattar del ben ch'i' vi trovai,
dirò de l'altre cose ch'i' v'ho scorte.

Io non so ben ridir com' i' v'intrai,   10
tant' era pien di sonno a quel punto
che la verace via abbandonai.

Ma poi ch'i' fui al piè d'un colle giunto,   13
là dove terminava quella valle
che m'avea di paura il cor compunto,

guardai in alto e vidi le sue spalle   16
vestite già de' raggi del pianeta
che mena dritto altrui per ogne calle.

Allor fu la paura un poco queta,   19
che nel lago del cor m'era durata
la notte ch'i' passai con tanta pieta.

E come quei che con lena affannata,   22
uscito fuor del pelago a la riva,
si volge a l'acqua perigliosa e guata,

così l'animo mio, ch'ancor fuggiva,   25
si volse a retro a rimirar lo passo
che non lasciò già mai persona viva.

Poi ch'èi posato un poco il corpo lasso,   28
ripresi via per la piaggia diserta,
sì che 'l piè fermo sempre era 'l più basso.

The voyager-narrator astray by night in a dark forest. Morning and the sunlit hill. Three beasts that impede his ascent. The encounter with Virgil, who offers his guidance and an alternative path through two of the three realms the voyager must visit.

W hen I had journeyed half of our life's way,
   I found myself within a shadowed forest,
for I had lost the path that does not stray.

Ah, it is hard to speak of what it was,   4
that savage forest, dense and difficult,
which even in recall renews my fear:

so bitter—death is hardly more severe!   7
But to retell the good discovered there,
I'll also tell the other things I saw.

I cannot clearly say how I had entered   10
the wood; I was so full of sleep just at
the point where I abandoned the true path.

But when I'd reached the bottom of a hill—   13
it rose along the boundary of the valley
that had harassed my heart with so much fear—

I looked on high and saw its shoulders clothed   16
already by the rays of that same planet
which serves to lead men straight along all roads.

At this my fear was somewhat quieted;   19
for through the night of sorrow I had spent,
the lake within my heart felt terror present.

And just as he who, with exhausted breath,   22
having escaped from sea to shore, turns back
to watch the dangerous waters he has quit,

so did my spirit, still a fugitive,   25
turn back to look intently at the pass
that never has let any man survive.

I let my tired body rest awhile.   28
Moving again, I tried the lonely slope—
my firm foot always was the one below.

Ed ecco, quasi al cominciar de l'erta,   31
una lonza leggiera e presta molto,
che di pel macolato era coverta;

e non mi si partia dinanzi al volto,   34
anzi 'mpediva tanto il mio cammino,
ch'i' fui per ritornar più volte vòlto.

Temp' era dal principio del mattino,   37
e 'l sol montava 'n sù con quelle stelle
ch'eran con lui quando l'amor divino

mosse di prima quelle cose belle;   40
sì ch'a bene sperar m'era cagione
di quella fiera a la gaetta pelle

l'ora del tempo e la dolce stagione;   43
ma non sì che paura non mi desse
la vista che m'apparve d'un leone.

Questi parea che contra me venisse   46
con la test' alta e con rabbiosa fame,
sì che parea che l'aere ne tremesse.

Ed una lupa, che di tutte brame   49
sembiava carca ne la sua magrezza,
e molte genti fé già viver grame,

questa mi porse tanto di gravezza   52
con la paura ch'uscia di sua vista,
ch'io perdei la speranza de l'altezza.

E qual è quei che volontieri acquista,   55
e giugne 'l tempo che perder lo face,
che 'n tutti suoi pensier piange e s'attrista;

tal mi fece la bestia sanza pace,   58
che, venendomi 'ncontro, a poco a poco
mi ripigneva là dove 'l sol tace.

Mentre ch'i' rovinava in basso loco,   61
dinanzi a li occhi mi si fu offerto
chi per lungo silenzio parea fioco.

Quando vidi costui nel gran diserto,   64
"Miserere di me," gridai a lui,
"qual che tu sii, od ombra od omo certo!"

Rispuosemi: "Non omo, omo già fui,   67
e li parenti miei furon lombardi,
mantoani per patrïa ambedui.

And almost where the hillside starts to rise—   31
look there!—a leopard, very quick and lithe,
a leopard covered with a spotted hide.

He did not disappear from sight, but stayed;   34
indeed, he so impeded my ascent
that I had often to turn back again.

The time was the beginning of the morning;   37
the sun was rising now in fellowship
with the same stars that had escorted it

when Divine Love first moved those things of beauty;   40
so that the hour and the gentle season
gave me good cause for hopefulness on seeing

that beast before me with his speckled skin;   43
but hope was hardly able to prevent
the fear I felt when I beheld a lion.

His head held high and ravenous with hunger—   46
even the air around him seemed to shudder—
this lion seemed to make his way against me.

And then a she-wolf showed herself; she seemed   49
to carry every craving in her leanness;
she had already brought despair to many.

The very sight of her so weighted me   52
with fearfulness that I abandoned hope
of ever climbing up that mountain slope.

Even as he who glories while he gains   55
will, when the time has come to tally loss,
lament with every thought and turn despondent,

so was I when I faced that restless beast,   58
which, even as she stalked me, step by step
had thrust me back to where the sun is speechless.

While I retreated down to lower ground,   61
before my eyes there suddenly appeared
one who seemed faint because of the long silence.

When I saw him in that vast wilderness,   64
"Have pity on me," were the words I cried,
"whatever you may be—a shade, a man."

He answered me: "Not man; I once was man.   67
Both of my parents came from Lombardy,
and both claimed Mantua as native city.

Nacqui *sub Iulio,* ancor che fosse tardi,   70
e vissi a Roma sotto 'l buono Augusto
nel tempo de li dèi falsi e bugiardi.

Poeta fui, e cantai di quel giusto   73
figliuol d'Anchise che venne di Troia,
poi che 'l superbo Ilïón fu combusto.

Ma tu perché ritorni a tanta noia?   76
perché non sali il dilettoso monte
ch'è principio e cagion di tutta gioia?"

"Or se' tu quel Virgilio e quella fonte   79
che spandi di parlar sì largo fiume?"
rispuòs' io lui con vergognosa fronte.

"O de li altri poeti onore e lume,   82
vagliami 'l lungo studio e 'l grande amore
che m'ha fatto cercar lo tuo volume.

Tu se' lo mio maestro e 'l mio autore,   85
tu se' solo colui da cu' io tolsi
lo bello stilo che m'ha fatto onore.

Vedi la bestia per cu' io mi volsi;   88
aiutami da lei, famoso saggio,
ch'ella mi fa tremar le vene e i polsi."

"A te convien tenere altro vïaggio,"   91
rispuose, poi che lagrimar mi vide,
"se vuo' campar d'esto loco selvaggio;

ché questa bestia, per la qual tu gride,   94
non lascia altrui passar per la sua via,
ma tanto lo 'mpedisce che l'uccide;

e ha natura sì malvagia e ria,   97
che mai non empie la bramosa voglia,
e dopo 'l pasto ha più fame che pria.

Molti son li animali a cui s'ammoglia,   100
e più saranno ancora, infin che 'l veltro
verrà, che la farà morir con doglia.

Questi non ciberà terra né peltro,   103
ma sapïenza, amore e virtute,
e sua nazion sarà tra feltro e feltro.

Di quella umile Italia fia salute   106
per cui morì la vergine Cammilla,
Eurialo e Turno e Niso di ferute.

And I was born, though late, *sub Julio,*   70
and lived in Rome under the good Augustus—
the season of the false and lying gods.

I was a poet, and I sang the righteous   73
son of Anchises who had come from Troy
when flames destroyed the pride of Ilium.

But why do you return to wretchedness?   76
Why not climb up the mountain of delight,
the origin and cause of every joy?"

"And are you then that Virgil, you the fountain   79
that freely pours so rich a stream of speech?"
I answered him with shame upon my brow.

"O light and honor of all other poets,   82
may my long study and the intense love
that made me search your volume serve me now.

You are my master and my author, you—   85
the only one from whom my writing drew
the noble style for which I have been honored.

You see the beast that made me turn aside;   88
help me, o famous sage, to stand against her,
for she has made my blood and pulses shudder."

"It is another path that you must take,"   91
he answered when he saw my tearfulness,
"if you would leave this savage wilderness;

the beast that is the cause of your outcry   94
allows no man to pass along her track,
but blocks him even to the point of death;

her nature is so squalid, so malicious   97
that she can never sate her greedy will;
when she has fed, she's hungrier than ever.

She mates with many living souls and shall   100
yet mate with many more, until the Greyhound
arrives, inflicting painful death on her.

That Hound will never feed on land or pewter,   103
but find his fare in wisdom, love, and virtue;
his place of birth shall be between two felts.

He will restore low-lying Italy   106
for which the maid Camilla died of wounds,
and Nisus, Turnus, and Euryalus.

Questi la caccerà per ogne villa,   109
fin che l'avrà rimessa ne lo 'nferno,
là onde 'nvidia prima dipartilla.

    Ond' io per lo tuo me' penso e discerno   112
che tu mi segui, e io sarò tua guida,
e trarrotti di qui per loco etterno,

    ove udirai le disperate strida,   115
vedrai li antichi spiriti dolenti,
ch'a la seconda morte ciascun grida;

    e vederai color che son contenti   118
nel foco, perché speran di venire
quando che sia a le beate genti.

    A le quai poi se tu vorrai salire,   121
anima fia a ciò più di me degna:
con lei ti lascerò nel mio partire;

    ché quello imperador che là sù regna,   124
perch' i' fu' ribellante a la sua legge,
non vuol che 'n sua città per me si vegna.

    In tutte parti impera e quivi regge;   127
quivi è la sua città e l'alto seggio:
oh felice colui cu' ivi elegge!"

    E io a lui: "Poeta, io ti richeggio   130
per quello Dio che tu non conoscesti,
a ciò ch'io fugga questo male e peggio,

    che tu mi meni là dov' or dicesti,   133
sì ch'io veggia la porta di san Pietro
e color cui tu fai cotanto mesti."

    Allor si mosse, e io li tenni dietro.   136

    And he will hunt that beast through every city   109
until he thrusts her back again to Hell,
from which she was first sent above by envy.

    Therefore, I think and judge it best for you   112
to follow me, and I shall guide you, taking
you from this place through an eternal place,

    where you shall hear the howls of desperation   115
and see the ancient spirits in their pain,
as each of them laments his second death;

    and you shall see those souls who are content   118
within the fire, for they hope to reach—
whenever that may be—the blessed people.

    If you would then ascend as high as these,   121
a soul more worthy than I am will guide you;
I'll leave you in her care when I depart,

    because that Emperor who reigns above,   124
since I have been rebellious to His law,
will not allow me entry to His city.

    He governs everywhere, but rules from there;   127
there is His city, His high capital:
o happy those He chooses to be there!"

    And I replied: "O poet—by that God   130
whom you had never come to know—I beg you,
that I may flee this evil and worse evils,

    to lead me to the place of which you spoke,   133
that I may see the gateway of Saint Peter
and those whom you describe as sorrowful."

    Then he set out, and I moved on behind him.   136

I·2

I · 22

II · 127

CANTO II

Lo giorno se n'andava, e l'aere bruno
toglieva li animai che sono in terra
da le fatiche loro; e io sol uno

m'apparecchiava a sostener la guerra   4
sì del cammino e sì de la pietate,
che ritrarrà la mente che non erra.

O Muse, o alto ingegno, or m'aiutate;   7
o mente che scrivesti ciò ch'io vidi,
qui si parrà la tua nobilitate.

Io cominciai: "Poeta che mi guidi,   10
guarda la mia virtù s'ell' è possente,
prima ch'a l'alto passo tu mi fidi.

Tu dici che di Silvïo il parente,   13
corruttibile ancora, ad immortale
secolo andò, e fu sensibilmente.

Però, se l'avversario d'ogne male   16
cortese i fu, pensando l'alto effetto
ch'uscir dovea di lui, e 'l chi e 'l quale,

non pare indegno ad omo d'intelletto;   19
ch'e' fu de l'alma Roma e di suo impero
ne l'empireo ciel per padre eletto:

la quale e 'l quale, a voler dir lo vero,   22
fu stabilita per lo loco santo
u' siede il successor del maggior Piero.

Per quest' andata onde li dai tu vanto,   25
intese cose che furon cagione
di sua vittoria e del papale ammanto.

Andovvi poi lo Vas d'elezïone,   28
per recarne conforto a quella fede
ch'è principio a la via di salvazione.

The following evening, Invocation to the Muses. The narrator's questioning of his worthiness to visit the deathless world. Virgil's comforting explanation that he has been sent to help Dante by three Ladies of Heaven. The voyager heartened. Their setting out.

The day was now departing; the dark air
released the living beings of the earth
from work and weariness; and I myself

alone prepared to undergo the battle   4
both of the journeying and of the pity,
which memory, mistaking not, shall show.

O Muses, o high genius, help me now;   7
o memory that set down what I saw,
here shall your excellence reveal itself!

I started: "Poet, you who are my guide,   10
see if the force in me is strong enough
before you let me face that rugged pass.

You say that he who fathered Sylvius,   13
while he was still corruptible, had journeyed
into the deathless world with his live body.

For, if the Enemy of every evil   16
was courteous to him, considering
all he would cause and who and what he was,

that does not seem incomprehensible,   19
since in the empyrean heaven he was chosen
to father honored Rome and her empire;

and if the truth be told, Rome and her realm   22
were destined to become the sacred place,
the seat of the successor of great Peter.

And through the journey you ascribe to him,   25
he came to learn of things that were to bring
his victory and, too, the papal mantle.

Later the Chosen Vessel travelled there,   28
to bring us back assurance of that faith
with which the way to our salvation starts.

Ma io, perché venirvi? o chi 'l concede?   31
Io non Enëa, io non Paulo sono;
me degno a ciò né io né altri 'l crede.

Per che, se del venire io m'abbandono,   34
temo che la venuta non sia folle.
Se' savio; intendi me' ch'i' non ragiono."

E qual è quei che disvuol ciò che volle   37
e per novi pensier cangia proposta,
sì che dal cominciar tutto si tolle,

tal mi fec' ïo 'n quella oscura costa,   40
perché, pensando, consumai la 'mpresa
che fu nel cominciar cotanto tosta.

"S'i' ho ben la parola tua intesa,"   43
rispuose del magnanimo quell' ombra,
"l'anima tua è da viltade offesa;

la qual molte fïate l'omo ingombra   46
sì che d'onrata impresa lo rivolve,
come falso veder bestia quand' ombra.

Da questa tema a ciò che tu ti solve,   49
dirotti perch' io venni e quel ch'io 'ntesi
nel primo punto che di te mi dolve.

Io era tra color che son sospesi,   52
e donna mi chiamò beata e bella,
tal che di comandare io la richiesi.

Lucevan li occhi suoi più che la stella;   55
e cominciommi a dir soave e piana,
con angelica voce, in sua favella:

"O anima cortese mantoana,   58
di cui la fama ancor nel mondo dura,
e durerà quanto 'l mondo lontana,

l'amico mio, e non de la ventura,   61
ne la diserta piaggia è impedito
sì nel cammin, che vòlt' è paura;

e temo che non sia già sì smarrito,   64
ch'io mi sia tardi al soccorso levata,
per quel ch'i' ho di lui nel cielo udito.

Or movi, e con la tua parola ornata   67
e con ciò c'ha mestieri al suo campare,
l'aiuta sì ch'i' ne sia consolata.

But why should I go there? Who sanctions it?   31
For I am not Aeneas, am not Paul;
nor I nor others think myself so worthy.

    Therefore, if I consent to start this journey,   34
I fear my venture may be wild and empty.
You're wise; you know far more than what I say."

    And just as he who unwills what he wills   37
and shifts what he intends to seek new ends
so that he's drawn from what he had begun,

    so was I in the midst of that dark land,   40
because, with all my thinking, I annulled
the task I had so quickly undertaken.

    "If I have understood what you have said,"   43
replied the shade of that great-hearted one,
"your soul has been assailed by cowardice,

    which often weighs so heavily on a man—   46
distracting him from honorable trials—
as phantoms frighten beasts when shadows fall.

    That you may be delivered from this fear,   49
I'll tell you why I came and what I heard
when I first felt compassion for your pain.

    I was among those souls who are suspended;   52
a lady called to me, so blessed, so lovely
that I implored to serve at her command.

    Her eyes surpassed the splendor of the star's;   55
and she began to speak to me—so gently
and softly—with angelic voice. She said:

    'O spirit of the courteous Mantuan,   58
whose fame is still a presence in the world
and shall endure as long as the world lasts,

    my friend, who has not been the friend of fortune,   61
is hindered in his path along that lonely
hillside; he has been turned aside by terror.

    From all that I have heard of him in Heaven,   64
he is, I fear, already so astray
that I have come to help him much too late.

    Go now; with your persuasive word, with all   67
that is required to see that he escapes,
bring help to him, that I may be consoled.

I' son Beatrice che ti faccio andare;   70
vegno del loco ove tornar disio;
amor mi mosse, che mi fa parlare.

Quando sarò dinanzi al segnor mio,   73
di te mi loderò sovente a lui.'
Tacette allora, e poi comincia' io:

'O donna di virtù sola per cui   76
l'umana spezie eccede ogne contento
di quel ciel c'ha minor li cerchi sui,

tanto m'aggrada il tuo comandamento,   79
che l'ubidir, se già fosse, m'è tardi;
più non t'è uo' ch'aprirmi il tuo talento.

Ma dimmi la cagion che non ti guardi   82
de lo scender qua giuso in questo centro
de l'ampio loco ove tornar tu ardi.'

'Da che tu vuo' saver cotanto a dentro,   85
dirotti brievemente,' mi rispuose,
'perch' i' non temo di venir qua entro.

Temer si dee di sole quelle cose   88
c'hanno potenza di fare altrui male;
de l'altre no, ché non son paurose.

I' son fatta da Dio, sua mercé, tale,   91
che la vostra miseria non mi tange,
né fiamma d'esto 'ncendio non m'assale.

Donna è gentil nel ciel che si compiange   94
di questo 'mpedimento ov' io ti mando,
sì che duro giudicio là sù frange.

Questa chiese Lucia in suo dimando   97
e disse:—Or ha bisogno il tuo fedele
di te, e io a te lo raccomando—.

Lucia, nimica di ciascun crudele,   100
si mosse, e venne al loco dov' i' era,
che mi sedea con l'antica Rachele.

Disse:—Beatrice, loda di Dio vera,   103
ché non soccorri quei che t'amò tanto,
ch'uscì per te de la volgare schiera?

Non odi tu la pieta del suo pianto,   106
non vedi tu la morte che 'l combatte
su la fiumana ove 'l mar non ha vanto?—

   For I am Beatrice who send you on;   70
I come from where I most long to return;
Love prompted me, that Love which makes me speak.

   When once again I stand before my Lord,   73
then I shall often let Him hear your praises.'
Now Beatrice was silent. I began:

   'O Lady of virtue, the sole reason why   76
the human race surpasses all that lies
beneath the heaven with the smallest spheres,

   so welcome is your wish, that even if   79
it were already done, it would seem tardy;
all you need do is let me know your will.

   But tell me why you have not been more prudent—   82
descending to this center, moving from
that spacious place where you long to return?'

   'Because you want to fathom things so deeply,   85
I now shall tell you promptly,' she replied,
'why I am not afraid to enter here.

   One ought to be afraid of nothing other   88
than things possessed of power to do us harm,
but things innocuous need not be feared.

   God, in His graciousness, has made me so   91
that this, your misery, cannot touch me;
I can withstand the fires flaming here.

   In Heaven there's a gentle lady—one   94
who weeps for the distress toward which I send you,
so that stern judgment up above is shattered.

   And it was she who called upon Lucia,   97
requesting of her: "Now your faithful one
has need of you, and I commend him to you."

   Lucia, enemy of every cruelty,   100
arose and made her way to where I was,
sitting beside the venerable Rachel.

   She said: "You, Beatrice, true praise of God,   103
why have you not helped him who loves you so
that—for your sake—he's left the vulgar crowd?

   Do you not hear the anguish in his cry?   106
Do you not see the death he wars against
upon that river ruthless as the sea?"

Al mondo non fur mai persone ratte   109
a far lor pro o a fuggir lor danno,
com' io, dopo cotai parole fatte,

    venni qua giù del mio beato scanno,   112
fidandomi del tuo parlare onesto,
ch'onora te e quei ch'udito l'hanno.'

    Poscia che m'ebbe ragionato questo,   115
li occhi lucenti lagrimando volse,
per che mi fece del venir più presto.

    E venni a te così com' ella volse: 118
d'inanzi a quella fiera ti levai
che del bel monte il corto andar ti tolse.

    Dunque: che è? perché, perché restai,   121
perché tanta viltà nel core allette,
perché ardire e franchezza non hai,

    poscia che tai tre donne benedette   124
curan di te ne la corte del cielo,
e 'l mio parlar tanto ben ti promette?"

    Quali fioretti dal notturno gelo   127
chinati e chiusi, poi che 'l sol li 'mbianca,
si drizzan tutti aperti in loro stelo,

    tal mi fec' io di mia virtude stanca,   130
e tanto buono ardire al cor mi corse,
ch'i' cominciai come persona franca:

    "Oh pietosa colei che mi soccorse!   133
e te cortese ch'ubidisti tosto
a le vere parole che ti porse!

    Tu m'hai con disiderio il cor disposto   136
sì al venir con le parole tue,
ch'i' son tornato nel primo proposto.

    Or va, ch'un sol volere è d'ambedue: 139
tu duca, tu segnore e tu maestro."
Così li dissi; e poi che mosso fue,

    intrai per lo cammino alto e silvestro.   142

No one within this world has ever been   109
so quick to seek his good or flee his harm
as I—when she had finished speaking thus—

to come below, down from my blessed station;   112
I trusted in your honest utterance,
which honors you and those who've listened to you.'

When she had finished with her words to me,   115
she turned aside her gleaming, tearful eyes,
which only made me hurry all the more.

And, just as she had wished, I came to you: 118
I snatched you from the path of the fierce beast
that barred the shortest way up the fair mountain.

What is it then? Why, why do you resist?   121
Why does your heart host so much cowardice?
Where are your daring and your openness

as long as there are three such blessed women   124
concerned for you within the court of Heaven
and my words promise you so great a good?"

As little flowers, which the chill of night   127
has bent and huddled, when the white sun strikes,
grow straight and open fully on their stems,

so did I, too, with my exhausted force;   130
and such warm daring rushed into my heart
that I—as one who has been freed—began:

"O she, compassionate, who has helped me!   133
And you who, courteous, obeyed so quickly
the true words that she had addressed to you!

You, with your words, have so disposed my heart   136
to longing for this journey—I return
to what I was at first prepared to do.

Now go; a single will fills both of us: 139
you are my guide, my governor, my master."
These were my words to him; when he advanced,

I entered on the steep and savage path.   142

CANTO III

PER ME SI VA NE LA CITTÀ DOLENTE,
  PER ME SI VA NE L'ETTERNO DOLORE,
PER ME SI VA TRA LA PERDUTA GENTE.

  GIUSTIZIA MOSSE IL MIO ALTO FATTORE;   4
FECEMI LA DIVINA PODESTATE,
LA SOMMA SAPÏENZA E 'L PRIMO AMORE.

  DINANZI A ME NON FUOR COSE CREATE   7
SE NON ETTERNE, E IO ETTERNO DURO.
LASCIATE OGNE SPERANZA, VOI CH'INTRATE.

  Queste parole di colore oscuro   10
vid' ïo scritte al sommo d'una porta;
per ch'io: "Maestro, il senso lor m'è duro."

  Ed elli a me, come persona accorta: 13
"Qui si convien lasciare ogne sospetto;
ogne viltà convien che qui sia morta.

  Noi siam venuti al loco ov' i' t'ho detto   16
che tu vedrai le genti dolorose
c'hanno perduto il ben de l'intelletto."

  E poi che la sua mano a la mia puose   19
con lieto volto, ond' io mi confortai,
mi mise dentro a le segrete cose.

  Quivi sospiri, pianti e alti guai   22
risonavan per l'aere sanza stelle,
per ch'io al cominciar ne lagrimai.

  Diverse lingue, orribili favelle,   25
parole di dolore, accenti d'ira,
voci alte e fioche, e suon di man con elle

  facevano un tumulto, il qual s'aggira   28
sempre in quell' aura sanza tempo tinta,
come la rena quando turbo spira.

The inscription above the Gate of Hell. The Ante-Inferno, where the shades of those who lived without praise and without blame now intermingle with the neutral angels. He who made the great refusal. The River Acheron. Charon. Dante's loss of his senses as the earth trembles.

THROUGH ME THE WAY INTO THE SUFFERING CITY,
  THROUGH ME THE WAY TO THE ETERNAL PAIN,
THROUGH ME THE WAY THAT RUNS AMONG THE LOST.

  JUSTICE URGED ON MY HIGH ARTIFICER;   4
MY MAKER WAS DIVINE AUTHORITY,
THE HIGHEST WISDOM, AND THE PRIMAL LOVE.

  BEFORE ME NOTHING BUT ETERNAL THINGS   7
WERE MADE, AND I ENDURE ETERNALLY.
ABANDON EVERY HOPE, WHO ENTER HERE.

  These words—their aspect was obscure—I read   10
inscribed above a gateway, and I said:
"Master, their meaning is difficult for me."

  And he to me, as one who comprehends: 13
"Here one must leave behind all hesitation;
here every cowardice must meet its death.

  For we have reached the place of which I spoke,   16
where you will see the miserable people,
those who have lost the good of the intellect."

  And when, with gladness in his face, he placed   19
his hand upon my own, to comfort me,
he drew me in among the hidden things.

  Here sighs and lamentations and loud cries   22
were echoing across the starless air,
so that, as soon as I set out, I wept.

  Strange utterances, horrible pronouncements,   25
accents of anger, words of suffering,
and voices shrill and faint, and beating hands—

  all went to make a tumult that will whirl   28
forever through that turbid, timeless air,
like sand that eddies when a whirlwind swirls.

    E io ch'avea d'orror la testa cinta,   31
dissi: "Maestro, che è quel ch'i' odo?
e che gent' è che par nel duol sì vinta?"

    Ed elli a me: "Questo misero modo   34
tegnon l'anime triste di coloro
che visser sanza 'nfamia e sanza lodo.

    Mischiate sono a quel cattivo coro   37
de li angeli che non furon ribelli
né fur fedeli a Dio, ma per sé fuoro.

    Caccianli i ciel per non esser men belli,   40
né lo profondo inferno li riceve,
ch'alcuna gloria i rei avrebber d'elli."

    E io: "Maestro, che è tanto greve   43
a lor che lamentar li fa sì forte?"
Rispuose: "Dicerolti molto breve.

    Questi non hanno speranza di morte,   46
e la lor cieca vita è tanto bassa,
che 'nvidïosi son d'ogne altra sorte.

    Fama di loro il mondo esser non lassa;   49
misericordia e giustizia li sdegna:
non ragioniam di lor, ma guarda e passa."

    E io, che riguardai, vidi una 'nsegna   52
che girando correva tanto ratta,
che d'ogne posa mi parea indegna;

    e dietro le venìa sì lunga tratta   55
di gente, ch'i' non averei creduto
che morte tanta n'avesse disfatta.

    Poscia ch'io v'ebbi alcun riconosciuto,   58
vidi e conobbi l'ombra di colui
che fece per viltade il gran rifiuto.

    Incontanente intesi e certo fui   61
che questa era la setta d'i cattivi,
a Dio spiacenti e a' nemici sui.

    Questi sciaurati, che mai non fur vivi,   64
erano ignudi e stimolati molto
da mosconi e da vespe ch'eran ivi.

    Elle rigavan lor di sangue il volto,   67
che, mischiato di lagrime, a' lor piedi
da fastidiosi vermi era ricolto.

And I—my head oppressed by horror—said: 31
"Master, what is it that I hear? Who are
those people so defeated by their pain?"

And he to me: "This miserable way   34
is taken by the sorry souls of those
who lived without disgrace and without praise.

They now commingle with the coward angels,   37
the company of those who were not rebels
nor faithful to their God, but stood apart.

The heavens, that their beauty not be lessened,   40
have cast them out, nor will deep Hell receive them—
even the wicked cannot glory in them."

And I: "What is it, master, that oppresses   43
these souls, compelling them to wail so loud?"
He answered: "I shall tell you in few words.

Those who are here can place no hope in death,   46
and their blind life is so abject that they
are envious of every other fate.

The world will let no fame of theirs endure;   49
both justice and compassion must disdain them;
let us not talk of them, but look and pass."

And I, looking more closely, saw a banner   52
that, as it wheeled about, raced on—so quick
that any respite seemed unsuited to it.

Behind that banner trailed so long a file   55
of people—I should never have believed
that death could have unmade so many souls.

After I had identified a few,   58
I saw and recognized the shade of him
who made, through cowardice, the great refusal.

At once I understood with certainty: 61
this company contained the cowardly,
hateful to God and to His enemies.

These wretched ones, who never were alive,   64
went naked and were stung again, again
by horseflies and by wasps that circled them.

The insects streaked their faces with their blood,   67
which, mingled with their tears, fell at their feet,
where it was gathered up by sickening worms.

   E poi ch'a riguardar oltre mi diedi,   70
vidi genti a la riva d'un gran fiume;
per ch'io dissi: "Maestro, or mi concedi

   ch'i' sappia quali sono, e qual costume   73
le fa di trapassar parer sì pronte,
com' i' discerno per lo fioco lume."

   Ed elli a me: "Le cose ti fier conte   76
quando noi fermerem li nostri passi
su la trista riviera d'Acheronte."

   Allor con li occhi vergognosi e bassi,   79
temendo no 'l mio dir li fosse grave,
infino al fiume del parlar mi trassi.

   Ed ecco verso noi venir per nave   82
un vecchio, bianco per antico pelo,
gridando: "Guai a voi, anime prave!

   Non isperate mai veder lo cielo: 85
i' vegno per menarvi a l'altra riva
ne le tenebre etterne, in caldo e 'n gelo.

   E tu che se' costì, anima viva,   88
pàrtiti da cotesti che son morti."
Ma poi che vide ch'io non mi partiva,

   disse: "Per altra via, per altri porti   91
verrai a piaggia, non qui, per passare:
più lieve legno convien che ti porti."

   E 'l duca lui: "Caron, non ti crucciare: 94
vuolsi così colà dove si puote
ciò che si vuole, e più non dimandare."

   Quinci fuor quete le lanose gote   97
al nocchier de la livida palude,
che 'ntorno a li occhi avea di fiamme rote.

   Ma quell' anime, ch'eran lasse e nude,   100
cangiar colore e dibattero i denti,
ratto che 'nteser le parole crude.

   Bestemmiavano Dio e lor parenti,   103
l'umana spezie e 'l loco e 'l tempo e 'l seme
di lor semenza e di lor nascimenti.

   Poi si ritrasser tutte quante insieme,   106
forte piangendo, a la riva malvagia
ch'attende ciascun uom che Dio non teme.

And then, looking beyond them, I could see   70
a crowd along the bank of a great river;
at which I said: "Allow me now to know

      who are these people—master—and what law   73
has made them seem so eager for the crossing,
as I can see despite the feeble light."

      And he to me: "When we have stopped along   76
the melancholy shore of Acheron,
then all these matters will be plain to you."

      At that, with eyes ashamed, downcast, and fearing   79
that what I said had given him offense,
I did not speak until we reached the river.

      And here, advancing toward us, in a boat,   82
an aged man—his hair was white with years—
was shouting: "Woe to you, corrupted souls!

      Forget your hope of ever seeing Heaven: 85
I come to lead you to the other shore,
to the eternal dark, to fire and frost.

      And you approaching there, you living soul,   88
keep well away from these—they are the dead."
But when he saw I made no move to go,

      he said: "Another way and other harbors—   91
not here—will bring you passage to your shore:
a lighter craft will have to carry you."

      My guide then: "Charon, don't torment yourself: 94
our passage has been willed above, where One
can do what He has willed; and ask no more."

      Now silence fell upon the wooly cheeks   97
of Charon, pilot of the livid marsh,
whose eyes were ringed about with wheels of flame.

      But all those spirits, naked and exhausted,   100
had lost their color, and they gnashed their teeth
as soon as they heard Charon's cruel words;

      they execrated God and their own parents   103
and humankind, and then the place and time
of their conception's seed and of their birth.

      Then they forgathered, huddled in one throng,   106
weeping aloud along that wretched shore
which waits for all who have no fear of God.

Caron dimonio, con occhi di bragia   109
loro accennando, tutte le raccoglie;
batte col remo qualunque s'adagia.

Come d'autunno si levan le foglie   112
l'una appresso de l'altra, fin che 'l ramo
vede a la terra tutte le sue spoglie,

similemente il mal seme d'Adamo   115
gittansi di quel lito ad una ad una,
per cenni come augel per suo richiamo.

Così sen vanno su per l'onda bruna,   118
e avanti che sien di là discese,
anche di qua nuova schiera s'auna.

"Figliuol mio," disse 'l maestro cortese,   121
"quelli che muoion ne l'ira di Dio
tutti convegnon qui d'ogne paese;

e pronti sono a trapassar lo rio,   124
ché la divina giustizia li sprona,
sì che la tema si volve in disio.

Quinci non passa mai anima buona;   127
e però, se Caron di te si lagna,
ben puoi sapere omai che 'l suo dir suona."

Finito questo, la buia campagna   130
tremò sì forte, che de lo spavento
la mente di sudore ancor mi bagna.

La terra lagrimosa diede vento,   133
che balenò una luce vermiglia
la qual mi vinse ciascun sentimento;

e caddi come l'uom cui sonno piglia.   136

The demon Charon, with his eyes like embers,
by signaling to them, has all embark;
his oar strikes anyone who stretches out.
109

As, in the autumn, leaves detach themselves,
first one and then the other, till the bough
sees all its fallen garments on the ground,
112

similarly, the evil seed of Adam
descended from the shoreline one by one,
when signaled, as a falcon—called—will come.
115

So do they move across the darkened waters;
even before they reach the farther shore,
new ranks already gather on this bank.
118

"My son," the gracious master said to me,
"those who have died beneath the wrath of God,
all these assemble here from every country;
121

and they are eager for the river crossing
because celestial justice spurs them on,
so that their fear is turned into desire.
124

No good soul ever takes its passage here;
therefore, if Charon has complained of you,
by now you can be sure what his words mean."
127

And after this was said, the darkened plain
quaked so tremendously—the memory
of terror then, bathes me in sweat again.
130

A whirlwind burst out of the tear-drenched earth,
a wind that crackled with a bloodred light,
a light that overcame all of my senses;
133

and like a man whom sleep has seized, I fell.
136

C H A R O N

III·112

V·46

IV·103

CANTO IV

Ruppemi l'alto sonno ne la testa
un greve truono, sì ch'io mi riscossi
come persona ch'è per forza desta;

e l'occhio riposato intorno mossi,   4
dritto levato, e fiso riguardai
per conoscer lo loco dov' io fossi.

Vero è che 'n su la proda mi trovai   7
de la valle d'abisso dolorosa
che 'ntrono accoglie d'infiniti guai.

Oscura e profonda era e nebulosa   10
tanto che, per ficcar lo viso a fondo,
io non vi discernea alcuna cosa.

"Or discendiam qua giù nel cieco mondo,"   13
cominciò il poeta tutto smorto.
"Io sarò primo, e tu sarai secondo."

E io, che del color mi fui accorto,   16
dissi: "Come verrò, se tu paventi
che suoli al mio dubbiare esser conforto?"

Ed elli a me: "L'angoscia de le genti   19
che son qua giù, nel viso mi dipigne
quella pietà che tu per tema senti.

Andiam, ché la via lunga ne sospigne."   22
Così si mise e così mi fé intrare
nel primo cerchio che l'abisso cigne.

Quivi, secondo che per ascoltare,   25
non avea pianto mai che di sospiri
che l'aura etterna facevan tremare;

ciò avvenia di duol sanza martìri,   28
ch'avean le turbe, ch'eran molte e grandi,
d'infanti e di femmine e di viri.

Dante's awakening to the First Circle, or Limbo, inhabited by those who were worthy but lived before Christianity and/or without baptism. The welcoming of Virgil and Dante by Homer, Horace, Ovid, Lucan. The catalogue of other great-hearted spirits in the noble castle of Limbo.

The heavy sleep within my head was smashed
by an enormous thunderclap, so that
I started up as one whom force awakens;

I stood erect and turned my rested eyes   4
from side to side, and I stared steadily
to learn what place it was surrounding me.

In truth I found myself upon the brink   7
of an abyss, the melancholy valley
containing thundering, unending wailings.

That valley, dark and deep and filled with mist,   10
is such that, though I gazed into its pit,
I was unable to discern a thing.

"Let us descend into the blind world now,"   13
the poet, who was deathly pale, began;
"I shall go first and you will follow me."

But I, who'd seen the change in his complexion,   16
said: "How shall I go on if you are frightened,
you who have always helped dispel my doubts?"

And he to me: "The anguish of the people   19
whose place is here below, has touched my face
with the compassion you mistake for fear.

Let us go on, the way that waits is long."   22
So he set out, and so he had me enter
on that first circle girdling the abyss.

Here, for as much as hearing could discover,   25
there was no outcry louder than the sighs
that caused the everlasting air to tremble.

The sighs arose from sorrow without torments,   28
out of the crowds—the many multitudes—
of infants and of women and of men.

Lo buon maestro a me: "Tu non dimandi   31
che spiriti son questi che tu vedi?
Or vo' che sappi, innanzi che più andi,

    ch'ei non peccaro; e s'elli hanno mercedi,   34
non basta, perché non ebber battesmo,
ch'è porta de la fede che tu credi;

    e s'e' furon dinanzi al cristianesmo,   37
non adorar debitamente a Dio:
e di questi cotai son io medesmo.

    Per tai difetti, non per altro rio,   40
semo perduti, e sol di tanto offesi
che sanza speme vivemo in disio."

    Gran duol mi prese al cor quando lo 'ntesi,   43
però che gente di molto valore
conobbi che 'n quel limbo eran sospesi.

    "Dimmi, maestro mio, dimmi, segnore,"   46
comincia' io per volere esser certo
di quella fede che vince ogne errore:

    "uscicci mai alcuno, o per suo merto   49
o per altrui, che poi fosse beato?"
E quei che 'ntese il mio parlar coverto,

    rispuose: "Io era nuovo in questo stato,   52
quando ci vidi venire un possente,
con segno di vittoria coronato.

    Trasseci l'ombra del primo parente,   55
d'Abèl suo figlio e quella di Noè,
di Moïsè legista e ubidente;

    Abraàm patrïarca e Davìd re,   58
Israèl con lo padre e co' suoi nati
e con Rachele, per cui tanto fé,

    e altri molti, e feceli beati.   61
E vo' che sappi che, dinanzi ad essi,
spiriti umani non eran salvati."

    Non lasciavam l'andar perch' ei dicessi,   64
ma passavam la selva tuttavia,
la selva, dico, di spiriti spessi.

    Non era lunga ancor la nostra via   67
di qua dal sonno, quand' io vidi un foco
ch'emisperio di tenebre vincia.

The kindly master said: "Do you not ask   31
who are these spirits whom you see before you?
I'd have you know, before you go ahead,

    they did not sin; and yet, though they have merits,   34
that's not enough, because they lacked baptism,
the portal of the faith that you embrace.

    And if they lived before Christianity,   37
they did not worship God in fitting ways;
and of such spirits I myself am one.

    For these defects, and for no other evil,   40
we now are lost and punished just with this:
we have no hope and yet we live in longing."

    Great sorrow seized my heart on hearing him,   43
for I had seen some estimable men
among the souls suspended in that limbo.

    "Tell me, my master, tell me, lord," I then   46
began because I wanted to be certain
of that belief which vanquishes all errors,

    "did any ever go—by his own merit   49
or others'—from this place toward blessedness?"
And he, who understood my covert speech,

    replied: "I was new-entered on this state   52
when I beheld a Great Lord enter here:
the crown he wore, a sign of victory.

    He carried off the shade of our first father,   55
of his son Abel, and the shade of Noah,
of Moses, the obedient legislator,

    of father Abraham, David the king,   58
of Israel, his father, and his sons,
and Rachel, she for whom he worked so long,

    and many others—and He made them blessed;   61
and I should have you know that, before them,
there were no human souls that had been saved."

    We did not stay our steps although he spoke;   64
we still continued onward through the wood—
the wood, I say, where many spirits thronged.

    Our path had not gone far beyond the point   67
where I had slept, when I beheld a fire
win out against a hemisphere of shadows.

Di lungi n'eravamo ancora un poco,   70
ma non sì ch'io non discernessi in parte
ch'orrevol gente possedea quel loco.

"O tu ch'onori scïenzïa e arte,   73
questi chi son c'hanno cotanta onranza,
che dal modo de li altri li diparte?"

E quelli a me: "L'onrata nominanza   76
che di lor suona sù ne la tua vita,
grazïa acquista in ciel che sì li avanza."

Intanto voce fu per me udita: 79
"Onorate l'altissimo poeta;
l'ombra sua torna, ch'era dipartita."

Poi che la voce fu restata e queta,   82
vidi quattro grand' ombre a noi venire:
sembianz' avevan né trista né lieta.

Lo buon maestro cominciò a dire: 85
"Mira colui con quella spada in mano,
che vien dinanzi ai tre sì come sire:

quelli è Omero poeta sovrano;   88
l'altro è Orazio satiro che vene;
Ovidio è 'l terzo, e l'ultimo Lucano.

Però che ciascun meco si convene   91
nel nome che sonò la voce sola,
fannomi onore, e di ciò fanno bene."

Così vid' i' adunar la bella scola   94
di quel segnor de l'altissimo canto
che sovra li altri com' aquila vola.

Da ch'ebber ragionato insieme alquanto,   97
volsersi a me con salutevol cenno,
e 'l mio maestro sorrise di tanto;

e più d'onore ancora assai mi fenno,   100
ch'e' sì mi fecer de la loro schiera,
sì ch'io fui sesto tra cotanto senno.

Così andammo infino a la lumera,   103
parlando cose che 'l tacere è bello,
sì com' era 'l parlar colà dov' era.

Venimmo al piè d'un nobile castello,   106
sette volte cerchiato d'alte mura,
difeso intorno d'un bel fiumicello.

    We still were at a little distance from it,   70
but not so far I could not see in part
that honorable men possessed that place.

    "O you who honor art and science both,   73
who are these souls whose dignity has kept
their way of being, separate from the rest?"

    And he to me: "The honor of their name,   76
which echoes up above within your life,
gains Heaven's grace, and that advances them."

    Meanwhile there was a voice that I could hear: 79
"Pay honor to the estimable poet;
his shadow, which had left us, now returns."

    After that voice was done, when there was silence,   82
I saw four giant shades approaching us;
in aspect, they were neither sad nor joyous.

    My kindly master then began by saying: 85
"Look well at him who holds that sword in hand,
who moves before the other three as lord.

    That shade is Homer, the consummate poet;   88
the other one is Horace, satirist;
the third is Ovid, and the last is Lucan.

    Because each of these spirits shares with me   91
the name called out before by the lone voice,
they welcome me—and, doing that, do well."

    And so I saw that splendid school assembled,   94
led by the lord of song incomparable,
who like an eagle soars above the rest.

    Soon after they had talked a while together,   97
they turned to me, saluting cordially;
and having witnessed this, my master smiled;

    and even greater honor then was mine,   100
for they invited me to join their ranks—
I was the sixth among such intellects.

    So did we move along and toward the light,   103
talking of things about which silence here
is just as seemly as our speech was there.

    We reached the base of an exalted castle,   106
encircled seven times by towering walls,
defended all around by a fair stream.

Questo passammo come terra dura;   109
per sette porte intrai con questi savi:
giugnemmo in prato di fresca verdura.

Genti v'eran con occhi tardi e gravi,   112
di grande autorità ne' lor sembianti:
parlavan rado, con voci soavi.

Traemmoci così da l'un de' canti,   115
in loco aperto, luminoso e alto,
sì che veder si potien tutti quanti.

Colà diritto, sovra 'l verde smalto,   118
mi fuor mostrati li spiriti magni,
che del vedere in me stesso m'essalto.

I' vidi Eletra con molti compagni,   121
tra ' quai conobbi Ettòr ed Enea,
Cesare armato con li occhi grifagni.

Vidi Cammilla e la Pantasilea;   124
da l'altra parte vidi 'l re Latino
che con Lavina sua figlia sedea.

Vidi quel Bruto che cacciò Tarquino,   127
Lucrezia, Iulia, Marzïa e Corniglia;
e solo, in parte, vidi 'l Saladino.

Poi ch'innalzai un poco più le ciglia,   130
vidi 'l maestro di color che sanno
seder tra filosofica famiglia.

Tutti lo miran, tutti onor li fanno: 133
quivi vid' ïo Socrate e Platone,
che 'nnanzi a li altri più presso li stanno;

Democrito che 'l mondo a caso pone,   136
Dïogenès, Anassagora e Tale,
Empedoclès, Eraclito e Zenone;

e vidi il buono accoglitor del quale,   139
Dïascoride dico; e vidi Orfeo,
Tulïo e Lino e Seneca morale;

Euclide geomètra e Tolomeo,   142
Ipocràte, Avicenna e Galïeno,
Averoìs che 'l gran comento feo.

Io non posso ritrar di tutti a pieno,   145
però che sì mi caccia il lungo tema,
che molte volte al fatto il dir vien meno.

We forded this as if upon hard ground; 109
I entered seven portals with these sages;
we reached a meadow of green flowering plants.

The people here had eyes both grave and slow; 112
their features carried great authority;
they spoke infrequently, with gentle voices.

We drew aside to one part of the meadow, 115
an open place both high and filled with light,
and we could see all those who were assembled.

Facing me there, on the enameled green, 118
great-hearted souls were shown to me and I
still glory in my having witnessed them.

I saw Electra with her many comrades, 121
among whom I knew Hector and Aeneas,
and Caesar, in his armor, falcon-eyed.

I saw Camilla and Penthesilea 124
and, on the other side, saw King Latinus,
who sat beside Lavinia, his daughter.

I saw that Brutus who drove Tarquin out, 127
Lucretia, Julia, Marcia, and Cornelia,
and, solitary, set apart, Saladin.

When I had raised my eyes a little higher, 130
I saw the master of the men who know,
seated in philosophic family.

There all look up to him, all do him honor: 133
there I beheld both Socrates and Plato,
closest to him, in front of all the rest;

Democritus, who ascribes the world to chance, 136
Diogenes, Empedocles, and Zeno,
and Thales, Anaxagoras, Heraclitus;

I saw the good collector of medicinals, 139
I mean Dioscorides; and I saw Orpheus,
and Tully, Linus, moral Seneca;

and Euclid the geometer, and Ptolemy, 142
Hippocrates and Galen, Avicenna,
Averroës, of the great Commentary.

I cannot here describe them all in full; 145
my ample theme impels me onward so:
what's told is often less than the event.

La sesta compagnia in due si scema: 148
per altra via mi mena il savio duca,
fuor de la queta, ne l'aura che trema.

E vegno in parte ove non è che luca.   151

The company of six divides in two;   148
my knowing guide leads me another way,
beyond the quiet, into trembling air.

And I have reached a part where no thing gleams.   151

CANTO V

Così discesi del cerchio primaio
    giù nel secondo, che men loco cinghia
e tanto più dolor, che punge a guaio.

Stavvi Minòs orribilmente, e ringhia: 4
essamina le colpe ne l'intrata;
giudica e manda secondo ch'avvinghia.

Dico che quando l'anima mal nata   7
li vien dinanzi, tutta si confessa;
e quel conoscitor de le peccata

vede qual loco d'inferno è da essa;   10
cignesi con la coda tante volte
quantunque gradi vuol che giù sia messa.

Sempre dinanzi a lui ne stanno molte: 13
vanno a vicenda ciascuna al giudizio,
dicono e odono e poi son giù volte.

"O tu che vieni al doloroso ospizio,"   16
disse Minòs a me quando mi vide,
lasciando l'atto di cotanto offizio,

"guarda com' entri e di cui tu ti fide;   19
non t'inganni l'ampiezza de l'intrare!"
E 'l duca mio a lui: "Perché pur gride?

Non impedir lo suo fatale andare: 22
vuolsi così colà dove si puote
ciò che si vuole, e più non dimandare."

Or incomincian le dolenti note   25
a farmisi sentire; or son venuto
là dove molto pianto mi percuote.

Io venni in loco d'ogne luce muto,   28
che mugghia come fa mar per tempesta,
se da contrari venti è combattuto.

The Second Circle, where the Lustful are forever buffeted by violent storms. Minos. The catalogue of carnal sinners. Francesca da Rimini and her brother-in-law, Paolo Malatesta. Francesca's tale of their love and death, at which Dante faints.

S o I descended from the first enclosure
     down to the second circle, that which girdles
less space but grief more great, that goads to weeping.

There dreadful Minos stands, gnashing his teeth: 4
examining the sins of those who enter,
he judges and assigns as his tail twines.

I mean that when the spirit born to evil   7
appears before him, it confesses all;
and he, the connoisseur of sin, can tell

the depth in Hell appropriate to it;   10
as many times as Minos wraps his tail
around himself, that marks the sinner's level.

Always there is a crowd that stands before him: 13
each soul in turn advances toward that judgment;
they speak and hear, then they are cast below.

Arresting his extraordinary task,   16
Minos, as soon as he had seen me, said:
"O you who reach this house of suffering,

be careful how you enter, whom you trust;   19
the gate is wide, but do not be deceived!"
To which my guide replied: "But why protest?

Do not attempt to block his fated path: 22
our passage has been willed above, where One
can do what He has willed; and ask no more."

Now notes of desperation have begun   25
to overtake my hearing; now I come
where mighty lamentation beats against me.

I reached a place where every light is muted,   28
which bellows like the sea beneath a tempest,
when it is battered by opposing winds.

La bufera infernal, che mai non resta, 31
mena li spirti con la sua rapina;
voltando e percotendo li molesta.

Quando giungon davanti a la ruina, 34
quivi le strida, il compianto, il lamento;
bestemmian quivi la virtù divina.

Intesi ch'a così fatto tormento 37
enno dannati i peccator carnali,
che la ragion sommettono al talento.

E come li stornei ne portan l'ali 40
nel freddo tempo, a schiera larga e piena,
così quel fiato li spiriti mali

di qua, di là, di giù, di sù li mena; 43
nulla speranza li conforta mai,
non che di posa, ma di minor pena.

E come i gru van cantando lor lai, 46
faccendo in aere di sé lunga riga,
così vid' io venir, traendo guai,

ombre portate da la detta briga; 49
per ch'i' dissi: "Maestro, chi son quelle
genti che l'aura nera sì gastiga?"

"La prima di color di cui novelle 52
tu vuo' saper," mi disse quelli allotta,
"fu imperadrice di molte favelle.

A vizio di lussuria fu sì rotta, 55
che libito fé licito in sua legge,
per tòrre il biasmo in che era condotta.

Ell' è Semiramìs, di cui si legge 58
che succedette a Nino e fu sua sposa:
tenne la terra che 'l Soldan corregge.

L'altra è colei che s'ancise amorosa, 61
e ruppe fede al cener di Sicheo;
poi è Cleopatràs lussurïosa.

Elena vedi, per cui tanto reo 64
tempo si volse, e vedi 'l grande Achille,
che con amore al fine combatteo.

Vedi Parìs, Tristano"; e più di mille 67
ombre mostrommi e nominommi a dito,
ch'amor di nostra vita dipartille.

The hellish hurricane, which never rests,   31
drives on the spirits with its violence:
wheeling and pounding, it harasses them.

When they come up against the ruined slope,   34
then there are cries and wailing and lament,
and there they curse the force of the divine.

I learned that those who undergo this torment   37
are damned because they sinned within the flesh,
subjecting reason to the rule of lust.

And as, in the cold season, starlings' wings   40
bear them along in broad and crowded ranks,
so does that blast bear on the guilty spirits:

now here, now there, now down, now up, it drives them.   43
There is no hope that ever comforts them—
no hope for rest and none for lesser pain.

And just as cranes in flight will chant their lays,   46
arraying their long file across the air,
so did the shades I saw approaching, borne

by that assailing wind, lament and moan;   49
so that I asked him: "Master, who are those
who suffer punishment in this dark air?"

"The first of those about whose history   52
you want to know," my master then told me,
"once ruled as empress over many nations.

Her vice of lust became so customary   55
that she made license licit in her laws
to free her from the scandal she had caused.

She is Semíramis, of whom we read   58
that she was Ninus' wife and his successor:
she held the land the Sultan now commands.

That other spirit killed herself for love,   61
and she betrayed the ashes of Sychaeus;
the wanton Cleopatra follows next.

See Helen, for whose sake so many years   64
of evil had to pass; see great Achilles,
who finally met love—in his last battle.

See Paris, Tristan . . ."—and he pointed out   67
and named to me more than a thousand shades
departed from our life because of love.

Poscia ch'io ebbi 'l mio dottore udito   70
nomar le donne antiche e' cavalieri,
pietà mi giunse, e fui quasi smarrito.

I' cominciai: "Poeta, volontieri   73
parlerei a quei due che 'nsieme vanno,
e paion sì al vento esser leggieri."

Ed elli a me: "Vedrai quando saranno   76
più presso a noi; e tu allor li priega
per quello amor che i mena, ed ei verranno."

Sì tosto come il vento a noi li piega,   79
mossi la voce: "O anime affannate,
venite a noi parlar, s'altri nol niega!"

Quali colombe dal disio chiamate   82
con l'ali alzate e ferme al dolce nido
vegnon per l'aere, dal voler portate;

cotali uscir de la schiera ov' è Dido,   85
a noi venendo per l'aere maligno,
sì forte fu l'affettüoso grido.

"O animal grazïoso e benigno   88
che visitando vai per l'aere perso
noi che tignemmo il mondo di sanguigno,

se fosse amico il re de l'universo,   91
noi pregheremmo lui de la tua pace,
poi c'hai pietà del nostro mal perverso.

Di quel che udire e che parlar vi piace,   94
noi udiremo e parleremo a voi,
mentre che 'l vento, come fa, ci tace.

Siede la terra dove nata fui   97
su la marina dove 'l Po discende
per aver pace co' seguaci sui.

Amor, ch'al cor gentil ratto s'apprende,   100
prese costui de la bella persona
che mi fu tolta; e 'l modo ancor m'offende.

Amor, ch'a nullo amato amar perdona,   103
mi prese del costui piacer sì forte,
che, come vedi, ancor non m'abbandona.

Amor condusse noi ad una morte.   106
Caina attende chi a vita ci spense."
Queste parole da lor ci fuor porte.

No sooner had I heard my teacher name   70
the ancient ladies and the knights, than pity
seized me, and I was like a man astray.

My first words: "Poet, I should willingly   73
speak with those two who go together there
and seem so lightly carried by the wind."

And he to me: "You'll see when they draw closer   76
to us, and then you may appeal to them
by that love which impels them. They will come."

No sooner had the wind bent them toward us   79
than I urged on my voice: "O battered souls,
if One does not forbid it, speak with us."

Even as doves when summoned by desire,   82
borne forward by their will, move through the air
with wings uplifted, still, to their sweet nest,

those spirits left the ranks where Dido suffers,   85
approaching us through the malignant air;
so powerful had been my loving cry.

"O living being, gracious and benign,   88
who through the darkened air have come to visit
our souls that stained the world with blood, if He

who rules the universe were friend to us,   91
then we should pray to Him to give you peace,
for you have pitied our atrocious state.

Whatever pleases you to hear and speak   94
will please us, too, to hear and speak with you,
now while the wind is silent, in this place.

The land where I was born lies on that shore   97
to which the Po together with the waters
that follow it descends to final rest.

Love, that can quickly seize the gentle heart,   100
took hold of him because of the fair body
taken from me—how that was done still wounds me.

Love, that releases no beloved from loving,   103
took hold of me so strongly through his beauty
that, as you see, it has not left me yet.

Love led the two of us unto one death.   106
Caïna waits for him who took our life."
These words were borne across from them to us.

Quand' io intesi quell' anime offense,   109
china' il viso, e tanto il tenni basso,
fin che 'l poeta mi disse: "Che pense?"

Quando rispuosi, cominciai: "Oh lasso,   112
quanti dolci pensier, quanto disio
menò costoro al doloroso passo!"

Poi mi rivolsi a loro e parla' io,   115
e cominciai: "Francesca, i tuoi martìri
a lagrimar mi fanno tristo e pio.

Ma dimmi: al tempo d'i dolci sospiri,   118
a che e come concedette amore
che conosceste i dubbiosi disiri?"

E quella a me: "Nessun maggior dolore   121
che ricordarsi del tempo felice
ne la miseria; e ciò sa 'l tuo dottore.

Ma s'a conoscer la prima radice   124
del nostro amor tu hai cotanto affetto,
dirò come colui che piange e dice.

Noi leggiavamo un giorno per diletto   127
di Lancialotto come amor lo strinse;
soli eravamo e sanza alcun sospetto.

Per più fïate li occhi ci sospinse   130
quella lettura, e scolorocci il viso;
ma solo un punto fu quel che ci vinse.

Quando leggemmo il disïato riso   133
esser basciato da cotanto amante,
questi, che mai da me non fia diviso,

la bocca mi basciò tutto tremante.   136
Galeotto fu 'l libro e chi lo scrisse:
quel giorno più non vi leggemmo avante."

Mentre che l'uno spirto questo disse,   139
l'altro piangëa; sì che di pietade
io venni men così com' io morisse.

E caddi come corpo morto cade.   142

When I had listened to those injured souls,   109
I bent my head and held it low until
the poet asked of me: "What are you thinking?"

When I replied, my words began: "Alas,   112
how many gentle thoughts, how deep a longing,
had led them to the agonizing pass!"

Then I addressed my speech again to them,   115
and I began: "Francesca, your afflictions
move me to tears of sorrow and of pity.

But tell me, in the time of gentle sighs,   118
with what and in what way did Love allow you
to recognize your still uncertain longings?"

And she to me: "There is no greater sorrow   121
than thinking back upon a happy time
in misery—and this your teacher knows.

Yet if you long so much to understand   124
the first root of our love, then I shall tell
my tale to you as one who weeps and speaks.

One day, to pass the time away, we read   127
of Lancelot—how love had overcome him.
We were alone, and we suspected nothing.

And time and time again that reading led   130
our eyes to meet, and made our faces pale,
and yet one point alone defeated us.

When we had read how the desired smile   133
was kissed by one who was so true a lover,
this one, who never shall be parted from me,

while all his body trembled, kissed my mouth.   136
A Gallehault indeed, that book and he
who wrote it, too; that day we read no more."

And while one spirit said these words to me,   139
the other wept, so that—because of pity—
I fainted, as if I had met my death.

And then I fell as a dead body falls.   142

VI·13

CANTO VI

Al tornar de la mente, che si chiuse
dinanzi a la pietà d'i due cognati,
che di trestizia tutto mi confuse,

novi tormenti e novi tormentati   4
mi veggio intorno, come ch'io mi mova
e ch'io mi volga, e come che io guati.

Io sono al terzo cerchio, de la piova   7
etterna, maladetta, fredda e greve;
regola e qualità mai non l'è nova.

Grandine grossa, acqua tinta e neve   10
per l'aere tenebroso si riversa;
pute la terra che questo riceve.

Cerbero, fiera crudele e diversa,   13
con tre gole caninamente latra
sovra la gente che quivi è sommersa.

Li occhi ha vermigli, la barba unta e atra,   16
e 'l ventre largo, e unghiate le mani;
graffia li spirti ed iscoia ed isquatra.

Urlar li fa la pioggia come cani;   19
de l'un de' lati fanno a l'altro schermo;
volgonsi spesso i miseri profani.

Quando ci scorse Cerbero, il gran vermo,   22
le bocche aperse e mostrocci le sanne;
non avea membro che tenesse fermo.

E 'l duca mio distese le sue spanne,   25
prese la terra, e con piene le pugna
la gittò dentro a le bramose canne.

Qual è quel cane ch'abbaiando agogna,   28
e si racqueta poi che 'l pasto morde,
ché solo a divorarlo intende e pugna,

*Dante's awakening to the Third Circle, where the Gluttonous,
supine, are flailed by cold and filthy rain and tormented by
Cerberus. Ciacco and his prophecy concerning Florence. The state
of the damned after the Resurrection.*

Upon my mind's reviving—it had closed
  on hearing the lament of those two kindred,
since sorrow had confounded me completely—

  I see new sufferings, new sufferers   4
surrounding me on every side, wherever
I move or turn about or set my eyes.

  I am in the third circle, filled with cold,   7
unending, heavy, and accursèd rain;
its measure and its kind are never changed.

  Gross hailstones, water gray with filth, and snow   10
come streaking down across the shadowed air;
the earth, as it receives that shower, stinks.

  Over the souls of those submerged beneath   13
that mess, is an outlandish, vicious beast,
his three throats barking, doglike: Cerberus.

  His eyes are bloodred; greasy, black, his beard;   16
his belly bulges, and his hands are claws;
his talons tear and flay and rend the shades.

  That downpour makes the sinners howl like dogs;   19
they use one of their sides to screen the other—
those miserable wretches turn and turn.

  When Cerberus, the great worm, noticed us,   22
he opened wide his mouths, showed us his fangs;
there was no part of him that did not twitch.

  My guide opened his hands to their full span,   25
plucked up some earth, and with his fists filled full
he hurled it straight into those famished jaws.

  Just as a dog that barks with greedy hunger   28
will then fall quiet when he gnaws his food,
intent and straining hard to cram it in,

cotai si fecer quelle facce lorde   31
de lo demonio Cerbero, che 'ntrona
l'anime sì, ch'esser vorrebber sorde.

Noi passavam su per l'ombre che adona   34
la greve pioggia, e ponavam le piante
sovra lor vanità che par persona.

Elle giacean per terra tutte quante,   37
fuor d'una ch'a seder si levò, ratto
ch'ella ci vide passarsi davante.

"O tu che se' per questo 'nferno tratto,"   40
mi disse, "riconoscimi, se sai:
tu fosti, prima ch'io disfatto, fatto."

E io a lui: "L'angoscia che tu hai   43
forse ti tira fuor de la mia mente,
sì che non par ch'i' ti vedessi mai.

Ma dimmi chi tu se' che 'n sì dolente   46
loco se' messo, e hai sì fatta pena,
che, s'altra è maggio, nulla è sì spiacente."

Ed elli a me: "La tua città, ch'è piena   49
d'invidia sì che già trabocca il sacco,
seco mi tenne in la vita serena.

Voi cittadini mi chiamaste Ciacco: 52
per la dannosa colpa de la gola,
come tu vedi, a la pioggia mi fiacco.

E io anima trista non son sola,   55
ché tutte queste a simil pena stanno
per simil colpa." E più non fé parola.

Io li rispuosi: "Ciacco, il tuo affanno   58
mi pesa sì, ch'a lagrimar mi 'nvita;
ma dimmi, se tu sai, a che verranno

li cittadin de la città partita;   61
s'alcun v'è giusto; e dimmi la cagione
per che l'ha tanta discordia assalita."

E quelli a me: "Dopo lunga tencione   64
verranno al sangue, e la parte selvaggia
caccerà l'altra con molta offensione.

Poi appresso convien che questa caggia   67
infra tre soli, e che l'altra sormonti
con la forza di tal che testé piaggia.

so were the filthy faces of the demon 31
Cerberus transformed—after he'd stunned
the spirits so, they wished that they were deaf.

We walked across the shades on whom there thuds 34
that heavy rain, and set our soles upon
their empty images that seem like persons.

And all those spirits lay upon the ground, 37
except for one who sat erect as soon
as he caught sight of us in front of him.

"O you who are conducted through this Hell," 40
he said to me, "recall me, if you can;
for you, before I was unmade, were made."

And I to him: "It is perhaps your anguish 43
that snatches you out of my memory,
so that it seems that I have never seen you.

But tell me who you are, you who are set 46
in such a dismal place, such punishment—
if other pains are more, none's more disgusting."

And he to me: "Your city—one so full 49
of envy that its sack has always spilled—
that city held me in the sunlit life.

The name you citizens gave me was Ciacco; 52
and for the damning sin of gluttony,
as you can see, I languish in the rain.

And I, a wretched soul, am not alone, 55
for all of these have this same penalty
for this same sin." And he said nothing more.

I answered him: "Ciacco, your suffering 58
so weights on me that I am forced to weep;
but tell me, if you know, what end awaits

the citizens of that divided city; 61
is any just man there? Tell me the reason
why it has been assailed by so much schism."

And he to me: "After long controversy, 64
they'll come to blood; the party of the woods
will chase the other out with much offense.

But then, within three suns, they too must fall; 67
at which the other party will prevail,
using the power of one who tacks his sails.

Alte terrà lungo tempo le fronti,   70
tenendo l'altra sotto gravi pesi,
come che di ciò pianga o che n'aonti.

Giusti son due, e non vi sono intesi;   73
superbia, invidia e avarizia sono
le tre faville c'hanno i cuori accesi."

Qui puose fine al lagrimabil suono.   76
E io a lui: "Ancor vo' che mi 'nsegni
e che di più parlar mi facci dono.

Farinata e 'l Tegghiaio, che fuor sì degni,   79
Iacopo Rusticucci, Arrigo e 'l Mosca
e li altri ch'a ben far puoser li 'ngegni

dimmi ove sono e fa ch'io li conosca;   82
ché gran disio mi stringe di savere
se 'l ciel li addolcia o lo 'nferno li attosca."

E quelli: "Ei son tra l'anime più nere;   85
diverse colpe giù li grava al fondo:
se tanto scendi, là i potrai vedere.

Ma quando tu sarai nel dolce mondo,   88
priegoti ch'a la mente altrui mi rechi:
più non ti dico e più non ti rispondo."

Li diritti occhi torse allora in biechi;   91
guardommi un poco e poi chinò la testa:
cadde con essa a par de li altri ciechi.

E 'l duca disse a me: "Più non si desta   94
di qua dal suon de l'angelica tromba,
quando verrà la nimica podesta:

ciascun riverderà la trista tomba,   97
ripiglierà sua carne e sua figura,
udirà quel ch'in etterno rimbomba."

Sì trapassammo per sozza mistura   100
de l'ombre e de la pioggia, a passi lenti,
toccando un poco la vita futura;

per ch'io dissi: "Maestro, esti tormenti   103
cresceran' ei dopo la gran sentenza,
o fier minori, o saran sì cocenti?"

Ed elli a me: "Ritorna a tua scïenza,   106
che vuol, quanto la cosa è più perfetta,
più senta il bene, e così la doglienza.

This party will hold high its head for long   70
and heap great weights upon its enemies,
however much they weep indignantly.

Two men are just, but no one listens to them.   73
Three sparks that set on fire every heart
are envy, pride, and avariciousness."

With this, his words, inciting tears, were done;   76
and I to him: "I would learn more from you;
I ask you for a gift of further speech:

Tegghiaio, Farinata, men so worthy,   79
Arrigo, Mosca, Jacopo Rusticucci,
and all the rest whose minds bent toward the good,

do tell me where they are and let me meet them;   82
for my great longing drives me on to learn
if Heaven sweetens or Hell poisons them."

And he: "They are among the blackest souls;   85
a different sin has dragged them to the bottom;
if you descend so low, there you can see them.

But when you have returned to the sweet world,   88
I pray, recall me to men's memory:
I say no more to you, answer no more."

Then his straight gaze grew twisted and awry;   91
he looked at me awhile, then bent his head;
he fell as low as all his blind companions.

And my guide said to me: "He'll rise no more   94
until the blast of the angelic trumpet
upon the coming of the hostile Judge:

each one shall see his sorry tomb again   97
and once again take on his flesh and form,
and hear what shall resound eternally."

So did we pass across that squalid mixture   100
of shadows and of rain, our steps slowed down,
talking awhile about the life to come.

At which I said: "And after the great sentence—   103
o master—will these torments grow, or else
be less, or will they be just as intense?"

And he to me: "Remember now your science,   106
which says that when a thing has more perfection,
so much the greater is its pain or pleasure.

Tutto che questa gente maladetta   109
in vera perfezion già mai non vada,
di là più che di qua essere aspetta."

Noi aggirammo a tondo quella strada,   112
parlando più assai ch'i' non ridico;
venimmo al punto dove si digrada:

quivi trovammo Pluto, il gran nemico.   115

Though these accursed sinners never shall   109
attain the true perfection, yet they can
expect to be more perfect then than now."

We took the circling way traced by that road;   112
we said much more than I can here recount;
we reached the point that marks the downward slope.

Here we found Plutus, the great enemy.   115

CANTO VII

*P*ape Satàn, pape Satàn, aleppe!"
   cominciò Pluto con la voce chioccia;
e quel savio gentil, che tutto seppe,

   disse per confortarmi: "Non ti noccia   4
la tua paura; ché, poder ch'elli abbia,
non ci torrà lo scender questa roccia."

   Poi si rivolse a quella 'nfiata labbia,   7
e disse: "Taci, maladetto lupo!
consuma dentro te con la tua rabbia.

   Non è sanza cagion l'andare al cupo: 10
vuolsi ne l'alto, là dove Michele
fé la vendetta del superbo strupo."

   Quali dal vento le gonfiate vele   13
caggiono avvolte, poi che l'alber fiacca,
tal cadde a terra la fiera crudele.

   Così scendemmo ne la quarta lacca,   16
pigliando più de la dolente ripa
che 'l mal de l'universo tutto insacca.

   Ahi giustizia di Dio! tante chi stipa   19
nove travaglie e pene quant' io viddi?
e perché nostra colpa sì ne scipa?

   Come fa l'onda là sovra Cariddi,   22
che si frange con quella in cui s'intoppa,
così convien che qui la gente riddi.

   Qui vid' i' gente più ch'altrove troppa,   25
e d'una parte e d'altra, con grand' urli,
voltando pesi per forza di poppa.

   Percotëansi 'ncontro; e poscia pur lì   28
si rivolgea ciascun, voltando a retro,
gridando: "Perché tieni?" e "Perché burli?"

*The demon Plutus. The Fourth Circle, where the Avaricious and the
Prodigal, in opposite directions, roll weights in semicircles. Fortune
and her ways. Descent into the Fifth Circle: the Wrathful and the
Sullen, the former besmirched by the muddy Styx, the latter immersed in it.*

*P*ape Satàn, pape Satàn aleppe!"
   so Plutus, with his grating voice, began.
The gentle sage, aware of everything,
   said reassuringly, "Don't let your fear   4
defeat you; for whatever power he has,
he cannot stop our climbing down this crag."

   Then he turned back to Plutus' swollen face   7
and said to him: "Be quiet, cursed wolf!
Let your vindictiveness feed on yourself.

   His is no random journey to the deep: 10
it has been willed on high, where Michael took
revenge upon the arrogant rebellion."

   As sails inflated by the wind collapse,   13
entangled in a heap, when the mast cracks,
so that ferocious beast fell to the ground.

   Thus we made our way down to the fourth ditch,   16
to take in more of that despondent shore
where all the universe's ill is stored.

   Justice of God! Who has amassed as many   19
strange tortures and travails as I have seen?
Why do we let our guilt consume us so?

   Even as waves that break above Charybdis,   22
each shattering the other when they meet,
so must the spirits here dance their round dance.

   Here, more than elsewhere, I saw multitudes   25
to every side of me; their howls were loud
while, wheeling weights, they used their chests to push.

   They struck against each other; at that point,   28
each turned around and, wheeling back those weights,
cried out: "Why do you hoard?" "Why do you squander?"

  Così tornavan per lo cerchio tetro   31
da ogne mano a l'opposito punto,
gridandosi anche loro ontoso metro;

  poi si volgea ciascun, quand' era giunto,   34
per lo suo mezzo cerchio a l'altra giostra.
E io, ch'avea lo cor quasi compunto,

  dissi: "Maestro mio, or mi dimostra   37
che gente è questa, e se tutti fuor cherci
questi chercuti a la sinistra nostra."

  Ed elli a me: "Tutti quanti fuor guerci   40
sì de la mente in la vita primaia,
che con misura nullo spendio ferci.

  Assai la voce lor chiaro l'abbaia,   43
quando vegnono a' due punti del cerchio
dove colpa contraria li dispaia.

  Questi fuor cherci, che non han coperchio   46
piloso al capo, e papi e cardinali,
in cui usa avarizia il suo soperchio."

  E io: "Maestro, tra questi cotali   49
dovre' io ben riconoscere alcuni
che furo immondi di cotesti mali."

  Ed elli a me: "Vano pensiero aduni: 52
la sconoscente vita che i fé sozzi,
ad ogne conoscenza or li fa bruni.

  In etterno verranno a li due cozzi: 55
questi resurgeranno del sepulcro
col pugno chiuso, e questi coi crin mozzi.

  Mal dare e mal tener lo mondo pulcro   58
ha tolto loro, e posti a questa zuffa:
qual ella sia, parole non ci appulcro.

  Or puoi, figliuol, veder la corta buffa   61
d'i ben che son commessi a la fortuna,
per che l'umana gente si rabuffa;

  ché tutto l'oro ch'è sotto la luna   64
e che già fu, di quest' anime stanche
non poterebbe farne posare una."

  "Maestro mio," diss' io, "or mi dì anche: 67
questa fortuna di che tu mi tocche,
che è, che i ben del mondo ha sì tra branche?"

So did they move around the sorry circle   31
from left and right to the opposing point;
again, again they cried their chant of scorn;

    and so, when each of them had changed positions,   34
he circled halfway back to his next joust.
And I, who felt my heart almost pierced through,

    requested: "Master, show me now what shades   37
are these and tell me if they all were clerics—
those tonsured ones who circle on our left."

    And he to me: "All these, to left and right   40
were so squint-eyed of mind in the first life—
no spending that they did was done with measure.

    Their voices bark this out with clarity   43
when they have reached the two points of the circle
where their opposing guilts divide their ranks.

    These to the left—their heads bereft of hair—   46
were clergymen, and popes and cardinals,
within whom avarice works its excess."

    And I to him: "Master, among this kind   49
I certainly might hope to recognize
some who have been bespattered by these crimes."

    And he to me: "That thought of yours is empty: 52
the undiscerning life that made them filthy
now renders them unrecognizable.

    For all eternity they'll come to blows: 55
these here will rise up from their sepulchers
with fists clenched tight; and these, with hair cropped close.

    Ill giving and ill keeping have robbed both   58
of the fair world and set them to this fracas—
what that is like, my words need not embellish.

    Now you can see, my son, how brief's the sport   61
of all those goods that are in Fortune's care,
for which the tribe of men contend and brawl;

    for all the gold that is or ever was   64
beneath the moon could never offer rest
to even one of these exhausted spirits."

    "Master," I asked of him, "now tell me too: 67
this Fortune whom you've touched upon just now—
what's she, who clutches so all the world's goods?"

    E quelli a me: "Oh creature sciocche,   70
quanta ignoranza è quella che v'offende!
Or vo' che tu mia sentenza ne 'mbocche.

    Colui lo cui saver tutto trascende,   73
fece li cieli e diè lor chi conduce
sì, ch'ogne parte ad ogne parte splende,

    distribuendo igualmente la luce.   76
Similemente a li splendor mondani
ordinò general ministra e duce

    che permutasse a tempo li ben vani   79
di gente in gente e d'uno in altro sangue,
oltre la difension d'i senni umani;

    per ch'una gente impera e l'altra langue,   82
seguendo lo giudicio di costei,
che è occulto come in erba l'angue.

    Vostro saver non ha contasto a lei: 85
questa provede, giudica, e persegue
suo regno come il loro li altri dèi.

    Le sue permutazion non hanno triegue: 88
necessità la fa esser veloce;
sì spesso vien chi vicenda consegue.

    Quest' è colei ch'è tanto posta in croce   91
pur da color che le dovrien dar lode,
dandole biasmo a torto e mala voce;

    ma ella s'è beata e ciò non ode: 94
con l'altre prime creature lieta
volve sua spera e beata si gode.

    Or discendiamo omai a maggior pieta;   97
già ogne stella cade che saliva
quand' io mi mossi, e 'l troppo star si vieta."

    Noi ricidemmo il cerchio a l'altra riva   100
sovr' una fonte che bolle e riversa
per un fossato che da lei deriva.

    L'acqua era buia assai più che persa;   103
e noi, in compagnia de l'onde bige,
intrammo giù per una via diversa.

    In la palude va c'ha nome Stige   106
questo tristo ruscel, quand' è disceso
al piè de le maligne piagge grige.

And he to me: "O unenlightened creatures,   70
how deep—the ignorance that hampers you!
I want you to digest my word on this.

Who made the heavens and who gave them guides   73
was He whose wisdom transcends everything;
that every part may shine unto the other,

He had the light apportioned equally;   76
similarly, for wordly splendors, He
ordained a general minister and guide

to shift, from time to time, those empty goods   79
from nation unto nation, clan to clan,
in ways that human reason can't prevent;

just so, one people rules, one languishes,   82
obeying the decision she has given,
which, like a serpent in the grass, is hidden.

Your knowledge cannot stand against her force;   85
for she foresees and judges and maintains
her kingdom as the other gods do theirs.

The changes that she brings are without respite: 88
it is necessity that makes her swift;
and for this reason, men change state so often.

She is the one so frequently maligned   91
even by those who should give praise to her—
they blame her wrongfully with words of scorn.

But she is blessed and does not hear these things;   94
for with the other primal beings, happy,
she turns her sphere and glories in her bliss.

But now let us descend to greater sorrow,   97
for every star that rose when I first moved
is setting now; we cannot stay too long."

We crossed the circle to the other shore;   100
we reached a foaming watercourse that spills
into a trench formed by its overflow.

That stream was even darker than deep purple;   103
and we, together with those shadowed waves,
moved downward and along a strange pathway.

When it has reached the foot of those malign   106
gray slopes, that melancholy stream descends,
forming a swamp that bears the name of Styx.

   E io, che di mirare stava inteso,   109
vidi genti fangose in quel pantano,
ignude tutte, con sembiante offeso.

   Queste si percotean non pur con mano,   112
ma con la testa e col petto e coi piedi,
troncandosi co' denti a brano a brano.

   Lo buon maestro disse: "Figlio, or vedi   115
l'anime di color cui vinse l'ira;
e anche vo' che tu per certo credi

   che sotto l'acqua è gente che sospira,   118
e fanno pullular quest' acqua al summo,
come l'occhio ti dice, u' che s'aggira.

   Fitti nel limo dicon: 'Tristi fummo   121
ne l'aere dolce che dal sol s'allegra,
portando dentro accidïoso fummo:

   or ci attristiam ne la belletta negra.'   124
Quest' inno si gorgoglian ne la strozza,
ché dir nol posson con parola integra."

   Così girammo de la lorda pozza   127
grand' arco, tra la ripa secca e 'l mézzo,
con li occhi vòlti a chi del fango ingozza.

   Vènimmo al piè d'una torre al da sezzo.   130

And I, who was intent on watching it,   109
could make out muddied people in that slime,
all naked and their faces furious.

These struck each other not with hands alone,   112
but with their heads and chests and with their feet,
and tore each other piecemeal with their teeth.

The kindly master told me: "Son, now see   115
the souls of those whom anger has defeated;
and I should also have you know for certain

that underneath the water there are souls   118
who sigh and make this plain of water bubble,
as your eye, looking anywhere, can tell.

Wedged in the slime, they say: 'We had been sullen   121
in the sweet air that's gladdened by the sun;
we bore the mist of sluggishness in us:

now we are bitter in the blackened mud.'   124
This hymn they have to gurgle in their gullets,
because they cannot speak it in full words."

And so, between the dry shore and the swamp,   127
we circled much of that disgusting pond,
our eyes upon the swallowers of slime.

We came at last upon a tower's base.   130

... the ranks where Dido suffers

V·85

So did the thousand ruined souls…

CANTO VIII

Io dico, seguitando, ch'assai prima
che noi fossimo al piè de l'alta torre,
li occhi nostri n'andar suso a la cima

per due fiammette che i vedemmo porre,   4
e un'altra da lungi render cenno,
tanto ch'a pena il potea l'occhio tòrre.

E io mi volsi al mar di tutto 'l senno;   7
dissi: "Questo che dice? e che risponde
quell' altro foco? e chi son quei che 'l fenno?"

Ed elli a me: "Su per le sucide onde   10
già scorgere puoi quello che s'aspetta,
se 'l fummo del pantan nol ti nasconde."

Corda non pinse mai da sé saetta   13
che sì corresse via per l'aere snella,
com' io vidi una nave piccioletta

venir per l'acqua verso noi in quella,   16
sotto 'l governo d'un sol galeoto,
che gridava: "Or se' giunta, anima fella!"

"Flegïàs, Flegïàs, tu gridi a vòto,"   19
disse lo mio segnore, "a questa volta:
più non ci avrai che sol passando il loto."

Qual è colui che grande inganno ascolta   22
che li sia fatto, e poi se ne rammarca,
fecesi Flegïàs ne l'ira accolta.

Lo duca mio discese ne la barca,   25
e poi mi fece intrare appresso lui;
e sol quand' io fui dentro parve carca.

Tosto che 'l duca e io nel legno fui,   28
segando se ne va l'antica prora
de l'acqua più che non suol con altrui.

Still the Fifth Circle: the Wrathful and the Sullen. The tall tower.
Phlegyas and the crossing of the Styx. Filippo Argenti and Dante's
fury. Approach to Dis, the lower part of Hell: its moat, its walls, its
gate. The demons, fallen angels, and their obstruction of the poets'
entry into Dis.

I say, continuing, that long before
  we two had reached the foot of that tall tower,
our eyes had risen upward, toward its summit,

    because of two small flames that flickered there,   4
while still another flame returned their signal,
so far off it was scarcely visible.

    And I turned toward the sea of all good sense;   7
I said: "What does this mean? And what reply
comes from that other fire? Who kindled it?"

    And he to me: "Above the filthy waters   10
you can already see what waits for us,
if it's not hid by vapors from the marsh."

    Bowstring has not thrust from itself an arrow   13
that ever rushed as swiftly through the air
as did the little bark that at that moment

    I saw as it skimmed toward us on the water,   16
a solitary boatman at its helm.
I heard him howl: "Now you are caught, foul soul!"

    "O Phlegyas, Phlegyas, such a shout is useless   19
this time," my master said; "we're yours no longer
than it will take to cross the muddy sluice."

    And just as one who hears some great deception   22
was done to him, and then resents it, so
was Phlegyas when he had to store his anger.

    My guide preceded me into the boat.   25
Once he was in, he had me follow him;
there seemed to be no weight until I boarded.

    No sooner were my guide and I embarked   28
than off that ancient prow went, cutting water
more deeply than it does when bearing others.

Mentre noi corravam la morta gora,   31
dinanzi mi si fece un pien di fango,
e disse: "Chi se' tu che vieni anzi ora?"

E io a lui: "S'i' vegno, non rimango;   34
ma tu chi se', che sì se' fatto brutto?"
Rispuose: "Vedi che son un che piango."

E io lui: "Con piangere e con lutto,   37
spirito maladetto, ti rimani;
chi'i' ti conosco, ancor sie lordo tutto."

Allor distese al legno ambo le mani;   40
per che 'l maestro accorto lo sospinse,
dicendo: "Via costà con li altri cani!"

Lo collo poi con le braccia mi cinse;   43
basciommi 'l volto e disse: "Alma sdegnosa,
benedetta colei che 'n te s'incinse!

Quei fu al mondo persona orgogliosa;   46
bontà non è che sua memoria fregi:
così s'è l'ombra sua qui furïosa.

Quanti si tegnon or là sù gran regi   49
che qui staranno come porci in brago,
di sé lasciando orribili dispregi!"

E io: "Maestro, molto sarei vago   52
di vederlo attuffare in questa broda
prima che noi uscissimo del lago."

Ed elli a me: "Avante che la proda   55
ti si lasci veder, tu sarai sazio:
di tal disïo convien che tu goda."

Dopo ciò poco vid' io quello strazio   58
far di costui a le fangose genti,
che Dio ancor ne lodo e ne ringrazio.

Tutti gridavano: "A Filippo Argenti!"   61
e 'l fiorentino spirito bizzarro
in sé medesmo si volvea co' denti.

Quivi il lasciammo, che più non ne narro;   64
ma ne l'orecchie mi percosse un duolo,
per ch'io avante l'occhio intento sbarro.

Lo buon maestro disse: "Omai, figliuolo,   67
s'appressa la città c'ha nome Dite,
coi gravi cittadin, col grande stuolo."

And while we steered across the stagnant channel,   31
before me stood a sinner thick with mud,
saying: "Who are you, come before your time?"

And I to him: "I've come, but I don't stay;   34
but who are you, who have become so ugly?"
He answered: "You can see—I'm one who weeps."

And I to him: "In weeping and in grieving,   37
accursèd spirit, may you long remain;
though you're disguised by filth, I know your name."

Then he stretched both his hands out toward the boat,   40
at which my master quickly shoved him back,
saying: "Be off there with the other dogs!"

That done, he threw his arms around my neck   43
and kissed my face and said: "Indignant soul,
blessèd is she who bore you in her womb!

When in the world, he was presumptuous;   46
there is no good to gild his memory,
and so his shade down here is hot with fury.

How many up above now count themselves   49
great kings, who'll wallow here like pigs in slime,
leaving behind foul memories of their crimes!"

And I: "O master, I am very eager   52
to see that spirit soused within this broth
before we've made our way across the lake."

And he to me: "Before the other shore   55
comes into view, you shall be satisfied;
to gratify so fine a wish is right."

Soon after I had heard these words, I saw   58
the muddy sinners so dismember him
that even now I praise and thank God for it.

They all were shouting: "At Filippo Argenti!"   61
At this, the Florentine, gone wild with spleen,
began to turn his teeth against himself.

We left him there; I tell no more of him.   64
But in my ears so loud a wailing pounded
that I lean forward, all intent to see.

The kindly master said: "My son, the city   67
that bears the name of Dis is drawing near,
with its grave citizens, its great battalions."

E io: "Maestro, già le sue meschite   70
là entro certe ne la valle cerno,
vermiglie come se di foco uscite

fossero." Ed ei mi disse: "Il foco etterno   73
ch'entro l'affoca le dimostra rosse,
come tu vedi in questo basso inferno."

Noi pur giugnemmo dentro a l'alte fosse   76
che vallan quella terra sconsolata:
le mura mi parean che ferro fosse.

Non sanza prima far grande aggirata,   79
venimmo in parte dove il nocchier forte
"Usciteci," gridò: "qui è l'intrata."

Io vidi più di mille in su le porte   82
da ciel piovuti, che stizzosamente
dicean: "Chi è costui che sanza morte

va per lo regno de la morta gente?"   85
E 'l savio mio maestro fece segno
di voler lor parlar segretamente.

Allor chiusero un poco il gran disdegno   88
e disser: "Vien tu solo, e quei sen vada
che sì ardito intrò per questo regno.

Sol si ritorni per la folle strada: 91
pruovi, se sa; ché tu qui rimarrai,
che li ha' iscorta sì buia contrada."

Pensa, lettor, se io mi sconfortai   94
nel suon de le parole maladette,
ché non credetti ritornarci mai.

"O caro duca mio, che più di sette   97
volte m'hai sicurtà renduta e tratto
d'alto periglio che 'ncontra mi stette,

non mi lasciar," diss' io, "così disfatto;   100
e se 'l passar più oltre ci è negato,
ritroviam l'orme nostre insieme ratto."

E quel segnor che lì m'avea menato,   103
mi disse: "Non temer; ché 'l nostro passo
non ci può tòrre alcun: da tal n'è dato.

Ma qui m'attendi, e lo spirito lasso   106
conforta e ciba di speranza buona,
ch'i' non ti lascerò nel mondo basso."

I said: "I can already see distinctly—   70
master—the mosques that gleam within the valley,
as crimson as if they had just been drawn

   out of the fire." He told me: "The eternal   73
flame burning there appears to make them red,
as you can see, within this lower Hell."

So we arrived inside the deep-cut trenches   76
that are the moats of this despondent land:
the ramparts seemed to me to be of iron.

But not before we'd ranged in a wide circuit   79
did we approach a place where that shrill pilot
shouted: "Get out; the entrance way is here."

About the gates I saw more than a thousand—   82
who once had rained from Heaven—and they cried
in anger: "Who is this who, without death,

   can journey through the kingdom of the dead?"   85
And my wise master made a sign that said
he wanted to speak secretly to them.

Then they suppressed—somewhat—their great disdain   88
and said: "You come alone; let him be gone—
for he was reckless, entering this realm.

Let him return alone on his mad road—   91
or try to, if he can, since you, his guide
across so dark a land, you are to stay."

Consider, reader, my dismay before   94
the sound of those abominable words:
returning here seemed so impossible.

"O my dear guide, who more than seven times   97
has given back to me my confidence
and snatched me from deep danger that had menaced,

   do not desert me when I'm so undone;   100
and if they will not let us pass beyond,
let us retrace our steps together, quickly."

These were my words; the lord who'd led me there   103
replied: "Forget your fear, no one can hinder
our passage; One so great has granted it.

But you wait here for me, and feed and comfort   106
your tired spirit with good hope, for I
will not abandon you in this low world."

Così sen va, e quivi m'abbandona   109
lo dolce padre, e io rimagno in forse,
che sì e no nel capo mi tenciona.

Udir non potti quello ch'a lor porse;   112
ma ei non stette là con essi guari,
che ciascun dentro a pruova si ricorse.

Chiuser le porte que' nostri avversari   115
nel petto al mio segnor, che fuor rimase
e rivolsesi a me con passi rari.

Li occhi a la terra e le ciglia avea rase   118
d'ogne baldanza, e dicea ne' sospiri:
"Chi m'ha negate le dolenti case!"

E a me disse: "Tu, perch' io m'adiri,   121
non sbigottir, ch'io vincerò la prova,
qual ch'a la difension dentro s'aggiri.

Questa lor tracotanza non è nova;   124
ché già l'usaro a men segreta porta,
la qual sanza serrame ancor si trova.

Sovr' essa vedestù la scritta morta: 127
e già di qua da lei discende l'erta,
passando per li cerchi sanza scorta,

    tal che per lui ne fia la terra aperta."   130

So he goes on his way; that gentle father   109
has left me there to wait and hesitate,
for *yes* and *no* contend within my head.

I could not hear what he was telling them;   112
but he had not been long with them when each
ran back into the city, scrambling fast.

And these, our adversaries, slammed the gates   115
in my lord's face; and he remained outside,
then, with slow steps, turned back again to me.

His eyes turned to the ground, his brows deprived   118
of every confidence, he said with sighs:
"See who has kept me from the house of sorrow!"

To me he added: "You—though I am vexed—   121
must not be daunted; I shall win this contest,
whoever tries—within—to block our way.

This insolence of theirs is nothing new;   124
they used it once before and at a gate
less secret—it is still without its bolts—

the place where you made out the fatal text;   127
and now, already well within that gate,
across the circles—and alone—descends

the one who will unlock this realm for us."   130

CANTO IX

Quel color che viltà di fuor mi pinse
veggendo il duca mio tornare in volta,
più tosto dentro il suo novo ristrinse.

Attento si fermò com' uom ch'ascolta;   4
ché l'occhio nol potea menare a lunga
per l'aere nero e per la nebbia folta.

"Pur a noi converrà vincer la punga,"   7
cominciò el, "se non... Tal ne s'offerse.
Oh quanto tarda a me ch'altri qui giunga!"

I' vidi ben sì com' ei ricoperse   10
lo cominciar con l'altro che poi venne,
che fur parole a le prime diverse;

ma nondimen paura il suo dir dienne,   13
perch' io traeva la parola tronca
forse a peggior sentenzia che non tenne.

"In questo fondo de la trista conca   16
discende mai alcun del primo grado,
che sol per pena ha la speranza cionca?"

Questa question fec' io; e quei "Di rado   19
incontra," mi rispuose, "che di noi
faccia il cammino alcun per qual io vado.

Ver è ch'altra fiata qua giù fui,   22
congiurato da quella Eritón cruda
che richiamava l'ombre a' corpi sui.

Di poco era di me la carne nuda,   25
ch'ella mi fece intrar dentr' a quel muro,
per trarne un spirto del cerchio di Giuda.

Quell' è 'l più basso loco e 'l più oscuro,   28
e 'l più lontan dal ciel che tutto gira:
ben so 'l cammin; però ti fa sicuro.

The gate of Dis. Dante's fear. The three Furies, invoking Medusa. Virgil's warning to Dante lest he look at Gorgon, Medusa's head. A heavenly messenger. The flight of the demons. Entry into Dis, where Virgil and Dante reach the Sixth Circle and its Arch-Heretics, entombed in red-hot sepulchers.

The color cowardice displayed in me
   when I saw that my guide was driven back,
made him more quickly mask his own new pallor.

He stood alert, like an attentive listener,   4
because his eye could hardly journey far
across the black air and the heavy fog.

"We have to win this battle," he began,   7
"if not ... But one so great had offered help.
How slow that someone's coming seems to me!"

But I saw well enough how he had covered   10
his first words with the words that followed after—
so different from what he had said before;

nevertheless, his speech made me afraid,   13
because I drew out from his broken phrase
a meaning worse—perhaps—than he'd intended.

"Does anyone from the first circle, one   16
whose only punishment is crippled hope,
ever descend so deep in this sad hollow?"

That was my question. And he answered so: 19
"It is quite rare for one of us to go
along the way that I have taken now.

But I, in truth, have been here once before: 22
that savage witch Erichtho, she who called
the shades back to their bodies, summoned me.

My flesh had not been long stripped off when she   25
had me descend through all the rings of Hell,
to draw a spirit back from Judas' circle.

That is the deepest and the darkest place,   28
the farthest from the heaven that girds all:
so rest assured, I know the pathway well.

Questa palude che 'l gran puzzo spira   31
cigne dintorno la città dolente,
u' non potemo intrare omai sanz' ira."

E altro disse, ma non l'ho a mente;   34
però che l'occhio m'avea tutto tratto
ver' l'alta torre a la cima rovente,

dove in un punto furon dritte ratto   37
tre furïe infernal di sangue tinte,
che membra feminine avieno e atto,

e con idre verdissime eran cinte;   40
serpentelli e ceraste avien per crine,
onde le fiere tempie erano avvinte.

E quei, che ben conobbe le meschine   43
de la regina de l'etterno pianto,
"Guarda," mi disse, "le feroci Erine.

Quest' è Megera dal sinistro canto;   46
quella che piange dal destro è Aletto;
Tesifón è nel mezzo"; e tacque a tanto.

Con l'unghie si fendea ciascuna il petto;   49
battiensi a palme e gridavan sì alto,
chi'i' mi strinsi al poeta per sospetto.

"Vegna Medusa: sì 'l farem di smalto,"   52
dicevan tutte riguardando in giuso;
"mal non vengiammo in Tesëo l'assalto."

"Volgiti 'n dietro e tien lo viso chiuso;   55
ché se 'l Gorgón si mostra e tu 'l vedessi,
nulla sarebbe di tornar mai suso."

Così disse 'l maestro; ed elli stessi   58
mi volse, e non si tenne a le mie mani,
che con le sue ancor non mi chiudessi.

O voi ch'avete li 'ntelletti sani,   61
mirate la dottrina che s'asconde
sotto 'l velame de li versi strani.

E già venìa su per le torbide onde   64
un fracasso d'un suon, pien di spavento,
per cui tremavano amendue le sponde,

non altrimenti fatto che d'un vento   67
impetüoso per li avversi ardori,
che fier la selva e sanz' alcun rattento

This swamp that breeds and breathes the giant stench   31
surrounds the city of the sorrowing,
which now we cannot enter without anger."

And he said more, but I cannot remember   34
because my eyes had wholly taken me
to that high tower with the glowing summit

where, at one single point, there suddenly   37
stood three infernal Furies flecked with blood,
who had the limbs of women and their ways

but wore, as girdles, snakes of deepest green;   40
small serpents and horned vipers formed their hairs,
and these were used to bind their bestial temples.

And he, who knew these handmaids well—they served   43
the Queen of never-ending lamentation—
said: "Look at the ferocious Erinyes!

That is Megaera on the left, and she   46
who weeps upon the right, that is Allecto;
Tisiphone's between them." He was done.

Each Fury tore her breast with taloned nails;   49
each, with her palms, beat on herself and wailed
so loud that I, in fear, drew near the poet.

"Just let Medusa come; then we shall turn   52
him into stone," they all cried, looking down;
"we should have punished Theseus' assault."

"Turn round and keep your eyes shut fast, for should   55
the Gorgon show herself and you behold her,
never again would you return above,"

my master said; and he himself turned me   58
around and, not content with just my hands,
used his as well to cover up my eyes.

O you possessed of sturdy intellects,   61
observe the teaching that is hidden here
beneath the veil of verses so obscure.

And now, across the turbid waves, there passed   64
a reboantic fracas—horrid sound,
enough to make both of the shorelines quake:

a sound not other than a wind's when, wild   67
because it must contend with warmer currents,
it strikes against the forest without let,

li rami schianta, abbatte e porta fori;   70
dinanzi polveroso va superbo,
e fa fuggir le fiere e li pastori.

Li occhi mi sciolse e disse: "Or drizza il nerbo   73
del viso su per quella schiuma antica
per indi ove quel fummo è più acerbo."

Come le rane innanzi a la nimica   76
biscia per l'acqua si dileguan tutte,
fin ch'a la terra ciascuna s'abbica,

vid' io più di mille anime distrutte   79
fuggir così dinanzi ad un ch'al passo
passava Stige con le piante asciutte.

Dal volto rimovea quell' aere grasso,   82
menando la sinistra innanzi spesso;
e sol di quell' angoscia parea lasso.

Ben m'accorsi ch'elli era da ciel messo,   85
e volsimi al maestro; e quei fé segno
ch'i' stessi queto ed inchinassi ad esso.

Ahi quanto mi parea pien di disdegno!   88
Venne a la porta e con una verghetta
l'aperse, che non v'ebbe alcun ritegno.

"O cacciati del ciel, gente dispetta,"   91
cominciò elli in su l'orribil soglia,
"ond' esta oltracotanza in voi s'alletta?

Perché recalcitrate a quella voglia   94
a cui non puote il fin mai esser mozzo,
e che più volte v'ha cresciuta doglia?

Che giova ne le fata dar di cozzo?   97
Cerbero vostro, se ben vi ricorda,
ne porta ancor pelato il mento e 'l gozzo."

Poi si rivolse per la strada lorda,   100
e non fé motto a noi, ma fé sembiante
d'omo cui altra cura stringa e morda

che quella di colui che li è davante;   103
e noi movemmo i piedi inver' la terra,
sicuri appresso le parole sante.

Dentro li 'ntrammo sanz' alcuna guerra;   106
e io, ch'avea di riguardar disio
la condizion che tal fortezza serra,

shattering, beating down, bearing off branches,   70
as it moves proudly, clouds of dust before it,
and puts to flight both animals and shepherds.

He freed my eyes and said: "Now let your optic   73
nerve turn directly toward that ancient foam,
there where the mist is thickest and most acrid."

As frogs confronted by their enemy,   76
the snake, will scatter underwater till
each hunches in a heap along the bottom,

so did the thousand ruined souls I saw   79
take flight before a figure crossing Styx
who walked as if on land and with dry soles.

He thrust away the thick air from his face,   82
waving his left hand frequently before him;
that seemed the only task that wearied him.

I knew well he was Heaven's messenger,   85
and I turned toward my master; and he made
a sign that I be still and bow before him.

How full of high disdain he seemed to me!   88
He came up to the gate, and with a wand,
he opened it, for there was no resistance.

"O you cast out of Heaven, hated crowd,"   91
were his first words upon that horrid threshold,
"why do you harbor this presumptuousness?

Why are you so reluctant to endure   94
that Will whose aim can never be cut short,
and which so often added to your hurts?

What good is it to thrust against the fates?   97
Your Cerberus, if you remember well,
for that, had both his throat and chin stripped clean."

At that he turned and took the filthy road,   100
and did not speak to us, but had the look
of one who is obsessed by other cares

than those that press and gnaw at those before him;   103
and we moved forward, on into the city,
in safety, having heard his holy words.

We made our way inside without a struggle;   106
and I, who wanted so much to observe
the state of things that such a fortress guarded,

com' io fui dentro, l'occhio intorno invio: 109
e veggio ad ogne man grande campagna,
piena di duolo e di tormento rio.

    Sì come ad Arli, ove Rodano stagna,   112
sì com' a Pola, presso del Carnaro
ch'Italia chiude e suoi termini bagna,

    fanno i sepulcri tutt' il loco varo,   115
così facevan quivi d'ogne parte,
salvo che 'l modo v'era più amaro;

    ché tra li avelli fiamme erano sparte,   118
per le quali eran sì del tutto accesi,
che ferro più non chiede verun' arte.

    Tutti li lor coperchi eran sospesi,   121
e fuor n'uscivan sì duri lamenti,
che ben parean di miseri e d'offesi.

    E io: "Maestro, quai son quelle genti   124
che, seppellite dentro da quell' arche,
si fan sentir coi sospiri dolenti?"

    E quelli a me: "Qui son li eresïarche   127
con lor seguaci, d'ogne setta, e molto
più che non credi son le tombe carche.

    Simile qui con simile è sepolto,   130
e i monimenti son più e men caldi."
E poi ch'a la man destra si fu vòlto,

    passammo tra i martìri e li alti spaldi.   133

as soon as I had entered, looked about.   109
I saw, on every side, a spreading plain
of lamentation and atrocious pain.

Just as at Arles, where Rhone becomes a marsh,   112
just as at Pola, near Quarnero's gulf,
that closes Italy and bathes its borders,

the sepulchers make all the plain uneven,   115
so they did here on every side, except
that here the sepulchers were much more harsh;

for flames were scattered through the tombs, and these 118
had kindled all of them to glowing heat;
no artisan could ask for hotter iron.

The lid of every tomb was lifted up,   121
and from each tomb such sorry cries arose
as could come only from the sad and hurt.

And I: "Master, who can these people be   124
who, buried in great chests of stone like these,
must speak by way of sighs in agony?"

And he to me: "Here are arch-heretics   127
and those who followed them, from every sect;
those tombs are much more crowded than you think.

Here, like has been ensepulchered with like;   130
some monuments are heated more, some less."
And then he turned around and to his right;

we passed between the torments and high walls.   133

XII·4

TISIPHONE

CANTO X

Ora sen va per un secreto calle,
tra 'l muro de la terra e li martìri,
lo mio maestro, e io dopo le spalle.

"O virtù somma, che per li empi giri   4
mi volvi," cominciai, "com' a te piace,
parlami, e sodisfammi a' miei disiri.

La gente che per li sepolcri giace   7
potrebbesi veder? già son levati
tutt' i coperchi, e nessun guardia face."

E quelli a me: "Tutti saran serrati   10
quando di Iosafàt qui torneranno
coi corpi che là sù hanno lasciati.

Suo cimitero da questa parte hanno   13
con Epicuro tutti suoi seguaci,
che l'anima col corpo morta fanno.

Però a la domanda che mi faci   16
quinc' entro satisfatto sarà tosto,
e al disio ancor che tu mi taci."

E io: "Buon duca, non tegno riposto   19
a te mio cuor se non per dicer poco,
e tu m'hai non pur mo a ciò disposto."

"O Tosco che per la città del foco   22
vivo ten vai così parlando onesto,
piacciati di restare in questo loco.

La tua loquela ti fa manifesto   25
di quella nobil patrïa natio,
a la qual forse fui troppo molesto."

Subitamente questo suono uscìo   28
d'una de l'arche; però m'accostai,
temendo, un poco più al duca mio.

N ow, by a narrow path that ran between
those torments and the ramparts of the city,
my master moves ahead, I following.

"O highest virtue, you who lead me through 4
these circles of transgression, at your will,
do speak to me, and satisfy my longings.

Can those who lie within the sepulchers 7
be seen? The lids—in fact—have all been lifted;
no guardian is watching over them."

And he to me: "They'll all be shuttered up 10
when they return here from Jehosaphat
together with the flesh they left above.

Within this region is the cemetery 13
of Epicurus and his followers,
all those who say the soul dies with the body.

And so the question you have asked of me 16
will soon find satisfaction while we're here,
as will the longing you have hid from me."

And I: "Good guide, the only reason I 19
have hid my heart was that I might speak briefly,
and you, long since, encouraged me in this."

"O Tuscan, you who pass alive across 22
the fiery city with such seemly words,
be kind enough to stay your journey here.

Your accent makes it clear that you belong 25
among the natives of the noble city
I may have dealt with too vindictively."

This sound had burst so unexpectedly 28
out of one sepulcher that, trembling, I
then drew a little closer to my guide.

Ed el mi disse: "Volgiti! Che fai?   31
Vedi là Farinata che s'è dritto:
da la cintola in sù tutto 'l vedrai."

Io avea già il mio viso nel suo fitto;   34
ed el s'ergea col petto e con la fronte
com' avesse l'inferno a gran dispitto.

E l'animose man del duca e pronte   37
mi pinser tra le sepulture a lui,
dicendo: "Le parole tue sien conte."

Com' io al piè de la sua tomba fui,   40
guardommi un poco, e poi, quasi sdegnoso,
mi dimandò: "Chi fuor li maggior tui?"

Io ch'era d'ubidir disideroso,   43
non gliel celai, ma tutto gliel' apersi;
ond' ei levò le ciglia un poco in suso;

poi disse: "Fieramente furo avversi   46
a me e a miei primi e a mia parte,
sì che per due fïate li dispersi."

"S'ei fur cacciati, ei tornar d'ogne parte,"   49
rispuos' io lui, "l'una e l'altra fïata;
ma i vostri non appreser ben quell' arte."

Allor surse a la vista scoperchiata   52
un'ombra, lungo questa, infino al mento:
credo che s'era in ginocchie levata.

Dintorno mi guardò, come talento   55
avesse di veder s'altri era meco;
e poi che 'l sospecciar fu tutto spento,

piangendo disse: "Se per questo cieco   58
carcere vai per altezza d'ingegno,
mio figlio ov' è? e perché non è teco?"

E io a lui: "Da me stesso non vegno: 61
colui ch'attende là per qui mi mena
forse cui Guido vostro ebbe a disdegno."

Le sue parole e 'l modo de la pena   64
m'avean di costui già letto il nome;
però fu la risposta così piena.

Di sùbito drizzato gridò: "Come?   67
dicesti 'elli ebbe'? non viv' elli ancora?
non fiere li occhi suoi lo dolce lume?"

But he told me: "Turn round! What are you doing?   31
That's Farinata who has risen there—
you will see all of him from the waist up."

My eyes already were intent on his;   34
and up he rose—his forehead and his chest—
as if he had tremendous scorn for Hell.

My guide—his hands encouraging and quick—   37
thrust me between the sepulchers toward him,
saying: "Your words must be appropriate."

When I'd drawn closer to his sepulcher,   40
he glanced at me, and as if in disdain,
he asked of me: "Who were your ancestors?"

Because I wanted so to be compliant,   43
I hid no thing from him: I told him all.
At this he lifted up his brows a bit,

then said: "They were ferocious enemies   46
of mine and of my parents and my party,
so that I had to scatter them twice over."

"If they were driven out," I answered him,   49
"they still returned, both times, from every quarter;
but yours were never quick to learn that art."

At this there rose another shade alongside,   52
uncovered to my sight down to his chin;
I think that he had risen on his knees.

He looked around me, just as if he longed   55
to see if I had come with someone else;
but then, his expectation spent, he said

in tears: "If it is your high intellect   58
that lets you journey here, through this blind prison,
where is my son? Why is he not with you?"

I answered: "My own powers have not brought me;   61
he who awaits me there, leads me through here
perhaps to one your Guido did disdain."

His words, the nature of his punishment—   64
these had already let me read his name;
therefore, my answer was so fully made.

Then suddenly erect, he cried: "What's that: 67
He *'did* disdain'? He is not still alive?
The sweet light does not strike against his eyes?"

Quando s'accorse d'alcuna dimora   70
ch'io facëa dinanzi a la risposta,
supin ricadde e più non parve fora.

Ma quell' altro magnanimo, a cui posta   73
restato m'era, non mutò aspetto,
né mosse collo, né piegò sua costa;

e sé continüando al primo detto,   76
"S'elli han quell' arte," disse, "male appresa,
ciò mi tormenta più che questo letto.

Ma non cinquanta volte fia raccesa   79
la faccia de la donna che qui regge,
che tu saprai quanto quell' arte pesa.

E se tu mai nel dolce mondo regge,   82
dimmi: perché quel popolo è sì empio
incontr' a' miei in ciascuna sua legge?"

Ond' io a lui: "Lo strazio e 'l grande scempio   85
che fece l'Arbia colorata in rosso,
tal orazion fa far nel nostro tempio."

Poi ch'ebbe sospirando il capo mosso,   88
"A ciò non fu' io sol," disse, "né certo
sanza cagion con li altri sarei mosso.

Ma fu' io solo, là dove sofferto   91
fu per ciascun di tòrre via Fiorenza,
colui che la difesi a viso aperto."

"Deh, se riposi mai vostra semenza,"   94
prega' io lui, "solvetemi quel nodo
che qui ha 'nviluppata mia sentenza.

El par che voi veggiate, se ben odo,   97
dinanzi quel che 'l tempo seco adduce,
e nel presente tenete altro modo."

"Noi veggiam, come quei c'ha mala luce,   100
le cose," disse, "che ne son lontano;
cotanto ancor ne splende il sommo duce.

Quando s'appressano o son, tutto è vano   103
nostro intelletto; e s'altri non ci apporta,
nulla sapem di vostro stato umano.

Però comprender puoi che tutta morta   106
fia nostra conoscenza da quel punto
che del futuro fia chiusa la porta."

And when he noticed how I hesitated   70
a moment in my answer, he fell back—
supine—and did not show himself again.

But that great-hearted one, the other shade   73
at whose request I'd stayed, did not change aspect
or turn aside his head or lean or bend;

and taking up his words where he'd left off,   76
"If they were slow," he said, "to learn that art,
that is more torment to me than this bed.

And yet the Lady who is ruler here   79
will not have her face kindled fifty times
before you learn how heavy is that art.

And so may you return to the sweet world,   82
tell me: why are those citizens so cruel
against my kin in all of their decrees?"

To which I said: "The carnage, the great bloodshed   85
that stained the waters of the Arbia red
have led us to such prayers in our temple."

He sighed and shook his head, then said: "In that,   88
I did not act alone, but certainly
I'd not have joined the others without cause.

But where I was alone was *there* where all   91
the rest would have annihilated Florence,
had I not interceded forcefully."

"Ah, as I hope your seed may yet find peace,"   94
I asked, "so may you help me to undo
the knot that here has snarled my course of thought.

It seems, if I hear right, that you can see   97
beforehand that which time is carrying,
but you're denied the sight of present things."

"We see, even as men who are farsighted,   100
those things," he said, "that are remote from us;
the Highest Lord allots us that much light.

But when events draw near or are, our minds   103
are useless; were we not informed by others,
we should know nothing of your human state.

So you can understand how our awareness   106
will die completely at the moment when
the portal of the future has been shut."

Allor, come di mia colpa compunto,   109
dissi: "Or direte dunque a quel caduto
che 'l suo nato è co' vivi ancor congiunto;

e s'i' fui, dianzi, a la risposta muto,   112
fate i saper che 'l fei perché pensava
già ne l'error che m'avete soluto."

E già 'l maestro mio mi richiamava;   115
per ch'i' pregai lo spirto più avaccio
che mi dicesse chi con lu' istava.

Dissemi: "Qui con più di mille giaccio: 118
qua dentro è 'l secondo Federico
e 'l Cardinale; e de li altri mi taccio."

Indi s'ascose; e io inver' l'antico   121
poeta volsi i passi, ripensando
a quel parlar che mi parea nemico.

Elli si mosse; e poi, così andando,   124
mi disse: "Perché se' tu sì smarrito?"
E io li sodisfeci al suo dimando.

"La mente tua conservi quel ch'udito   127
hai contra te," mi comandò quel saggio;
"e ora attendi qui," e drizzò 'l dito:

"quando sarai dinanzi al dolce raggio   130
di quella il cui bell' occhio tutto vede,
da lei saprai di tua vita il vïaggio."

Appresso mosse a man sinistra il piede: 133
lasciammo il muro e gimmo inver' lo mezzo
per un sentier ch'a una valle fiede,

che 'nfin là sù facea spiacer suo lezzo.   136

Then, as if penitent for my omission,   109
I said: "Will you now tell that fallen man
his son is still among the living ones;

    and if, a while ago, I held my tongue   112
before his question, let him know it was
because I had in mind the doubt you've answered."

    And now my master was recalling me;   115
so that, more hurriedly, I asked the spirit
to name the others who were there with him.

    He said: "More than a thousand lie with me: 118
the second Frederick is but one among them,
as is the Cardinal; I name no others."

    With that, he hid himself; and pondering   121
the speech that seemed to me so menacing,
I turned my steps to meet the ancient poet.

    He moved ahead, and as we made our way,   124
he said to me: "Why are you so dismayed?"
I satisfied him, answering him fully.

    And then that sage exhorted me: "Remember   127
the words that have been spoken here against you.
Now pay attention," and he raised his finger;

    "when you shall stand before the gentle splendor   130
of one whose gracious eyes see everything,
then you shall learn—from her—your lifetime's journey."

    Following that, his steps turned to the left,   133
leaving the wall and moving toward the middle
along a path that strikes into a valley

    whose stench, as it rose up, disgusted us.   136

CANTO XI

In su l'estremità d'un'alta ripa
che facevan gran pietre rotte in cerchio,
venimmo sopra più crudele stipa;

e quivi, per l'orribile soperchio   4
del puzzo che 'l profondo abisso gitta,
ci raccostammo, in dietro, ad un coperchio

d'un grand' avello, ov' io vidi una scritta   7
che dicea: "Anastasio papa guardo,
lo qual trasse Fotin de la via dritta."

"Lo nostro scender conviene esser tardo,   10
sì che s'ausi un poco in prima il senso
al tristo fiato; e poi no i fia riguardo."

Così 'l maestro; e io "Alcun compenso,"   13
dissi lui, "trova che 'l tempo non passi
perduto." Ed elli: "Vedi ch'a ciò penso."

"Figliuol mio, dentro da cotesti sassi,"   16
cominciò poi a dir, "son tre cerchietti
di grado in grado, come que' che lassi.

Tutti son pien di spirti maladetti;   19
ma perché poi ti basti pur la vista,
intendi come e perché son costretti.

D'ogne malizia, ch'odio in cielo acquista,   22
ingiuria è 'l fine, ed ogne fin cotale
o con forza o con frode altrui contrista.

Ma perché frode è de l'uom proprio male,   25
più spiace a Dio; e però stan di sotto
li frodolenti, e più dolor li assale.

Di vïolenti il primo cerchio è tutto;   28
ma perché si fa forza a tre persone,
in tre gironi è distinto e costrutto.

Along the upper rim of a high bank
formed by a ring of massive broken boulders,
we came above a crowd more cruelly pent.

And here, because of the outrageous stench   4
thrown up in excess by that deep abyss,
we drew back till we were behind the lid

of a great tomb, on which I made out this,   7
inscribed: "I hold Pope Anastasius,
enticed to leave the true path by Photinus."

"It would be better to delay descent   10
so that our senses may grow somewhat used
to this foul stench; and then we can ignore it."

So said my master, and I answered him: 13
"Do find some compensation, lest this time
be lost." And he: "You see, I've thought of that."

"My son, within this ring of broken rocks,"   16
he then began, "there are three smaller circles;
like those that you are leaving, they range down.

Those circles are all full of cursed spirits;   19
so that your seeing of them may suffice,
learn now the how and why of their confinement.

Of every malice that earns hate in Heaven,   22
injustice is the end; and each such end
by force or fraud brings harm to other men.

However, fraud is man's peculiar vice;   25
God finds it more displeasing—and therefore,
the fraudulent are lower, suffering more.

The violent take all of the first circle;   28
but since one uses force against three persons,
that circle's built of three divided rings.

A Dio, a sé, al prossimo si pòne   31
far forza, dico in loro e in lor cose,
come udirai con aperta ragione.

Morte per forza e ferute dogliose   34
nel prossimo si danno, e nel suo avere
ruine, incendi e tollette dannose;

onde omicide e ciascun che mal fiere,   37
guastatori e predon, tutti tormenta
lo giron primo per diverse schiere.

Puote omo aver in sé man vïolenta   40
e ne' suoi beni; e però nel secondo
giron convien che sanza pro si penta

qualunque priva sé del vostro mondo,   43
biscazza e fonde la sua facultade,
e piange là dov' esser de' giocondo.

Puossi far forza ne la deïtade,   46
col cor negando e bestemmiando quella,
e spregiando natura e sua bontade;

e però lo minor giron suggella   49
del segno suo e Soddoma e Caorsa
e chi, spregiando Dio col cor, favella.

La frode, ond' ogne coscïenza è morsa,   52
pùo l'omo usare in colui che 'n lui fida
e in quel che fidanza non imborsa.

Questo modo di retro par ch'incida   55
pur lo vinco d'amor che fa natura;
onde nel cerchio secondo s'annida

ipocresia, lusinghe e chi affattura,   58
falsità, ladroneccio e simonia,
ruffian, baratti e simile lordura.

Per l'altro modo quell' amor s'oblia   61
che fa natura, e quel ch'è poi aggiunto,
di che la fede spezïal si cria;

onde nel cerchio minore, ov' è 'l punto   64
de l'universo in su che Dite siede,
qualunque trade in etterno è consunto."

E io: "Maestro, assai chiara procede   67
la tua ragione, e assai ben distingue
questo baràtro e 'l popol ch'e' possiede.

To God and to one's self and to one's neighbor—   31
I mean, to them or what is theirs—one can
do violence, as you shall now hear clearly.

  Violent death and painful wounds may be   34
inflicted on one's neighbor; his possessions
may suffer ruin, fire, and extortion;

    thus, murderers and those who strike in malice, 37
as well as plunderers and robbers—these,
in separated ranks, the first ring racks.

  A man can set violent hands against   40
himself or his belongings; so within
the second ring repents, though uselessly,

    whoever would deny himself your world,   43
gambling away, wasting his patrimony,
and weeping where he should instead be happy.

  One can be violent against the Godhead,   46
one's heart denying and blaspheming Him
and scorning nature and the good in her;

    so, with its sign, the smallest ring has sealed 49
both Sodom and Cahors and all of those
who speak in passionate contempt of God.

  Now fraud, that eats away at every conscience,   52
is practiced by a man against another
who trusts in him, or one who has no trust.

  This latter way seems only to cut off   55
the bond of love that nature forges; thus,
nestled within the second circle are:

    hypocrisy and flattery, sorcerers,   58
and falsifiers, simony, and theft,
and barrators and panders and like trash.

  But in the former way of fraud, not only   61
the love that nature forges is forgotten,
but added love that builds a special trust;

    thus, in the tightest circle, where there is   64
the universe's center, seat of Dis,
all traitors are consumed eternally."

  "Master, your reasoning is clear indeed,"   67
I said; "it has made plain for me the nature
of this pit and the population in it.

Ma dimmi: quei de la palude pingue,   70
che mena il vento, e che batte la pioggia,
e che s'incontran con sì aspre lingue,

   perché non dentro da la città roggia   73
sono ei puniti, se Dio li ha in ira?
e se non li ha, perché sono a tal foggia?"

   Ed elli a me "Perché tanto delira,"   76
disse, "lo 'ngegno tuo da quel che sòle?
o ver la mente dove altrove mira?

   Non ti rimembra di quelle parole   79
con le quai la tua Etica pertratta
le tre disposizion che 'l ciel non vole,

   incontenenza, malizia e la matta   82
bestialitade? e come incontenenza
men Dio offende e men biasimo accatta?

   Se tu riguardi ben questa sentenza,   85
e rechiti a la mente chi son quelli
che sù di fuor sostegnon penitenza,

   tu vedrai ben perché da questi felli   88
sien dipartiti, e perché men crucciata
la divina vendetta li martelli."

   "O sol che sani ogne vista turbata,   91
tu mi contenti sì quando tu solvi,
che, non men che saver, dubbiar m'aggrata.

   Ancora in dietro un poco ti rivolvi,"   94
diss' io, "là dove di' ch'usura offende
la divina bontade, e 'l groppo solvi."

   "Filosofia," mi disse, "a chi la 'ntende,   97
nota, non pure in una sola parte,
come natura lo suo corso prende

   dal divino 'ntelletto e da sua arte;   100
e se tu ben la tua Fisica note,
tu troverai, non dopo molte carte,

   che l'arte vostra quella, quanto pote,   103
segue, come 'l maestro fa 'l discente;
sì che vostr' arte a Dio quasi è nepote.

   Da queste due, se tu ti rechi a mente   106
lo Genesì dal principio, convene
prender sua vita e avanzar la gente;

But tell me: those the dense marsh holds, or those   70
driven before the wind, or those on whom
rain falls, or those who clash with such harsh tongues,

why are they not all punished in the city   73
of flaming red if God is angry with them?
And if He's not, why then are they tormented?"

And then to me, "Why does your reason wander   76
so far from its accustomed course?" he said.
"Or of what other things are you now thinking?

Have you forgotten, then, the words with which   79
your *Ethics* treats of those three dispositions
that strike at Heaven's will: incontinence

and malice and mad bestiality?   82
And how the fault that is the least condemned
and least offends God is incontinence?

If you consider carefully this judgment   85
and call to mind the souls of upper Hell,
who bear their penalties outside this city,

you'll see why they have been set off from these   88
unrighteous ones, and why, when heaven's vengeance
hammers at them, it carries lesser anger."

"O sun that heals all sight that is perplexed,   91
when I ask you, your answer so contents
that doubting pleases me as much as knowing.

Go back a little to that point," I said,   94
"where you told me that usury offends
divine goodness; unravel now that knot."

"Philosophy, for one who understands,   97
points out, and not in just one place," he said,
"how nature follows—as she takes her course—

the Divine Intellect and Divine Art;   100
and if you read your *Physics* carefully,
not many pages from the start, you'll see

that when it can, your art would follow nature,   103
just as a pupil imitates his master;
so that your art is almost God's grandchild.

From these two, art and nature, it is fitting,   106
if you recall how *Genesis* begins,
for men to make their way, to gain their living;

e perché l'usuriere altra via tene,   109
per sé natura e per la sua seguace
dispregia, poi ch'in altro pon la spene.

Ma seguimi oramai che 'l gir mi piace;   112
ché i Pesci guizzan su per l'orizzonta,
e 'l Carro tutto sovra 'l Coro giace,

e 'l balzo via là oltra si dismonta."   115

and since the usurer prefers another 109
pathway, he scorns both nature in herself
and art, her follower; his hope is elsewhere.

But follow me, for it is time to move; 112
the Fishes glitter now on the horizon
and all the Wain is spread out over Caurus;

only beyond, can one climb down the cliff." 115

XII·12

XII·63

CANTO XII

Era lo loco ov' a scender la riva
venimmo, alpestro e, per quel che v'er' anco,
tal, ch'ogne vista ne sarebbe schiva.

    Qual è quella ruina che nel fianco   4
di qua da Trento l'Adice percosse,
o per tremoto o per sostegno manco,

    che da cima del monte, onde si mosse,   7
al piano è sì la roccia discoscesa,
ch'alcuna via darebbe a chi sù fosse:

    cotal di quel burrato era la scesa;   10
e 'n su la punta de la rotta lacca
l'infamïa di Creti era distesa

    che fu concetta ne la falsa vacca;   13
e quando vide noi, sé stesso morse,
sì come quei cui l'ira dentro fiacca.

    Lo savio mio inver' lui gridò: "Forse   16
tu credi che qui sia 'l duca d'Atene,
che sù nel mondo la morte ti porse?

    Pàrtiti, bestia, ché questi non vene   19
ammaestrato da la tua sorella,
ma vassi per veder le vostre pene."

    Qual è quel toro che si slaccia in quella   22
c'ha ricevuto già 'l colpo mortale,
che gir non sa, ma qua e là saltella,

    vid' io lo Minotauro far cotale;   25
e quello accorto gridò: "Corri al varco;
mentre ch'e' 'nfuria, è buon che tu ti cale."

    Così prendemmo via giù per lo scarco   28
di quelle pietre, che spesso moviensi
sotto i miei piedi per lo novo carco.

The Seventh Circle, First Ring: the Violent against their Neighbors.
The Minotaur. The Centaurs, led by Chiron, who assigns Nessus to
guide Dante and Virgil across the boiling river of blood
(Phlegethon). In that river, Tyrants and Murderers, immersed,
watched over by the Centaurs.

T he place that we had reached for our descent
  along the bank was alpine; what reclined
upon that bank would, too, repel all eyes.

Just like the toppled mass of rock that struck—   4
because of earthquake or eroded props—
the Adige on its flank, this side of Trent,

where from the mountain top from which it thrust   7
down to the plain, the rock is shattered so
that it permits a path for those above:

such was the passage down to that ravine.   10
And at the edge above the cracked abyss,
there lay outstretched the infamy of Crete,

conceived within the counterfeited cow;   13
and, catching sight of us, he bit himself
like one whom fury devastates within.

Turning to him, my sage cried out: "Perhaps   16
you think this is the Duke of Athens here,
who, in the world above, brought you your death.

Be off, you beast; this man who comes has not   19
been tutored by your sister; all he wants
in coming here is to observe your torments."

Just as the bull that breaks loose from its halter   22
the moment it receives the fatal stroke,
and cannot run but plunges back and forth,

so did I see the Minotaur respond;   25
and my alert guide cried: "Run toward the pass;
it's better to descend while he's berserk."

And so we made our way across that heap   28
of stones, which often moved beneath my feet
because my weight was somewhat strange for them.

Io gia pensando; e quei disse: "Tu pensi   31
forse a questa ruina, ch'è guardata
da quell' ira bestial ch'i' ora spensi.

Or vo' che sappi che l'altra fïata   34
ch'i' discesi qua giù nel basso inferno,
questa roccia non era ancor cascata.

Ma certo poco pria, se ben discerno,   37
che venisse colui che la gran preda
levò a Dite del cerchio superno,

da tutte parti l'alta valle feda   40
tremò sì, ch'i' pensai che l'universo
sentisse amor, per lo qual è chi creda

più volte il mondo in caòsso converso;   43
e in quel punto questa vecchia roccia,
qui e altrove, tal fece riverso.

Ma ficca li occhi a valle, ché s'approccia   46
la riviera del sangue in la qual bolle
qual che per vïolenza in altrui noccia."

Oh cieca cupidigia e ira folle,   49
che sì ci sproni ne la vita corta,
e ne l'etterna poi sì mal c'immolle!

Io vidi un'ampia fossa in arco torta,   52
come quella che tutto 'l piano abbraccia,
secondo ch'avea detto la mia scorta;

e tra 'l piè de la ripa ed essa, in traccia   55
corrien centauri, armati di saette,
come solien nel mondo andare a caccia.

Veggendoci calar, ciascun ristette,   58
e de la schiera tre si dipartiro
con archi e asticciuole prima elette;

e l'un gridò da lungi: "A qual martiro   61
venite voi che scendete la costa?
Ditel costinci; se non, l'arco tiro."

Lo mio maestro disse: "La risposta   64
farem noi a Chirón costà di presso:
mal fu la voglia tua sempre sì tosta."

Poi mi tentò, e disse: "Quelli è Nesso,   67
che morì per la bella Deianira,
e fé di sé la vendetta elli stesso.

While climbing down, I thought. He said: "You wonder, 31
perhaps, about that fallen mass, watched over
by the inhuman rage I have just quenched.

Now I would have you know: the other time 34
that I descended into lower Hell,
this mass of boulders had not yet collapsed;

but if I reason rightly, it was just 37
before the coming of the One who took
from Dis the highest circle's splendid spoils

that, on all sides, the steep and filthy valley 40
had trembled so, I thought the universe
felt love (by which, as some believe, the world

has often been converted into chaos); 43
and at that moment, here as well as elsewhere,
these ancient boulders toppled, in this way.

But fix your eyes below, upon the valley, 46
for now we near the stream of blood, where those
who injure others violently, boil."

O blind cupidity and insane anger, 49
which goad us on so much in our short life,
then steep us in such grief eternally!

I saw a broad ditch bent into an arc 52
so that it could embrace all of that plain,
precisely as my guide had said before;

between it and the base of the embankment 55
raced files of Centaurs who were armed with arrows,
as, in the world above, they used to hunt.

On seeing us descend, they all reined in; 58
and, after they had chosen bows and shafts,
three of their number moved out from their ranks;

and still far off, one cried: "What punishment 61
do you approach as you descend the slope?
But speak from there: if not, I draw my bow."

My master told him: "We shall make reply 64
only to Chiron, when we reach his side;
your hasty will has never served you well."

Then he nudged me and said: "That one is Nessus, 67
who died because of lovely Deianira
and of himself wrought vengeance for himself.

E quel di mezzo, ch'al petto si mira,   70
è il gran Chirón, il qual nodrì Achille;
quell' altro è Folo, che fu sì pien d'ira.

Dintorno al fosso vanno a mille a mille,   73
saettando qual anima si svelle
del sangue più che sua colpa sortille."

Noi ci appressammo a quelle fiere isnelle: 76
Chirón prese uno strale, e con la cocca
fece la barba in dietro a le mascelle.

Quando s'ebbe scoperta la gran bocca,   79
disse a' compagni: "Siete voi accorti
che quel di retro move ciò ch'el tocca?

Così non soglion far li piè d'i morti."   82
E 'l mio buon duca, che già li er' al petto,
dove le due nature son consorti,

rispuose: "Ben è vivo, e sì soletto   85
mostrar li mi convien la valle buia;
necessità 'l ci 'nduce, e non diletto.

Tal si partì da cantare alleluia   88
che mi commise quest' officio novo:
non è ladron, né io anima fuia.

Ma per quella virtù per cu' io movo   91
li passi miei per sì selvaggia strada,
danne un de' tuoi, a cui noi siamo a provo,

e che ne mostri là dove si guada,   94
e che porti costui in su la groppa,
ché non è spirto che per l'aere vada."

Chirón si volse in su la destra poppa,   97
e disse a Nesso: "Torna, e sì li guida,
e fa cansar s'altra schiera v'intoppa."

Or ci movemmo con la scorta fida   100
lungo la proda del bollor vermiglio,
dove i bolliti facieno alte strida.

Io vidi gente sotto infino al ciglio;   103
e 'l gran centauro disse: "E' son tiranni
che dier nel sangue e ne l'aver di piglio.

Quivi si piangon li spietati danni;   106
quivi è Alessandro, e Dïonisio fero
che fé Cicilia aver dolorosi anni.

And in the middle, gazing at his chest,   70
is mighty Chiron, tutor of Achilles;
the third is Pholus, he who was so frenzied.

And many thousands wheel around the moat,   73
their arrows aimed at any soul that thrusts
above the blood more than its guilt allots."

By now we had drawn near those agile beasts;   76
Chiron drew out an arrow; with the notch,
he parted his beard back upon his jaws.

When he'd uncovered his enormous mouth,   79
he said to his companions: "Have you noticed
how he who walks behind moves what he touches?

Dead soles are not accustomed to do that."   82
And my good guide—now near the Centaur's chest,
the place where his two natures met—replied:

"He is indeed alive, and so alone   85
it falls to me to show him the dark valley.
Necessity has brought him here, not pleasure.

For she who gave me this new task was one   88
who had just come from singing halleluiah:
he is no robber; I am not a thief.

But by the Power that permits my steps   91
to journey on so wild a path, give us
one of your band, to serve as our companion;

and let him show us where to ford the ditch,   94
and let him bear this man upon his back,
for he's no spirit who can fly through air."

Then Chiron wheeled about and right and said   97
to Nessus: "Then, return and be their guide;
if other troops disturb you, fend them off."

Now, with our faithful escort, we advanced   100
along the bloodred, boiling ditch's banks,
beside the piercing cries of those who boiled.

I saw some who were sunk up to their brows,   103
and that huge Centaur said: "These are the tyrants
who plunged their hands in blood and plundering.

Here they lament their ruthless crimes; here are   106
both Alexander and the fierce Dionysius,
who brought such years of grief to Sicily.

E quella fronte c'ha 'l pel così nero,   109
è Azzolino; e quell' altro ch'è biondo,
è Opizzo da Esti, il qual per vero
    fu spento dal figliastro sù nel mondo."   112
Allor mi volsi al poeta, e quei disse:
"Questi ti sia or primo, e io secondo."

    Poco più oltre il centauro s'affisse   115
sovr' una gente che 'nfino a la gola
parea che di quel bulicame uscisse.

    Mostrocci un'ombra da l'un canto sola,   118
dicendo: "Colui fesse in grembo a Dio
lo cor che 'n su Tamisi ancor si cola."

    Poi vidi gente che di fuor del rio   121
tenean la testa e ancor tutto 'l casso;
e di costoro assai riconobb' io.

    Così a più a più si facea basso   124
quel sangue, sì che cocea pur li piedi;
e quindi fu del fosso il nostro passo.

    "Sì come tu da questa parte vedi   127
lo bulicame che sempre si scema,"
disse 'l centauro, "voglio che tu credi

    che da quest' altra a più a più giù prema   130
lo fondo suo, infin ch'el si raggiunge
ove la tirannia convien che gema.

    La divina giustizia di qua punge   133
quell' Attila che fu flagello in terra,
e Pirro e Sesto; e in etterno munge

    le lagrime, che col bollor diserra,   136
a Rinier da Corneto, a Rinier Pazzo,
che fecero a le strade tanta guerra."

    Poi si rivolse e ripassossi 'l guazzo.   139

That brow with hair so black is Ezzelino;   109
that other there, the blonde one, is Obizzo
of Este, he who was indeed undone,

within the world above, by his fierce son."   112
Then I turned to the poet, and he said:
"Now let him be your first guide, me your second."

A little farther on, the Centaur stopped   115
above a group that seemed to rise above
the boiling blood as far up as their throats.

He pointed out one shade, alone, apart,   118
and said: "Within God's bosom, he impaled
the heart that still drips blood upon the Thames."

Then I caught sight of some who kept their heads   121
and even their full chests above the tide;
among them—many whom I recognized.

And so the blood grew always shallower   124
until it only scorched the feet; and here
we found a place where we could ford the ditch.

"Just as you see that, on this side, the brook   127
continually thins," the Centaur said,
"so I should have you know the rivulet,

along the other side, will slowly deepen   130
its bed, until it reaches once again
the depth where tyranny must make lament.

And there divine justice torments Attila   133
he who was such a scourge upon the earth,
and Pyrrhus, Sextus; to eternity

it milks the tears that boiling brook unlocks   136
from Rinier of Corneto, Rinier Pazzo,
those two who waged such war upon the highroads."

Then he turned round and crossed the ford again.   139

CANTO XIII

Non era ancor di là Nesso arrivato,
quando noi ci mettemmo per un bosco
che da neun sentiero era segnato.

Non fronda verde, ma di color fosco;   4
non rami schietti, ma nodosi e 'nvolti;
non pomi v'eran, ma stecchi con tòsco.

Non han sì aspri sterpi né sì folti   7
quelle fiere selvagge che 'n odio hanno
tra Cecina e Corneto i luoghi cólti.

Quivi le brutte Arpie lor nidi fanno,   10
che cacciar de le Strofade i Troiani
con tristo annunzio di futuro danno.

Ali hanno late, e colli e visi umani,   13
piè con artigli, e pennuto 'l gran ventre;
fanno lamenti in su li alberi strani.

E 'l buon maestro "Prima che più entre,   16
sappi che se' nel secondo girone,"
mi cominciò a dire, "e sarai mentre

che tu verrai ne l'orribil sabbione.   19
Però riguarda ben; sì vederai
cose che torrien fede al mio sermone."

Io sentia d'ogne parte trarre guai   22
e non vedea persona che 'l facesse;
per ch'io tutto smarrito m'arrestai.

Cred' ïo ch'ei credette ch'io credesse   25
che tante voci uscisser, tra quei bronchi,
da gente che per noi si nascondesse.

Però disse 'l maestro: "Se tu tronchi   28
qualche fraschetta d'una d'este piante,
li pensier c'hai si faran tutti monchi."

Nessus had not yet reached the other bank
  when we began to make our way across
a wood on which no path had left its mark.

  No green leaves in that forest, only black;   4
no branches straight and smooth, but knotted, gnarled;
no fruits were there, but briers bearing poison.

  Even those savage beasts that roam between   7
Cécina and Corneto, beasts that hate
tilled lands, do not have holts so harsh and dense.

  This is the nesting place of the foul Harpies,   10
who chased the Trojans from the Strophades
with sad foretelling of their future trials.

  Their wings are wide, their necks and faces human;   13
their feet are taloned, their great bellies feathered;
they utter their laments on the strange trees.

  And my kind master then instructed me: 16
"Before you enter farther know that now
you are within the second ring and shall

  be here until you reach the horrid sand;   19
therefore look carefully; you'll see such things
as would deprive my speech of all belief."

  From every side I heard the sound of cries,   22
but I could not see any source for them,
so that, in my bewilderment, I stopped.

  I think that he was thinking that I thought   25
so many voices moaned among those trunks
from people who had been concealed from us.

  Therefore my master said: "If you would tear   28
a little twig from any of these plants,
the thoughts you have will also be cut off."

Allor porsi la mano un poco avante   31
e colsi un ramicel da un gran pruno;
e 'l tronco suo gridò: "Perché mi schiante?"

Da che fatto fu poi di sangue bruno,   34
ricominciò a dir: "Perché mi scerpi?
non hai tu spirto di pietade alcuno?

Uomini fummo, e or siam fatti sterpi: 37
ben dovrebb' esser la tua man più pia,
se state fossimo anime di serpi."

Come d'un stizzo verde ch'arso sia   40
da l'un de' capi, che da l'altro geme
e cigola per vento che va via,

sì de la scheggia rotta usciva insieme   43
parole e sangue; ond' io lasciai la cima
cadere, e stetti come l'uom che teme.

"S'elli avesse potuto creder prima,"   44
rispuose 'l savio mio, "anima lesa,
ciò c'ha veduto pur con la mia rima,

non averebbe in te la man distesa;   49
ma la cosa incredibile mi fece
indurlo ad ovra ch'a me stesso pesa.

Ma dilli chi tu fosti, sì che 'n vece   52
d'alcun' ammenda tua fama rinfreschi
nel mondo sù, dove tornar li lece."

E 'l tronco: "Sì col dolce dir m'adeschi,   55
ch'i' non posso tacere; e voi non gravi
perch' ïo un poco a ragionar m'inveschi.

Io son colui che tenni ambo le chiavi   58
del cor di Federigo, e che le volsi,
serrando e diserrando, sì soavi,

che dal secreto suo quasi ogn' uom tolsi;   61
fede portai al glorïoso offizio,
tanto ch'i' ne perde' li sonni e ' polsi.

La meretrice che mai da l'ospizio   64
di Cesare non torse li occhi putti,
morte comune e de le corti vizio,

infiammò contra me li animi tutti;   67
e li 'nfiammati infiammar sì Augusto,
che ' lieti onor tornaro in tristi lutti.

Then I stretched out my hand a little way 31
and from a great thornbush snapped off a branch,
at which its trunk cried out: "Why do you tear me?"

And then, when it had grown more dark with blood, 34
it asked again: "Why do you break me off?
Are you without all sentiment of pity?

We once were men and now are arid stumps: 37
your hand might well have shown us greater mercy
had we been nothing more than souls of serpents."

As from a sapling log that catches fire 40
along one of its ends, while at the other
it drips and hisses with escaping vapor,

so from that broken stump issued together 43
both words and blood; at which I let the branch
fall, and I stood like one who is afraid.

My sage said: "Wounded soul, if, earlier, 46
he had been able to believe what he
had only glimpsed within my poetry,

then he would not have set his hand against you; 49
but its incredibility made me
urge him to do a deed that grieves me deeply.

But tell him who you were, so that he may, 52
to make amends, refresh your fame within
the world above, where he can still return."

To which the trunk: "Your sweet speech draws me so 55
that I cannot be still; and may it not
oppress you, if I linger now in talk.

I am the one who guarded both the keys 58
of Frederick's heart and turned them, locking and
unlocking them with such dexterity

that none but I could share his confidence; 61
and I was faithful to my splendid office,
so faithful that I lost both sleep and strength.

The whore who never turned her harlot's eyes 64
away from Caesar's dwelling, she who is
the death of all and vice of every court,

inflamed the minds of everyone against me; 67
and those inflamed, then so inflamed Augustus
that my delighted honors turned to sadness.

L'animo mio, per disdegnoso gusto,   70
credendo col morir fuggir disdegno,
ingiusto fece me contra me giusto.

Per le nove radici d'esto legno   73
vi giuro che già mai non ruppi fede
al mio segnor, che fu d'onor sì degno.

E se di voi alcun nel mondo riede,   76
conforti la memoria mia, che giace
ancor del colpo che 'nvidia le diede."

Un poco attese, e poi "Da ch'el si tace,"   79
disse 'l poeta a me, "non perder l'ora;
ma parla, e chiedi a lui, se più ti piace."

Ond' ïo a lui: "Domandal tu ancora   82
di quel che credi ch'a me satisfaccia;
ch'i' non potrei, tanta pietà m'accora."

Perciò ricominciò: "Se l'om ti faccia   85
liberamente ciò che 'l tuo dir priega,
spirito incarcerato, ancor ti piaccia

di dirne come l'anima si lega   88
in questi nocchi; e dinne, se tu puoi,
s'alcuna mai di tai membra si spiega."

Allor soffiò il tronco forte, e poi   91
si convertì quel vento in cotal voce:
"Brievemente sarà risposto a voi.

Quando si parte l'anima feroce   94
dal corpo ond' ella stessa s'è disvelta,
Minòs la manda a la settima foce.

Cade in la selva, e non l'è parte scelta;   97
ma là dove fortuna la balestra,
quivi germoglia come gran di spelta.

Surge in vermena e in pianta silvestra: 100
l'Arpie, pascendo poi de le sue foglie,
fanno dolore, e al dolor fenestra.

Come l'altre verrem per nostre spoglie,   103
ma non però ch'alcuna sen rivesta,
ché non è giusto aver ciò ch'om si toglie.

Qui le strascineremo, e per la mesta   106
selva saranno i nostri corpi appesi,
ciascuno al prun de l'ombra sua molesta."

My mind, because of its disdainful temper,   70
believing it could flee disdain through death,
made me unjust against my own just self.

I swear to you by the peculiar roots   73
of this thornbush, I never broke my faith
with him who was so worthy—with my lord.

If one of you returns into the world,   76
then let him help my memory, which still
lies prone beneath the battering of envy."

The poet waited briefly, then he said   79
to me: "Since he is silent, do not lose
this chance, but speak and ask what you would know."

And I: "Do you continue; ask of him   82
whatever you believe I should request;
I cannot, so much pity takes my heart."

Then he began again: "Imprisoned spirit,   85
so may this man do freely what you ask,
may it please you to tell us something more

of how the soul is bound into these knots;   88
and tell us, if you can, if any one
can ever find his freedom from these limbs."

At this the trunk breathed violently, then   91
that wind became this voice: "You shall be answered
promptly. When the savage spirit quits

the body from which it has torn itself,   94
then Minos sends it to the seventh maw.
It falls into the wood, and there's no place

to which it is allotted, but wherever   97
fortune has flung that soul, that is the space
where, even as a grain of spelt, it sprouts.

It rises as a sapling, a wild plant;   100
and then the Harpies, feeding on its leaves,
cause pain and for that pain provide a vent.

Like other souls, we shall seek out the flesh   103
that we have left, but none of us shall wear it;
it is not right for any man to have

what he himself has cast aside. We'll drag   106
our bodies here; they'll hang in this sad wood,
each on the stump of its vindictive shade."

Noi eravamo ancora al tronco attesi,   109
credendo ch'altro ne volesse dire,
quando noi fummo d'un romor sorpresi,

  similemente a colui che venire   112
sente 'l porco e la caccia a la sua posta,
ch'ode le bestie, e le frasche stormire.

  Ed ecco due da la sinistra costa,   115
nudi e graffiati, fuggendo sì forte,
che de la selva rompieno ogne rosta.

  Quel dinanzi: "Or accorri, accorri, morte!"   118
E l'altro, cui pareva tardar troppo,
gridava: "Lano, sì non furo accorte

  le gambe tue a le giostre dal Toppo!"   121
E poi che forse li fallia la lena,
di sé e d'un cespuglio fece un groppo.

  Di rietro a loro era la selva piena   124
di nere cagne, bramose e correnti
come veltri ch'uscisser di catena.

  In quel che s'appiattò miser li denti,   127
e quel dilaceraro a brano a brano;
poi sen portar quelle membra dolenti.

  Presemi allor la mia scorta per mano,   130
e menommi al cespuglio che piangea
per le rotture sanguinenti in vano.

  "O Iacopo," dicea, "da Santo Andrea,   133
che t'è giovato di me fare schermo?
che colpa ho io de la tua vita rea?"

  Quando 'l maestro fu sovr' esso fermo,   136
disse: "Chi fosti, che per tante punte
soffi con sangue doloroso sermo?"

  Ed elli a noi: "O anime che giunte   139
siete a veder lo strazio disonesto
c'ha le mie fronde sì da me disgiunte,

  raccoglietele al piè del tristo cesto.   142
I' fui de la città che nel Batista
mutò 'l primo padrone; ond' ei per questo

  sempre con l'arte sua la farà trista;   145
e se non fosse che 'n sul passo d'Arno
rimane ancor di lui alcuna vista,

And we were still intent upon the trunk—   109
believing it had wanted to say more—
when we were overtaken by a roar,

   just as the hunter is aware of chase   112
and boar as they draw near his post—he hears
the beasts and then the branches as they crack.

And there upon the left were two who, scratched   115
and naked, fled so violently that
they tore away each forest bough they passed.

The one in front: "Now come, death, quickly come!"   118
The other shade, who thought himself too slow,
was shouting after him: "Lano, your legs

   were not so nimble at the jousts of Toppo!"   121
And then, perhaps because he'd lost his breath,
he fell into one tangle with a bush.

Behind these two, black bitches filled the wood,   124
and they were just as eager and as swift
as greyhounds that have been let off their leash.

They set their teeth in him where he had crouched;   127
and, piece by piece, those dogs dismembered him
and carried off his miserable limbs.

Then he who was my escort took my hand;   130
he led me to the lacerated thorn
that wept in vain where it was bleeding, broken.

"O Jacopo," it said, "da Santo Andrea,   133
what have you gained by using me as screen?
Am I to blame for your indecent life?"

When my good master stood beside that bush,   136
he said: "Who were you, who through many wounds
must breathe with blood your melancholy words?"

And he to us: "O spirits who have come   139
to witness the outrageous laceration
that leaves so many of my branches torn,

   collect them at the foot of this sad thorn.   142
My home was in the city whose first patron
gave way to John the Baptist; for this reason,

   he'll always use his art to make it sorrow;   145
and if—along the crossing of the Arno—
some effigy of Mars had not remained,

que' cittadin che poi la rifondarno   148
sovra 'l cener che d'Attila rimase,
avrebber fatto lavorare indarno.

Io fei gibetto a me de le mie case."   151

those citizens who afterward rebuilt   148
their city on the ashes that Attila
had left to them, would have travailed in vain.
    I made—of my own house—my gallows place."   151

XIII · 5

CANTO XIV

Poi che la carità del natio loco
   mi strinse, raunai le fronde sparte
e rende'le a colui, ch'era già fioco.

   Indi venimmo al fine ove si parte   4
lo secondo giron dal terzo, e dove
si vede di giustizia orribil arte.

   A ben manifestar le cose nove,   7
dico che arrivammo ad una landa
che dal suo letto ogne pianta rimove.

   La dolorosa selva l'è ghirlanda   10
intorno, come 'l fosso tristo ad essa;
quivi fermammo i passi a randa a randa.

   Lo spazzo era una rena arida e spessa,   13
non d'altra foggia fatta che colei
che fu da' piè di Caton già soppressa.

   O vendetta di Dio, quanto tu dei   16
esser temuta da ciascun che legge
ciò che fu manifesto a li occhi mei!

   D'anime nude vidi molte gregge   19
che piangean tutte assai miseramente,
e parea posta lor diversa legge.

   Supin giacea in terra alcuna gente,   22
alcuna si sedea tutta raccolta,
e altra andava continüamente.

   Quella che giva 'ntorno era più molta,   25
e quella men che giacëa al tormento,
ma più al duolo avea la lingua sciolta.

   Sovra tutto 'l sabbion, d'un cader lento,   28
piovean di foco dilatate falde,
come di neve in alpe sanza vento.

L ove of our native city overcame me;
 I gathered up the scattered boughs and gave
them back to him whose voice was spent already.

 From there we reached the boundary that divides   4
the second from the third ring—and the sight
of a dread work that justice had devised.

 To make these strange things clear, I must explain   7
that we had come upon an open plain
that banishes all green things from its bed.

 The wood of sorrow is a garland round it,   10
just as that wood is ringed by a sad channel;
here, at the very edge, we stayed our steps.

 The ground was made of sand, dry and compact,   13
a sand not different in kind from that
on which the feet of Cato had once tramped.

 O vengeance of the Lord, how you should be   16
dreaded by everyone who now can read
whatever was made manifest to me!

 I saw so many flocks of naked souls,   19
all weeping miserably, and it seemed
that they were ruled by different decrees.

 Some lay upon the ground, flat on their backs;   22
some huddled in a crouch, and there they sat;
and others moved about incessantly.

 The largest group was those who walked about,   25
the smallest, those supine in punishment;
but these had looser tongues to tell their torment.

 Above that plain of sand, distended flakes   28
of fire showered down; their fall was slow—
as snow descends on alps when no wind blows.

Quali Alessandro in quelle parti calde   31
d'Indïa vide sopra 'l süo stuolo
fiamme cadere infino a terra salde,

   per ch'ei provide a scalpitar lo suolo   34
con le sue schiere, acciò che lo vapore
mei si stingueva mentre ch'era solo:

   tale scendeva l'etternale ardore;   37
onde la rena s'accendea, com' esca
sotto focile, a doppiar lo dolore.

   Sanza riposo mai era la tresca   40
de le misere mani, or quindi or quinci
escotendo da sé l'arsura fresca.

   I' cominciai: "Maestro, tu che vinci   43
tutte le cose, fuor che ' demon duri
ch'a l'intrar de la porta incontra uscinci,

   chi è quel grande che non par che curi   46
lo 'ncendio e giace dispettoso e torto,
sì che la pioggia non par che 'l maturi?"

   E quel medesmo, che si fu accorto   49
ch'io domandava il mio duca di lui,
gridò: "Qual io fui vivo, tal son morto.

   Se Giove stanchi 'l suo fabbro da cui   52
crucciato prese la folgore aguta
onde l'ultimo dì percosso fui;

   o s'elli stanchi li altri a muta a muta   55
in Mongibello a la focina negra,
chiamando 'Buon Vulcano, aiuta, aiuta!'

   sì com' el fece a la pugna di Flegra,   58
e me saetti con tutta sua forza:
non ne potrebbe aver vendetta allegra."

   Allora il duca mio parlò di forza   61
tanto, ch'i' non l'avea sì forte udito:
"O Capaneo, in ciò che non s'ammorza

   la tua superbia, se' tu più punito;   64
nullo martiro, fuor che la tua rabbia,
sarebbe al tuo furor dolor compito."

   Poi si rivolse a me con miglior labbia,   67
dicendo: "Quei fu l'un d'i sette regi
ch'assiser Tebe; ed ebbe e par ch'elli abbia

Just like the flames that Alexander saw 31
in India's hot zones, when fires fell,
intact and to the ground, on his battalions,

for which—wisely—he had his soldiers tramp 34
the soil to see that every fire was spent
before new flames were added to the old;

so did the never-ending heat descend; 37
with this, the sand was kindled just as tinder
on meeting flint will flame—doubling the pain.

The dance of wretched hands was never done; 40
now here, now there, they tried to beat aside
the fresh flames as they fell. And I began

to speak: "My master, you who can defeat 43
all things except for those tenacious demons
who tried to block us at the entryway,

who is that giant there, who does not seem 46
to heed the singeing—he who lies and scorns
and scowls, he whom the rains can't seem to soften?"

And he himself, on noticing that I 49
was querying my guide about him, cried:
"That which I was in life, I am in death.

Though Jove wear out the smith from whom he took, 52
in wrath, the keen-edged thunderbolt with which
on my last day I was to be transfixed;

or if he tire the others, one by one, 55
in Mongibello, at the sooty forge,
while bellowing: 'O help, good Vulcan, help!'—

just as he did when there was war at Phlegra— 58
and casts his shafts at me with all his force,
not even then would he have happy vengeance."

Then did my guide speak with such vehemence 61
as I had never heard him use before:
"O Capaneus, for your arrogance

that is not quenched, you're punished all the more: 64
no torture other than your own madness
could offer pain enough to match your wrath."

But then, with gentler face he turned to me 67
and said: "That man was one of seven kings
besieging Thebes; he held—and still, it seems,

Dio in disdegno, e poco par che 'l pregi;   70
ma, com' io dissi lui, li suoi dispetti
sono al suo petto assai debiti fregi.

Or mi vien dietro, e guarda che non metti,   73
ancor, li piedi ne la rena arsiccia;
ma sempre al bosco tien li piedi stretti."

Tacendo divenimmo là 've spiccia   76
fuor de la selva un picciol fiumicello,
lo cui rossore ancor mi raccapriccia.

Quale del Bulicame esce ruscello   79
che parton poi tra lor le peccatrici,
tal per la rena giù sen giva quello.

Lo fondo suo e ambo le pendici   82
fatt' era 'n pietra, e ' margini da lato;
per ch'io m'accorsi che 'l passo era lici.

"Tra tutto l'altro ch'i' t'ho dimostrato,   85
poscia che noi intrammo per la porta
lo cui sogliare a nessuno è negato,

cosa non fu da li tuoi occhi scorta   88
notabile com' è 'l presente rio,
che sovra sé tutte fiammelle ammorta."

Queste parole fuor del duca mio;   91
per ch'io 'l pregai che mi largisse 'l pasto
di cui largito m'avēa il disio.

"In mezzo mar siede un paese guasto,"   94
diss' elli allora, "che s'appella Creta,
sotto 'l cui rege fu già 'l mondo casto.

Una montagna v'è che già fu lieta   97
d'acqua e di fronde, che si chiamò Ida;
or è diserta come cosa vieta.

Rëa la scelse già per cuna fida   100
del suo figliuolo, e per celarlo meglio,
quando piangea, vi facea far le grida.

Dentro dal monte sta dritto un gran veglio,   103
che tien volte le spalle inver' Dammiata
e Roma guarda come süo speglio.

La sua testa è di fin oro formata,   106
e puro argento son le braccia e 'l petto,
poi è di rame infino a la forcata;

holds—God in great disdain, disprizing Him;   70
but as I told him now, his maledictions
sit well as ornaments upon his chest.

Now follow me and—take care—do not set   73
your feet upon the sand that's burning hot,
but always keep them back, close to the forest."

In silence we had reached a place where flowed   76
a slender watercourse out of the wood—
a stream whose redness makes me shudder still.

As from the Bulicame pours a brook   79
whose waters then are shared by prostitutes,
so did this stream run down across the sand.

Its bed and both its banks were made of stone,   82
together with the slopes along its shores,
so that I saw our passageway lay there.

"Among all other things that I have shown you   85
since we first made our way across the gate
whose threshold is forbidden to no one,

no thing has yet been witnessed by your eyes   88
as notable as this red rivulet,
which quenches every flame that burns above it."

These words were spoken by my guide; at this,   91
I begged him to bestow the food for which
he had already given me the craving.

"A devastated land lies in midsea,   94
a land that is called Crete," he answered me.
"Under its king the world once lived chastely.

Within that land there was a mountain blessed   97
with leaves and waters, and they called it Ida;
but it is withered now like some old thing.

It once was chosen as a trusted cradle   100
by Rhea for her son; to hide him better,
when he cried out, she had her servants clamor.

Within the mountain is a huge Old Man,   103
who stands erect—his back turned toward Damietta—
and looks at Rome as if it were his mirror.

The Old Man's head is fashioned of fine gold,   106
the purest silver forms his arms and chest,
but he is made of brass down to the cleft;

da indi in giuso è tutto ferro eletto,   109
salvo che 'l destro piede è terra cotta;
e sta 'n su quel, più che 'n su l'altro, eretto.

   Ciascuna parte, fuor che l'oro, è rotta   112
d'una fessura che lagrime goccia,
le quali, accolte, fóran quella grotta.

   - Lor corso in questa valle si diroccia;   115
fanno Acheronte, Stige e Flegetonta;
poi sen van giù per questa stretta doccia,

   infin, là dove più non si dismonta,   118
fanno Cocito; e qual sia quello stagno
tu lo vedrai, però qui non si conta."

   E io a lui: "Se 'l presente rigagno   121
si diriva così dal nostro mondo,
perché ci appar pur a questo vivagno?"

   Ed elli a me: "Tu sai che 'l loco è tondo;   124
e tutto che tu sie venuto molto,
pur a sinistra, giù calando al fondo,

   non se' ancor per tutto 'l cerchio vòlto;   127
per che, se cosa n'apparisce nova,
non de' addur maraviglia al tuo volto."

   E io ancor: "Maestro, ove si trova   130
Flegetonta e Letè? ché de l'un taci,
e l'altro di' che si fa d'esta piova."

   "In tutte tue question certo mi piaci,"   133
rispuose, "ma 'l bollor de l'acqua rossa
dovea ben solver l'una che tu faci.

   Letè vedrai, ma fuor di questa fossa,   136
là dove vanno l'anime a lavarsi
quando la colpa pentuta è rimossa."

   Poi disse: "Omai è tempo da scostarsi   139
dal bosco; fa che di retro a me vegne:
li margini fan via, che non son arsi,

   e sopra loro ogne vapor si spegne."   142

below that point he is of choicest iron   109
except for his right foot, made of baked clay;
and he rests more on this than on the left.

Each part of him, except the gold, is cracked;   112
and down that fissure there are tears that drip;
when gathered, they pierce through that cavern's floor

and, crossing rocks into this valley, form   115
the Acheron and Styx and Phlegethon;
and then they make their way down this tight channel,

and at the point past which there's no descent,   118
they form Cocytus; since you are to see
what that pool is, I'll not describe it here."

And I asked him: "But if the rivulet   121
must follow such a course down from our world,
why can we see it only at this boundary?"

And he to me: "You know this place is round;   124
and though the way that you have come is long,
and always toward the left and toward the bottom,

you still have not completed all the circle: 127
so that, if something new appears to us,
it need not bring such wonder to your face."

And I again: "Master, where's Phlegethon   130
and where is Lethe? You omit the second
and say this rain of tears has formed the first."

"I'm pleased indeed," he said, "with all your questions; 133
yet one of them might well have found its answer
already—when you saw the red stream boiling.

You shall see Lethe, but past this abyss,   136
there where the spirits go to cleanse themselves
when their repented guilt is set aside."

Then he declared: "The time has come to quit   139
this wood; see that you follow close behind me;
these margins form a path that does not scorch,

and over them, all flaming vapor is quenched."   142

CANTO XV

Ora cen porta l'un de' duri margini;
   e 'l fummo del ruscel di sopra aduggia,
sì che dal foco salva l'acqua e li argini.

   Quali Fiamminghi tra Guizzante e Bruggia,   4
temendo 'l fiotto che 'nver' lor s'avventa,
fanno lo schermo perché 'l mar si fuggia;

   e quali Padoan lungo la Brenta,   7
per difender lor ville e lor castelli,
anzi che Carentana il caldo senta:

   a tale imagine eran fatti quelli,   10
tutto che né sì alti né sì grossi,
qual che si fosse, lo maestro félli.

   Già eravam da la selva rimossi   13
tanto ch'i' non avrei visto dov' era,
perch' io in dietro rivolto mi fossi,

   quando incontrammo d'anime una schiera   16
che venian lungo l'argine, e ciascuna
ci riguardava come suol da sera

   guardare uno altro sotto nuova luna;   19
e sì ver' noi aguzzavan le ciglia
come 'l vecchio sartor fa ne la cruna.

   Così adocchiato da cotal famiglia,   22
fui conosciuto da un, che mi prese
per lo lembo e gridò: "Qual maraviglia!"

   E io, quando 'l suo braccio a me distese,   25
ficcaï li occhi per lo cotto aspetto,
sì che 'l viso abbrusciato non difese

   la conoscenza süa al mio 'ntelletto;   28
e chinando la mano a la sua faccia,
rispuosi: "Siete voi qui, ser Brunetto?"

Now one of the hard borders bears us forward;
  the river mist forms shadows overhead
and shields the shores and water from the fire.

  Just as between Wissant and Bruges, the Flemings,   4
in terror of the tide that floods toward them,
have built a wall of dykes to daunt the sea;

  and as the Paduans, along the Brenta,   7
build bulwarks to defend their towns and castles
before the dog days fall on Carentana;

  just so were these embankments, even though   10
they were not built so high and not so broad,
whoever was the artisan who made them.

  By now we were so distant from the wood   13
that I should not have made out where it was—
not even if I'd turned around to look—

  when we came on a company of spirits   16
who made their way along the bank; and each
stared steadily at us, as in the dusk,

  beneath the new moon, men look at each other.   19
They knit their brows and squinted at us—just
as an old tailor at his needle's eye.

  And when that family looked harder, I   22
was recognized by one, who took me by
the hem and cried out: "This is marvelous!"

  That spirit having stretched his arm toward me,   25
I fixed my eyes upon his baked, brown features,
so that the scorching of his face could not

  prevent my mind from recognizing him;   28
and lowering my face to meet his face,
I answered him: "Are you here, Ser Brunetto?"

E quelli: "O figliuol mio, non ti dispiaccia   31
se Brunetto Latino un poco teco
ritorna 'n dietro e lascia andar la traccia."

I' dissi lui: "Quanto posso, ven preco;   34
e se volete che con voi m'asseggia,
faròl, se piace a costui che vo seco."

"O figliuol," disse, "qual di questa greggia   37
s'arresta punto, giace poi cent' anni
sanz' arrostarsi quando 'l foco il feggia.

Però va oltre: i' ti verrò a' panni;   40
e poi rigiugnerò la mia masnada,
che va piangendo i suoi etterni danni."

Io non osava scender de la strada   43
per andar par di lui; ma 'l capo chino
tenea com' uom che reverente vada.

El cominciò: "Qual fortuna o destino   46
anzi l'ultimo dì qua giù ti mena?
e chi è questi che mostra 'l cammino?"

"Là sù di sopra, in la vita serena,"   49
rispuos' io lui, "mi smarri' in una valle,
avanti che l'età mia fosse piena.

Pur ier mattina le volsi le spalle: 52
questi m'apparve, tornand' ïo in quella,
e reducemi a ca per questo calle."

Ed elli a me: "Se tu segui tua stella,   55
non puoi fallire a glorïoso porto,
se ben m'accorsi ne la vita bella;

e s'io non fossi sì per tempo morto,   58
veggendo il cielo a te così benigno,
dato t'avrei a l'opera conforto.

Ma quello ingrato popolo maligno   61
che discese di Fiesole ab antico,
e tiene ancor del monte e del macigno,

ti si farà, per tuo ben far, nimico;   64
ed è ragion, ché tra li lazzi sorbi
si disconvien fruttare al dolce fico.

Vecchia fama nel mondo li chiama orbi;   67
gent' è avara, invidiosa e superba:
dai lor costumi fa che tu ti forbi.

    And he: "My son, do not mind if Brunetto   31
Latino lingers for a while with you
and lets the file he's with pass on ahead."

    I said: "With all my strength I pray you, stay;   34
and if you'd have me rest awhile with you,
I shall, if that please him with whom I go."

    "O son," he said, "whoever of this flock   37
stops but a moment, stays a hundred years
and cannot shield himself when fire strikes.

    Therefore move on; below—but close—I'll follow;   40
and then I shall rejoin my company,
who go lamenting their eternal sorrows."

    I did not dare to leave my path for his   43
own level; but I walked with head bent low
as does a man who goes in reverence.

    And he began: "What destiny or chance   46
has led you here below before your last
day came, and who is he who shows the way?"

    "There, in the sunlit life above," I answered,   49
"before my years were full, I went astray
within a valley. Only yesterday

    at dawn I turned my back upon it—but   52
when I was newly lost, he here appeared,
to guide me home again along this path."

    And he to me: "If you pursue your star,   55
you cannot fail to reach a splendid harbor,
if in fair life, I judged you properly;

    and if I had not died too soon for this,   58
on seeing Heaven was so kind to you,
I should have helped sustain you in your work.

    But that malicious, that ungrateful people   61
come down, in ancient times, from Fiesole—
still keeping something of the rock and mountain—

    for your good deeds, will be your enemy: 64
and there is cause—among the sour sorbs,
the sweet fig is not meant to bear its fruit.

    The world has long since called them blind, a people 67
presumptuous, avaricious, envious;
be sure to cleanse yourself of their foul ways.

La tua fortuna tanto onor ti serba,   70
che l'una parte e l'altra avranno fame
di te; ma lungi fia dal becco l'erba.

Faccian le bestie fiesolane strame   73
di lor medesme, e non tocchin la pianta,
s'alcuna surge ancora in lor letame,

in cui riviva la sementa santa   76
di que' Roman che vi rimaser quando
fu fatto il nido di malizia tanta."

"Se fosse tutto pieno il mio dimando,"   79
rispuos' io lui, "voi non sareste ancora
de l'umana natura posto in bando;

ché 'n la mente m'è fitta, e or m'accora,   82
la cara e buona imagine paterna
di voi quando nel mondo ad ora ad ora

m'insegnavate come l'uom s'etterna: 85
e quant' io l'abbia in grado, mentr' io vivo
convien che ne la mia lingua si scerna.

Ciò che narrate di mio corso scrivo,   88
e serbolo a chiosar con altro testo
a donna che saprà, s'a lei arrivo.

Tanto vogl' io che vi sia manifesto,   91
pur che mia coscïenza non mi garra,
ch'a la Fortuna, come vuol, son presto.

Non è nuova a li orecchi miei tal arra: 94
però giri Fortuna la sua rota
come le piace, e 'l villan la sua marra."

Lo mio maestro allora in su la gota   97
destra si volse in dietro e riguardommi;
poi disse: "Bene ascolta chi la nota."

Né per tanto di men parlando vommi   100
con ser Brunetto, e dimando chi sono
li suoi compagni più noti e più sommi.

Ed elli a me: "Saper d'alcuno è buono;   103
de li altri fia laudabile tacerci,
ché 'l tempo saria corto a tanto suono.

In somma sappi che tutti fur cherci   106
e litterati grandi e di gran fama,
d'un peccato medesmo al mondo lerci.

Your fortune holds in store such honor for you,   70
one party and the other will be hungry
for you—but keep the grass far from the goat.

For let the beasts of Fiesole find forage   73
among themselves, and leave the plant alone—
if still, among their dung, it rises up—

in which there lives again the sacred seed   76
of those few Romans who remained in Florence
when such a nest of wickedness was built."

"If my desire were answered totally,"   79
I said to Ser Brunetto, "you'd still be
among, not banished from, humanity.

Within my memory is fixed—and now   82
moves me—your dear, your kind paternal image
when, in the world above, from time to time

you taught me how man makes himself eternal;   85
and while I live, my gratitude for that
must always be apparent in my words.

What you have told me of my course, I write;   88
I keep it with another text, for comment
by one who'll understand, if I may reach her.

One thing alone I'd have you plainly see: 91
so long as I am not rebuked by conscience,
I stand prepared for Fortune, come what may.

My ears find no new pledge in that prediction;   94
therefore, let Fortune turn her wheel as she
may please, and let the peasant turn his mattock."

At this, my master turned his head around   97
and toward the right, and looked at me and said:
"He who takes note of this has listened well."

But nonetheless, my talk with Ser Brunetto   100
continues, and I ask of him who are
his comrades of repute and excellence.

And he to me: "To know of some is good;   103
but for the rest, silence is to be praised;
the time we have is short for so much talk.

In brief, know that my company has clerics   106
and men of letters and of fame—and all
were stained by one same sin upon the earth.

Priscian sen va con quella turba grama,   109
e Francesco d'Accorso anche; e vedervi,
s'avessi avuto di tal tigna brama,

colui potei che dal servo de' servi   112
fu trasmutato d'Arno in Bacchiglione,
dove lasciò li mal protesi nervi.

Di più direi; ma 'l venire e 'l sermone   115
più lungo esser non può, però ch'i' veggio
là surger nuovo fummo del sabbione.

Gente vien con la quale esser non deggio.   118
Sieti raccomandato il mio Tesoro,
nel qual io vivo ancora, e più non cheggio."

Poi si rivolse e parve di coloro   121
che corrono a Verona il drappo verde
per la campagna; e parve di costoro

quelli che vince, non colui che perde.   124

That sorry crowd holds Priscian and Francesco   109
d'Accorso; and among them you can see,
if you have any longing for such scurf,

the one the Servant of His Servants sent   112
from the Arno to the Bacchiglione's banks,
and there he left his tendons strained by sin.

I would say more; but both my walk and words   115
must not be longer, for—beyond—I see
new smoke emerging from the sandy bed.

Now people come with whom I must not be.   118
Let my *Tesoro,* in which I still live,
be precious to you; and I ask no more."

And then he turned and seemed like one of those   121
who race across the fields to win the green
cloth at Verona; of those runners, he

appeared to be the winner, not the loser.   124

XIV · 1

XIV · 103

CANTO XVI

Già era in loco onde s'udia 'l rimbombo
de l'acqua che cadea ne l'altro giro,
simile a quel che l'arnie fanno rombo,

quando tre ombre insieme si partiro,   4
correndo, d'una torma che passava
sotto la pioggia de l'aspro martiro.

Venian ver' noi, e ciascuna gridava: 7
"Sòstati tu ch'a l'abito ne sembri
essere alcun di nostra terra prava."

Ahimè, che piaghe vidi ne' lor membri,   10
ricenti e vecchie, da le fiamme incese!
Ancor men duol pur ch'i' me ne rimembri.

A le lor grida il mio dottor s'attese;   13
volse 'l viso ver' me, e "Or aspetta,"
disse, "a costor si vuole esser cortese.

E se non fosse il foco che saetta   16
la natura del loco, i' dicerei
che meglio stesse a te che a lor la fretta."

Ricominciar, come noi restammo, ei   19
l'antico verso; e quando a noi fuor giunti,
fenno una rota di sé tutti e trei.

Qual sogliono i campion far nudi e unti,   22
avvisando lor presa e lor vantaggio,
prima che sien tra lor battuti e punti,

così rotando, ciascuno il visaggio   25
drizzava a me, sì che 'n contraro il collo
faceva ai piè continüo vïaggio.

E "Se miseria d'esto loco sollo   28
rende in dispetto noi e nostri prieghi,"
cominciò l'uno, "e 'l tinto aspetto e brollo,

N o sooner had I reached the place where one
   could hear a murmur, like a beehive's hum,
of waters as they fell to the next circle,

when, setting out together, three shades ran,   4
leaving another company that passed
beneath the rain of bitter punishment.

They came toward us, and each of them cried out: 7
"Stop, you who by your clothing seem to be
someone who comes from our indecent country!"

Ah me, what wounds I saw upon their limbs,   10
wounds new and old, wounds that the flames seared in!
It pains me still as I remember it.

When they cried out, my master paid attention;   13
he turned his face toward me and then he said:
"Now wait: to these one must show courtesy.

And were it not the nature of this place   16
for shafts of fire to fall, I'd say that haste
was seemlier for you than for those three."

As soon as we stood still, they started up   19
their ancient wail again; and when they reached us,
they formed a wheel, all three of them together.

As champions, naked, oiled, will always do,   22
each studying the grip that serves him best
before the blows and wounds begin to fall,

while wheeling so, each one made sure his face   25
was turned to me, so that their necks opposed
their feet in one uninterrupted flow.

And, "If the squalor of this shifting sand,   28
together with our baked and barren features,
makes us and our requests contemptible,"

la fama nostra il tuo animo pieghi   31
a dirne chi tu se', che i vivi piedi
così sicuro per lo 'nferno freghi.

    Questi, l'orme di cui pestar mi vedi,   34
tutto che nudo e dipelato vada,
fu di grado maggior che tu non credi:

    nepote fu de la buona Gualdrada;   37
Guido Guerra ebbe nome, e in sua vita
fece col senno assai e con la spada.

    L'altro, ch'appresso me la rena trita,   40
è Tegghiaio Aldobrandi, la cui voce
nel mondo sù dovria esser gradita.

    E io, che posto son con loro in croce,   43
Iacopo Rusticucci fui, e certo
la fiera moglie più ch'altro mi nuoce."

    S'i' fossi stato dal foco coperto,   46
gittato mi sarei tra lor di sotto,
e credo che 'l dottor l'avria sofferto;

    ma perch' io mi sarei brusciato e cotto,   49
vinse paura la mia buona voglia
che di loro abbracciar mi facea ghiotto.

    Poi cominciai: "Non dispetto, ma doglia   52
la vostra condizion dentro mi fisse,
tanta che tardi tutta si dispoglia,

    tosto che questo mio segnor mi disse   55
parole per le quali i' mi pensai
che qual voi siete, tal gente venisse.

    Di vostra terra sono, e sempre mai   58
l'ovra di voi e li onorati nomi
con affezion ritrassi e ascoltai.

    Lascio lo fele e vo per dolci pomi   61
promessi a me per lo verace duca;
ma 'nfino al centro pria convien ch'i' tomi."

    "Se lungamente l'anima conduca   64
le membra tue," rispuose quelli ancora,
"e se la fama tua dopo te luca,

    cortesia e valor dì se dimora   67
ne la nostra città sì come suole,
o se del tutto se n'è gita fora;

one said, "then may our fame incline your mind   31
to tell us who you are, whose living feet
can make their way through Hell with such assurance.

He in whose steps you see me tread, although   34
he now must wheel about both peeled and naked,
was higher in degree than you believe:

he was a grandson of the good Gualdrada,   37
and Guido Guerra was his name; in life
his sword and his good sense accomplished much.

The other who, behind me, tramples sand—   40
Tegghiaio Aldobrandi, one whose voice
should have been heeded in the world above.

And I, who share this punishment with them,   43
was Jacopo Rusticucci; certainly,
more than all else, my savage wife destroyed me."

If I'd had shield and shelter from the fire,   46
I should have thrown myself down there among them—
I think my master would have sanctioned that;

but since that would have left me burned and baked,   49
my fear won out against the good intention
that made me so impatient to embrace them.

Then I began: "Your present state had fixed   52
not scorn but sorrow in me—and so deeply
that it will only disappear slowly—

as soon as my lord spoke to me with words   55
that made me understand what kind of men
were coming toward us, men of worth like yours.

For I am of your city; and with fondness,   58
I've always told and heard the others tell
of both your actions and your honored names.

I leave the gall and go for the sweet apples   61
that I was promised by my truthful guide;
but first I must descend into the center."

"So may your soul long lead your limbs and may   64
your fame shine after you," he answered then,
"tell us if courtesy and valor still

abide within our city as they did   67
when we were there, or have they disappeared
completely; for Guiglielmo Borsiere,

ché Guiglielmo Borsiere, il qual si duole   70
con noi per poco e va là coi compagni,
assai ne cruccia con le sue parole."

"La gente nuova e i sùbiti guadagni   73
orgoglio e dismisura han generata,
Fiorenza, in te, sì che tu già ten piagni."

Così gridai con la faccia levata;   76
e i tre, che ciò inteser per risposta,
guardar l'un l'altro com' al ver si guata.

"Se l'altre volte sì poco ti costa,"   79
rispuoser tutti, "il satisfare altrui,
felice te se sì parli a tua posta!

Però, se campi d'esti luoghi bui   82
e torni a riveder le belle stelle,
quando ti gioverà dicere 'I' fui,'

fa che di noi a la gente favelle."   85
Indi rupper la rota, e a fuggirsi
ali sembiar le gambe loro isnelle.

Un amen non saria possuto dirsi   88
tosto così com' e' fuoro spariti;
per ch'al maestro parve di partirsi.

Io lo seguiva, e poco eravam iti,   91
che 'l suon de l'acqua n'era sì vicino,
che per parlar saremmo a pena uditi.

Come quel fiume c'ha proprio cammino   94
prima dal Monte Viso 'nver' levante,
da la sinistra costa d'Apennino,

che si chiama Acquacheta suso, avante   97
che si divalli giù nel basso letto,
e a Forlì di quel nome è vacante,

rimbomba là sovra San Benedetto   100
de l'Alpe per cadere ad una scesa
ove dovea per mille esser recetto;

così, giù d'una ripa discoscesa,   103
trovammo risonar quell' acqua tinta,
sì che 'n poc' ora avria l'orecchia offesa.

Io avea una corda intorno cinta,   106
e con essa pensai alcuna volta
prender la lonza a la pelle dipinta.

who only recently has come to share   70
our torments, and goes there with our companions,
has caused us much affliction with his words."

"Newcomers to the city and quick gains   73
have brought excess and arrogance to you,
o Florence, and you weep for it already!"

So I cried out with face upraised; the three   76
looked at each other when they heard my answer
as men will stare when they have heard the truth.

"If you can always offer a reply   79
so readily to others," said all three,
"then happy you who speak, at will, so clearly.

So, if you can escape these lands of darkness   82
and see the lovely stars on your return,
when you repeat with pleasure, 'I was there,'

be sure that you remember us to men."   85
At this they broke their wheel; and as they fled,
their swift legs seemed to be no less than wings.

The time it took for them to disappear—   88
more brief than time it takes to say "amen";
and so, my master thought it right to leave.

I followed him. We'd only walked a little   91
when roaring water grew so near to us
we hardly could have heard each other speak.

And even as the river that is first   94
to take its own course eastward from Mount Viso,
along the left flank of the Apennines

(which up above is called the Acquacheta,   97
before it spills into its valley bed
and flows without that name beyond Forlì),

reverberates above San Benedetto   100
dell'Alpe as it cascades in one leap,
where there is space enough to house a thousand;

so did we hear that blackened water roar   103
as it plunged down a steep and craggy bank,
enough to deafen us in a few hours.

Around my waist I had a cord as girdle,   106
and with it once I thought I should be able
to catch the leopard with the painted hide.

Poscia ch'io l'ebbi tutta da me sciolta,   109
sì come 'l duca m'avea comandato,
porsila a lui aggroppata e ravvolta.

Ond' ei si volse inver' lo destro lato,   112
e alquanto di lunge da la sponda
la gittò giuso in quell' alto burrato.

"E' pur convien che novità risponda,"   115
dicea fra me medesmo, "al novo cenno
che 'l maestro con l'occhio sì seconda."

Ahi quanto cauti li uomini esser dienno   118
presso a color che non veggion pur l'ovra,
ma per entro i pensier miran col senno!

El disse a me: "Tosto verrà di sovra   121
ciò ch'io attendo e che il tuo pensier sogna;
tosto convien ch'al tuo viso si scovra."

Sempre a quel ver c'ha faccia di menzogna   124
de' l'uom chiuder le labbra fin ch'el puote,
però che sanza colpa fa vergogna;

ma qui tacer nol posso; e per le note   127
di questa comedìa, lettor, ti giuro,
s'elle non sien di lunga grazia vòte,

ch'i' vidi per quell' aere grosso e scuro   130
venir notando una figura in suso,
maravigliosa ad ogne cor sicuro,

sì come torna colui che va giuso   133
talora a solver l'àncora ch'aggrappa
o scoglio o altro che nel mare è chiuso,

che 'n sù si stende e da piè si rattrappa.   136

And after I had loosened it completely,   109
just as my guide commanded me to do,
I handed it to him, knotted and coiled.

At this, he wheeled around upon his right   112
and cast it, at some distance from the edge,
straight down into the depth of the ravine.

"And surely something strange must here reply,"   115
I said within myself, "to this strange sign—
the sign my master follows with his eye."

Ah, how much care men ought to exercise   118
with those whose penetrating intellect
can see our thoughts—not just our outer act!

He said to me: "Now there will soon emerge   121
what I await and what your thought has conjured:
it soon must be discovered to your sight."

Faced with that truth which seems a lie, a man   124
should always close his lips as long as he can—
to tell it shames him, even though he's blameless;

but here I can't be still; and by the lines   127
of this my Comedy, reader, I swear—
and may my verse find favor for long years—

that through the dense and darkened air I saw   130
a figure swimming, rising up, enough
to bring amazement to the firmest heart,

like one returning from the waves where he   133
went down to loose an anchor snagged upon
a reef or something else hid in the sea,

who stretches upward and draws in his feet.   136

CANTO XVII

Ecco la fiera con la coda aguzza,
    che passa i monti e rompe i muri e l'armi!
Ecco colei che tutto 'l mondo appuzza!"

    Sì cominciò lo mio duca a parlarmi;   4
e accennolle che venisse a proda,
vicino al fin d'i passeggiati marmi.

    E quella sozza imagine di froda   7
sen venne, e arrivò la testa e 'l busto,
ma 'n su la riva non trasse la coda.

    La faccia sua era faccia d'uom giusto,   10
tanto benigna avea di fuor la pelle,
e d'un serpente tutto l'altro fusto;

    due branche avea pilose insin l'ascelle;   13
lo dosso e 'l petto e ambedue le coste
dipinti avea di nodi e di rotelle.

    Con più color, sommesse e sovraposte   16
non fer mai drappi Tartari né Turchi,
né fuor tai tele per Aragne imposte.

    Come talvolta stanno a riva i burchi,   19
che parte sono in acqua e parte in terra,
e come là tra li Tedeschi lurchi

    lo bivero s'assetta a far sua guerra,   22
così la fiera pessima si stava
su l'orlo ch'è di pietra e 'l sabbion serra.

    Nel vano tutta sua coda guizzava,   25
torcendo in sù la venenosa forca
ch'a guisa di scorpion la punta armava.

    Lo duca disse: "Or convien che si torca   28
la nostra via un poco insino a quella
bestia malvagia che colà si corca."

The monster Geryon. The Seventh Circle, Third Ring, Third Zone: the Violent against Nature and Art (Usurers), each seated beneath the rain of fire with a purse—bearing his family's heraldic emblem—around his neck. Descent to the Eighth Circle on the back of Geryon.

Behold the beast who bears the pointed tail,
who crosses mountains, shatters weapons, walls!
Behold the one whose stench fills all the world!"

So did my guide begin to speak to me,   4
and then he signaled him to come ashore
close to the end of those stone passageways.

And he came on, that filthy effigy   7
of fraud, and landed with his head and torso
but did not draw his tail onto the bank.

The face he wore was that of a just man,   10
so gracious was his features' outer semblance;
and all his trunk, the body of a serpent;

he had two paws, with hair up to the armpits;   13
his back and chest as well as both his flanks
had been adorned with twining knots and circlets.

No Turks or Tartars ever fashioned fabrics   16
more colorful in background and relief,
nor had Arachne ever loomed such webs.

As boats will sometimes lie along the shore,   19
with part of them on land and part in water,
and just as there, among the guzzling Germans,

the beaver sets himself when he means war,   22
so did that squalid beast lie on the margin
of stone that serves as border for the sand.

And all his tail was quivering in the void   25
while twisting upward its envenomed fork,
which had a tip just like a scorpion's.

My guide said: "Now we'd better bend our path   28
a little, till we reach as far as that
malicious beast which crouches over there."

Però scendemmo a la destra mammella,   31
e diece passi femmo in su lo stremo,
per ben cessar la rena e la fiammella.

E quando noi a lei venuti semo,   34
poco più oltre veggio in su la rena
gente seder propinqua al loco scemo.

Quivi 'l maestro "Acciò che tutta piena   37
esperïenza d'esto giron porti,"
mi disse, "va, e vedi la lor mena.

Li tuoi ragionamenti sian là corti;   40
mentre che torni, parlerò con questa,
che ne conceda i suoi omeri forti."

Così ancor su per la strema testa   43
di quel settimo cerchio tutto solo
andai, dove sedea la gente mesta.

Per li occhi fora scoppiava lor duolo;   46
di qua, di là soccorrien con le mani
quando a' vapori, e quando al caldo suolo:

non altrimenti fan di state i cani   49
or col ceffo or col piè, quando son morsi
o da pulci o da mosche o da tafani.

Poi che nel viso a certi li occhi porsi,   52
ne' quali 'l doloroso foco casca,
non ne conobbi alcun; ma io m'accorsi

che dal collo a ciascun pendea una tasca   55
ch'avea certo colore e certo segno,
e quindi par che 'l loro occhio si pasca.

E com' io riguardando tra lor vegno,   58
in una borsa gialla vidi azzurro
che d'un leone avea faccia e contegno.

Poi, procedendo di mio sguardo il curro,   61
vidine un'altra come sangue rossa,
mostrando un'oca bianca più che burro.

E un che d'una scrofa azzurra e grossa   64
segnato avea lo suo sacchetto bianco,
mi disse: "Che fai tu in questa fossa?

Or te ne va; e perché se' vivo anco,   67
sappi che 'l mio vicin Vitalïano
sederà qui dal mio sinistro fianco.

Thus we descended on the right hand side   31
and moved ten paces on the stony brink
in order to avoid the sand and fire.

When we had reached the sprawling beast, I saw—   34
a little farther on, upon the sand—
some sinners sitting near the fissured rock.

And here my master said to me: "So that   37
you may experience this ring in full,
go now, and see the state in which they are.

But keep your conversation with them brief;   40
till you return, I'll parley with this beast,
to see if he can lend us his strong shoulders."

So I went on alone and even farther   43
along the seventh circle's outer margin,
to where the melancholy people sat.

Despondency was bursting from their eyes;   46
this side, then that, their hands kept fending off,
at times the flames, at times the burning soil:

not otherwise do dogs in summer—now   49
with muzzle, now with paw—when they are bitten
by fleas or gnats or by the sharp gadfly.

When I had set my eyes upon the faces   52
of some on whom that painful fire falls,
I recognized no one; but I did notice

that from the neck of each a purse was hung   55
that had a special color and an emblem,
and their eyes seemed to feast upon these pouches.

Looking about—when I had come among them—   58
I saw a yellow purse with azure on it
that had the face and manner of a lion.

Then, as I let my eyes move farther on,   61
I saw another purse that was bloodred,
and it displayed a goose more white than butter.

And one who had an azure, pregnant sow   64
inscribed as emblem on his white pouch, said
to me: "What are you doing in this pit?

Now you be off; and since you're still alive,   67
remember that my neighbor Vitaliano
shall yet sit here, upon my left hand side.

Con questi Fiorentin son padoano: 70
spesse fïate mi 'ntronan li orecchi
gridando: 'Vegna 'l cavalier sovrano,

che recherà la tasca con tre becchi!' "   73
Qui distorse la bocca e di fuor trasse
la lingua, come bue che 'l naso lecchi.

E io, temendo no 'l più star crucciasse   76
lui che di poco star m'avea 'mmonito,
torna'mi in dietro da l'anime lasse.

Trova' il duca mio ch'era salito   79
già su la groppa del fiero animale,
e disse a me: "Or sie forte e ardito.

Omai si scende per sì fatte scale;   82
monta dinanzi, chi'i' voglio esser mezzo,
sì che la coda non possa far male."

Qual è colui che sì presso ha 'l riprezzo   85
de la quartana, c'ha già l'unghie smorte,
e triema tutto pur guardando 'l rezzo,

tal divenn' io a le parole porte;   88
ma vergogna mi fé le sue minacce,
che innanzi a buon segnor fa servo forte.

I' m'assettai in su quelle spallacce;   91
sì volli dir, ma la voce non venne
com' io credetti: "Fa che tu m'abbracce."

Ma esso, ch'altra volta mi sovvenne   94
ad altro forse, tosto ch'i' montai
con le braccia m'avvinse e mi sostenne;

e disse: "Gerïon, moviti omai: 97
le rote larghe, e lo scender sia poco;
pensa la nova soma che tu hai."

Come la navicella esce di loco   100
in dietro in dietro, sì quindi si tolse;
e poi ch'al tutto si sentì a gioco,

là 'v' era 'l petto, la coda rivolse,   103
e quella tesa, come anguilla, mosse,
e con le branche l'aere a sé raccolse.

Maggior paura non credo che fosse   106
quando Fetonte abbandonò li freni,
per che 'l ciel, come pare ancor, si cosse;

Among these Florentines, I'm Paduan;   70
I often hear them thunder in my ears,
shouting, 'Now let the sovereign cavalier,

    the one who'll bring the purse with three goats, come!'" 73
At this he slewed his mouth, and then he stuck
his tongue out, like an ox that licks its nose.

    And I, afraid that any longer stay   76
might anger him who'd warned me to be brief,
made my way back from those exhausted souls.

    I found my guide, who had already climbed   79
upon the back of that brute animal,
and he told me: "Be strong and daring now,

    for our descent is by this kind of stairs: 82
you mount in front; I want to be between,
so that the tail can't do you any harm."

    As one who feels the quartan fever near   85
and shivers, with his nails already blue,
the sight of shade enough to make him shudder,

    so I became when I had heard these words;   88
but then I felt the threat of shame, which makes
a servant—in his kind lord's presence—brave.

    I settled down on those enormous shoulders;   91
I wished to say (and yet my voice did not
come as I thought): "See that you hold me tight."

    But he who—other times, in other dangers—   94
sustained me, just as soon as I had mounted,
clasped me within his arms and propped me up,

    and said: "Now, Geryon, move on; take care   97
to keep your circles wide, your landing slow;
remember the new weight you're carrying."

    Just like a boat that, starting from its moorings, 100
moves backward, backward, so that beast took off;
and when he felt himself completely clear,

    he turned his tail to where his chest had been   103
and, having stretched it, moved it like an eel,
and with his paws he gathered in the air.

    I do not think that there was greater fear   106
in Phaethon when he let his reins go free—
for which the sky, as one still sees, was scorched—

  né quando Icaro misero le reni   109
sentì spennar per la scaldata cera,
gridando il padre a lui "Mala via tieni!"

  che fu la mia, quando vidi ch'i' era   112
ne l'aere d'ogne parte, e vidi spenta
ogne veduta fuor che de la fera.

  Ella sen va notando lenta lenta;   115
rota e discende, ma non me n'accorgo
se non che al viso e di sotto mi venta.

  Io sentia già da la man destra il gorgo   118
far sotto noi un orribile scroscio,
per che con li occhi 'n giù la testa sporgo.

  Allor fu' io più timido a lo stoscio,   121
però ch'i' vidi fuochi e senti' pianti;
ond' io tremando tutto mi raccoscio.

  E vidi poi, ché nol vedea davanti,   124
lo scendere e 'l girar per li gran mali
che s'appressavan da diversi canti.

  Come 'l falcon ch'è stato assai su l'ali,   127
che sanza veder logoro o uccello
fa dire al falconiere "Omè, tu cali!"

  discende lasso onde si move isnello,   130
per cento rote, e da lunge si pone
dal suo maestro, disdegnoso e fello;

  così ne puose al fondo Gerïone   133
al piè al piè de la stagliata rocca,
e, discarcate le nostre persone,

  si dileguò come da corda cocca.   136

   nor in poor Icarus when he could feel   109
his sides unwinged because the wax was melting,
his father shouting to him, "That way's wrong!"

   than was in me when, on all sides, I saw   112
that I was in the air, and everything
had faded from my sight—except the beast.

   Slowly, slowly, swimming, he moves on;   115
he wheels and he descends, but I feel only
the wind upon my face and the wind rising.

   Already, on our right, I heard the torrent   118
resounding, there beneath us, horribly,
so that I stretched my neck and looked below.

   Then I was more afraid of falling off,   121
for I saw fires and I heard laments,
at which I tremble, crouching, and hold fast.

   And now I saw what I had missed before: 124
his wheeling and descent—because great torments
were drawing closer to us on all sides.

   Just as a falcon long upon the wing—   127
who, seeing neither lure nor bird, compels
the falconer to cry, "Ah me, you fall!"—

   descends, exhausted, in a hundred circles,   130
where he had once been swift, and sets himself,
embittered and enraged, far from his master;

   such, at the bottom of the jagged rock,   133
was Geryon, when he had set us down.
And once our weight was lifted from his back,

   he vanished like an arrow from a bow.   136

XVII · 3

and he came on, that filthy effigy of fraud

XVII · 50   XVII · 127

CANTO XVIII

Luogo è in inferno detto Malebolge,
  tutto di pietra di color ferrigno,
come la cerchia che dintorno il volge.

  Nel dritto mezzo del campo maligno   4
vaneggia un pozzo assai largo e profondo,
di cui *suo loco* dicerò l'ordigno.

  Quel cinghio che rimane adunque è tondo   7
tra 'l pozzo e 'l piè de l'alta ripa dura,
e ha distinto in dieci valli il fondo.

  Quale, dove per guardia de le mura   10
più e più fossi cingon li castelli,
la parte dove son rende figura,

  tale imagine quivi facean quelli;   13
e come a tai fortezze da' lor sogli
a la ripa di fuor son ponticelli,

  così da imo de la roccia scogli   16
movien che ricidien li argini e ' fossi
infino al pozzo che i tronca e raccogli.

  In questo luogo, de la schiena scossi   19
di Gerïon, trovammoci; e 'l poeta
tenne a sinistra, e io dietro mi mossi.

  A la man destra vidi nova pieta,   22
novo tormento e novi frustatori,
di che la prima bolgia era repleta.

  Nel fondo erano ignudi i peccatori;   25
dal mezzo in qua ci venien verso 'l volto,
di là con noi, ma con passi maggiori,

  come i Roman per l'essercito molto,   28
l'anno del giubileo, su per lo ponte
hanno a passar la gente modo colto,

There is a place in Hell called Malebolge,
made all of stone the color of crude iron,
as is the wall that makes its way around it.

Right in the middle of this evil field   4
is an abyss, a broad and yawning pit,
whose structure I shall tell in its due place.

The belt, then, that extends between the pit   7
and that hard, steep wall's base is circular;
its bottom has been split into ten valleys.

Just as, where moat on moat surrounds a castle   10
in order to keep guard upon the walls,
the ground they occupy will form a pattern,

so did the valleys here form a design;   13
and as such fortresses have bridges running
right from their thresholds toward the outer bank,

so here, across the banks and ditches, ridges   16
ran from the base of that rock wall until
the pit that cuts them short and joins them all.

This was the place in which we found ourselves   19
when Geryon had put us down; the poet
held to the left, and I walked at his back.

Upon the right I saw new misery,   22
I saw new tortures and new torturers,
filling the first of Malebolge's moats.

Along its bottom, naked sinners moved,   25
to our side of the middle, facing us;
beyond that, they moved with us, but more quickly—

as, in the year of Jubilee, the Romans,   28
confronted by great crowds, contrived a plan
that let the people pass across the bridge,

che da l'un lato tutti hanno la fronte   31
verso 'l castello e vanno a Santo Pietro,
da l'altra sponda vanno verso 'l monte.

Di qua, di là, su per lo sasso tetro   34
vidi demon cornuti con gran ferze,
che li battien crudelmente di retro.

Ahi come facean lor levar le berze   37
a le prime percosse! già nessuno
le seconde aspettava né le terze.

Mentr' io andava, li occhi miei in uno   40
furo scontrati; e io sì tosto dissi:
"Già di veder costui non son digiuno."

Per ch'ïo a figurarlo i piedi affissi;   43
e 'l dolce duca meco si ristette,
e assentio ch'alquanto in dietro gissi.

E quel frustato celar si credette   46
bassando 'l viso; ma poco li valse,
ch'io dissi: "O tu che l'occhio a terra gette,

se le fazion che porti non son false,   49
Venedico se' tu Caccianemico.
Ma che ti mena a sì pungenti salse?"

Ed elli a me: "Mal volontier lo dico;   52
ma sforzami la tua chiara favella,
che mi fa sovvenir del mondo antico.

I' fui colui che la Ghisolabella   55
condussi a far la voglia del marchese,
come che suoni la sconcia novella.

E non pur io qui piango bolognese;   58
anzi n'è questo loco tanto pieno,
che tante lingue non son ora apprese

a dicer 'sipa' tra Sàvena e Reno;   61
e se di ciò vuoi fede o testimonio,
rècati a mente il nostro avaro seno."

Così parlando il percosse un demonio   64
de la sua scurïada, e disse: "Via,
ruffian! qui non son femmine da conio."

I' mi raggiunsi con la scorta mia;   67
poscia con pochi passi divenimmo
là 'v' uno scoglio de la ripa uscia.

for to one side went all who had their eyes   31
upon the Castle, heading toward St. Peter's,
and to the other, those who faced the Mount.

Both left and right, along the somber rock,   34
I saw horned demons with enormous whips,
who lashed those spirits cruelly from behind.

Ah, how their first strokes made those sinners lift   37
their heels! Indeed no sinner waited for
a second stroke to fall—or for a third.

And as I moved ahead, my eyes met those   40
of someone else, and suddenly I said:
"I was not spared the sight of him before."

And so I stayed my steps, to study him;   43
my gentle guide had stopped together with me
and gave me leave to take a few steps back.

That scourged soul thought that he could hide himself   46
by lowering his face; it helped him little,
for I said: "You, who cast your eyes upon

the ground, if these your features are not false,   49
must be Venèdico Caccianemico;
but what brings you to sauces so piquant?"

And he to me: "I speak unwillingly;   52
but your plain speech, that brings the memory
of the old world to me, is what compels me;

For it was I who led Ghisolabella   55
to do as the Marquis would have her do—
however they retell that filthy tale.

I'm not the only Bolognese who weeps here;   58
indeed, this place is so crammed full of us
that not so many tongues have learned to say

sipa between the Sàvena and Reno;   61
if you want faith and testament of that,
just call to mind our avaricious hearts."

And as he spoke, a demon cudgeled him   64
with his horsewhip and cried: "Be off, you pimp,
there are no women here for you to trick."

I joined my escort once again; and then   67
with but few steps, we came upon a place
where, from the bank, a rocky ridge ran out.

Assai leggeramente quel salimmo;   70
e vòlti a destra su per la sua scheggia,
da quelle cerchie etterne ci partimmo.

Quando noi fummo là dov' el vaneggia   73
di sotto per dar passo a li sferzati,
lo duca disse: "Attienti, e fa che feggia

lo viso in te di quest' altri mal nati,   76
ai quali ancor non vedesti la faccia
però che son con noi insieme andati."

Del vecchio ponte guardavam la traccia   79
che venìa verso noi da l'altra banda,
e che la ferza similmente scaccia.

E 'l buon maestro, sanza mia dimanda,   82
mi disse: "Guarda quel grande che vene,
e per dolor non par lagrime spanda:

quanto aspetto reale ancor ritene!   85
Quelli è Iasón, che per cuore e per senno
li Colchi del monton privati féne.

Ello passò per l'isola di Lenno   88
poi che l'ardite femmine spietate
tutti li maschi loro a morte dienno.

Ivi con segni e con parole ornate   91
Isifile ingannò, la giovinetta
che prima avea tutte l'altre ingannate.

Lasciolla quivi, gravida, soletta;   94
tal colpa a tal martiro lui condanna;
e anche di Medea si fa vendetta.

Con lui sen va chi da tal parte inganna;   97
e questo basti de la prima valle
sapere e di color che 'n sé assanna."

Già eravam là 've lo stretto calle   100
con l'argine secondo s'incrocicchia,
e fa di quello ad un altr' arco spalle.

Quindi sentimmo gente che si nicchia   103
ne l'altra bolgia e che col muso scuffa,
e sé medesma con le palme picchia.

Le ripe eran grommate d'una muffa,   106
per l'alito di giù che vi s'appasta,
che con li occhi e col naso facea zuffa.

We climbed quite easily along that height;   70
and turning right upon its jagged back,
we took our leave of those eternal circlings.

When we had reached the point where that ridge opens   73
below to leave a passage for the lashed,
my guide said: "Stay, and make sure that the sight

of still more ill-born spirits strikes your eyes,   76
for you have not yet seen their faces, since
they have been moving in our own direction."

From the old bridge we looked down at the ranks   79
of those approaching from the other side;
they too were driven onward by the lash.

And my good master, though I had not asked,   82
urged me: "Look at that mighty one who comes
and does not seem to shed a tear of pain:

how he still keeps the image of a king!   85
That shade is Jason, who with heart and head
deprived the men of Colchis of their ram.

He made a landfall on the isle of Lemnos   88
after its women, bold and pitiless,
had given all their island males to death.

With polished words and love signs he took in   91
Hypsipyle, the girl whose own deception
had earlier deceived the other women.

And he abandoned her, alone and pregnant;   94
such guilt condemns him to such punishment;
and for Medea, too, revenge is taken.

With him go those who cheated so: this is   97
enough for you to know of that first valley
and of the souls it clamps within its jaws."

We were already where the narrow path   100
reaches and intersects the second bank
and serves as shoulder for another bridge.

We heard the people whine in the next pouch   103
and heard them as they snorted with their snouts;
we heard them use their palms to beat themselves.

And exhalations, rising from below,   106
stuck to the banks, encrusting them with mold,
and so waged war against both eyes and nose.

Lo fondo è cupo sì, che non ci basta   109
loco a veder sanza montare al dosso
de l'arco, ove lo scoglio più sovrasta.

Quivi venimmo; e quindi giù nel fosso   112
vidi gente attuffata in uno sterco
che da li uman privadi parea mosso.

E mentre ch'io là giù con l'occhio cerco,   115
vidi un col capo sì di merda lordo,
che non parëa s'era laico o cherco.

Quei mi sgridò: "Perché se' tu sì gordo   118
di riguardar più me che li altri brutti?"
E io a lui: "Perché, se ben ricordo,

già t'ho veduto coi capelli asciutti,   121
e se' Alessio Interminei da Lucca:
però t'adocchio più che li altri tutti."

Ed elli allor, battendosi la zucca: 124
"Qua giù m'hanno sommerso le lusinghe
ond' io non ebbi mai la lingua stucca."

Appresso ciò lo duca "Fa che pinghe,"   127
mi disse, "il viso un poco più avante,
sì che la faccia ben con l'occhio attinghe

di quella sozza e scapigliata fante   130
che là si graffia con l'unghie merdose,
e or s'accoscia e ora è in piedi stante.

Taïde è, la puttana che rispuose   133
al drudo suo quando disse 'Ho io grazie
grandi apo te?': 'Anzi maravigliose!'

E quinci sian le nostre viste sazie."   136

The bottom is so deep, we found no spot   109
to see it from, except by climbing up
the arch until the bridge's highest point.

This was the place we reached; the ditch beneath   112
held people plunged in excrement that seemed
as if it had been poured from human privies.

And while my eyes searched that abysmal sight,   115
I saw one with a head so smeared with shit,
one could not see if he were lay or cleric.

He howled: "Why do you stare more greedily   118
at me than at the others who are filthy?"
And I: "Because, if I remember right,

I have seen you before, with your hair dry;   121
and so I eye you more than all: you are
Alessio Interminei of Lucca."

Then he continued, pounding on his pate: 124
"I am plunged here because of flatteries—
of which my tongue had such sufficiency."

At which my guide advised me: "See you thrust   127
your head a little farther to the front,
so that your eyes can clearly glimpse the face

of that besmirched, bedraggled harridan   130
who scratches at herself with shit-filled nails,
and now she crouches, now she stands upright.

That is Thaïs, the harlot who returned   133
her lover's question, 'Are you very grateful
to me?' by saying, 'Yes, enormously.'"

And now our sight has had its fill of this."   136

CANTO XIX

O Simon mago, o miseri seguaci
   che le cose di Dio, che di bontate
deon essere spose, e voi rapaci

   per oro e per argento avolterate,   4
or convien che per voi suoni la tromba,
però che ne la terza bolgia state.

   Già eravamo, a la seguente tomba,   7
montati de lo scoglio in quella parte
ch'a punto sovra mezzo 'l fosso piomba.

   O somma sapïenza, quanta è l'arte   10
che mostri in cielo, in terra e nel mal mondo,
e quanto giusto tua virtù comparte!

   Io vidi per le coste e per lo fondo   13
piena la pietra livida di fóri,
d'un largo tutti e ciascun era tondo.

   Non mi parean men ampi né maggiori   16
che que' che son nel mio bel San Giovanni,
fatti per loco d'i battezzatori;

   l'un de li quali, ancor non è molt' anni,   19
rupp' io per un che dentro v'annegava:
e questo sia suggel ch'ogn' omo sganni.

   Fuor de la bocca a ciascun soperchiava   22
d'un peccator li piedi e de le gambe
infino al grosso, e l'altro dentro stava.

   Le piante erano a tutti accese intrambe;   25
per che sì forte guizzavan le giunte,
che spezzate averien ritorte e strambe.

   Qual suole il fiammeggiar de le cose unte   28
muoversi pur su per la strema buccia,
tal era lì dai calcagni a le punte.

O Simon Magus! O his sad disciples!
Rapacious ones, who take the things of God,
that ought to be the brides of Righteousness,

and make them fornicate for gold and silver!   4
The time has come to let the trumpet sound
for you; your place is here in this third pouch.

We had already reached the tomb beyond   7
and climbed onto the ridge, where its high point
hangs just above the middle of the ditch.

O Highest Wisdom, how much art you show   10
in heaven, earth, and this sad world below,
how just your power is when it allots!

Along the sides and down along the bottom,   13
I saw that livid rock was perforated:
the openings were all one width and round.

They did not seem to me less broad or more   16
than those that in my handsome San Giovanni
were made to serve as basins for baptizing;

and one of these, not many years ago,   19
I broke for someone who was drowning in it:
and let this be my seal to set men straight.

Out from the mouth of each hole there emerged   22
a sinner's feet and so much of his legs
up to the thigh; the rest remained within.

Both soles of every sinner were on fire;   25
their joints were writhing with such violence,
they would have severed withes and ropes of grass.

As flame on oily things will only stir   28
along the outer surface, so there, too,
that fire made its way from heels to toes.

"Chi è colui, maestro, che si cruccia   31
guizzando più che li altri suoi consorti,"
diss' io, "e cui più roggia fiamma succia?"

Ed elli a me: "Se tu vuo' ch'i' ti porti   34
là giù per quella ripa che più giace,
da lui saprai di sé e de' suoi torti."

E io: "Tanto m'è bel, quanto a te piace: 37
tu se' segnore, e sai ch'i' non mi parto
dal tuo volere, e sai quel che si tace."

Allor venimmo in su l'argine quarto;   40
volgemmo e discendemmo a mano stanca
là giù nel fondo foracchiato e arto.

Lo buon maestro ancor de la sua anca   43
non mi dipuose, sì mi giunse al rotto
di quel che si piangeva con la zanca.

"O qual che se' che 'l di sù tien di sotto,   46
anima trista come pal commessa,"
comincia' io a dir, "se puoi, fa motto."

Io stava come 'l frate che confessa   49
lo perfido assessin, che, poi ch'è fitto,
richiama lui per che la morte cessa.

Ed el gridò: "Se' tu già costì ritto,   52
se' tu già costì ritto, Bonifazio?
Di parecchi anni mi mentì lo scritto.

Se' tu sì tosto di quell' aver sazio   55
per lo qual non temesti tòrre a 'nganno
la bella donna, e poi di farne strazio?"

Tal mi fec' io, quai son color che stanno,   58
per non intender ciò ch'è lor risposto,
quasi scornati, e risponder non sanno.

Allor Virgilio disse: "Dilli tosto: 61
'Non son colui, non son colui che credi' ";
e io rispuosi come a me fu imposto.

Per che lo spirto tutti storse i piedi;   64
poi, sospirando e con voce di pianto,
mi disse: "Dunque che a me richiedi?

Se di saper ch'i' sia ti cal cotanto,   67
che tu abbi però la ripa corsa,
sappi ch'i' fui vestito del gran manto;

"Master," I said, "who is that shade who suffers   31
and quivers more than all his other comrades,
that sinner who is licked by redder flames?"

And he to me: "If you would have me lead   34
you down along the steepest of the banks,
from him you'll learn about his self and sins."

And I: "What pleases you will please me too: 37
you are my lord; you know I do not swerve
from what you will; you know what is unspoken."

At this we came upon the fourth embankment;   40
we turned and, keeping to the left, descended
into the narrow, perforated bottom.

My good lord did not let me leave his side   43
until he'd brought me to the hole that held
that sinner who lamented with his legs.

"Whoever you may be, dejected soul,   46
whose head is downward, planted like a pole,"
my words began, "do speak if you are able."

I stood as does the friar who confesses   49
the foul assassin who, fixed fast, head down,
calls back the friar, and so delays his death;

and he cried out: "Are you already standing,   52
already standing there, o Boniface?
The book has lied to me by several years.

Are you so quickly sated with the riches   55
for which you did not fear to take by guile
the Lovely Lady, then to violate her?"

And I became like those who stand as if   58
they have been mocked, who cannot understand
what has been said to them and can't respond.

But Virgil said: "Tell this to him at once: 61
'I am not he—not whom you think I am.'"
And I replied as I was told to do.

At this the spirit twisted both his feet,   64
and sighing and with a despairing voice,
he said: "What is it, then, you want of me?

If you have crossed the bank and climbed so far   67
to find out who I am, then know that I
was one of those who wore the mighty mantle,

e veramente fui figliuol de l'orsa,   70
cupido sì per avanzar li orsatti,
che sù l'avere e qui me misi in borsa.

Di sotto al capo mio son li altri tratti   73
che precedetter me simoneggiando,
per le fessure de la pietra piatti.

Là giù cascherò io altresì quando   76
verrà colui ch'i' credea che tu fossi,
allor ch'i' feci 'l sùbito dimando.

Ma più è 'l tempo già che i piè mi cossi   79
e ch'i' son stato così sottosopra,
ch'el non starà piantato coi piè rossi:

ché dopo lui verrà di più laida opra,   82
di ver' ponente, un pastor sanza legge,
tal che convien che lui e me ricuopra.

Nuovo Iasón sarà, di cui si legge   85
ne' Maccabei; e come a quel fu molle
suo re, così fia lui chi Francia regge."

Io non so s'i' mi fui qui troppo folle,   88
ch'i' pur rispuosi lui a questo metro:
"Deh, or mi dì: quanto tesoro volle

Nostro Segnore in prima da san Pietro   91
ch'ei ponesse le chiavi in sua balìa?
Certo non chiese se non 'Viemmi retro.'

Né Pier né li altri tolsero a Matia   94
oro od argento, quando fu sortito
al loco che perdé l'anima ria.

Però ti sta, ché tu se' ben punito;   97
e guarda ben la mal tolta moneta
ch'esser ti fece contra Carlo ardito.

E se non fosse ch'ancor lo mi vieta   100
la reverenza de le somme chiavi
che tu tenesti ne la vita lieta,

io userei parole ancor più gravi;   103
ché la vostra avarizia il mondo attrista,
calcando i buoni e sollevando i pravi.

Di voi pastor s'accorse il Vangelista,   106
quando colei che siede sopra l'acque
puttaneggiar coi regi a lui fu vista;

    and surely was a son of the she-bear,   70
so eager to advance the cubs that I
pursed wealth above while here I purse myself.

    Below my head there is the place of those   73
who took the way of simony before me;
and they are stuffed within the clefts of stone.

    I, too, shall yield my place and fall below   76
when he arrives, the one for whom I had
mistaken you when I was quick to question.

    But I have baked my feet a longer time,   79
have stood like this, upon my head, than he
is to stand planted here with scarlet feet:

    for after him, one uglier in deeds   82
will come, a lawless shepherd from the west,
worthy to cover him and cover me.

    He'll be a second Jason, of whom we read   85
in *Maccabees*; and just as Jason's king
was soft to him, so shall the king of France

    be soft to this one." And I do not know   88
if I was too rash here—I answered so:
"Then tell me now, how much gold did our Lord

    ask that Saint Peter give to him before   91
he placed the keys within his care? Surely
the only thing he said was: 'Follow me.'

    And Peter and the others never asked   94
for gold or silver when they chose Matthias
to take the place of the transgressing soul.

    Stay as you are, for you are rightly punished;   97
and guard with care the money got by evil
that made you so audacious against Charles.

    And were it not that I am still prevented   100
by reverence for those exalted keys
that you had held within the happy life,

    I'd utter words much heavier than these,   103
because your avarice afflicts the world:
it tramples on the good, lifts up the wicked.

    You, shepherds, the Evangelist had noticed   106
when he saw her who sits upon the waters
and realized she fornicates with kings,

quella che con le sette teste nacque,   109
e da le diece corna ebbe argomento,
fin che virtute al suo marito piacque.

Fatto v'avete dio d'oro e d'argento;   112
e che altro è da voi a l'idolatre,
se non ch'elli uno, e voi ne orate cento?

Ahi, Costantin, di quanto mal fu matre,   115
non la tua conversion, ma quella dote
che da te prese il primo ricco patre!"

E mentr' io li cantava cotai note,   118
o ira o coscïenza che 'l mordesse,
forte spingava con ambo le piote.

I' credo ben ch'al mio duca piacesse,   121
con sì contenta labbia sempre attese
lo suon de le parole vere espresse.

Però con ambo le braccia mi prese;   124
e poi che tutto su mi s'ebbe al petto,
rimontò per la via onde discese.

Né si stancò d'avermi a sé distretto,   127
sì men portò sovra 'l colmo de l'arco
che dal quarto al quinto argine è tragetto.

Quivi soavemente spuose il carco,   130
soave per lo scoglio sconcio ed erto
che sarebbe a le capre duro varco.

Indi un altro vallon mi fu scoperto.   133

she who was born with seven heads and had 109
the power and support of the ten horns,
as long as virtue was her husband's pleasure.

    You've made yourselves a god of gold and silver; 112
how are you different from idolaters,
save that they worship one and you a hundred?

    Ah, Constantine, what wickedness was born— 115
and not from your conversion—from the dower
that you bestowed upon the first rich father!"

    And while I sang such notes to him—whether 118
it was his indignation or his conscience
that bit him—he kicked hard with both his soles.

    I do indeed believe it pleased my guide: 121
he listened always with such satisfied
expression to the sound of those true words.

    And then he gathered me in both his arms 124
and, when he had me fast against his chest,
where he climbed down before, climbed upward now;

    nor did he tire of clasping me until 127
he brought me to the summit of the arch
that crosses from the fourth to the fifth rampart.

    And here he gently set his burden down— 130
gently because the ridge was rough and steep,
and would have been a rugged pass for goats.

    From there another valley lay before me. 133

XXI · 7

DANTE & VIRGIL

CANTO XX

D i nova pena mi conven far versi
    e dar matera al ventesimo canto
de la prima canzon, ch'è d'i sommersi.

Io era già disposto tutto quanto   4
a riguardar ne lo scoperto fondo,
che si bagnava d'angoscioso pianto;

e vidi gente per lo vallon tondo   7
venir, tacendo e lagrimando, al passo
che fanno le letane in questo mondo.

Come 'l viso mi scese in lor più basso,   10
mirabilmente apparve esser travolto
ciascun tra 'l mento e 'l principio del casso,

ché da le reni era tornato 'l volto,   13
e in dietro venir li convenia,
perché 'l veder dinanzi era lor tolto.

Forse per forza già di parlasia   16
si travolse così alcun del tutto;
ma io nol vidi, né credo che sia.

Se Dio ti lasci, lettor, prender frutto   19
di tua lezione, or pensa per te stesso
com' io potea tener lo viso asciutto,

quando la nostra imagine di presso   22
vidi sì torta, che 'l pianto de li occhi
le natiche bagnava per lo fesso.

Certo io piangea, poggiato a un de' rocchi   25
del duro scoglio, sì che la mia scorta
mi disse: "Ancor se' tu de li altri sciocchi?

Qui vive la pietà quand' è ben morta;   28
chi è più scellerato che colui
che al giudicio divin passion comporta?

I must make verses of new punishment
and offer matter now for Canto Twenty
of this first canticle—of the submerged.

    I was already well prepared to stare   4
below, into the depth that was disclosed,
where tears of anguished sorrow bathed the ground;

    and in the valley's circle I saw souls   7
advancing, mute and weeping, at the pace
that, in our world, holy processions take.

    As I inclined my head still more, I saw   10
that each, amazingly, appeared contorted
between the chin and where the chest begins;

    they had their faces twisted toward their haunches   13
and found it necessary to walk backward,
because they could not see ahead of them.

    Perhaps the force of palsy has so fully   16
distorted some, but that I've yet to see,
and I do not believe that that can be.

    May God so let you, reader, gather fruit   19
from what you read; and now think for yourself
how I could ever keep my own face dry

    when I beheld our image so nearby   22
and so awry that tears, down from the eyes,
bathed the buttocks, running down the cleft.

    Of course I wept, leaning against a rock   25
along that rugged ridge, so that my guide
told me: "Are you as foolish as the rest?

    Here pity only lives when it is dead: 28
for who can be more impious than he
who links God's judgment to passivity?

Drizza la testa, drizza, e vedi a cui   31
s'aperse a li occhi d'i Teban la terra;
per ch'ei gridavan tutti: 'Dove rui,

Anfïarao? perché lasci la guerra?'   34
E non restò di ruinare a valle
fino a Minòs che ciascheduno afferra.

Mira c'ha fatto petto de le spalle;   37
perché volse veder troppo davante,
di retro guarda e fa retroso calle.

Vedi Tiresia, che mutò sembiante   40
quando di maschio femmina divenne,
cangiandosi le membra tutte quante;

e prima, poi, ribatter li convenne   43
li duo serpenti avvolti, con la verga,
che rïavesse le maschili penne.

Aronta è quel ch'al ventre li s'atterga,   46
che ne' monti di Luni, dove ronca
lo Carrarese che di sotto alberga,

ebbe tra ' bianchi marmi la spelonca   49
per sua dimora; onde a guardar le stelle
e 'l mar non li era la veduta tronca.

E quella che ricuopre le mammelle,   52
che tu non vedi, con le trecce sciolte,
e ha di là ogne pilosa pelle,

Manto fu, che cercò per terre molte;   55
poscia si puose là dove nacqu' io;
onde un poco mi piace che m'ascolte.

Poscia che 'l padre suo di vita uscìo   58
e venne serva la città di Baco,
questa gran tempo per lo mondo gio.

Suso in Italia bella giace un laco,   61
a piè de l'Alpe che serra Lamagna
sovra Tiralli, c'ha nome Benaco.

Per mille fonti, credo, e più si bagna   64
tra Garda e Val Camonica e Pennino
de l'acqua che nel detto laco stagna.

Loco è nel mezzo là dove 'l trentino   67
pastore e quel di Brescia e 'l veronese
segnar poria, s'e' fesse quel cammino.

Lift, lift your head and see the one for whom   31
the earth was opened while the Thebans watched,
so that they all cried: 'Amphiaraus,

where are you rushing? Have you quit the fight?'   34
Nor did he interrupt his downward plunge
to Minos, who lays hands on every sinner.

See how he's made a chest out of his shoulders;   37
and since he wanted so to see ahead,
he looks behind and walks a backward path.

And see Tiresias, who changed his mien   40
when from a man he turned into a woman,
so totally transforming all his limbs

that then he had to strike once more upon   43
the two entwining serpents with his wand
before he had his manly plumes again.

And Aruns is the one who backs against   46
the belly of Tiresias—Aruns who,
in Luni's hills, tilled by the Carrarese,

who live below, had as his home, a cave   49
among white marbles, from which he could gaze
at stars and sea with unimpeded view.

And she who covers up her breasts—which you   52
can't see—with her disheveled locks, who keeps
all of her hairy parts to the far side,

was Manto, who had searched through many lands,   55
then settled in the place where I was born;
on this, I'd have you hear me now a while.

When Manto's father took his leave of life,   58
and Bacchus' city found itself enslaved,
she wandered through the world for many years.

High up, in lovely Italy, beneath   61
the Alps that shut in Germany above
Tirolo, lies a lake known as Benaco.

A thousand springs and more, I think, must flow   64
out of the waters of that lake to bathe
Pennino, Garda, Val Camonica.

And at its middle is a place where three—   67
the bishops of Verona, Brescia, Trento—
may bless if they should chance to come that way.

Siede Peschiera, bello e forte arnese   70
da fronteggiar Bresciani e Bergamaschi,
ove la riva 'ntorno più discese.

Ivi convien che tutto quanto caschi   73
ciò che 'n grembo a Benaco star non può,
e fassi fiume giù per verdi paschi.

Tosto che l'acqua a correr mette co,   76
non più Benaco, ma Mencio si chiama
fino a Governol, dove cade in Po.

Non molto ha corso, ch'el trova una lama,   79
ne la qual si distende e la 'mpaluda;
e suol di state talor esser grama.

Quindi passando la vergine cruda   82
vide terra, nel mezzo del pantano,
sanza coltura e d'abitanti nuda.

Lì, per fuggire ogne consorzio umano,   85
ristette con suoi servi a far sue arti,
e visse, e vi lasciò suo corpo vano.

Li uomini poi che 'ntorno erano sparti   88
s'accolsero a quel loco, ch'era forte
per lo pantan ch'avea da tutte parti.

Fer la città sovra quell' ossa morte;   91
e per colei che 'l loco prima elesse,
Mantüa l'appellar sanz' altra sorte.

Già fuor le genti sue dentro più spesse,   94
prima che la mattia da Casalodi
da Pinamonte inganno ricevesse.

Però t'assenno che, se tu mai odi   97
originar la mia terra altrimenti,
la verità nulla menzogna frodi."

E io: "Maestro, i tuoi ragionamenti   100
mi son sì certi e prendon sì mia fede,
che li altri mi sarien carboni spenti.

Ma dimmi, de la gente che procede,   103
se tu ne vedi alcun degno di nota;
ché solo a ciò la mia mente rifiede."

Allor mi disse: "Quel che da la gota   106
porge la barba in su le spalle brune,
fu—quando Grecia fu di maschi vòta,

Peschiera, strong and handsome fortress, built   70
to face the Brescians and the Bergamasques
stands where the circling shore is at its lowest.

There, all the waters that cannot be held   73
within the bosom of Benaco fall,
to form a river running through green meadows.

No sooner has that stream begun to flow   76
than it is called the Mincio, not Benaco—
until Govèrnolo, where it joins the Po.

It's not flowed far before it finds flat land;   79
and there it stretches out to form a fen
that in the summer can at times be fetid.

And when she passed that way, the savage virgin   82
saw land along the middle of the swamp,
untilled and stripped of its inhabitants.

And there, to flee all human intercourse,   85
she halted with her slaves to ply her arts;
and there she lived, there left her empty body.

And afterward, the people of those parts   88
collected at that place, because the marsh—
surrounding it on all sides—made it strong.

They built a city over her dead bones;   91
and after her who first had picked that spot,
they called it Mantua—they cast no lots.

There once were far more people in its walls,   94
before the foolishness of Casalodi
was tricked by the deceit of Pinamonte.

Therefore, I charge you, if you ever hear   97
a different tale of my town's origin,
do not let any falsehood gull the truth."

And I: "O master, that which you have spoken   100
convinces me and so compels my trust
that others' words would only be spent coals.

But tell me if among the passing souls   103
you see some spirits worthy of our notice,
because my mind is bent on that alone."

Then he to me: "That shade who spreads his beard   106
down from his cheeks across his swarthy shoulders—
when Greece had been so emptied of its males

sì ch'a pena rimaser per le cune—   109
augure, e diede 'l punto con Calcanta
in Aulide a tagliar la prima fune.

   Euripilo ebbe nome, e così 'l canta   112
l'alta mia tragedìa in alcun loco:
ben lo sai tu che la sai tutta quanta.

   Quell' altro che ne' fianchi è così poco,   115
Michele Scotto fu, che veramente
de le magiche frode seppe 'l gioco.

   Vedi Guido Bonatti; vedi Asdente,   118
ch'avere inteso al cuoio e a lo spago
ora vorrebbe, ma tardi si pente.

   Vedi le triste che lasciaron l'ago,   121
la spuola e 'l fuso, e fecersi 'ndivine;
fecer malie con erbe e con imago.

   Ma vienne omai, ché già tiene 'l confine   124
d'amendue li emisperi e tocca l'onda
sotto Sobilia Caino e le spine;

   e già iernotte fu la luna tonda: 127
ben ten de' ricordar, ché non ti nocque
alcuna volta per la selva fonda."

   Sì mi parlava, e andavamo introcque.   130

    that hardly any cradle held a son,   109
he was an augur; and at Aulis, he
and Calchas set the time to cut the cables.

    His name's Eurypylus; a certain passage   112
of my high tragedy has sung it so;
you know that well enough, who know the whole.

    That other there, his flanks extremely spare,   115
was Michael Scot, a man who certainly
knew how the game of magic fraud was played.

    See there Guido Bonatti; see Asdente,   118
who now would wish he had attended to
his cord and leather, but repents too late.

    See those sad women who had left their needle, 121
shuttle, and spindle to become diviners;
they cast their spells with herbs and effigies.

    But let us go; Cain with his thorns already   124
is at the border of both hemispheres
and there, below Seville, touches the sea.

    Last night the moon was at its full; you should 127
be well aware of this, for there were times
when it did you no harm in the deep wood."

    These were his words to me; meanwhile we journeyed. 130

CANTO XXI

Così di ponte in ponte, altro parlando
che la mia comedìa cantar non cura,
venimmo; e tenavamo 'l colmo, quando

restammo per veder l'altra fessura   4
di Malebolge e li altri pianti vani;
e vidila mirabilmente oscura.

Quale ne l'arzanà de' Viniziani   7
bolle l'inverno la tenace pece
a rimpalmare i legni lor non sani,

ché navicar non ponno—in quella vece   10
chi fa suo legno novo e chi ristoppa
le coste a quel che più vïaggi fece;

chi ribatte da proda e chi da poppa;   13
altri fa remi e altri volge sarte;
chi terzeruolo e artimon rintoppa—:

tal, non per foco ma per divin' arte,   16
bollia là giuso una pegola spessa,
che 'nviscava la ripa d'ogne parte.

I' vedea lei, ma non vedëa in essa   19
mai che le bolle che 'l bollor levava,
e gonfiar tutta, e riseder compressa.

Mentr' io là giù fisamente mirava,   22
lo duca mio, dicendo "Guarda, guarda!"
mi trasse a sé del loco dov' io stava.

Allor mi volsi come l'uom cui tarda   25
di veder quel che li convien fuggire
e cui paura sùbita sgagliarda,

che, per veder, non indugia 'l partire: 28
e vidi dietro a noi un diavol nero
correndo su per lo scoglio venire.

The Eighth Circle, Fifth Pouch, with Barrators plunged into boiling pitch and guarded by demons armed with prongs. A newly arrived magistrate from Lucca. Ten demons assigned by Malacoda ("Evil-Tail"), the chief of the Malebranche ("Evil-Claws"), to escort Dante and Virgil. The remarkable signal for their march.

We came along from one bridge to another,
   talking of things my Comedy is not
concerned to sing. We held fast to the summit,

   then stayed our steps to spy the other cleft   4
of Malebolge and other vain laments.
I saw that it was wonderfully dark.

   As in the arsenal of the Venetians,   7
all winter long a stew of sticky pitch
boils up to patch their sick and tattered ships

   that cannot sail (instead of voyaging,   10
some build new keels, some tow and tar the ribs
of hulls worn out by too much journeying;

   some hammer at the prow, some at the stern,   13
and some make oars, and some braid ropes and cords;
one mends the jib, another, the mainsail);

   so, not by fire but by the art of God,   16
below there boiled a thick and tarry mass
that covered all the banks with clamminess.

   I saw it, but I could not see within it;   19
no thing was visible but boiling bubbles,
the swelling of the pitch; and then it settled.

   And while I watched below attentively,   22
my guide called out to me: "Take care! Take care!"
And then, from where I stood, he drew me near.

   I turned around as one who is impatient   25
to see what he should shun but is dashed down
beneath the terror he has undergone,

   who does not stop his flight and yet would look.   28
And then in back of us I saw a black
demon as he came racing up the crags.

Ahi quant' elli era ne l'aspetto fero!   31
e quanto mi parea ne l'atto acerbo,
con l'ali aperte e sovra i piè leggero!

L'omero suo, ch'era aguto e superbo,   34
carcava un peccator con ambo l'anche,
e quei tenea de' piè ghermito 'l nerbo.

Del nostro ponte disse: "O Malebranche,   37
ecco un de li anzïan di Santa Zita!
Mettetel sotto, ch'i' torno per anche

a quella terra, che n'è ben fornita: 40
ogn' uom v'è barattier, fuor che Bonturo;
del no, per li denar, vi si fa *ita*."

Là giù 'l buttò, e per lo scoglio duro   43
si volse; e mai non fu mastino sciolto
con tanta fretta a seguitar lo furo.

Quel s'attuffò, e tornò sù convolto;   46
ma i demon che del ponte avean coperchio,
gridar: "Qui non ha loco il Santo Volto!

qui si nuota altrimenti che nel Serchio!   49
Però, se tu non vuo' di nostri graffi,
non far sopra la pegola soverchio."

Poi l'addentar con più di cento raffi,   52
disser: "Coverto convien che qui balli,
sì che, se puoi, nascosamente accaffi."

Non altrimenti i cuochi a' lor vassalli   55
fanno attuffare in mezzo la caldaia
la carne con li uncin, perché non galli.

Lo buon maestro "Acciò che non si paia   58
che tu ci sia," mi disse, "giù t'acquatta
dopo uno scheggio, ch'alcun schermo t'aia;

e per nulla offension che mi sia fatta,   61
non temer tu, ch'i' ho le cose conte,
per ch'altra volta fui a tal baratta."

Poscia passò di là dal co del ponte;   64
e com' el giunse in su la ripa sesta,
mestier li fu d'aver sicura fronte.

Con quel furore e con quella tempesta   67
ch'escono i cani a dosso al poverello
che di sùbito chiede ove s'arresta,

Ah, he was surely barbarous to see!   31
And how relentless seemed to me his acts!
His wings were open and his feet were lithe;

    across his shoulder, which was sharp and high,   34
he had slung a sinner, upward from the thighs;
in front, the demon gripped him by the ankles.

    Then from our bridge, he called: "O Malebranche,   37
I've got an elder of Saint Zita for you!
Shove this one under—I'll go back for more—

    his city is well furnished with such stores;   40
there, everyone's a grafter but Bonturo;
and there—for cash—they'll change a *no* to *yes*."

    He threw the sinner down, then wheeled along   43
the stony cliff: no mastiff's ever been
unleashed with so much haste to chase a thief.

    The sinner plunged, then surfaced, black with pitch;   46
but now the demons, from beneath the bridge,
shouted: "The Sacred Face has no place here;

    here we swim differently than in the Serchio;   49
if you don't want to feel our grappling hooks,
don't try to lift yourself above that ditch."

    They pricked him with a hundred prongs and more,   52
then taunted: "Here one dances under cover,
so try to grab your secret graft below."

    The demons did the same as any cook   55
who has his urchins force the meat with hooks
deep down into the pot, that it not float.

    Then my good master said to me: "Don't let   58
those demons see that you are here; take care
to crouch behind the cover of a crag.

    No matter what offense they offer me,   61
don't be afraid; I know how these things go—
I've had to face such fracases before."

    When this was said, he moved beyond the bridgehead.   64
And on the sixth embankment, he had need
to show his imperturbability.

    With the same frenzy, with the brouhaha   67
of dogs, when they beset a poor wretch who
then stops dead in his tracks as if to beg,

usciron quei di sotto al ponticello,   70
e volser contra lui tutt' i runcigli;
ma el gridò: "Nessun di voi sia fello!

Innanzi che l'uncin vostro mi pigli,   73
traggasi avante l'un di voi che m'oda,
e poi d'arruncigliarmi si consigli."

Tutti gridaron: "Vada Malacoda!";   76
per ch'un si mosse—e li altri stetter fermi—
e venne a lui dicendo: "Che li approda?"

"Credi tu, Malacoda, qui vedermi   79
esser venuto," disse 'l mio maestro,
"sicuro già da tutti vostri schermi,

sanza voler divino e fato destro?   82
Lascian' andar, ché nel cielo è voluto
ch'i' mostri altrui questo cammin silvestro."

Allor li fu l'orgoglio sì caduto,   85
ch'e' si lasciò cascar l'uncino a' piedi,
e disse a li altri: "Omai non sia feruto."

E 'l duca mio a me: "O tu che siedi   88
tra li scheggion del ponte quatto quatto,
sicuramente omai a me ti riedi."

Per ch'io mi mossi e a lui venni ratto;   91
e i diavoli si fecer tutti avanti,
sì ch'io temetti ch'ei tenesser patto;

così vid' ïo già temer li fanti   94
ch'uscivan patteggiati di Caprona,
veggendo sé tra nemici cotanti.

I' m'accostai con tutta la persona   97
lungo 'l mio duca, e non torceva li occhi
da la sembianza lor ch'era non buona.

Ei chinavan li raffi e "Vuo' che 'l tocchi,"   100
diceva l'un con l'altro, "in sul groppone?"
E rispondien: "Sì, fa che gliel' accocchi."

Ma quel demonio che tenea sermone   103
col duca mio, si volse tutto presto
e disse: "Posa, posa, Scarmiglione!"

Poi disse a noi: "Più oltre andar per questo   106
iscoglio non si può, però che giace
tutto spezzato al fondo l'arco sesto.

so, from beneath the bridge, the demons rushed   70
against my guide with all their prongs, but he
called out: "Can't you forget your savagery!

Before you try to maul me, just let one   73
of all your troop step forward. Hear me out,
and then decide if I am to be hooked."

At this they howled, "Let Malacoda go!"   76
And one of them moved up—the others stayed—
and as he came, he asked: "How can he win?"

"O Malacoda, do you think I've come,"   79
my master answered him, "already armed—
as you can see—against your obstacles,

without the will of God and helpful fate?   82
Let us move on; it is the will of Heaven
for me to show this wild way to another."

At this the pride of Malacoda fell;   85
his prong dropped to his feet. He told his fellows:
"Since that's the way things stand, let us not wound him."

My guide then spoke to me: "O you, who crouch,   88
bent low among the bridge's splintered rocks,
you can feel safe—and now return to me."

At this I moved and quickly came to him.   91
The devils had edged forward, all of them;
I feared that they might fail to keep their word:

just so, I saw the infantry when they   94
marched out, under safe conduct, from Caprona;
they trembled when they passed their enemies.

My body huddled closer to my guide;   97
I did not let the demons out of sight;
the looks they cast at us were less than kind.

They bent their hooks and shouted to each other: 100
"And shall I give it to him on the rump?"
And all of them replied, "Yes, let him have it!"

But Malacoda, still in conversation   103
with my good guide, turned quickly to his squadron
and said: "Be still, Scarmiglione, still!"

To us he said: "There is no use in going   106
much farther on this ridge, because the sixth
bridge—at the bottom there—is smashed to bits.

E se l'andare avante pur vi piace,   109
andatevene su per questa grotta;
presso è un altro scoglio che via face.

Ier, più oltre cinqu' ore che quest' otta,   112
mille dugento con sessanta sei
anni compié che qui la via fu rotta.

Io mando verso là di questi miei   115
a riguardar s'alcun se ne sciorina;
gite con lor, che non saranno rei."

"Tra'ti avante, Alichino, e Calcabrina,"   118
cominciò elli a dire, "e tu, Cagnazzo;
e Barbariccia guidi la decina.

Libicocco vegn' oltre e Draghignazzo,   121
Cirïatto sannuto e Graffiacane
e Farfarello e Rubicante pazzo.

Cercate 'ntorno le boglienti pane;   124
costor sian salvi infino a l'altro scheggio
che tutto intero va sovra le tane."

"Omè, maestro, che è quel ch'i' veggio?"   127
diss' io, "deh, sanza scorta andianci soli,
se tu sa' ir; ch'i' per me non la cheggio.

Se tu se' sì accorto come suoli,   130
non vedi tu ch'e' digrignan li denti
e con le ciglia ne minaccian duoli?"

Ed elli a me: "Non vo' che tu paventi;   133
lasciali digrignar pur a lor senno,
ch'e' fanno ciò per li lessi dolenti."

Per l'argine sinistro volta dienno;   136
ma prima avea ciascun la lingua stretta
coi denti, verso lor duca, per cenno;

ed elli avea del cul fatto trombetta.   139

Yet if you two still want to go ahead,   109
move up and walk along this rocky edge;
nearby, another ridge will form a path.

Five hours from this hour yesterday,   112
one thousand and two hundred sixty-six
years passed since that roadway was shattered here.

I'm sending ten of mine out there to see   115
if any sinner lifts his head for air;
go with my men—there is no malice in them."

"Step forward, Alichino and Calcabrina,"   118
he then began to say, "and you, Cagnazzo;
and Barbariccia, who can lead the ten.

Let Libicocco go, and Draghignazzo   121
and tusky Ciriatto and Graffiacane
and Farfarello and mad Rubicante.

Search all around the clammy stew of pitch;   124
keep these two safe and sound till the next ridge
that rises without break across the dens."

"Ah me! What is this, master, that I see?"   127
I said. "Can't we do without company?
If you know how to go, I want no escort.

If you are just as keen as usual,   130
can't you see how those demons grind their teeth?
Their brows are menacing, they promise trouble."

And he to me: "I do not want you frightened: 133
just let them gnash away as they may wish;
they do it for the wretches boiled in pitch."

They turned around along the left hand bank: 136
but first each pressed his tongue between his teeth
as signal for their leader, Barbariccia.

And he had made a trumpet of his ass.   139

XX·52

SCARMIGLIONE

BARBARICCIA

CANTO XXII

Io vidi già cavalier muover campo,
e cominciare stormo e far lor mostra,
e talvolta partir per loro scampo;

corridor vidi per la terra vostra,   4
o Aretini, e vidi gir gualdane,
fedir torneamenti e correr giostra;

quando con trombe, e quando con campane,   7
con tamburi e con cenni di castella,
e con cose nostrali e con istrane;

né già con sì diversa cennamella   10
cavalier vidi muover né pedoni,
né nave a segno di terra o di stella.

Noi andavam con li diece demoni.   13
Ahi fiera compagnia! ma ne là chiesa
coi santi, e in taverna coi ghiottoni.

Pur a la pegola era la mia 'ntesa,   16
per veder de la bolgia ogne contegno
e de la gente ch'entro v'era incesa.

Come i dalfini, quando fanno segno   19
a' marinar con l'arco de la schiena
che s'argomentin di campar lor legno,

talor così, ad alleggiar la pena,   22
mostrav' alcun de' peccatori 'l dosso
e nascondea in men che non balena.

E come a l'orlo de l'acqua d'un fosso   25
stanno i ranocchi pur col muso fuori,
sì che celano i piedi e l'altro grosso,

sì stavan d'ogne parte i peccatori;   28
ma come s'appressava Barbariccia,
così si ritraén sotto i bollori.

Still the Eighth Circle, Fifth Pouch: the Barrators. The Barrator from Navarre. Fra Gomita and Michele Zanche, two Sardinians. The astuteness of the Navarrese that leads two demons to fall into the pitch.

B efore this I've seen horsemen start to march
and open the assault and muster ranks
and seen them, too, at times beat their retreat;

    and on your land, o Aretines, I've seen   4
rangers and raiding parties galloping,
the clash of tournaments, the rush of jousts,

    now done with trumpets, now with bells, and now   7
with drums, and now with signs from castle walls,
with native things and with imported ware;

    but never yet have I seen horsemen or   10
seen infantry or ship that sails by signal
of land or star move to so strange a bugle!

    We made our way together with ten demons: 13
ah, what ferocious company! And yet
"in church with saints, with rotters in the tavern."

    But I was all intent upon the pitch,   16
to seek out every feature of the pouch
and of the people who were burning in it.

    Just as the dolphins do, when with arched back,   19
they signal to the seamen to prepare
for tempest, that their vessel may be spared,

    so here from time to time, to ease his torment,   22
some sinner showed his back above the surface,
then hid more quickly than a lightning flash.

    And just as on the margin of a ditch,   25
frogs crouch, their snouts alone above the water,
so as to hide their feet and their plump flesh,

    so here on every side these sinners crouched;   28
but faster than a flash, when Barbariccia
drew near, they plunged beneath the boiling pitch.

I' vidi, e anco il cor me n'accapriccia,   31
uno aspettar così, com' elli 'ncontra
ch'una rana rimane e l'altra spiccia;

e Graffiacan, che li era più di contra,   34
li arrunciglò le 'mpegolate chiome
e trassel sù, che mi parve una lontra.

I' sapea già di tutti quanti 'l nome,   37
sì li notai quando fuorono eletti,
e poi ch'e' si chiamaro, attesi come.

"O Rubicante, fa che tu li metti   40
li unghioni a dosso, sì che tu lo scuoi!"
gridavan tutti insieme i maladetti.

E io: "Maestro mio, fa, se tu puoi,   43
che tu sappi chi è lo sciagurato
venuto a man de li avversari suoi."

Lo duca mio li s'accostò allato;   46
domandollo ond' ei fosse, e quei rispuose:
"I' fui del regno di Navarra nato.

Mia madre a servo d'un segnor mi puose,   49
che m'avea generato d'un ribaldo,
distruggitor di sé e di sue cose.

Poi fui famiglia del buon re Tebaldo;   52
quivi mi misi a far baratteria,
di ch'io rendo ragione in questo caldo."

E Cirïatto, a cui di bocca uscia   55
d'ogne parte una sanna come a porco,
li fé sentir come l'una sdruscia.

Tra male gatte era venuto 'l sorco;   58
ma Barbariccia il chiuse con le braccia
e disse: "State in là, mentr' io lo 'nforco."

E al maestro mio volse la faccia;   61
"Domanda," disse, "ancor, se più disii
saper da lui, prima ch'altri 'l disfaccia."

Lo duca dunque: "Or dì: de li altri rii   64
conosci tu alcun che sia latino
sotto la pece?" E quelli: "I' mi partii,

poco è, da un che fu di là vicino.   67
Così foss' io ancor con lui coperto,
ch'i' non temerei unghia né uncino!"

I saw—my heart still shudders in recall—   31
one who delayed, just as at times a frog
is left behind while others dive below;

   and Graffiacane, who was closest to him,   34
then hooked him by his pitch-entangled locks
and hauled him up; he seemed to me an otter.

   By now I knew the names of all those demons—   37
I'd paid attention when the fiends were chosen;
I'd watched as they stepped forward one by one.

   "O Rubicante, see you set your talons   40
right into him, so you can flay his flesh!"
So did those cursed ones cry out together.

   And I: "My master, if you can, find out   43
what is the name of that unfortunate
who's fallen victim to his enemies."

   My guide, who then drew near that sinner's side,   46
asked him to tell his birthplace. He replied:
"My homeland was the kingdom of Navarre.

   My mother, who had had me by a wastrel,   49
destroyer of himself and his possessions,
had placed me in the service of a lord.

   Then I was in the household of the worthy   52
King Thibault; there I started taking graft;
with this heat I pay reckoning for that."

   And Ciriatto, from whose mouth there bulged   55
to right and left two tusks like a wild hog's,
then let him feel how one of them could mangle.

   The mouse had fallen in with evil cats;   58
but Barbariccia clasped him in his arms
and said: "Stand off there, while I fork him fast."

   And turning toward my master then, he said: 61
"Ask on, if you would learn some more from him
before one of the others does him in."

   At which my guide: "Now tell: among the sinners   64
who hide beneath the pitch, are any others
Italian?" And he: "I have just left

   one who was nearby there; and would I were   67
still covered by the pitch as he is hidden,
for then I'd have no fear of hook or talon."

E Libicocco "Troppo avem sofferto,"   70
disse; e preseli 'l braccio col runciglio,
sì che, stracciando, ne portò un lacerto.

Draghignazzo anco i volle dar di piglio   73
giuso a le gambe; onde 'l decurio loro
si volse intorno intorno con mal piglio.

Quand' elli un poco rappaciati fuoro,   76
a lui, ch'ancor mirava sua ferita,
domandò 'l duca mio sanza dimoro:

"Chi fu colui da cui mala partita   79
di' che facesti per venire a proda?"
Ed ei rispuose: "Fu frate Gomita,

quel di Gallura, vasel d'ogne froda,   82
ch'ebbe i nemici di suo donno in mano,
e fé sì lor, che ciascun se ne loda.

Danar si tolse e lasciolli di piano,   85
sì com' e' dice; e ne li altri offici anche
barattier fu non picciol, ma sovrano.

Usa con esso donno Michel Zanche   88
di Logodoro; e a dir di Sardigna
le lingue lor non si sentono stanche.

Omè, vedete l'altro che digrigna;   91
i' direi anche, ma i' temo ch'ello
non s'apparecchi a grattarmi la tigna."

E 'l gran proposto, vòlto a Farfarello   94
che stralunava li occhi per fedire,
disse: "Fatti 'n costà, malvagio uccello!"

"Se voi volete vedere o udire,"   97
ricominciò lo spaürato appresso,
"Toschi o Lombardi, io ne farò venire;

ma stieno i Malebranche un poco in cesso,   100
sì ch'ei non teman de le lor vendette;
e io, seggendo in questo loco stesso,

per un ch'io son, ne farò venir sette   103
quand' io suffolerò, com' è nostro uso
di fare allor che fori alcun si mette."

Cagnazzo a cotal motto levò 'l muso,   106
crollando 'l capo, e disse: "Odi malizia
ch'elli ha pensata per gittarsi giuso!"

And Libicocco said, "We've been too patient!"   70
and, with his grapple, grabbed him by the arm
and, ripping, carried off a hunk of flesh.

But Draghignazzo also looked as if   73
to grab his legs; at which, their captain wheeled
and threatened all of them with raging looks.

When they'd grown somewhat less tumultuous,   76
without delay my guide asked of that one
who had his eyes still fixed upon his wound:

"Who was the one you left to come ashore—   79
unluckily—as you just said before?"
He answered: "Fra Gomita of Gallura,

who was a vessel fit for every fraud;   82
he had his master's enemies in hand,
but handled them in ways that pleased them all.

He took their gold and smoothly let them off,   85
as he himself says; and in other matters,
he was a sovereign, not a petty, swindler.

His comrade there is Don Michele Zanche   88
of Logodoro; and their tongues are never
too tired to talk of their Sardinia.

Ah me, see that one there who grinds his teeth!   91
If I were not afraid, I'd speak some more,
but he is getting set to scratch my scurf."

And their great marshal, facing Farfarello—   94
who was so hot to strike he rolled his eyes,
said: "Get away from there, you filthy bird!"

"If you perhaps would like to see or hear,"   97
that sinner, terrified, began again,
"Lombards or Tuscans, I can fetch you some;

but let the Malebranche stand aside   100
so that my comrades need not fear their vengeance.
Remaining in this very spot, I shall,

although alone, make seven more appear   103
when I have whistled, as has been our custom
when one of us has managed to get out."

At that, Cagnazzo lifted up his snout   106
and shook his head, and said: "Just listen to
that trick by which he thinks he can dive back!"

Ond' ei, ch'avea lacciuoli a gran divizia,   109
rispuose: "Malizioso son io troppo,
quand' io procuro a' mia maggior trestizia."

Alichin non si tenne e, di rintoppo   112
a li altri, disse a lui: "Se tu ti cali,
io non ti verrò dietro di gualoppo,

ma batterò sovra la pece l'ali.   115
Lascisi 'l collo, e sia la ripa scudo,
a veder se tu sol più di noi vali."

O tu che leggi, udirai nuovo ludo: 118
ciascun da l'altra costa li occhi volse,
quel prima, ch'a ciò fare era più crudo.

Lo Navarrese ben suo tempo colse;   121
fermò le piante a terra, e in un punto
saltò e dal proposto lor si sciolse.

Di che ciascun di colpa fu compunto,   124
ma quei più che cagion fu del difetto;
però si mosse e gridò: "Tu se' giunto!"

Ma poco i valse: ché l'ali al sospetto   127
non potero avanzar; quelli andò sotto,
e quei drizzò volando suso il petto:

non altrimenti l'anitra di botto,   130
quando 'l falcon s'appressa, giù s'attuffa,
ed ei ritorna sù crucciato e rotto.

Irato Calcabrina de la buffa,   133
volando dietro li tenne, invaghito
che quei campasse per aver la zuffa;

e come 'l barattier fu disparito,   136
così volse li artigli al suo compagno,
e fu con lui sopra 'l fosso ghermito.

Ma l'altro fu bene sparvier grifagno   139
ad artigliar ben lui, e amendue
cadder nel mezzo del bogliente stagno.

Lo caldo sghermitor sùbito fue;   142
ma però di levarsi era neente,
sì avieno inviscate l'ali sue.

Barbariccia, con li altri suoi dolente,   145
quattro ne fé volar da l'altra costa
con tutt' i raffi, e assai prestamente

To this, he who was rich in artifice   109
replied: "Then I must have too many tricks,
if I bring greater torment to my friends."

This was too much for Alichino and,   112
despite the others, he cried out: "If you
dive back, I shall not gallop after you

but beat my wings above the pitch; we'll leave   115
this height; with the embankment as a screen,
we'll see if you—alone—can handle us."

O you who read, hear now of this new sport: 118
each turned his eyes upon the other shore,
he first who'd been most hesitant before.

The Navarrese, in nick of time, had planted   121
his feet upon the ground; then in an instant
he jumped and freed himself from their commander.

At this each demon felt the prick of guilt,   124
and most, he who had led his band to blunder;
so he took off and shouted: "You are caught!"

But this could help him little; wings were not   127
more fast than fear; the sinner plunged right under;
the other, flying up, lifted his chest:

not otherwise the wild duck when it plunges   130
precipitously, when the falcon nears
and then—exhausted, thwarted—flies back up.

But Calcabrina, raging at the trick,   133
flew after Alichino; he was keen
to see the sinner free and have a brawl;

and once the Navarrese had disappeared,   136
he turned his talons on his fellow demon
and tangled with him just above the ditch.

But Alichino clawed him well—he was   139
indeed a full-grown kestrel; and both fell
into the middle of the boiling pond.

The heat was quick to disentangle them,   142
but still there was no way they could get out;
their wings were stuck, enmeshed in glue-like pitch.

And Barbariccia, grieving with the rest,   145
sent four to fly out toward the other shore
with all their forks, and speedily enough

di qua, di là discesero a la posta;   148
porser li uncini verso li 'mpaniati,
ch'eran già cotti dentro da la crosta.

E noi lasciammo lor così 'mpacciati.   151

on this side and on that they took their posts;   148
and toward those two—stuck fast, already cooked
beneath that crust—they stretched their grappling hooks.

We left them still contending with that mess.   151

CANTO XXIII

Taciti, soli, sanza compagnia
n'andavam l'un dinanzi e l'altro dopo,
come frati minor vanno per via.

Vòlt' era in su la favola d'Isopo   4
lo mio pensier per la presente rissa,
dov' el parlò de la rana e del topo;

ché più non si pareggia "mo" e "issa"   7
che l'un con l'altro fa, se ben s'accoppia
principio e fine con la mente fissa.

E come l'un pensier de l'altro scoppia,   10
così nacque di quello un altro poi,
che la prima paura mi fé doppia.

Io pensava così: "Questi per noi   13
sono scherniti con danno e con beffa
sì fatta, ch'assai credo che lor nòi.

Se l'ira sovra 'l mal voler s'aggueffa,   16
ei ne verranno dietro più crudeli
che 'l cane a quella lievre ch'elli acceffa."

Già mi sentia tutti arricciar li peli   19
de la paura e stava in dietro intento,
quand' io dissi: "Maestro, se non celi

te e me tostamente, i' ho pavento   22
d'i Malebranche. Noi li avem già dietro;
io li 'magino sì, che già li sento."

E quei: "S'i' fossi di piombato vetro,   25
l'imagine di fuor tua non trarrei
più tosto a me, che quella dentro 'mpetro.

Pur mo venieno i tuo' pensier tra ' miei,   28
con simile atto e con simile faccia,
sì che d'intrambi un sol consiglio fei.

Silent, alone, no one escorting us,
we made our way—one went before, one after—
as Friars Minor when they walk together.

The present fracas made me think of Aesop—   4
that fable where he tells about the mouse
and frog; for "near" and "nigh" are not more close

than are that fable and this incident,   7
if you compare with care how each begins
and then compare the endings that they share.

And even as one thought springs from another,   10
so out of that was still another born,
which made the fear I felt before redouble.

I thought: "Because of us, they have been mocked,   13
and this inflicted so much hurt and scorn
that I am sure they feel deep indignation.

If anger's to be added to their malice,   16
they'll hunt us down with more ferocity
than any hound whose teeth have trapped a hare."

I could already feel my hair curl up   19
from fear, and I looked back attentively,
while saying: "Master, if you don't conceal

yourself and me at once—they terrify me,   22
those Malebranche; they are after us;
I so imagine them, I hear them now."

And he to me: "Were I a leaded mirror,   25
I could not gather in your outer image
more quickly than I have received your inner.

For even now your thoughts have joined my own;   28
in both our acts and aspects we are kin—
with both our minds I've come to one decision.

S'elli è che sì la destra costa giaccia,   31
che noi possiam ne l'altra bolgia scendere,
noi fuggirem l'imaginata caccia."

Già non compié di tal consiglio rendere,   34
ch'io li vidi venir con l'ali tese
non molto lungi, per volerne prendere.

Lo duca mio di sùbito mi prese,   37
come la madre ch'al romore è desta
e vede presso a sé le fiamme accese,

che prende il figlio e fugge e non s'arresta,   40
avendo più di lui che di sé cura,
tanto che solo una camiscia vesta;

e giù dal collo de la ripa dura   43
supin si diede a la pendente roccia,
che l'un de' lati a l'altra bolgia tura.

Non corse mai sì tosto acqua per doccia   46
a volger ruota di molin terragno,
quand' ella più verso le pale approccia,

come 'l maestro mio per quel vivagno,   49
portandosene me sovra 'l suo petto,
come suo figlio, non come compagno.

A pena fuoro i piè suoi giunti al letto   52
del fondo giù, ch'e' furon in sul colle
sovresso noi; ma non lì era sospetto:

ché l'alta provedenza che lor volle   55
porre ministri de la fossa quinta,
poder di partirs' indi a tutti tolle.

Là giù trovammo una gente dipinta   58
che giva intorno assai con lenti passi,
piangendo e nel sembiante stanca e vinta.

Elli avean cappe con cappucci bassi   61
dinanzi a li occhi, fatte de la taglia
che in Clugnì per li monaci fassi.

Di fuor dorate son, sì ch'elli abbaglia;   64
ma dentro tutte piombo, e gravi tanto,
che Federigo le mettea di paglia.

Oh in etterno faticoso manto!   67
Noi ci volgemmo ancor pur a man manca
con loro insieme, intenti al tristo pianto;

If that right bank is not extremely steep,   31
we can descend into the other moat
and so escape from the imagined chase."

He'd hardly finished telling me his plan   34
when I saw them approach with outstretched wings,
not too far off, and keen on taking us.

My guide snatched me up instantly, just as   37
the mother who is wakened by a roar
and catches sight of blazing flames beside her,

will lift her son and run without a stop—   40
she cares more for the child than for herself—
not pausing even to throw on a shift;

and down the hard embankment's edge—his back   43
lay flat along the sloping rock that closes
one side of the adjacent moat—he slid.

No water ever ran so fast along   46
a sluice to turn the wheels of a land mill,
not even when its flow approached the paddles,

as did my master race down that embankment   49
while bearing me with him upon his chest,
just like a son, and not like a companion.

His feet had scarcely reached the bed that lies   52
along the deep below, than those ten demons
were on the edge above us; but there was

nothing to fear; for that High Providence   55
that willed them ministers of the fifth ditch,
denies to all of them the power to leave it.

Below that point we found a painted people,   58
who moved about with lagging steps, in circles,
weeping, with features tired and defeated.

And they were dressed in cloaks with cowls so low   61
they fell before their eyes, of that same cut
that's used to make the clothes for Cluny's monks.

Outside, these cloaks were gilded and they dazzled; 64
but inside they were all of lead, so heavy
that Frederick's capes were straw compared to them.

A tiring mantle for eternity!   67
We turned again, as always, to the left,
along with them, intent on their sad weeping;

ma per lo peso quella gente stanca   70
venìa sì pian, che noi eravam nuovi
di compagnia ad ogne mover d'anca.

Per ch'io al duca mio: "Fa che tu trovi   73
alcun ch'al fatto o al nome si conosca,
e li occhi, sì andando, intorno movi."

E un che 'ntese la parola tosca,   76
di retro a noi gridò: "Tenete i piedi,
voi che correte sì per l'aura fosca!

Forse ch'avrai da me quel che tu chiedi."   79
Onde 'l duca si volse e disse: "Aspetta,
e poi secondo il suo passo procedi."

Ristetti, e vidi due mostrar gran fretta   82
de l'animo, col viso, d'esser meco;
ma tardavali 'l carco e la via stretta.

Quando fuor giunti, assai con l'occhio bieco   85
mi rimiraron sanza far parola;
poi si volsero in sé, e dicean seco:

"Costui par vivo a l'atto de la gola;   88
e s'e' son morti, per qual privilegio
vanno scoperti de la grave stola?"

Poi disser me: "O Tosco, ch'al collegio   91
de l'ipocriti tristi se' venuto,
dir chi tu se' non avere in dispregio."

E io a loro: "I' fui nato e cresciuto   94
sovra 'l bel fiume d'Arno a la gran villa,
e son col corpo ch'i' ho sempre avuto.

Ma voi chi siete, a cui tanto distilla   97
quant' i' veggio dolor giù per le guance?
e che pena è in voi che sì sfavilla?"

E l'un rispuose a me: "Le cappe rance   100
son di piombo sì grosse, che li pesi
fan così cigolar le lor bilance.

Frati godenti fummo, e bolognesi;   103
io Catalano e questi Loderingo
nomati, e da tua terra insieme presi

come suole esser tolto un uom solingo,   106
per conservar sua pace; e fummo tali,
ch'ancor si pare intorno dal Gardingo."

but with their weights that weary people paced   70
so slowly that we found ourselves among
new company each time we took a step.

At which I told my guide: "Please try to find   73
someone whose name or deed I recognize;
and while we walk, be watchful with your eyes."

And one who'd taken in my Tuscan speech   76
cried out behind us: "Stay your steps, o you
who hurry so along this darkened air!

Perhaps you'll have from me that which you seek."   79
At which my guide turned to me, saying: "Wait,
and then continue, following his pace."

I stopped, and I saw two whose faces showed   82
their minds were keen to be with me; but both
their load and the tight path forced them to slow.

When they came up, they looked askance at me   85
a long while, and they uttered not a word
until they turned to one another, saying:

"The throbbing of his throat makes this one seem   88
alive; and if they're dead, what privilege
lets them appear without the heavy mantle?"

Then they addressed me: "Tuscan, you who come   91
to this assembly of sad hypocrites,
do not disdain to tell us who you are."

I answered: "Where the lovely Arno flows,   94
there I was born and raised, in the great city;
I'm with the body I have always had.

But who are you, upon whose cheeks I see   97
such tears distilled by grief? And let me know
what punishment it is that glitters so."

And one of them replied: "The yellow cloaks   100
are of a lead so thick, their heaviness
makes us, the balances beneath them, creak.

We both were Jovial Friars, and Bolognese;   103
my name was Catalano, Loderingo
was his, and we were chosen by your city

together, for the post that's usually   106
one man's, to keep the peace; and what we were
is still to be observed around Gardingo."

Io cominciai: "O frati, i vostri mali...";   109
ma più non dissi, ch'a l'occhio mi corse
un, crucifisso in terra con tre pali.

Quando mi vide, tutto si distorse,   112
soffiando ne la barba con sospiri;
e 'l frate Catalan, ch'a ciò s'accorse,

mi disse: "Quel confitto che tu miri,   115
consigliò i Farisei che convenia
porre un uom per lo popolo a' martìri.

Attraversato è, nudo, ne la via,   118
come tu vedi, ed è mestier ch'el senta
qualunque passa, come pesa, pria.

E a tal modo il socero si stenta   121
in questa fossa, e li altri dal concilio
che fu per li Giudei mala sementa."

Allor vid' io maravigliar Virgilio   124
sovra colui ch'era disteso in croce
tanto vilmente ne l'etterno essilio.

Poscia drizzò al frate cotal voce: 127
"Non vi dispiaccia, se vi lece, dirci
s'a la man destra giace alcuna foce

onde noi amendue possiamo uscirci,   130
sanza costrigner de li angeli neri
che vegnan d'esto fondo a dipartirci."

Rispuose adunque: "Più che tu non speri   133
s'appressa un sasso che da la gran cerchia
si move e varca tutt' i vallon feri,

salvo che 'n questo è rotto e nol coperchia;   136
montar potrete su per la ruina,
che giace in costa e nel fondo soperchia."

Lo duca stette un poco a testa china;   139
poi disse: "Mal contava la bisogna
colui che i peccator di qua uncina."

E 'l frate: "Io udi' già dire a Bologna   142
del diavol vizi assai, tra ' quali udi'
ch'elli è bugiardo e padre di menzogna."

Appresso il duca a gran passi sen gì,   145
turbato un poco d'ira nel sembiante;
ond' io da li 'ncarcati mi parti'

dietro a le poste de le care piante.   148

I then began, "O Friars, your misdeeds…"   109
but said no more, because my eyes had caught
one crucified by three stakes on the ground.

When he saw me, that sinner writhed all over,   112
and he breathed hard into his beard with sighs;
observing that, Fra Catalano said

to me: "That one impaled there, whom you see,   115
counseled the Pharisees that it was prudent
to let one man—and not one nation—suffer.

Naked, he has been stretched across the path,   118
as you can see, and he must feel the weight
of anyone who passes over him.

Like torment, in this ditch, afflicts both his   121
father-in-law and others in that council,
which for the Jews has seeded so much evil."

Then I saw Virgil stand amazed above   124
that one who lay stretched out upon a cross
so squalidly in his eternal exile.

And he addressed the friar in this way: 127
"If it does not displease you—if you may—
tell us if there's some passage on the right

that would allow the two of us to leave   130
without our having to compel black angels
to travel to this deep, to get us out."

He answered: "Closer than you hope, you'll find   133
a rocky ridge that stretches from the great
round wall and crosses all the savage valleys,

except that here it's broken—not a bridge.   136
But where its ruins slope along the bank
and heap up at the bottom, you can climb."

My leader stood a while with his head bent,   139
then said: "He who hooks sinners over there
gave us a false account of this affair."

At which the Friar: "In Bologna, I   142
once heard about the devil's many vices—
they said he was a liar and father of lies."

And then my guide moved on with giant strides,   145
somewhat disturbed, with anger in his eyes;
at this I left those overburdened spirits,

while following the prints of his dear feet.   148

C A I A P H A S

CANTO XXIV

In quella parte del giovanetto anno
   che 'l sole i crin sotto l'Aquario tempra
e già le notti al mezzo dì sen vanno,

   quando la brina in su la terra assempra   4
l'imagine di sua sorella bianca,
ma poco dura a la sua penna tempra,

   lo villanello a cui la roba manca,   7
si leva, e guarda, e vede la campagna
biancheggiar tutta; ond' ei si batte l'anca,

   ritorna in casa, e qua e là si lagna,   10
come 'l tapin che non sa che si faccia;
poi riede, e la speranza ringavagna,

   veggendo 'l mondo aver cangiata faccia   13
in poco d'ora, e prende suo vincastro
e fuor le pecorelle a pascer caccia.

   Così mi fece sbigottir lo mastro   16
quand' io li vidi sì turbar la fronte,
e così tosto al mal giunse lo 'mpiastro;

   ché, come noi venimmo al guasto ponte,   19
lo duca a me si volse con quel piglio
dolce ch'io vidi prima a piè del monte.

   Le braccia aperse, dopo alcun consiglio   22
eletto seco riguardando prima
ben la ruina, e diedemi di piglio.

   E come quei ch'adopera ed estima,   25
che sempre par che 'nnanzi si proveggia,
così, levando me sù ver' la cima

   d'un ronchione, avvisava un'altra scheggia   28
dicendo: "Sovra quella poi t'aggrappa;
ma tenta pria s'è tal ch'ella ti reggia."

I n that part of the young year when the sun
begins to warm its locks beneath Aquarius
and nights grow shorter, equaling the days,

    when hoarfrost mimes the image of his white   4
sister upon the ground—but not for long,
because the pen he uses is not sharp—

    the farmer who is short of fodder rises   7
and looks and sees the fields all white, at which
he slaps his thigh, turns back into the house,

    and here and there complains like some poor wretch   10
who doesn't know what can be done, and then
goes out again and gathers up new hope

    on seeing that the world has changed its face   13
in so few hours, and he takes his staff
and hurries out his flock of sheep to pasture.

    So did my master fill me with dismay   16
when I saw how his brow was deeply troubled,
yet then the plaster soothed the sore as quickly:

    for soon as we were on the broken bridge,   19
my guide turned back to me with that sweet manner
I first had seen along the mountain's base.

    And he examined carefully the ruin;   22
then having picked the way we would ascend,
he opened up his arms and thrust me forward.

    And just as he who ponders as he labors,   25
who's always ready for the step ahead,
so, as he lifted me up toward the summit

    of one great crag, he'd see another spur,   28
saying: "That is the one you will grip next,
but try it first to see if it is firm."

Non era via da vestito di cappa,   31
ché noi a pena, ei lieve e io sospinto,
potavam sù montar di chiappa in chiappa.

E se non fosse che da quel precinto   34
più che da l'altro era la costa corta,
non so di lui, ma io sarei ben vinto.

Ma perché Malebolge inver' la porta   37
del bassissimo pozzo tutta pende,
lo sito di ciascuna valle porta

che l'una costa surge e l'altra scende;   40
noi pur venimmo al fine in su la punta
onde l'ultima pietra si scoscende.

La lena m'era del polmon sì munta   43
quand' io fui sù, ch'i' non potea più oltre,
anzi m'assisi ne la prima giunta.

"Omai convien che tu così ti spoltre,"   46
disse 'l maestro; "ché, seggendo in piuma,
in fama non si vien, né sotto coltre;

sanza la qual chi sua vita consuma,   49
cotal vestigio in terra di sé lascia,
qual fummo in aere e in acqua la schiuma.

E però leva sù; vinci l'ambascia   52
con l'animo che vince ogne battaglia,
se col suo grave corpo non s'accascia.

Più lunga scala convien che si saglia;   55
non basta da costoro esser partito.
Se tu mi 'ntendi, or fa sì che ti vaglia."

Leva'mi allor, mostrandomi fornito   58
meglio di lena ch'i' non mi sentia,
e dissi: "Va, ch'i' son forte e ardito."

Su per lo scoglio prendemmo la via,   61
ch'era ronchioso, stretto e malagevole,
ed erto più assai che quel di pria.

Parlando andava per non parer fievole;   64
onde una voce uscì de l'altro fosso,
a parole formar disconvenevole.

Non so che disse, ancor che sovra 'l dosso   67
fossi de l'arco già che varca quivi;
ma chi parlava ad ire parea mosso.

I had bent downward, but my living eyes 70
could not see to the bottom through that dark;
at which I said: "O master, can we reach

the other belt? Let us descend the wall, 73
for as I hear and cannot understand,
so I see down but can distinguish nothing."

"The only answer that I give to you 76
is doing it," he said. "A just request
is to be met in silence, by the act."

We then climbed down the bridge, just at the end 79
where it runs right into the eighth embankment,
and now the moat was plain enough to me;

and there within I saw a dreadful swarm 82
of serpents so extravagant in form—
remembering them still drains my blood from me.

Let Libya boast no more about her sands; 85
for if she breeds chelydri, jaculi,
cenchres with amphisbaena, pareae,

she never showed—with all of Ethiopia 88
or all the land that borders the Red Sea—
so many, such malignant, pestilences.

Among this cruel and depressing swarm, 91
ran people who were naked, terrified,
with no hope of a hole or heliotrope.

Their hands were tied behind by serpents; these 94
had thrust their head and tail right through the loins,
and then were knotted on the other side.

And—there!—a serpent sprang with force at one 97
who stood upon our shore, transfixing him
just where the neck and shoulders form a knot.

No *o* or *i* has ever been transcribed 100
so quickly as that soul caught fire and burned
and, as he fell, completely turned to ashes;

and when he lay, undone, upon the ground, 103
the dust of him collected by itself
and instantly returned to what it was:

just so, it is asserted by great sages, 106
that, when it reaches its five-hundredth year,
the phoenix dies and then is born again;

    erba né biado in sua vita non pasce,   109
ma sol d'incenso lagrime e d'amomo,
e nardo e mirra son l'ultime fasce.

    E qual è quel che cade, e non sa como,   112
per forza di demon ch'a terra il tira,
o d'altra oppilazion che lega l'omo,

    quando si leva, che 'ntorno si mira   115
tutto smarrito de la grande angoscia
ch'elli ha sofferta, e guardando sospira:

    tal era 'l peccator levato poscia.   118
Oh potenza di Dio, quant' è severa,
che cotai colpi per vendetta croscia!

    Lo duca il domandò poi chi ello era;   121
per ch'ei rispuose: "Io piovvi di Toscana,
poco tempo è, in questa gola fiera.

    Vita bestial mi piacque e non umana,   124
sì come a mul ch'i' fui; son Vanni Fucci
bestia, e Pistoia mi fu degna tana."

    E ïo al duca: "Dilli che non mucci,   127
e domanda che colpa qua giù 'l pinse;
ch'io 'l vidi omo di sangue e di crucci."

    E 'l peccator, che 'ntese, non s'infinse,   130
ma drizzò verso me l'animo e 'l volto,
e di trista vergogna si dipinse;

    poi disse: "Più mi duol che tu m'hai colto   133
ne la miseria dove tu mi vedi,
che quando fui de l'altra vita tolto.

    Io non posso negar quel che tu chiedi;   136
in giù son messo tanto perch' io fui
ladro a la sagrestia d'i belli arredi,

    e falsamente già fu apposto altrui.   139
Ma perché di tal vista tu non godi,
se mai sarai di fuor da' luoghi bui,

    apri li orecchi al mio annunzio, e odi.   142
Pistoia in pria d'i Neri si dimagra;
poi Fiorenza rinova gente e modi.

    Tragge Marte vapor di Val di Magra   145
ch'è di torbidi nuvoli involuto;
e con tempesta impetüosa e agra

lifelong it never feeds on grass or grain,   109
only on drops of incense and amomum;
its final winding sheets are nard and myrrh.

    And just as he who falls, and knows not how—   112
by demon's force that drags him to the ground
or by some other hindrance that binds man—

    who, when he rises, stares about him, all   115
bewildered by the heavy anguish he
has suffered, sighing as he looks around;

    so did this sinner stare when he arose.   118
Oh, how severe it is, the power of God
that, as its vengeance, showers down such blows!

    My guide then asked that sinner who he was;   121
to this he answered: "Not long since, I rained
from Tuscany into this savage maw.

    Mule that I was, the bestial life pleased me   124
and not the human; I am Vanni Fucci,
beast; and the den that suited me—Pistoia."

    And I to Virgil: "Tell him not to slip   127
away, and ask what sin has thrust him here;
I knew him as a man of blood and anger."

    The sinner heard and did not try to feign   130
but turned his mind and face, intent, toward me;
and coloring with miserable shame,

    he said: "I suffer more because you've caught me   133
in this, the misery you see, than I
suffered when taken from the other life.

    I can't refuse to answer what you ask: 136
I am set down so far because I robbed
the sacristy of its fair ornaments,

    and someone else was falsely blamed for that.   139
But lest this sight give you too much delight,
if you can ever leave these lands of darkness,

    open your ears to my announcement, hear: 142
Pistoia first will strip herself of Blacks,
then Florence will renew her men and manners.

    From Val di Magra, Mars will draw a vapor   145
which turbid clouds will try to wrap; the clash
between them will be fierce, impetuous,

sovra Campo Picen fia combattuto;   148
ond' ei repente spezzerà la nebbia,
sì ch'ogne Bianco ne sarà feruto.

    E detto l'ho perché doler ti debbia!"   151

a tempest, fought upon Campo Piceno,   148
until that vapor, vigorous, shall crack
the mist, and every White be struck by it.

And I have told you this to make you grieve."   151

CANTO XXV

Al fine de le sue parole il ladro
le mani alzò con amendue le fiche,
gridando: "Togli, Dio, ch'a te le squadro!"

Da indi in qua mi fuor le serpi amiche,   4
perch' una li s'avvolse allora al collo,
come dicesse "Non vo' che più diche";

e un'altra a la braccia, e rilegollo,   7
ribadendo sé stessa sì dinanzi,
che non potea con esse dare un crollo.

Ahi Pistoia, Pistoia, ché non stanzi   10
d'incenerarti sì che più non duri,
poi che 'n mal fare il seme tuo avanzi?

Per tutt' i cerchi de lo 'nferno scuri   13
non vidi spirto in Dio tanto superbo,
non quel che cadde a Tebe giù da' muri.

El si fuggì che non parlò più verbo;   16
e io vidi un centauro pien di rabbia
venir chiamando: "Ov' è, ov' è l'acerbo?"

Maremma non cred' io che tante n'abbia,   19
quante bisce elli avea su per la groppa
infin ove comincia nostra labbia.

Sovra le spalle, dietro da la coppa,   22
con l'ali aperte li giacea un draco;
e quello affuoca qualunque s'intoppa.

Lo mio maestro disse: "Questi è Caco,   25
che, sotto 'l sasso di monte Aventino,
di sangue fece spesse volte laco.

Non va co' suoi fratei per un cammino,   28
per lo furto che frodolente fece
del grand armento ch'elli ebbe a vicino;

When he had finished with his words, the thief
raised high his fists with both figs cocked and cried:
"Take that, o God; I square them off for you!"

From that time on, those serpents were my friends,   4
for one of them coiled then around his neck,
as if to say, "I'll have you speak no more";

another wound about his arms and bound him   7
again and wrapped itself in front so firmly,
he could not even make them budge an inch.

Pistoia, ah, Pistoia, must you last: 10
why not decree your self-incineration,
since you surpass your seed in wickedness?

Throughout the shadowed circles of deep Hell,   13
I saw no soul against God so rebel,
not even he who fell from Theban walls.

He fled and could not say another word;   16
and then I saw a Centaur full of anger,
shouting: "Where is he, where's that bitter one?"

I do not think Maremma has the number   19
of snakes that Centaur carried on his haunch
until the part that takes our human form.

Upon his shoulders and behind his nape   22
there lay a dragon with its wings outstretched;
it sets ablaze all those it intercepts.

My master said: "That Centaur there is Cacus,   25
who often made a lake of blood within
a grotto underneath Mount Aventine.

He does not ride the same road as his brothers   28
because he stole—and most deceitfully—
from the great herd nearby; his crooked deeds

onde cessar le sue opere biece   31
sotto la mazza d'Ercule, che forse
gliene diè cento, e non sentì le diece."

    Mentre che sì parlava, ed el trascorse,   34
e tre spiriti venner sotto noi,
de' quai né io né 'l duca mio s'accorse,

    se non quando gridar: "Chi siete voi?"   37
per che nostra novella si ristette,
e intendemmo pur ad essi poi.

    Io non li conoscea; ma ei seguette,   40
come suol seguitar per alcun caso,
che l'un nomar un altro convenette,

    dicendo: "Cianfa dove fia rimaso?"   43
per ch'io, acciò che 'l duca stesse attento,
mi puosi 'l dito su dal mento al naso.

    Se tu se' or, lettore, a creder lento   46
ciò ch'io dirò, non sarà maraviglia,
ché io che 'l vidi, a pena il mi consento.

    Com' io tenea levate in lor le ciglia,   49
e un serpente con sei piè si lancia
dinanzi a l'uno, e tutto a lui s'appiglia.

    Co' piè di mezzo li avvinse la pancia   52
e con li anterïor le braccia prese;
poi li addentò e l'una e l'altra guancia;

    li diretani a le cosce distese,   55
e miseli la coda tra 'mbedue
e dietro per le ren sù la ritese.

    Ellera abbarbicata mai non fue   58
ad alber sì, come l'orribil fiera
per l'altrui membra avviticchiò le sue.

    Poi s'appiccar, come di calda cera   61
fossero stati, e mischiar lor colore,
né l'un né l'altro già parea quel ch'era:

    come procede innanzi da l'ardore,   64
per lo papiro suso, un color bruno
che non è nero ancora e 'l bianco more.

    Li altri due 'l riguardavano, e ciascuno   67
gridava: "Omè, Agnel, come ti muti!
Vedi che già non se' né due né uno."

ended beneath the club of Hercules,   31
who may have given him a hundred blows—
but he was not alive to feel the tenth."

While he was talking so, Cacus ran by   34
and, just beneath our ledge, three souls arrived;
but neither I nor my guide noticed them

until they had cried out: "And who are you?"   37
At this the words we shared were interrupted,
and we attended only to those spirits.

I did not recognize them, but it happened,   40
as chance will usually bring about,
that one of them called out the other's name,

exclaiming: "Where was Cianfa left behind?"   43
At this, so that my guide might be alert,
I raised my finger up from chin to nose.

If, reader, you are slow now to believe   46
what I shall tell, that is no cause for wonder,
for I who saw it hardly can accept it.

As I kept my eyes fixed upon those sinners,   49
a serpent with six feet springs out against
one of the three, and clutches him completely.

It gripped his belly with its middle feet,   52
and with its forefeet grappled his two arms;
and then it sank its teeth in both his cheeks;

it stretched its rear feet out along his thighs   55
and ran its tail along between the two,
then straightened it again behind his loins.

No ivy ever gripped a tree so fast   58
as when that horrifying monster clasped
and intertwined the other's limbs with its.

Then just as if their substance were warm wax,   61
they stuck together and they mixed their colors,
so neither seemed what he had been before;

just as, when paper's kindled, where it still   64
has not caught flame in full, its color's dark
though not yet black, while white is dying off.

The other two souls stared, and each one cried: 67
"Ah me, Agnello, how you change! Just see,
you are already neither two nor one!"

Già eran li due capi un divenuti,   70
quando n'apparver due figure miste
in una faccia, ov' eran due perduti.

Fersi le braccia due di quattro liste;   73
le cosce con le gambe e 'l ventre e 'l casso
divenner membra che non fuor mai viste.

Ogne primaio aspetto ivi era casso: 76
due e nessun l'imagine perversa
parea; e tal sen gio con lento passo.

Come 'l ramarro sotto la gran fersa   79
dei dì canicular, cangiando sepe,
folgore par se la via attraversa,

sì pareva, venendo verso l'epe   82
de li altri due, un serpentello acceso,
livido e nero come gran di pepe;

e quella parte onde prima è preso   85
nostro alimento, a l'un di lor trafisse;
poi cadde giuso innanzi lui disteso.

Lo trafitto 'l mirò, ma nulla disse;   88
anzi, co' piè fermati, sbadigliava
pur come sonno o febbre l'assalisse.

Elli 'l serpente e quei lui riguardava;   91
l'un per la piaga e l'altro per la bocca
fummavan forte, e 'l fummo si scontrava.

Taccia Lucano omai là dov' e' tocca   94
del misero Sabello e di Nasidio,
e attenda a udir quel ch'or si scocca.

Taccia di Cadmo e d'Aretusa Ovidio,   97
ché se quello in serpente e quella in fonte
converte poetando, io non lo 'nvidio;

ché due nature mai a fronte a fronte   100
non trasmutò sì ch'amendue le forme
a cambiar lor matera fosser pronte.

Insieme si rispuosero a tai norme,   103
che 'l serpente la coda in forca fesse,
e 'l feruto ristrinse insieme l'orme.

Le gambe con le cosce seco stesse   106
s'appiccar sì, che 'n poco la giuntura
non facea segno alcun che si paresse.

Then two heads were already joined in one,   70
when in one face where two had been dissolved,
two intermingled shapes appeared to us.

Two arms came into being from four lengths;   73
the thighs and legs, the belly and the chest
became such limbs as never had been seen.

And every former shape was canceled there: 76
that perverse image seemed to share in both—
and none; and so, and slowly, it moved on.

Just as the lizard, when it darts from hedge   79
to hedge, beneath the dog days' giant lash,
seems, if it cross one's path, a lightning flash,

so seemed a blazing little serpent moving   82
against the bellies of the other two,
as black and livid as a peppercorn.

Attacking one of them, it pierced right through   85
the part where we first take our nourishment;
and then it fell before him at full length.

The one it had transfixed stared but said nothing;   88
in fact he only stood his ground and yawned
as one whom sleep or fever has undone.

The serpent stared at him, he at the serpent;   91
one through his wound, the other through his mouth
were smoking violently; their smoke met.

Let Lucan now be silent, where he sings   94
of sad Sabellus and Nasidius,
and wait to hear what flies off from my bow.

Let Ovid now be silent, where he tells   97
of Cadmus, Arethusa; if his verse
has made of one a serpent, one a fountain,

I do not envy him; he never did   100
transmute two natures, face to face, so that
both forms were ready to exchange their matter.

These were the ways they answered to each other: 103
the serpent split its tail into a fork;
the wounded sinner drew his steps together.

The legs and then the thighs along with them   106
so fastened to each other that the juncture
soon left no sign that was discernible.

Togliea la coda fessa la figura   109
che si perdeva là, e la sua pelle
si facea molle, e quella di là dura.

Io vidi intrar le braccia per l'ascelle,   112
e i due piè de la fiera, ch'eran corti,
tanto allungar quanto accorciavan quelle.

Poscia li piè di rietro, insieme attorti,   115
diventaron lo membro che l'uom cela,
e 'l misero del suo n'avea due porti.

Mentre che 'l fummo l'uno e l'altro vela   118
di color novo, e genera 'l pel suso
per l'una parte e da l'altra il dipela,

l'un si levò e l'altro cadde giuso,   121
non torcendo però le lucerne empie,
sotto le quai ciascun cambiava muso.

Quel ch'era dritto, il trasse ver' le tempie,   124
e di troppa matera ch'in là venne
uscir li orecchi de le gote scempie;

ciò che non corse in dietro e si ritenne   127
di quel soverchio, fé naso a la faccia
e le labbra ingrossò quanto convenne.

Quel che giacëa, il muso innanzi caccia,   130
e li orecchi ritira per la testa
come face le corna la lumaccia;

e la lingua, ch'avëa unita e presta   133
prima a parlar, si fende, e la forcuta
ne l'altro si richiude; e 'l fummo resta.

L'anima ch'era fiera divenuta,   136
suffolando si fugge per la valle,
e l'altro dietro a lui parlando sputa.

Poscia li volse le novelle spalle,   139
e disse a l'altro: "I' vo' che Buoso corra,
com' ho fatt' io, carpon per questo calle."

Così vid' io la settima zavorra   142
mutare e trasmutare; e qui mi scusi
la novità se fior la penna abborra.

E avvegna che li occhi miei confusi   145
fossero alquanto e l'animo smagato,
non poter quei fuggirsi tanto chiusi,

Meanwhile the cleft tail took upon itself   109
the form the other gradually lost;
its skin grew soft, the other's skin grew hard.

I saw the arms that drew in at his armpits   112
and also saw the monster's two short feet
grow long for just as much as those were shortened.

The serpent's hind feet, twisted up together,   115
became the member that man hides; just as
the wretch put out two hind paws from his member.

And while the smoke veils each with a new color,   118
and now breeds hair upon the skin of one,
just as it strips the hair from off the other,

the one rose up, the other fell; and yet   121
they never turned aside their impious eyelamps,
beneath which each of them transformed his snout:

he who stood up drew his back toward the temples,   124
and from the excess matter growing there
came ears upon the cheeks that had been bare;

whatever had not been pulled back but kept,   127
superfluous, then made his face a nose
and thickened out his lips appropriately.

He who was lying down thrust out his snout;   130
and even as the snail hauls in its horns,
he drew his ears straight back into his head;

his tongue, which had before been whole and fit   133
for speech, now cleaves; the other's tongue, which had
been forked, now closes up; and the smoke stops.

The soul that had become an animal,   136
now hissing, hurried off along the valley;
the other one, behind him, speaks and spits.

And then he turned aside his new-made shoulders   139
and told the third soul: "I'd have Buoso run
on all fours down this road, as I have done."

And so I saw the seventh ballast change   142
and rechange; may the strangeness plead for me
if there's been some confusion in my pen.

And though my eyes were somewhat blurred, my mind   145
bewildered, those three sinners did not flee
so secretly that I could not perceive

ch'i' non scorgessi ben Puccio Sciancato;   148
ed era quel che sol, di tre compagni
che venner prima, non era mutato;

l'altr' era quel che tu, Gaville, piagni.   151

Puccio Sciancato clearly, he who was   148
the only soul who'd not been changed among
the three companions we had met at first;
    the other one made you, Gaville, grieve.   151

XXV · 49

ULYSSES & DIOMEDE

CANTO XXVI

Godi, Fiorenza, poi che se' sì grande
che per mare e per terra batti l'ali,
e per lo 'nferno tuo nome si spande!

Tra li ladron trovai cinque cotali   4
tuoi cittadini onde mi ven vergogna,
e tu in grande orranza non ne sali.

Ma se presso al mattin del ver si sogna,   7
tu sentirai, di qua da picciol tempo,
di quel che Prato, non ch'altri, t'agogna.

E se già fosse, non saria per tempo.   10
Così foss' ei, da che pur esser dee!
ché più mi graverà, com' più m'attempo.

Noi ci partimmo, e su per le scalee   13
che n'avea fatte i borni a scender pria,
rimontò 'l duca mio e trasse mee;

e proseguendo la solinga via,   16
tra le schegge e tra ' rocchi de lo scoglio
lo piè sanza la man non si spedia.

Allor mi dolsi, e ora mi ridoglio   19
quando drizzo la mente a ciò ch'io vidi,
e più lo 'ngegno affreno ch'i' non soglio,

perché non corra che virtù nol guidi;   22
sì che, se stella bona o miglior cosa
m'ha dato 'l ben, ch'io stessi nol m'invidi.

Quante 'l villan ch'al poggio si riposa,   25
nel tempo che colui che 'l mondo schiara
la faccia sua a noi tien meno ascosa,

come la mosca cede a la zanzara,   28
vede lucciole giù per la vallea,
forse colà dov' e' vendemmia e ara:

B e joyous, Florence, you are great indeed,
   for over sea and land you beat your wings;
through every part of Hell your name extends!

    Among the thieves I found five citizens   4
of yours—and such, that shame has taken me;
with them, you can ascend to no high honor.

    But if the dreams dreamt close to dawn are true,   7
then little time will pass before you feel
what Prato and the others crave for you.

    Were that already come, it would not be   10
too soon—and let it come, since it must be!
As I grow older, it will be more heavy.

    We left that deep and, by protruding stones   13
that served as stairs for our descent before,
my guide climbed up again and drew me forward;

    and as we took our solitary path   16
among the ridge's jagged spurs and rocks,
our feet could not make way without our hands.

    It grieved me then and now grieves me again   19
when I direct my mind to what I saw;
and more than usual, I curb my talent,

    that it not run where virtue does not guide;   22
so that, if my kind star or something better
has given me that gift, I not abuse it.

    As many as the fireflies the peasant   25
(while resting on a hillside in the season
when he who lights the world least hides his face),

    just when the fly gives way to the mosquito,   28
sees glimmering below, down in the valley,
there where perhaps he gathers grapes and tills—

di tante fiamme tutta risplendea   31
l'ottava bolgia, sì com' io m'accorsi
tosto che fui là 've 'l fondo parea.

E qual colui che si vengiò con li orsi   34
vide 'l carro d'Elia al dipartire,
quando i cavalli al cielo erti levorsi,

che nol potea sì con li occhi seguire,   37
ch'el vedesse altro che la fiamma sola,
sì come nuvoletta, in sù salire:

tal si move ciascuna per la gola   40
del fosso, ché nessuna mostra 'l furto,
e ogne fiamma un peccatore invola.

Io stava sovra 'l ponte a veder surto,   43
sì che s'io non avessi un ronchion preso,
caduto sarei giù sanz' esser urto.

E 'l duca, che mi vide tanto atteso,   46
disse: "Dentro dai fuochi son li spirti;
catun si fascia di quel ch'elli è inceso."

"Maestro mio," rispuos' io, "per udirti   49
son io più certo; ma già m'era avviso
che così fosse, e già volvea dirti:

chi è 'n quel foco che vien sì diviso   52
di sopra, che par surger de la pira
dov' Eteòcle col fratel fu miso?"

Rispuose a me: "Là dentro si martira   55
Ulisse e Dïomede, e così insieme
a la vendetta vanno come a l'ira;

e dentro da la lor fiamma si geme   58
l'agguato del caval che fé la porta
onde uscì de' Romani il gentil seme.

Piangevisi entro l'arte per che, morta,   61
Deïdamìa ancor si duol d'Achille,
e del Palladio pena vi si porta."

"S'ei posson dentro da quelle faville   64
parlar," diss' io, "maestro, assai ten priego
e ripriego, che 'l priego vaglia mille,

che non mi facci de l'attender niego   67
fin che la fiamma cornuta qua vegna;
vedi che del disio ver' lei mi piego!"

    so many were the flames that glittered in   31
the eighth abyss; I made this out as soon
as I had come to where one sees the bottom.

    Even as he who was avenged by bears   34
saw, as it left, Elijah's chariot—
its horses rearing, rising right to heaven—

    when he could not keep track of it except   37
by watching one lone flame in its ascent,
just like a little cloud that climbs on high:

    so, through the gullet of that ditch, each flame   40
must make its way; no flame displays its prey,
though every flame has carried off a sinner.

    I stood upon the bridge and leaned straight out   43
to see; and if I had not gripped a rock,
I should have fallen off—without a push.

    My guide, who noted how intent I was,   46
told me: "Within those fires there are souls;
each one is swathed in that which scorches him."

    "My master," I replied, "on hearing you,   49
I am more sure; but I'd already thought
that it was so, and I had meant to ask:

    Who is within the flame that comes so twinned   52
above that it would seem to rise out of
the pyre Eteocles shared with his brother?"

    He answered me: "Within that flame, Ulysses   55
and Diomedes suffer; they, who went
as one to rage, now share one punishment.

    And there, together in their flame, they grieve   58
over the horse's fraud that caused a breach—
the gate that let Rome's noble seed escape.

    There they regret the guile that makes the dead   61
Deïdamia still lament Achilles;
and there, for the Palladium, they pay."

    "If they can speak within those sparks," I said,   64
"I pray you and repray and, master, may
my prayer be worth a thousand pleas, do not

    forbid my waiting here until the flame   67
with horns approaches us; for you can see
how, out of my desire, I bend toward it."

Ed elli a me: "La tua preghiera è degna   70
di molta loda, e io però l'accetto;
ma fa che la tua lingua si sostegna.

Lascia parlare a me, ch'i' ho concetto   73
ciò che tu vuoi; ch'ei sarebbero schivi,
perch' e' fuor greci, forse del tuo detto."

Poi che la fiamma fu venuta quivi   76
dove parve al mio duca tempo e loco,
in questa forma lui parlare audivi:

"O voi che siete due dentro ad un foco,   79
s'io meritai di voi mentre ch'io vissi,
s'io meritai di voi assai o poco

quando nel mondo li alti versi scrissi,   82
non vi movete; ma l'un di voi dica
dove, per lui, perduto a morir gissi."

Lo maggior corno de la fiamma antica   85
cominciò a crollarsi mormorando,
pur come quella cui vento affatica;

indi la cima qua e là menando,   88
come fosse la lingua che parlasse,
gittò voce di fuori e disse: "Quando

mi diparti' da Circe, che sottrasse   91
me più d'un anno là presso a Gaeta,
prima che sì Enëa la nomasse,

né dolcezza di figlio, né la pieta   94
del vecchio padre, né 'l debito amore
lo qual dovea Penelopè far lieta,

vincer potero dentro a me l'ardore   97
ch'i' ebbi a divenir del mondo esperto
e de li vizi umani e del valore;

ma misi me per l'alto mare aperto   100
sol con un legno e con quella compagna
picciola da la qual non fui diserto.

L'un lito e l'altro vidi infin la Spagna,   103
fin nel Morrocco, e l'isola d'i Sardi,
e l'altre che quel mare intorno bagna.

Io e ' compagni eravam vecchi e tardi   106
quando venimmo a quella foce stretta
dov' Ercule segnò li suoi riguardi

And he to me: "What you have asked is worthy   70
of every praise; therefore, I favor it.
I only ask you this: refrain from talking.

Let me address them—I have understood   73
what you desire of them. Since they were Greek,
perhaps they'd be disdainful of your speech."

And when my guide adjudged the flame had reached   76
a point where time and place were opportune,
this was the form I heard his words assume:

"You two who move as one within the flame,   79
if I deserved of you while I still lived,
if I deserved of you much or a little

when in the world I wrote my noble lines,   82
do not move on; let one of you retell
where, having gone astray, he found his death."

The greater horn within that ancient flame   85
began to sway and tremble, murmuring
just like a fire that struggles in the wind;

and then he waved his flame-tip back and forth   88
as if it were a tongue that tried to speak,
and flung toward us a voice that answered: "When

I sailed away from Circe, who'd beguiled me   91
to stay more than a year there, near Gaeta—
before Aeneas gave that place a name—

neither my fondness for my son nor pity   94
for my old father nor the love I owed
Penelope, which would have gladdened her,

was able to defeat in me the longing   97
I had to gain experience of the world
and of the vices and the worth of men.

Therefore, I set out on the open sea   100
with but one ship and that small company
of those who never had deserted me.

I saw as far as Spain, far as Morocco,   103
along both shores; I saw Sardinia
and saw the other islands that sea bathes.

And I and my companions were already   106
old and slow, when we approached the narrows
where Hercules set up his boundary stones

acciò che l'uom più oltre non si metta;   109
da la man destra mi lasciai Sibilia,
da l'altra già m'avea lasciata Setta.

'O frati,' dissi, 'che per cento milia   112
perigli siete giunti a l'occidente,
a questa tanto picciola vigilia

d'i nostri sensi ch'è del rimanente   115
non vogliate negar l'esperïenza
di retro al sol, del mondo sanza gente.

Considerate la vostra semenza: 118
fatti non foste a viver come bruti,
ma per seguir virtute e canoscenza.'

Li miei compagni fec' io sì aguti,   121
con questa orazion picciola, al cammino,
che a pena poscia li avrei ritenuti;

e volta nostra poppa nel mattino,   124
de' remi facemmo ali al folle volo,
sempre acquistando dal lato mancino.

Tutte le stelle già de l'altro polo   127
vedea la notte, e 'l nostro tanto basso,
che non surgëa fuor del marin suolo.

Cinque volte racceso e tante casso   130
lo lume era di sotto da la luna,
poi che 'ntrati eravam ne l'alto passo,

quando n'apparve una montagna, bruna   133
per la distanza, e parvemi alta tanto
quanto veduta non avëa alcuna.

Noi ci allegrammo, e tosto tornò in pianto;   136
ché de la nova terra un turbo nacque
e percosse del legno il primo canto.

Tre volte il fé girar con tutte l'acque;   139
a la quarta levar la poppa in suso
e la prora ire in giù, com' altrui piacque,

infin che 'l mar fu sovra noi richiuso."   142

that men might heed and never reach beyond: 109
upon my right, I had gone past Seville,
and on the left, already passed Ceüta.

   'Brothers,' I said, 'o you, who having crossed   112
a hundred thousand dangers, reach the west,
to this brief waking-time that still is left

   unto your senses, you must not deny   115
experience of that which lies beyond
the sun, and of the world that is unpeopled.

   Consider well the seed that gave you birth: 118
you were not made to live your lives as brutes,
but to be followers of worth and knowledge.'

   I spurred my comrades with this brief address   121
to meet the journey with such eagerness
that I could hardly, then, have held them back;

   and having turned our stern toward morning, we   124
made wings out of our oars in a wild flight
and always gained upon our left-hand side.

   At night I now could see the other pole   127
and all its stars; the star of ours had fallen
and never rose above the plain of the ocean.

   Five times the light beneath the moon had been   130
rekindled, and, as many times, was spent,
since that hard passage faced our first attempt,

   when there before us rose a mountain, dark   133
because of distance, and it seemed to me
the highest mountain I had ever seen.

   And we were glad, but this soon turned to sorrow,   136
for out of that new land a whirlwind rose
and hammered at our ship, against her bow.

   Three times it turned her round with all the waters;   139
and at the fourth, it lifted up the stern
so that our prow plunged deep, as pleased an Other,

   until the sea again closed—over us."   142

CANTO XXVII

Già era dritta in sù la fiamma e queta
  per non dir più, e già da noi sen gia
con la licenza del dolce poeta,

    quand' un'altra, che dietro a lei venìa,   4
ne fece volger li occhi a la sua cima
per un confuso suon che fuor n'uscia.

    Come 'l bue cicilian che mugghiò prima   7
col pianto di colui, e ciò fu dritto,
che l'avea temperato con sua lima,

    mugghiava con la voce de l'afflitto,   10
sì che, con tutto che fosse di rame,
pur el pareva dal dolor trafitto;

    così, per non aver via né forame   13
dal principio nel foco, in suo linguaggio
si convertïan le parole grame.

    Ma poscia ch'ebber colto lor vïaggio   16
su per la punta, dandole quel guizzo
che dato avea la lingua in lor passaggio,

    udimmo dire: "O tu a cu' io drizzo   19
la voce e che parlavi mo lombardo,
dicendo 'Istra ten va, più non t'adizzo,'

    perch' io sia giunto forse alquanto tardo,   22
non t'incresca restare a parlar meco;
vedi che non incresce a me, e ardo!

    Se tu pur mo in questo mondo cieco   25
caduto se' di quella dolce terra
latina ond' io mia colpa tutta reco,

    dimmi se Romagnuoli han pace o guerra;   28
ch'io fui d'i monti là intra Orbino
e 'l giogo di che Tever si diserra."

T he flame already was erect and silent—
it had no more to say. Now it had left us
with the permission of the gentle poet,

    when, just behind it, came another flame   4
that drew our eyes to watch its tip because
of the perplexing sound that it sent forth.

    Even as the Sicilian bull (that first   7
had bellowed with the cry—and this was just—
of him who shaped it with his instruments)

    would always bellow with its victim's voice,   10
so that, although that bull was only brass,
it seemed as if it were pierced through by pain;

    so were the helpless words that, from the first,   13
had found no path or exit from the flame,
transformed into the language of the fire.

    But after they had found their way up toward   16
the tip, and given it that movement which
the tongue had given them along their passage,

    we heard: "O you to whom I turn my voice,   19
who only now were talking Lombard, saying,
'Now you may leave—I'll not provoke more speech,'

    though I have come perhaps a little late,   22
may it not trouble you to stop and speak
with me; see how I stay—and I am burning!

    If you have fallen into this blind world   25
but recently, out of the sweet Italian
country from which I carry all my guilt,

    do tell me if the Romagnoles have peace   28
or war; I was from there—the hills between
Urbino and the ridge where Tiber springs."

Io era in giuso ancora attento e chino,   31
quando il mio duca mi tentò di costa,
dicendo: "Parla tu; questi è latino."

E io, ch'avea già pronta la risposta,   34
sanza indugio a parlare incominciai:
"O anima che se' là giù nascosta,

Romagna tua non è, e non fu mai,   37
sanza guerra ne' cuor de' suoi tiranni;
ma 'n palese nessuna or vi lasciai.

Ravenna sta come stata è molt' anni: 40
l'aguglia da Polenta la si cova,
sì che Cervia ricuopre co' suoi vanni.

La terra che fé già la lunga prova   43
e di Franceschi sanguinoso mucchio,
sotto le branche verdi si ritrova.

E 'l mastin vecchio e 'l nuovo da Verrucchio,   46
che fecer di Montagna il mal governo,
là dove soglion fan d'i denti succhio.

Le città di Lamone e di Santerno   49
conduce il lïoncel dal nido bianco,
che muta parte da la state al verno.

E quella cu' il Savio bagna il fianco,   52
così com' ella sie' tra 'l piano e 'l monte,
tra tirannia si vive e stato franco.

Ora chi se', ti priego che ne conte;   55
non esser duro più ch'altri sia stato,
se 'l nome tuo nel mondo tegna fronte."

Poscia che 'l foco alquanto ebbe rugghiato   58
al modo suo, l'aguta punta mosse
di qua, di là, e poi diè cotal fiato:

"S'i' credesse che mia risposta fosse   61
a persona che mai tornasse al mondo,
questa fiamma staria sanza più scosse;

ma però che già mai di questo fondo   64
non tornò vivo alcun, s'i' odo il vero,
sanza tema d'infamia ti rispondo.

Io fui uom d'arme, e poi fui cordigliero,   67
credendomi, sì cinto, fare ammenda;
e certo il creder mio venìa intero,

I still was bent, attentive, over him,
when my guide nudged me lightly at the side
and said: "You speak; he is Italian." 31

And I, who had my answer set already,
without delay began to speak to him:
"O soul that is concealed below in flame, 34

Romagna is not now and never was
quite free of war inside its tyrants' hearts;
but when I left her, none had broken out. 37

Ravenna stands as it has stood for years;
the eagle of Polenta shelters it
and also covers Cervia with his wings. 40

The city that already stood long trial
and made a bloody heap out of the French,
now finds itself again beneath green paws. 43

Both mastiffs of Verruchio, old and new,
who dealt so badly with Montagna, use
their teeth to bore where they have always gnawed. 46

The cities on Lamone and Santerno
are led by the young lion of the white lair;
from summer unto winter, he shifts factions. 49

That city with its side bathed by the Savio,
just as it lies between the plain and mountain,
lives somewhere between tyranny and freedom. 52

And now, I pray you, tell me who you are:
do not be harder than I've been with you,
that in the world your name may still endure." 55

After the flame, in customary fashion,
had roared awhile, it moved its pointed tip
this side and that and then set free this breath: 58

"If I thought my reply were meant for one
who ever could return into the world,
this flame would stir no more; and yet, since none— 61

if what I hear is true—ever returned
alive from this abyss, then without fear
of facing infamy, I answer you. 64

I was a man of arms, then wore the cord,
believing that, so girt, I made amends;
and surely what I thought would have been true 67

se non fosse il gran prete, a cui mal prenda!,   70
che mi rimise ne le prime colpe;
e come e *quare,* voglio che m'intenda.

Mentre ch'io forma fui d'ossa e di polpe   73
che la madre mi diè, l'opere mie
non furon leonine, ma di volpe.

Li accorgimenti e le coperte vie   76
io seppi tutte, e sì menai lor arte,
ch'al fine de la terra il suono uscie.

Quando mi vidi giunto in quella parte   79
di mia etade ove ciascun dovrebbe
calar le vele e raccoglier le sarte,

ciò che pria mi piacëa, allor m'increbbe,   82
e pentuto e confesso mi rendei;
ahi miser lasso! e giovato sarebbe.

Lo principe d'i novi Farisei,   85
avendo guerra presso a Laterano,
e non con Saracin né con Giudei,

ché ciascun suo nimico era Cristiano,   88
e nessun era stato a vincer Acri
né mercatante in terra di Soldano,

né sommo officio né ordini sacri   91
guardò in sé, né in me quel capestro
che solea fare i suoi cinti più macri.

Ma come Costantin chiese Silvestro   94
d'entro Siratti a guerir de la lebbre,
così mi chiese questi per maestro

a guerir de la sua superba febbre;   97
domandommi consiglio, e io tacetti
perché le sue parole parver ebbre.

E' poi ridisse: 'Tuo cuor non sospetti;   100
finor t'assolvo, e tu m'insegna fare
sì come Penestrino in terra getti.

Lo ciel poss' io serrare e diserrare,   103
come tu sai; però son due le chiavi
che 'l mio antecessor non ebbe care.'

Allor mi pinser li argomenti gravi   106
là 've 'l tacer mi fu avviso 'l peggio,
e dissi: 'Padre, da che tu mi lavi

had not the Highest Priest—may he be damned!—   70
made me fall back into my former sins;
and how and why, I'd have you hear from me.

While I still had the form of bones and flesh   73
my mother gave to me, my deeds were not
those of the lion but those of the fox.

The wiles and secret ways—I knew them all   76
and so employed their arts that my renown
had reached the very boundaries of earth.

But when I saw myself come to that part   79
of life when it is fitting for all men
to lower sails and gather in their ropes,

what once had been my joy was now dejection;   82
repenting and confessing, I became
a friar; and—poor me—it would have helped.

The prince of the new Pharisees, who then   85
was waging war so near the Lateran—
and not against the Jews or Saracens,

for every enemy of his was Christian,   88
and none of them had gone to conquer Acre
or been a trader in the Sultan's lands—

took no care for the highest office or   91
the holy orders that were his, or for
my cord, which used to make its wearers leaner.

But just as Constantine, on Mount Soracte,   94
to cure his leprosy, sought out Sylvester,
so this one sought me out as his instructor,

to ease the fever of his arrogance.   97
He asked me to give counsel. I was silent—
his words had seemed to me delirious.

And then he said: 'Your heart must not mistrust: 100
I now absolve you in advance—teach me
to batter Penestrino to the ground.

You surely know that I possess the power   103
to lock and unlock Heaven; for the keys
my predecessor did not prize are two.'

Then his grave arguments compelled me so,   106
my silence seemed a worse offense than speech,
and I said: 'Since you cleanse me of the sin

di quel peccato ov' io mo cader deggio,   109
lunga promessa con l'attender corto
ti farà trïunfar ne l'alto seggio.'

Francesco venne poi, com' io fu' morto,   112
per me; ma un d'i neri cherubini
li disse: 'Non portar; non mi far torto.

Venir se ne dee giù tra ' miei meschini   115
perché diede 'l consiglio frodolente,
dal quale in qua stato li sono a' crini;

ch'assolver non si può chi non si pente,   118
né pentere e volere insieme puossi
per la contradizion che nol consente.'

Oh me dolente! come mi riscossi   121
quando mi prese dicendomi: 'Forse
tu non pensavi ch'io löico fossi!'

A Minòs mi portò; e quelli attorse   124
otto volte la coda al dosso duro;
e poi che per gran rabbia la si morse,

disse: 'Questi è d'i rei del foco furo';   127
per ch'io là dove vedi son perduto,
e sì vestito, andando, mi rancuro."

Quand' elli ebbe 'l suo dir così compiuto,   130
la fiamma dolorando si partio,
torcendo e dibattendo 'l corno aguto.

Noi passamm' oltre, e io e 'l duca mio,   133
su per lo scoglio infino in su l'altr' arco
che cuopre 'l fosso in che si paga il fio

a quei che scommettendo acquistan carco.   136

that I must now fall into, Father, know: 109
long promises and very brief fulfillments
will bring a victory to your high throne.'

   Then Francis came, as soon as I was dead,   112
for me; but one of the black cherubim
told him: 'Don't bear him off; do not cheat me.

   He must come down among my menials;   115
the counsel that he gave was fraudulent;
since then, I've kept close track, to snatch his scalp;

   one can't absolve a man who's not repented,   118
and no one can repent and will at once;
the law of contradiction won't allow it.'

   O miserable me, for how I started   121
when he took hold of me and said: 'Perhaps
you did not think that I was a logician!'

   He carried me to Minos; and that monster   124
twisted his tail eight times around his hide
and then, when he had bit it in great anger,

   announced: 'This one is for the thieving fire';   127
for which—and where, you see—I now am lost,
and in this garb I move in bitterness."

   And when, with this, his words were at an end,   130
the flame departed, sorrowing and writhing
and tossing its sharp horn. We moved beyond;

   I went together with my guide, along   133
the ridge until the other arch that bridges
the ditch where payment is imposed on those

   who, since they brought such discord, bear such loads. 136

XXVIII · 22

CANTO XXVIII

Chi poria mai pur con parole sciolte
dicer del sangue e de le piaghe a pieno
ch'i' ora vidi, per narrar più volte?

Ogne lingua per certo verria meno   4
per lo nostro sermone e per la mente
c'hanno a tanto comprender poco seno.

S'el s'aunasse ancor tutta la gente   7
che già, in su la fortunata terra
di Puglia, fu del suo sangue dolente

per li Troiani e per la lunga guerra   10
che de l'anella fé sì alte spoglie,
come Livïo scrive, che non erra,

con quella che sentio di colpi doglie   13
per contastare a Ruberto Guiscardo;
e l'altra il cui ossame ancor s'accoglie

a Ceperan, là dove fu bugiardo   16
ciascun Pugliese, e là da Tagliacozzo,
dove sanz' arme vinse il vecchio Alardo;

e qual forato suo membro e qual mozzo   19
mostrasse, d'aequar sarebbe nulla
il modo de la nona bolgia sozzo.

Già veggia, per mezzul perdere o lulla,   22
com' io vidi un, così non si pertugia,
rotto dal mento infin dove si trulla.

Tra le gambe pendevan le minugia;   25
la corata pareva e 'l tristo sacco
che merda fa di quel che si trangugia.

Mentre che tutto in lui veder m'attacco,   28
guardommi e con le man s'aperse il petto,
dicendo: "Or vedi com' io mi dilacco!

The Eighth Circle, Ninth Pouch, where the Sowers of Scandal and Schism, perpetually circling, are wounded and—after each healing—wounded again by a demon with a sword. Mohammed and Alì. Warning to Fra Dolcino. Curio. Mosca. Bertran de Born.

W ho, even with untrammeled words and many
    attempts at telling, ever could recount
in full the blood and wounds that I now saw?

    Each tongue that tried would certainly fall short   4
because the shallowness of both our speech
and intellect cannot contain so much.

    Were you to reassemble all the men   7
who once, within Apulia's fateful land,
had mourned their blood, shed at the Trojans' hands,

    as well as those who fell in the long war   10
where massive mounds of rings were battle spoils—
even as Livy writes, who does not err—

    and those who felt the thrust of painful blows   13
when they fought hard against Robert Guiscard;
with all the rest whose bones are still piled up

    at Ceperano—each Apulian was   16
a traitor there—and, too, at Tagliacozzo,
where old Alardo conquered without weapons;

    and then, were one to show his limb pierced through   19
and one his limb hacked off, that would not match
the hideousness of the ninth abyss.

    No barrel, even though it's lost a hoop   22
or end-piece, ever gapes as one whom I
saw ripped right from his chin to where we fart:

    his bowels hung between his legs, one saw   25
his vitals and the miserable sack
that makes of what we swallow excrement.

    While I was all intent on watching him,   28
he looked at me, and with his hands he spread
his chest and said: "See how I split myself!

    vedi come storpiato è Mäometto!   31
Dinanzi a me sen va piangendo Alì,
fesso nel volto dal mento al ciuffetto.

    E tutti li altri che tu vedi qui,   34
seminator di scandalo e di scisma
fuor vivi, e però son fessi così.

    Un diavolo è qua dietro che n'accisma   37
sì crudelmente, al taglio de la spada
rimettendo ciascun di questa risma,

    quand' avem volta la dolente strada;   40
però che le ferite son richiuse
prima ch'altri dinanzi li rivada.

    Ma tu chi se' che 'n su lo scoglio muse,   43
forse per indugiar d'ire a la pena
ch'è giudicata in su le tue accuse?"

    "Né morte 'l giunse ancor, né colpa 'l mena," 46
rispuose 'l mio maestro, "a tormentarlo;
ma per dar lui esperïenza piena,

    a me, che morto son, convien menarlo   49
per lo 'nferno qua giù di giro in giro;
e quest' è ver così com' io ti parlo."

    Più fuor di cento che, quando l'udiro,   52
s'arrestaron nel fosso a riguardarmi
per maraviglia, oblïando il martiro.

    "Or dì a fra Dolcin dunque che s'armi,   55
tu che forse vedra' il sole in breve,
s'ello non vuol qui tosto seguitarmi,

    sì di vivanda, che stretta di neve   58
non rechi la vittoria al Noarese,
ch'altrimenti acquistar non saria leve."

    Poi che l'un piè per girsene sospese,   61
Mäometto mi disse esta parola;
indi a partirsi in terra lo distese.

    Un altro, che forata avea la gola   64
e tronco 'l naso infin sotto le ciglia,
e non avea mai ch'una orecchia sola,

    ristato a riguardar per maraviglia   67
con li altri, innanzi a li altri aprì la canna,
ch'era di fuor d'ogne parte vermiglia,

See now how maimed Mohammed is! And he   31
who walks and weeps before me is Alì,
whose face is opened wide from chin to forelock.

And all the others here whom you can see   34
were, when alive, the sowers of dissension
and scandal, and for this they now are split.

Behind us here, a devil decks us out   37
so cruelly, re-placing every one
of this throng underneath the sword edge when

we've made our way around the road of pain,   40
because our wounds have closed again before
we have returned to meet his blade once more.

But who are you who dawdle on this ridge,   43
perhaps to slow your going to the verdict
that was pronounced on your self-accusations?"

"Death has not reached him yet," my master answered,   46
"nor is it guilt that summons him to torment;
but that he may gain full experience,

I, who am dead, must guide him here below,   49
to circle after circle, throughout Hell:
this is as true as that I speak to you."

More than a hundred, when they heard him, stopped   52
within the ditch and turned to look at me,
forgetful of their torture, wondering.

"Then you, who will perhaps soon see the sun,   55
tell Fra Dolcino to provide himself
with food, if he has no desire to join me

here quickly, lest when snow besieges him,   58
it bring the Novarese the victory
that otherwise they would not find too easy."

When he had raised his heel, as if to go,   61
Mohammed said these words to me, and then
he set it on the ground and off he went.

Another sinner, with his throat slit through   64
and with his nose hacked off up to his eyebrows,
and no more than a single ear remaining,

had—with the others—stayed his steps in wonder;   67
he was the first, before the rest, to open
his windpipe—on the outside, all bloodred—

e disse: "O tu cui colpa non condanna   70
e cu' io vidi in su terra latina,
se troppa simiglianza non m'inganna,

rimembriti di Pier da Medicina,   73
se mai torni a veder lo dolce piano
che da Vercelli a Marcabò dichina.

E fa sapere a' due miglior da Fano,   76
a messer Guido e anco ad Angiolello,
che, se l'antiveder qui non è vano,

gittati saran fuor di lor vasello   79
e mazzerati presso a la Cattolica
per tradimento d'un tiranno fello.

Tra l'isola di Cipri e di Maiolica   82
non vide mai sì gran fallo Nettuno,
non da pirate, non da gente argolica.

Quel traditor che vede pur con l'uno,   85
e tien la terra che tale qui meco
vorrebbe di vedere esser digiuno,

farà venirli a parlamento seco;   88
poi farà sì, ch'al vento di Focara
non sarà lor mestier voto né preco."

E io a lui: "Dimostrami e dichiara,   91
se vuo' ch'i' porti sù di te novella,
chi è colui da la veduta amara."

Allor puose la mano a la mascella   94
d'un suo compagno e la bocca li aperse,
gridando: "Questi è desso, e non favella.

Questi, scacciato, il dubitar sommerse   97
in Cesare, affermando che 'l fornito
sempre con danno l'attender sofferse."

Oh quanto mi pareva sbigottito   100
con la lingua tagliata ne la strozza
Curïo, ch'a dir fu così ardito!

E un ch'avea l'una e l'altra man mozza,   103
levando i moncherin per l'aura fosca,
sì che 'l sangue facea la faccia sozza,

gridò: "Ricordera'ti anche del Mosca,   106
che disse, lasso!, 'Capo ha cosa fatta,'
che fu mal seme per la gente tosca."

and said: "O you whom guilt does not condemn,   70
and whom, unless too close resemblance cheats me,
I've seen above upon Italian soil,

remember Pier da Medicina if   73
you ever see again the gentle plain
that from Vercelli slopes to Marcabò.

And let the two best men of Fano know—   76
I mean both Messer Guido and Angiolello—
that, if the foresight we have here's not vain,

they will be cast out of their ship and drowned,   79
weighed down with stones, near La Cattolica,
because of a foul tyrant's treachery.

Between the isles of Cyprus and Majorca,   82
Neptune has never seen so cruel a crime
committed by the pirates or the Argives.

That traitor who sees only with one eye   85
and rules the land which one who's here with me
would wish his sight had never seen, will call

Guido and Angiolello to a parley,   88
and then will so arrange it that they'll need
no vow or prayer to Focara's wind!"

And I to him: "If you would have me carry   91
some news of you above, then tell and show me
who so detests the sight of Rimini."

And then he set his hand upon the jaw   94
of a companion, opening his mouth
and shouting: "This is he, and he speaks not.

A man cast out, he quenched the doubt in Caesar,   97
insisting that the one who is prepared
can only suffer harm if he delays."

Oh, how dismayed and pained he seemed to me,   100
his tongue slit in his gullet: Curio,
who once was so audacious in his talk!

And one who walked with both his hands hacked off,   103
while lifting up his stumps through the dark air,
so that his face was hideous with blood,

cried out: "You will remember Mosca, too,   106
who said—alas—'What's done is at an end,'
which was the seed of evil for the Tuscans."

E io li aggiunsi: "E morte di tua schiatta";   109
per ch'elli, accumulando duol con duolo,
sen gio come persona trista e matta.

　　Ma io rimasi a riguardar lo stuolo,   112
e vidi cosa ch'io avrei paura,
sanza più prova, di contarla solo;

　　se non che coscïenza m'assicura,   115
la buona compagnia che l'uom francheggia
sotto l'asbergo del sentirsi pura.

　　Io vidi certo, e ancor par ch'io 'l veggia,   118
un busto sanza capo andar sì come
andavan li altri de la trista greggia;

　　e 'l capo tronco tenea per le chiome,   121
pesol con mano a guisa di lanterna:
e quel mirava noi e dicea: "Oh me!"

　　Di sé facea a sé stesso lucerna,   124
ed eran due in uno e uno in due;
com' esser può, quei sa che sì governa.

　　Quando diritto al piè del ponte fue,   127
levò 'l braccio alto con tutta la testa
per appressarne le parole sue,

　　che fuoro: "Or vedi la pena molesta,   130
tu che, spirando, vai veggendo i morti:
vedi s'alcuna è grande come questa.

　　E perché tu di me novella porti,   133
sappi ch'i' son Bertram dal Bornio, quelli
che diedi al re giovane i ma' conforti.

　　Io feci il padre e 'l figlio in sé ribelli;   136
Achitofèl non fé più d'Absalone
e di Davìd coi malvagi punzelli.

　　Perch' io parti' così giunte persone,   139
partito porto il mio cerebro, lasso!,
dal suo principio ch'è in questo troncone.

　　Così s'osserva in me lo contrapasso."   142

I added: "—and brought death to your own kinsmen";   109
then having heard me speak, grief heaped on grief,
he went his way as one gone mad with sadness.

But I stayed there to watch that company   112
and saw a thing that I should be afraid
to tell with no more proof than my own self—

except that I am reassured by conscience,   115
that good companion, heartening a man
beneath the breastplate of its purity.

I surely saw, and it still seems I see,   118
a trunk without a head that walked just like
the others in that melancholy herd;

it carried by the hair its severed head,   121
which swayed within its hand just like a lantern;
and that head looked at us and said: "Ah me!"

Out of itself it made itself a lamp,   124
and they were two in one and one in two;
how that can be, He knows who so decrees.

When it was just below the bridge, it lifted   127
its arm together with its head, so that
its words might be more near us, words that said:

"Now you can see atrocious punishment,   130
you who, still breathing, go to view the dead:
see if there's any pain as great as this.

And so that you may carry news of me,   133
know that I am Bertran de Born, the one
who gave bad counsel to the fledgling king.

I made the son and father enemies: 136
Achitophel with his malicious urgings
did not do worse with Absalom and David.

Because I severed those so joined, I carry—   139
alas—my brain disseevered from its source,
which is within my trunk. And thus, in me

one sees the law of counter-penalty."   142

CANTO XXIX

La molta gente e le diverse piaghe
  avean le luci mie sì inebrïate,
che de lo stare a piangere eran vaghe.

  Ma Virgilio mi disse: "Che pur guate?   4
perché la vista tua pur si soffolge
là giù tra l'ombre triste smozzicate?

  Tu non hai fatto sì a l'altre bolge;   7
pensa, se tu annoverar le credi,
che miglia ventidue la valle volge.

  E già la luna è sotto i nostri piedi;   10
lo tempo è poco omai che n'è concesso,
e altro è da veder che tu non vedi."

  "Se tu avessi," rispuos' io appresso,   13
"atteso a la cagion per ch'io guardava,
forse m'avresti ancor lo star dimesso."

  Parte sen giva, e io retro li andava,   16
lo duca, già faccendo la risposta,
e soggiugnendo: "Dentro a quella cava

  dov' io tenea or li occhi sì a posta,   19
credo ch'un spirto del mio sangue pianga
la colpa che là giù cotanto costa."

  Allor disse 'l maestro: "Non si franga   22
lo tuo pensier da qui innanzi sovr' ello.
Attendi ad altro, ed ei là si rimanga;

  ch'io vidi lui a piè del ponticello   25
mostrarti e minacciar forte col dito,
e udi' 'l nominar Geri del Bello.

  Tu eri allor sì del tutto impedito   28
sovra colui che già tenne Altaforte,
che non guardasti in là, sì fu partito."

So many souls and such outlandish wounds
had made my eyes inebriate—they longed
to stay and weep. But Virgil said to me:

"Why are you staring so insistently?   4
Why does your vision linger there below
among the lost and mutilated shadows?

You did not do so at the other moats.   7
If you would count them all, consider: twenty-two
miles make up the circuit of the valley.

The moon already is beneath our feet;   10
the time alloted to us now is short,
and there is more to see than you see here."

"Had you," I answered him without a pause,   13
"been able to consider why I looked,
you might have granted me a longer stay."

Meanwhile my guide had moved ahead; I went   16
behind him, answering as I walked on,
and adding: "In that hollow upon which

just now, I kept my eyes intent, I think   19
a spirit born of my own blood laments
the guilt which, down below, costs one so much."

At this my master said: "Don't let your thoughts   22
about him interrupt you from here on:
attend to other things, let him stay there;

for I saw him below the little bridge,   25
his finger pointing at you, threatening,
and heard him called by name—Geri del Bello.

But at that moment you were occupied   28
with him who once was lord of Hautefort;
you did not notice Geri—he moved off."

"O duca mio, la vïolenta morte   31
che non li è vendicata ancor," diss' io,
"per alcun che de l'onta sia consorte,

      fece lui disdegnoso; ond' el sen gio   34
sanza parlarmi, sì com' ïo estimo:
e in ciò m'ha el fatto a sé più pio."

      Così parlammo infino al loco primo   37
che de lo scoglio l'altra valle mostra,
se più lume vi fosse, tutto ad imo.

      Quando noi fummo sor l'ultima chiostra   40
di Malebolge, sì che suoi conversi
potean parere a la veduta nostra,

      lamenti saettaron me diversi,   43
che di pietà ferrati avean li strali;
ond' io li orecchi con le man copersi.

      Qual dolor fora, se de li spedali   46
di Valdichiana tra 'l luglio e 'l settembre
e di Maremma e di Sardigna i mali

      fossero in una fossa tutti 'nsembre,   49
tal era quivi, e tal puzzo n'usciva
qual suol venir de le marcite membre.

      Noi discendemmo in su l'ultima riva   52
del lungo scoglio, pur da man sinistra;
e allor fu la mia vista più viva

      giù ver' lo fondo, là 've la ministra   55
de l'alto Sire infallibil giustizia
punisce i falsador che qui registra.

      Non credo ch'a veder maggior tristizia   58
fosse in Egina il popol tutto infermo,
quando fu l'aere sì pien di malizia,

      che li animali, infino al picciol vermo,   61
cascaron tutti, e poi le genti antiche,
secondo che i poeti hanno per fermo,

      si ristorar di seme di formiche;   64
ch'era a veder per quella oscura valle
languir li 'spirti per diverse biche.

      Qual sovra 'l ventre e qual sovra le spalle   67
l'un de l'altro giacea, e qua' carpone
si trasmutava per lo tristo calle.

"My guide, it was his death by violence,   31
for which he still is not avenged," I said,
"by anyone who shares his shame, that made

him so disdainful now; and—I suppose—   34
for this he left without a word to me,
and this has made me pity him the more."

And so we talked until we found the first   37
point of the ridge that, if there were more light,
would show the other valley to the bottom.

When we had climbed above the final cloister   40
of Malebolge, so that its lay brothers
were able to appear before our eyes,

I felt the force of strange laments, like arrows   43
whose shafts are barbed with pity; and at this,
I had to place my hands across my ears.

Just like the sufferings that all the sick   46
of Val di Chiana's hospitals, Maremma's,
Sardina's, from July until September

would muster if assembled in one ditch—   49
so was it here, and such a stench rose up
as usually comes from festering limbs.

And keeping always to the left, we climbed   52
down to the final bank of the long ridge,
and then my sight could see more vividly

into the bottom, where unerring Justice,   55
the minister of the High Lord, punishes
the falsifiers she had registered.

I do not think that there was greater grief   58
in seeing all Aegina's people sick
(then, when the air was so infected that

all animals, down to the little worm,   61
collapsed; and afterward, as poets hold
to be the certain truth, those ancient peoples

received their health again through seed of ants)   64
than I felt when I saw, in that dark valley,
the spirits languishing in scattered heaps.

Some lay upon their bellies, some upon   67
the shoulders of another spirit, some
crawled on all fours along that squalid road.

Passo passo andavam sanza sermone,   70
guardando e ascoltando li ammalati,
che non potean levar le lor persone.

   Io vidi due sedere a sé poggiati,   73
com' a scaldar si poggia tegghia a tegghia,
dal capo al piè di schianze macolati;

   e non vidi già mai menare stregghia   76
a ragazzo aspettato dal segnorso,
né a colui che mal volontier vegghia,

   come ciascun menava spesso il morso   79
de l'unghie sora sé per la gran rabbia
del pizzicor, che non ha più soccorso;

   e sì traevan giù l'unghie la scabbia,   82
come coltel di scardova le scaglie
o d'altro pesce che più larghe l'abbia.

   "O tu che con le dita ti dismaglie,"   85
cominciò 'l duca mio a l'un di loro,
"e che fai d'esse tal volta tanaglie,

   dinne s'alcun Latino è tra costoro   88
che son quinc' entro, se l'unghia ti basti
etternalmente a cotesto lavoro."

   "Latin siam noi, che tu vedi sì guasti   91
qui ambedue," rispuose l'un piangendo;
"ma tu chi se' che di noi dimandasti?"

   E 'l duca disse: "I' son un che discendo   94
con questo vivo giù di balzo in balzo,
e di mostrar lo 'nferno a lui intendo."

   Allor si ruppe lo comun rincalzo;   97
e tremando ciascuno a me si volse
con altri che l'udiron di rimbalzo.

   Lo buon maestro a me tutto s'accolse,   100
dicendo: "Dì a lor ciò che tu vuoli";
e io incominciai, poscia ch'ei volse:

   "Se la vostra memoria non s'imboli   103
nel primo mondo da l'umane menti,
ma s'ella viva sotto molti soli,

   ditemi chi voi siete e di che genti;   106
la vostra sconcia e fastidiosa pena
di palesarvi a me non vi spaventi."

We journeyed step by step without a word,   70
watching and listening to those sick souls,
who had not strength enough to lift themselves.

I saw two sitting propped against each other—   73
as pan is propped on pan to heat them up—
and each, from head to foot, spotted with scabs;

and I have never seen a stableboy   76
whose master waits for him, or one who stays
awake reluctantly, so ply a horse

with currycomb, as they assailed themselves   79
with clawing nails—their itching had such force
and fury, and there was no other help.

And so their nails kept scraping off the scabs,   82
just as a knife scrapes off the scales of carp
or of another fish with scales more large.

"O you who use your nails to strip yourself,"   85
my guide began to say to one of them,
"and sometimes have to turn them into pincers,

tell us if there are some Italians   88
among the sinners in this moat—so may
your nails hold out, eternal, at their work."

"We two whom you see so disfigured here,   91
we are Italians," one said, in tears.
"But who are you who have inquired of us?"

My guide replied: "From circle down to circle,   94
together with this living man, I am
one who descends; I mean to show him Hell."

At this their mutual support broke off;   97
and, quivering, each spirit turned toward me
with others who, by chance, had heard his words.

Then my good master drew more close to me,   100
saying: "Now tell them what it is you want."
And I began to speak, just as he wished:

"So that your memory may never fade   103
within the first world from the minds of men,
but still live on—and under many suns—

do tell me who you are and from what city,   106
and do not let your vile and filthy torment
make you afraid to let me know your names."

"Io fui d'Arezzo, e Albero da Siena,"   109
rispuose l'un, "mi fé mettere al foco;
ma quel per ch'io mori' qui non mi mena.

    Vero è ch'i' dissi lui, parlando a gioco: 112
'I' mi saprei levar per l'aere a volo';
e quei, ch'avea vaghezza e senno poco,

    volle ch'i' li mostrassi l'arte; e solo   115
perch' io nol feci Dedalo, mi fece
ardere a tal che l'avea per figliuolo.

    Ma ne l'ultima bolgia de le diece   118
me per l'alchìmia che nel mondo usai
dannò Minòs, a cui fallar non lece."

    E io dissi al poeta: "Or fu già mai   121
gente sì vana come la sanese?
Certo non la francesca sì d'assai!"

    Onde l'altro lebbroso, che m'intese,   124
rispuose al detto mio: "Tra'mene Stricca
che seppe far le temperate spese,

    e Niccolò che la costuma ricca   127
del garofano prima discoverse
ne l'orto dove tal seme s'appicca;

    e tra'ne la brigata in che disperse   130
Caccia d'Ascian la vigna e la gran fonda,
e l'Abbagliato suo senno proferse.

    Ma perché sappi chi sì ti seconda   133
contra i Sanesi, aguzza ver' me l'occhio,
sì che la faccia mia ben ti risponda:

    sì vedrai ch'io son l'ombra di Capocchio,   136
che falsai li metalli con l'alchìmia;
e te dee ricordar, se ben t'adocchio,

    com' io fui di natura buona scimia."   139

One answered me: "My city was Arezzo   109
and Albero of Siena had me burned;
but what I died for does not bring me here.

It's true that I had told him—jestingly—   112
'I'd know enough to fly through air'; and he,
with curiosity, but little sense,

wished me to show that art to him and, just   115
because I had not made him Daedalus,
had one who held him as a son burn me.

But Minos, who cannot mistake, condemned   118
my spirit to the final pouch of ten
for alchemy I practiced in the world."

And then I asked the poet: "Was there ever   121
so vain a people as the Sienese?
Even the French can't match such vanity."

At this, the other leper, who had heard me,   124
replied to what I'd said: "Except for Stricca,
for he knew how to spend most frugally;

and Niccolò, the first to make men see   127
that cloves can serve as luxury (such seed,
in gardens where it suits, can take fast root);

and, too, Caccia d'Asciano's company,   130
with whom he squandered vineyards and tilled fields,
while Abbagliato showed such subtlety.

But if you want to know who joins you so   133
against the Sienese, look hard at me—
that way, my face can also answer rightly—

and see that I'm the shade of that Capocchio   136
whose alchemy could counterfeit fine metals.
And you, if I correctly take your measure,

recall how apt I was at aping nature."   139

XXIX · 73 · 84

E P H I A L T E S

CANTO XXX

Nel tempo che Iunone era crucciata
    per Semelè contra 'l sangue tebano,
come mostrò una e altra fïata,

    Atamante divenne tanto insano,   4
che veggendo la moglie con due figli
andar carcata da ciascuna mano,

    gridò: "Tendiam le reti, sì ch'io pigli   7
la leonessa e' leoncini al varco";
e poi distese i dispietati artigli,

    prendendo l'un ch'avea nome Learco,   10
e rotollo e percbsselo ad un sasso;
e quella s'annegò con l'altro carco.

    E quando la fortuna volse in basso   13
l'altezza de' Troian che tutto ardiva,
sì che 'nsieme col regno il re fu casso,

    Ecuba trista, misera e cattiva,   16
poscia che vide Polissena morta,
e del suo Polidoro in su la riva

    del mar si fu la dolorosa accorta,   19
forsennata latrò sì come cane;
tanto il dolor le fé la mente torta.

    Ma né di Tebe furie né troiane   22
si vider mäi in alcun tanto crude,
non punger bestie, nonché membra umane,

    quant' io vidi in due ombre smorte e nude,   25
che mordendo correvan di quel modo
che 'l porco quando del porcil si schiude.

    L'una giunse a Capocchio, e in sul nodo   28
del collo l'assannò, sì che, tirando,
grattar li fece il ventre al fondo sodo.

When Juno was incensed with Semele
and, thus, against the Theban family
had shown her fury time and time again,

then Athamas was driven so insane   4
that, seeing both his wife and their two sons,
as she bore one upon each arm, he cried:

"Let's spread the nets, to take the lioness   7
together with her cubs along the pass";
and he stretched out his talons, pitiless,

and snatched the son who bore the name Learchus,   10
whirled him around and dashed him on a rock;
she, with her other burden, drowned herself.

And after fortune turned against the pride   13
of Troy, which had dared all, so that the king
together with his kingdom, was destroyed,

then Hecuba was wretched, sad, a captive;   16
and after she had seen Polyxena
dead and, in misery, had recognized

her Polydorus lying on the shore,   19
she barked, out of her senses, like a dog—
her agony had so deformed her mind.

But neither fury—Theban, Trojan—ever   22
was seen to be so cruel against another,
in rending beasts and even human limbs,

as were two shades I saw, both pale and naked,   25
who, biting, ran berserk in just the way
a hog does when it's let loose from its sty.

The one came at Capocchio and sank   28
his tusks into his neck so that, by dragging,
he made the hard ground scrape against his belly.

E l'Aretin che rimase, tremando   31
mi disse: "Quel folletto è Gianni Schicchi,
e va rabbioso altrui così conciando."

"Oh," diss' io lui, "se l'altro non ti ficchi   34
li denti a dosso, non ti sia fatica
a dir chi è, pria che di qui si spicchi."

Ed elli a me: "Quell' è l'anima antica   37
di Mirra scellerata, che divenne
al padre, fuor del dritto amore, amica.

Questa a peccar con esso così venne,   40
falsificando sé in altrui forma,
come l'altro che là sen va, sostenne,

per guadagnar la donna de la torma,   43
falsificare in sé Buoso Donati,
testando e dando al testamento norma."

E poi che i due rabbiosi fuor passati   46
sovra cu' io avea l'occhio tenuto,
rivolsilo a guardar li altri mal nati.

Io vidi un, fatto a guisa di lëuto,   49
pur ch'elli avesse avuta l'anguinaia
tronca da l'altro che l'uomo ha forcuto.

La grave idropesì, che sì dispaia   52
le membra con l'omor che mal converte,
che 'l viso non risponde a la ventraia,

faceva lui tener le labbra aperte   55
come l'etico fa, che per la sete
l'un verso 'l mento e l'altro in sù rinverte.

"O voi che sanz' alcuna pena siete,   58
e non so io perché, nel mondo gramo,"
diss' elli a noi, "guardate e attendete

a la miseria del maestro Adamo: 61
io ebbi, vivo, assai di quel ch'i' volli,
e ora, lasso!, un gocciol d'acqua bramo.

Li ruscelletti che d'i verdi colli   64
del Casentin discendon giuso in Arno,
faccendo i lor canali freddi e molli,

sempre mi stanno innanzi, e non indarno,   67
ché l'imagine lor vie più m'asciuga
che 'l male ond' io nel volto mi discarno.

And he who stayed behind, the Aretine, 31
trembled and said: "That phantom's Gianni Schicchi,
and he goes raging, rending others so."

And, "Oh," I said to him, "so may the other 34
not sink its teeth in you, please tell me who
it is before it hurries off from here."

And he to me: "That is the ancient soul 37
of the indecent Myrrha, she who loved
her father past the limits of just love.

She came to sin with him by falsely taking 40
another's shape upon herself, just as
the other phantom who goes there had done,

that he might gain the lady of the herd, 43
when he disguised himself as Buoso Donati,
making a will as if most properly."

And when the pair of raging ones had passed, 46
those two on whom my eyes were fixed, I turned
around to see the rest of the ill-born.

I saw one who'd be fashioned like a lute 49
if he had only had his groin cut off
from that part of his body where it forks.

The heavy dropsy, which so disproportions 52
the limbs with unassimilated humors
that there's no match between the face and belly,

had made him part his lips like a consumptive, 55
who will, because of thirst, let one lip drop
down to his chin and lift the other up.

"O you exempt from every punishment 58
in this grim world, and I do not know why,"
he said to us, "look now and pay attention

to this, the misery of Master Adam: 61
alive, I had enough of all I wanted;
alas, I now long for one drop of water.

The rivulets that fall into the Arno 64
down from the green hills of the Casentino
with channels cool and moist, are constantly

before me; I am racked by memory— 67
the image of their flow parches me more
than the disease that robs my face of flesh.

La rigida giustizia che mi fruga   70
tragge cagion del loco ov' io peccai
a metter più li miei sospiri in fuga.

Ivi è Romena, là dov' io falsai   73
la lega suggellata del Batista;
per ch'io il corpo sù arso lasciai.

Ma s'io vedessi qui l'anima trista   76
di Guido o d'Alessandro o di lor frate,
per Fonte Branda non darei la vista.

Dentro c'è l'una già, se l'arrabbiate   79
ombre che vanno intorno dicon vero;
ma che mi val, c'ho le membra legate?

S'io fossi pur di tanto ancor leggero   82
ch'i' potessi in cent' anni andare un'oncia,
io sarei messo già per lo sentiero,

cercando lui tra questa gente sconcia,   85
con tutto ch'ella volge undici miglia,
e men d'un mezzo di traverso non ci ha.

Io son per lor tra sì fatta famiglia;   88
e' m'indussero a batter li fiorini
ch'avean tre carati di mondiglia."

E io a lui: "Chi son li due tapini   91
che fumman come man bagnate 'l verno,
giacendo stretti a' tuoi destri confini?"

"Qui li trovai—e poi volta non dierno—,"   94
rispuose, "quando piovvi in questo greppo,
e non credo che dieno in sempiterno.

L'una è la falsa ch'accusò Gioseppo;   97
l'altr' è 'l falso Sinon greco di Troia:
per febbre aguta gittan tanto leppo."

E l'un di lor, che si recò a noia   100
forse d'esser nomato sì oscuro,
col pugno li percosse l'epa croia.

Quella sonò come fosse un tamburo;   103
e mastro Adamo li percosse il volto
col braccio suo, che non parve men duro,

dicendo a lui: "Ancor che mi sia tolto   106
lo muover per le membra che son gravi,
ho io il braccio a tal mestiere sciolto."

The rigid Justice that would torment me
uses, as most appropriate, the place
where I had sinned, to draw swift sighs from me.
                                                          70

There is Romena, there I counterfeited
the currency that bears the Baptist's seal;
for this I left my body, burned, above.
                                                          73

But could I see the miserable souls
of Guido, Alessandro, or their brother,
I'd not give up the sight for Fonte Branda.
                                                          76

And one of them is in this moat already,
if what the angry shades report is true.
What use is that to me whose limbs are tied?
                                                          79

Were I so light that, in a hundred years,
I could advance an inch, I should already
be well upon the road to search for him
                                                          82

among the mutilated ones, although
this circuit measures some eleven miles
and is at least a half a mile across.
                                                          85

Because of them I'm in this family;
it was those three who had incited me
to coin the florins with three carats' dross."
                                                          88

And I to him: "Who are those two poor sinners
who give off smoke like wet hands in the winter
and lie so close to you upon the right?"
                                                          91

"I found them here," he answered, "when I rained
down to this rocky slope; they've not stirred since
and will not move, I think, eternally.
                                                          94

One is the lying woman who blamed Joseph;
the other, lying Sinon, Greek from Troy:
because of raging fever they reek so."
                                                          97

And one of them, who seemed to take offense,
perhaps at being named so squalidly,
struck with his fist at Adam's rigid belly.
                                                          100

It sounded as if it had been a drum;
and Master Adam struck him in the face,
using his arm, which did not seem less hard,
                                                          103

saying to him: "Although I cannot move
my limbs because they are too heavy, I
still have an arm that's free to serve that need."
                                                          106

Ond' ei rispuose: "Quando tu andavi   109
al fuoco, non l'avei tu così presto;
ma sì e più l'avei quando coniavi."

E l'idropico: "Tu di' ver di questo: 112
ma tu non fosti sì ver testimonio
là 've del ver fosti a Troia richesto."

"S'io dissi falso, e tu falsasti il conio,"   115
disse Sinon; "e son qui per un fallo,
e tu per più ch'alcun altro demonio!"

"Ricorditi, spergiuro, del cavallo,"   118
rispuose quel ch'avëa infiata l'epa;
"e sieti reo che tutto il mondo sallo!"

"E te sia rea la sete onde ti crepa,"   121
disse 'l Greco, "la lingua, e l'acqua marcia
che 'l ventre innanzi a li occhi sì t'assiepa!"

Allora il monetier: "Così si squarcia   124
la bocca tua per tuo mal come suole;
ché, s'i' ho sete e omor mi rinfarcia,

tu hai l'arsura e 'l capo che ti duole,   127
e per leccar lo specchio di Narcisso,
non vorresti a 'nvitar molte parole."

Ad ascoltarli er' io del tutto fisso,   130
quando 'l maestro mi disse: "Or pur mira,
che per poco che teco non mi risso!"

Quand' io 'l senti' a me parlar con ira,   133
volsimi verso lui con tal vergogna,
ch'ancor per la memoria mi si gira.

Qual è colui che suo dannaggio sogna,   136
che sognando desidera sognare,
sì che quel ch'è, come non fosse, agogna,

tal mi fec' io, non possendo parlare,   139
che disïava scusarmi, e scusava
me tuttavia, e nol mi credea fare.

"Maggior difetto men vergogna lava,"   142
disse 'l maestro, "che 'l tuo non è stato;
però d'ogne trestizia ti disgrava.

E fa ragion ch'io ti sia sempre allato,   145
se più avvien che fortuna t'accoglia
dove sien genti in simigliante piato:

ché voler ciò udire è bassa voglia."   148

And he replied: "But when you went to burning,   109
your arm was not as quick as it was now;
though when you coined, it was as quick and more."

To which the dropsied one: "Here you speak true;   112
but you were not so true a witness there,
when you were asked to tell the truth at Troy."

"If I spoke false, you falsified the coin,"   115
said Sinon: "I am here for just one crime—
but you've committed more than any demon."

"Do not forget the horse, you perjurer,"   118
replied the one who had the bloated belly,
"may you be plagued because the whole world knows it."

The Greek: "And you be plagued by thirst that cracks   121
your tongue, and putrid water that has made
your belly such a hedge before your eyes."

And then the coiner: "So, as usual,   124
your mouth, because of racking fever, gapes;
for if I thirst and if my humor bloats me,

you have both dryness and a head that aches;   127
few words would be sufficient invitation
to have you lick the mirror of Narcissus."

I was intent on listening to them   130
when this was what my master said: "If you
insist on looking more, I'll quarrel with you!"

And when I heard him speak so angrily,   133
I turned around to him with shame so great
that it still stirs within my memory.

Even as one who dreams that he is harmed   136
and, dreaming, wishes he were dreaming, thus
desiring that which is, as if it were not,

so I became within my speechlessness: 139
I wanted to excuse myself and did
excuse myself, although I knew it not.

"Less shame would wash away a greater fault   142
than was your fault," my master said to me;
"therefore release yourself from all remorse

and see that I am always at your side,   145
should it so happen—once again—that fortune
brings you where men would quarrel in this fashion:

to want to hear such bickering is base."   148

CANTO XXXI

Una medesma lingua pria mi morse,
sì che mi tinse l'una e l'altra guancia,
e poi la medicina mi riporse;

così od' io che solea far la lancia   4
d'Achille e del suo padre esser cagione
prima di trista e poi di buona mancia.

Noi demmo il dosso al misero vallone   7
su per la ripa che 'l cinge dintorno,
attraversando sanza alcun sermone.

Quiv' era men che notte e men che giorno,   10
sì che 'l viso m'andava innanzi poco;
ma io senti' sonare un alto corno,

tanto ch'avrebbe ogne tuon fatto fioco,   13
che, contra sé la sua via seguitando,
dirizzò li occhi miei tutti ad un loco.

Dopo la dolorosa rotta, quando   16
Carlo Magno perdé la santa gesta,
non sonò sì terribilmente Orlando.

Poco portäi in là volta la testa,   19
che me parve veder molte alte torri;
ond' io: "Maestro, dì, che terra è questa?"

Ed elli a me: "Però che tu trascorri   22
per le tenebre troppo da la lungi,
avvien che poi nel maginare abborri.

Tu vedrai ben, se tu là ti congiungi,   25
quanto 'l senso s'inganna di lontano;
però alquanto più te stesso pungi."

Poi caramente mi prese per mano   28
e disse: "Pria che noi siam più avanti,
acciò che 'l fatto men ti paia strano,

Passage to the Ninth Circle. The central pit or well of Hell, where Cocytus, the last river of Hell, freezes. The Giants: Nimrod, Ephialtes, Briareus, Antaeus. Antaeus's compliance with Virgil's request to lower the two poets into the pit.

The very tongue that first had wounded me,
    sending the color up in both my cheeks,
was then to cure me with its medicine—

    as did Achilles' and his father's lance,   4
even as I have heard, when it dispensed
a sad stroke first and then a healing one.

    We turned our backs upon that dismal valley   7
by climbing up the bank that girdles it;
we made our way across without a word.

    Here it was less than night and less than day,   10
so that my sight could only move ahead
slightly, but then I heard a bugle blast

    so strong, it would have made a thunder clap   13
seem faint; at this, my eyes—which doubled back
upon their path—turned fully toward one place.

    Not even Roland's horn, which followed on   16
the sad defeat when Charlemagne had lost
his holy army, was as dread as this.

    I'd only turned my head there briefly when   19
I seemed to make out many high towers; then
I asked him: "Master, tell me, what's this city?"

    And he to me: "It is because you try   22
to penetrate from far into these shadows
that you have formed such faulty images.

    When you have reached that place, you shall see clearly   25
how much the distance has deceived your sense;
and, therefore, let this spur you on your way."

    Then lovingly he took me by the hand   28
and said: "Before we have moved farther on,
so that the fact may seem less strange to you,

sappi che non son torri, ma giganti,   31
e son nel pozzo intorno da la ripa
da l'umbilico in giuso tutti quanti."

    Come quando la nebbia si dissipa,   34
lo sguardo a poco a poco raffigura
ciò che cela 'l vapor che l'aere stipa,

    così forando l'aura grossa e scura,   37
più e più appressando ver' la sponda,
fuggiemi errore e cresciemi paura;

    però che, come su la cerchia tonda   40
Montereggioni di torri si corona,
così la proda che 'l pozzo circonda

    torreggiavan di mezza la persona   43
li orribili giganti, cui minaccia
Giove del cielo ancora quando tuona.

    E io scorgeva già d'alcun la faccia,   46
le spalle e 'l petto e del ventre gran parte,
e per le coste giù ambo le braccia.

    Natura certo, quando lasciò l'arte   49
di sì fatti animali, assai fé bene
per tòrre tali essecutori a Marte.

    E s'ella d'elefanti e di balene   52
non si pente, chi guarda sottilmente,
più giusta e più discreta la ne tene;

    ché dove l'argomento de la mente   55
s'aggiugne al mal volere e a la possa,
nessun riparo vi può far la gente.

    La faccia sua mi parea lunga e grossa   58
come la pina di San Pietro a Roma,
e a sua proporzione eran l'altre ossa;

    sì che la ripa, ch'era perizoma   61
dal mezzo in giù, ne mostrava ben tanto
di sovra, che di giugnere a la chioma

    tre Frison s'averien dato mal vanto;   64
però ch'i' ne vedea trenta gran palmi
dal loco in giù dov' omo affibbia 'l manto.

    "Raphèl maì amècche zabì almi,"   67
cominciò a gridar la fiera bocca,
cui non si convenia più dolci salmi.

I'd have you know they are not towers, but giants,   31
and from the navel downward, all of them
are in the central pit, at the embankment."

Just as, whenever mists begin to thin,   34
when, gradually, vision finds the form
that in the vapor-thickened air was hidden,

so I pierced through the dense and darkened fog;   37
as I drew always nearer to the shore,
my error fled from me, my terror grew;

for as, on its round wall, Montereggioni   40
is crowned with towers, so there towered here,
above the bank that runs around the pit,

with half their bulk, the terrifying giants,   43
whom Jove still menaces from Heaven when
he sends his bolts of thunder down upon them.

And I could now make out the face of one,   46
his shoulders and his chest, much of his belly,
and both his arms that hung along his sides.

Surely when she gave up the art of making   49
such creatures, Nature acted well indeed,
depriving Mars of instruments like these.

And if she still produces elephants   52
and whales, whoever sees with subtlety
holds her—for this—to be more just and prudent;

for where the mind's acutest reasoning   55
is joined to evil will and evil power,
there human beings can't defend themselves.

His face appeared to me as broad and long   58
as Rome can claim for its St. Peter's pine cone;
his other bones shared in that same proportion;

so that the bank, which served him as an apron   61
down from his middle, showed so much of him
above, that three Frieslanders would in vain

have boasted of their reaching to his hair;   64
for downward from the place where one would buckle
a mantle, I saw thirty spans of him.

"Raphèl maì amècche zabì almi,"   67
began to bellow that brute mouth, for which
no sweeter psalms would be appropriate.

    E 'l duca mio ver' lui: "Anima sciocca,   70
tienti col corno, e con quel ti disfoga
quand' ira o altra passïon ti tocca!

    Cércati al collo, e troverai la soga   73
che 'l tien legato, o anima confusa,
e vedi lui che 'l gran petto ti doga."

    Poi disse a me: "Elli stessi s'accusa;   76
questi è Nembrotto per lo cui mal coto
pur un linguaggio nel mondo non s'usa.

    Lasciànlo stare e non parliamo a vòto;   79
ché così è a lui ciascun linguaggio
come 'l suo ad altrui, ch'a nulla è noto."

    Facemmo adunque più lungo vïaggio,   82
vòlti a sinistra; e al trar d'un balestro
trovammo l'altro assai più fero e maggio.

    A cigner lui qual che fosse 'l maestro,   85
non so io dir, ma el tenea soccinto
dinanzi l'altro e dietro il braccio destro

    d'una catena che 'l tenea avvinto   88
dal collo in giù, sì che 'n su lo scoperto
si ravvolgëa infino al giro quinto.

    "Questo superbo volle esser esperto   91
di sua potenza contra 'l sommo Giove,"
disse 'l mio duca, "ond' elli ha cotal merto.

    Fïalte ha nome, e fece le gran prove   94
quando i giganti fer paura a' dèi;
le braccia ch'el menò, già mai non move."

    E io a lui: "S'esser puote, io vorrei   97
che de lo smisurato Brïareo
esperïenza avesser li occhi mei."

    Ond' ei rispuose: "Tu vedrai Anteo   100
presso di qui che parla ed è disciolto,
che ne porrà nel fondo d'ogne reo.

    Quel che tu vuo' veder, più là è molto   103
ed è legato e fatto come questo,
salvo che più feroce par nel volto."

    Non fu tremoto già tanto rubesto,   106
che scotesse una torre così forte,
come Fïalte a scuotersi fu presto.

And my guide turned to him: "O stupid soul,   70
keep to your horn and use that as an outlet
when rage or other passion touches you!

Look at your neck, and you will find the strap   73
that holds it fast; and see, bewildered spirit,
how it lies straight across your massive chest."

And then to me: "He is his own accuser;   76
for this is Nimrod, through whose wicked thought
one single language cannot serve the world.

Leave him alone—let's not waste time in talk;   79
for every language is to him the same
as his to others—no one knows his tongue."

So, turning to the left, we journeyed on   82
and, at the distance of a bow-shot, found
another giant, far more huge and fierce.

Who was the master who had tied him so,   85
I cannot say, but his left arm was bent
behind him and his right was bent in front,

both pinioned by a chain that held him tight   88
down from the neck; and round the part of him
that was exposed, it had been wound five times.

"This giant in his arrogance had tested   91
his force against the force of highest Jove,"
my guide said, "so he merits this reward.

His name is Ephialtes; and he showed   94
tremendous power when the giants frightened
the gods; the arms he moved now move no more."

And I to him: "If it is possible,   97
I'd like my eyes to have experience
of the enormous one, Briareus."

At which he answered: "You shall see Antaeus   100
nearby. He is unfettered and can speak;
he'll take us to the bottom of all evil.

The one you wish to see lies far beyond   103
and is bound up and just as huge as this one,
and even more ferocious in his gaze."

No earthquake ever was so violent   106
when called to shake a tower so robust,
as Ephialtes quick to shake himself.

Allor temett' io più che mai la morte,   109
e non v'era mestier più che la dotta,
s'io non avessi viste le ritorte.

Noi procedemmo più avante allotta,   112
e venimmo ad Anteo, che ben cinque alle,
sanza la testa, uscia fuor de la grotta.

"O tu che ne la fortunata valle   115
che fece Scipïon di gloria reda,
quand' Anibàl co' suoi diede le spalle,

recasti già mille leon per preda,   118
e che, se fossi stato a l'alta guerra
de' tuoi fratelli, ancor par che si creda

ch'avrebber vinto i figli de la terra: 121
mettine giù, e non ten vegna schifo,
dove Cocito la freddura serra.

Non ci fare ire a Tizio né a Tifo: 124
questi può dar di quel che qui si brama;
però ti china e non torcer lo grifo.

Ancor ti può nel mondo render fama,   127
ch'el vive, e lunga vita ancor aspetta
se 'nnanzi tempo grazia a sé nol chiama."

Così disse 'l maestro; e quelli in fretta   130
le man distese, e prese 'l duca mio,
ond' Ercule sentì già grande stretta.

Virgilio, quando prender si sentio,   133
disse a me: "Fatti qua, sì ch'io ti prenda";
poi fece sì ch'un fascio era elli e io.

Qual pare a riguardar la Carisenda   136
sotto 'l chinato, quando un nuvol vada
sov'r essa sì, ched ella incontro penda:

tal parve Antëo a me che stava a bada   139
di vederlo chinare, e fu tal ora
ch'i' avrei voluto ir per altra strada.

Ma lievemente al fondo che divora   142
Lucifero con Giuda, ci sposò;
né, sì chinato, lì fece dimora,

e come albero in nave si levò.   145

Then I was more afraid of death than ever;   109
that fear would have been quite enough to kill me,
had I not seen how he was held by chains.

    And we continued on until we reached   112
Antaeus, who, not reckoning his head,
stood out above the rock wall full five ells.

    "O you, who lived within the famous valley   115
(where Scipio became the heir of glory
when Hannibal retreated with his men),

    who took a thousand lions as your prey—   118
and had you been together with your brothers
in their high war, it seems some still believe

    the sons of earth would have become the victors—   121
do set us down below, where cold shuts in
Cocytus, and do not disdain that task.

    Don't send us on to Tityus or Typhon;   124
this man can give you what is longed for here;
therefore bend down and do not curl your lip.

    He still can bring you fame within the world,   127
for he's alive and still expects long life,
unless grace summon him before his time."

    So said my master; and in haste Antaeus   130
stretched out his hands, whose massive grip had once
been felt by Hercules, and grasped my guide.

    And Virgil, when he felt himself caught up,   133
called out to me: "Come here, so I can hold you,"
then made one bundle of himself and me.

    Just as the Garisenda seems when seen   136
beneath the leaning side, when clouds run past
and it hangs down as if about to crash,

    so did Antaeus seem to me as I   139
watched him bend over me—a moment when
I'd have preferred to take some other road.

    But gently—on the deep that swallows up   142
both Lucifer and Judas—he placed us;
nor did he, so bent over, stay there long,

    but, like a mast above a ship, he rose.   145

XXXIV · 28

CANTO XXXII

S'ïo avessi le rime aspre e chiocce,
 come si converrebbe al tristo buco
sovra 'l qual pontan tutte l'altre rocce,

io premerei di mio concetto il suco   4
più pienamente; ma perch' io non l'abbo,
non sanza tema a dicer mi conduco;

ché non è impresa da pigliare a gabbo   7
discriver fondo a tutto l'universo,
né da lingua che chiami mamma o babbo.

Ma quelle donne aiutino il mio verso   10
ch'aiutaro Anfïone a chiuder Tebe,
sì che dal fatto il dir non sia diverso.

Oh sovra tutte mal creata plebe   13
che stai nel loco onde parlare è duro,
mei foste state qui pecore o zebe!

Come noi fummo giù nel pozzo scuro   16
sotto i piè del gigante assai più bassi,
e io mirava ancora a l'alto muro,

dicere udi'mi: "Guarda come passi: 19
va sì, che tu non calchi con le piante
le teste de' fratei miseri lassi."

Per ch'io mi volsi, e vidimi davante   22
e sotto i piedi un lago che per gelo
avea di vetro e non d'acqua sembiante.

Non fece al corso suo sì grosso velo   25
di verno la Danoia in Osterlicchi,
né Tanaï là sotto 'l freddo cielo,

com' era quivi; che se Tambernicchi   28
vi fosse sù caduto, o Pietrapana,
non avria pur da l'orlo fatto cricchi.

The Ninth Circle, First Ring, called Caïna, where Traitors to their Kin are immersed in the ice, heads bent down. Camiscione dei Pazzi. The Second Ring, called Antenora: the Traitors to their Homeland or Party. Bocca degli Abati's provocation of Dante. Two traitors, one gnawing at the other's head.

Had I the crude and scrannel rhymes to suit
the melancholy hole upon which all
the other circling crags converge and rest,

   the juice of my conception would be pressed   4
more fully; but because I feel their lack,
I bring myself to speak, yet speak in fear;

   for it is not a task to take in jest,   7
to show the base of all the universe—
nor for a tongue that cries out, "mama," "papa."

   But may those ladies now sustain my verse   10
who helped Amphion when he walled up Thebes,
so that my tale not differ from the fact.

   O rabble, miscreated past all others,   13
there in the place of which it's hard to speak,
better if here you had been goats or sheep!

   When we were down below in the dark well,   16
beneath the giant's feet and lower yet,
with my eyes still upon the steep embankment,

   I heard this said to me: "Watch how you pass;   19
walk so that you not trample with your soles
the heads of your exhausted, wretched brothers."

   At this I turned and saw in front of me,   22
beneath my feet, a lake that, frozen fast,
had lost the look of water and seemed glass.

   The Danube where it flows in Austria,   25
the Don beneath its frozen sky, have never
made for their course so thick a veil in winter

   as there was here; for had Mount Tambernic   28
or Pietrapana's mountain crashed upon it,
not even at the edge would it have creaked.

    E come a gracidar si sta la rana   31
col muso fuor de l'acqua, quando sogna
di spigolar sovente la villana,

    livide, insin là dove appar vergogna   34
eran l'ombre dolenti ne la ghiaccia,
mettendo i denti in nota di cicogna.

    Ognuna in giù tenea volta la faccia;   37
da bocca il freddo, e da li occhi il cor tristo
tra lor testimonianza si procaccia.

    Quand' io m'ebbi dintorno alquanto visto,   40
volsimi a' piedi, e vidi due sì stretti,
che 'l pel del capo avieno insieme misto.

    "Ditemi, voi che sì strignete i petti,"   43
diss' io, "chi siete?" E quei piegaro i colli;
e poi ch'ebber li visi a me eretti,

    li occhi lor, ch'eran pria pur dentro molli,   46
gocciar su per le labbra, e 'l gelo strinse
le lagrime tra essi e riserrolli.

    Con legno legno spranga mai non cinse   49
forte così; ond' ei come due becchi
cozzaro insieme, tanta ira li vinse.

    E un ch'avea perduti ambo li orecchi   52
per la freddura, pur col viso in giùe,
disse: "Perché cotanto in noi ti specchi?

    Se vuoi saper chi son cotesti due,   55
la valle onde Bisenzo si dichina
del padre loro Alberto e di lor fue.

    D'un corpo usciro; e tutta la Caina   58
potrai cercare, e non troverai ombra
degna più d'esser fitta in gelatina:

    non quelli a cui fu rotto il petto e l'ombra   61
con esso un colpo per la man d'Artù;
non Focaccia; non questi che m'ingombra

    col capo sì, ch'i' non veggio oltre più,   64
e fu nomato Sassol Mascheroni;
se tosco se', ben sai omai chi fu.

    E perché non mi metti in più sermoni,   67
sappi ch'i' fu' il Camiscion de' Pazzi;
e aspetto Carlin che mi scagioni."

And as the croaking frog sits with its muzzle   31
above the water, in the season when
the peasant woman often dreams of gleaning,

    so, livid in the ice, up to the place   34
where shame can show itself, were those sad shades,
whose teeth were chattering with notes like storks'.

    Each kept his face bent downward steadily;   37
their mouths bore witness to the cold they felt,
just as their eyes proclaimed their sorry hearts.

    When I had looked around a while, my eyes   40
turned toward my feet and saw two locked so close,
the hair upon their heads had intermingled.

    "Do tell me, you whose chests are pressed so tight,"   43
I said, "who are you?" They bent back their necks,
and when they'd lifted up their faces toward me,

    their eyes, which wept upon the ground before,   46
shed tears down on their lips until the cold
held fast the tears and locked their lids still more.

    No clamp has ever fastened plank to plank   49
so tightly; and because of this, they butted
each other like two rams, such was their fury.

    And one from whom the cold had taken both   52
his ears, who kept his face bent low, then said:
"Why do you keep on staring so at us?

    If you would like to know who these two are: 55
that valley where Bisenzio descends,
belonged to them and to their father Alberto.

    They came out of one body; and you can   58
search all Caïna, you will never find
a shade more fit to sit within this ice—

    not him who, at one blow, had chest and shadow   61
shattered by Arthur's hand; and not Focaccia;
and not this sinner here who so impedes

    my vision with his head, I can't see past him;   64
his name was Sassol Mascheroni; if
you're Tuscan, now you know who he has been.

    And lest you keep me talking any longer,   67
know that I was Camiscion de' Pazzi;
I'm waiting for Carlino to absolve me."

Poscia vid' io mille visi cagnazzi   70
fatti per freddo; onde mi vien riprezzo,
e verrà sempre, de' gelati guazzi.

E mentre ch'andavamo inver' lo mezzo   73
al quale ogne gravezza si rauna,
e io tremava ne l'etterno rezzo;

se voler fu o destino o fortuna,   76
non so; ma, passeggiando tra le teste,
forte percossi 'l piè nel viso ad una.

Piangendo mi sgridò: "Perché mi peste?   79
se tu non vieni a crescer la vendetta
di Montaperti, perché mi moleste?"

E io: "Maestro mio, or qui m'aspetta,   82
sì ch'io esca d'un dubbio per costui;
poi mi farai, quantunque vorrai, fretta."

Lo duca stette, e io dissi a colui   85
che bestemmiava duramente ancora:
"Qual se' tu che così rampogni altrui?"

"Or tu chi se' che vai per l'Antenora,   88
percotendo," rispuose, "altrui le gote,
sì che, se fossi vivo, troppo fora?"

"Vivo son io, e caro esser ti puote,"   91
fu mia risposta, "se dimandi fama,
ch'io metta il nome tuo tra l'altra note."

Ed elli a me: "Del contrario ho io brama.   94
Lèvati quinci e non mi dar più lagna,
ché mal sai lusingar per questa lama!"

Allor lo presi per la cuticagna   97
e dissi: "El converrà che tu ti nomi,
o che capel qui sù non ti rimagna."

Ond' elli a me: "Perché tu mi dischiomi,   100
né ti dirò ch'io sia, né mosterrolti
se mille fiate in sul capo mi tomi."

Io avea già i capelli in mano avvolti,   103
e tratti glien' avea più d'una ciocca,
latrando lui con li occhi in giù raccolti,

quando un altro gridò: "Che hai tu, Bocca?   106
non ti basta sonar con le mascelle,
se tu non latri? qual diavol ti tocca?"

  And after that I saw a thousand faces   70
made doglike by the cold; for which I shudder—
and always will—when I face frozen fords.

  And while we were advancing toward the center   73
to which all weight is drawn—I, shivering
in that eternally cold shadow—I

  know not if it was will or destiny   76
or chance, but as I walked among the heads,
I struck my foot hard in the face of one.

  Weeping, he chided then: "Why trample me?   79
If you've not come to add to the revenge
of Montaperti, why do you molest me?"

  And I: "My master, now wait here for me,   82
that I may clear up just one doubt about him;
then you can make me hurry as you will."

  My guide stood fast, and I went on to ask   85
of him who still was cursing bitterly:
"Who are you that rebukes another so?"

  "And who are you who go through Antenora,   88
striking the cheeks of others," he replied,
"too roughly—even if you were alive?"

  "I am alive, and can be precious to you   91
if you want fame," was my reply, "for I
can set your name among my other notes."

  And he to me: "I want the contrary;   94
so go away and do not harass me—
your flattery is useless in this valley."

  At that I grabbed him by the scruff and said: 97
"You'll have to name yourself to me or else
you won't have even one hair left up here."

  And he to me: "Though you should strip me bald,   100
I shall not tell you who I am or show it,
not if you pound my head a thousand times."

  His hairs were wound around my hand already,   103
and I had plucked from him more than one tuft
while he was barking and his eyes stared down,

  when someone else cried out: "What is it, Bocca?   106
Isn't the music of your jaws enough
for you without your bark? What devil's at you?"

"Omai," diss' io, "non vo' che più favelle,   109
malvagio traditor; ch'a la tua onta
io porterò di te vere novelle."

"Va via," rispuose, "e ciò che tu vuoi conta;   112
ma non tacer, se tu di qua entro eschi,
di quel ch'ebbe or così la lingua pronta,

El piange qui l'argento de' Franceschi: 115
'Io vidi,' potrai dir, 'quel da Duera
là dove i peccatori stanno freschi.'

Se fossi domandato 'Altri chi v'era?'   118
tu hai dallato quel di Beccheria
di cui segò Fiorenza la gorgiera.

Gianni de' Soldanier credo che sia   121
più là con Ganellone e Tebaldello,
ch'aprì Faenza quando si dormia."

Noi eravam partiti già da ello,   124
ch'io vidi due ghiacciati in una buca,
sì che l'un capo a l'altro era cappello;

e come 'l pan per fame si manduca,   127
così 'l sovran li denti a l'altro pose
là 've 'l cervel s'aggiugne con la nuca:

non altrimenti Tidëo si rose   130
le tempie a Menalippo per disdegno,
che quei faceva il teschio e l'altre cose.

"O tu che mostri per sì bestial segno   133
odio sovra colui che tu ti mangi,
dimmi 'l perché," diss' io, "per tal convegno,

che se tu a ragion di lui ti piangi,   136
sappiendo chi voi siete e la sua pecca,
nel mondo suso ancora io te ne cangi,

se quella con ch'io parlo non si secca."   139

"And now," I said, "you traitor bent on evil,   109
I do not need your talk, for I shall carry
true news of you, and that will bring you shame."

"Be off," he answered; "tell them what you like,   112
but don't be silent, if you make it back,
about the one whose tongue was now so quick.

Here he laments the silver of the Frenchmen;   115
'I saw,' you then can say, 'him of Duera,
down there, where all the sinners are kept cool.'

And if you're asked who else was there in ice,   118
one of the Beccheria is beside you—
he had his gullet sliced right through by Florence.

Gianni de' Soldanieri, I believe,   121
lies there with Ganelon and Tebaldello,
he who unlocked Faenza while it slept."

We had already taken leave of him,   124
when I saw two shades frozen in one hole,
so that one's head served as the other's cap;

and just as he who's hungry chews his bread,   127
one sinner dug his teeth into the other
right at the place where brain is joined to nape:

no differently had Tydeus gnawed the temples   130
of Menalippus, out of indignation,
than this one chewed the skull and other parts.

"O you who show, with such a bestial sign,   133
your hatred for the one on whom you feed,
tell me the cause," I said; "we can agree

that if your quarrel with him is justified,   136
then knowing who you are and what's his sin,
I shall repay you yet on earth above,

if that with which I speak does not dry up."   139

CANTO XXXIII

La bocca sollevò dal fiero pasto
quel peccator, forbendola a' capelli
del capo ch'elli avea di retro guasto.

Poi cominciò: "Tu vuo' ch'io rinovelli   4
disperato dolor che 'l cor mi preme
già pur pensando, pria ch'io ne favelli.

Ma se le mie parole esser dien seme   7
che frutti infamia al traditor ch'i' rodo,
parlare e lagrimar vedrai insieme.

Io non so chi tu se' né per che modo   10
venuto se' qua giù; ma fiorentino
mi sembri veramente quand' io t'odo.

Tu dei saper ch'i' fui conte Ugolino,   13
e questi è l'arcivescovo Ruggieri:
or ti dirò perché i son tal vicino.

Che per l'effetto de' suo' mai pensieri,   16
fidandomi di lui, io fossi preso
e poscia morto, dir non è mestieri;

però quel che non puoi avere inteso,   19
cioè come la morte mia fu cruda,
udirai, e saprai s'e' m'ha offeso.

Breve pertugio dentro da la Muda,   22
la qual per me ha 'l titol de la fame,
e che conviene ancor ch'altrui si chiuda,

m'avea mostrato per lo suo forame   25
più lune già, quand' io feci 'l mal sonno
che del futuro mi squarciò 'l velame.

Questi pareva a me maestro e donno,   28
cacciando il lupo e ' lupicini al monte
per che i Pisan veder Lucca non ponno.

That sinner raised his mouth from his fierce meal,
then used the head that he had ripped apart
in back: he wiped his lips upon its hair.

Then he began: "You want me to renew   4
despairing pain that presses at my heart
even as I think back, before I speak.

But if my words are seed from which the fruit 7
is infamy for this betrayer whom
I gnaw, you'll see me speak and weep at once.

I don't know who you are or in what way   10
you've come down here; and yet you surely seem—
from what I hear—to be a Florentine.

You are to know I was Count Ugolino,   13
and this one here, Archbishop Ruggieri;
and now I'll tell you why I am his neighbor.

There is no need to tell you that, because   16
of his malicious tricks, I first was taken
and then was killed—since I had trusted him;

however, that which you cannot have heard—   19
that is, the cruel death devised for me—
you now shall hear and know if he has wronged me.

A narrow window in the Eagles' Tower,   22
which now, through me, is called the Hunger Tower,
a cage in which still others will be locked,

had, through its opening, already showed me   25
several moons, when I dreamed that bad dream
which rent the curtain of the future for me.

This man appeared to me as lord and master;   28
he hunted down the wolf and its young whelps
upon the mountain that prevents the Pisans

Con cagne magre, studïose e conte   31
Gualandi con Sismondi e con Lanfranchi
s'avea messi dinanzi da la fronte.

In picciol corso mi parieno stanchi   34
lo padre e ' figli, e con l'agute scane
mi parea lor veder fender li fianchi.

Quando fui desto innanzi la dimane,   37
pianger senti' fra 'l sonno i miei figliuoli
ch'eran con meco, e dimandar del pane.

Ben se' crudel, se tu già non ti duoli   40
pensando ciò che 'l mio cor s'annunziava;
e se non piangi, di che pianger suoli?

Già eran desti, e l'ora s'appressava   43
che 'l cibo ne solëa essere addotto,
e per suo sogno ciascun dubitava;

e io senti' chiavar l'uscio di sotto   46
a l'orribile torre; ond' io guardai
nel viso a' mie' figliuoi sanza far motto.

Io non piangëa, sì dentro impetrai: 49
piangevan elli; e Anselmuccio mio
disse: 'Tu guardi sì, padre! che hai?'

Perciò non lagrimai né rispuos' io   52
tutto quel giorno né la notte appresso,
infin che l'altro sol nel mondo uscìo.

Come un poco di raggio si fu messo   55
nel doloroso carcere, e io scorsi
per quattro visi il mio aspetto stesso,

ambo le man per lo dolor mi morsi;   58
ed ei, pensando ch'io 'l fessi per voglia
di manicar, di sùbito levorsi

e disser: 'Padre, assai ci fia men doglia   61
se tu mangi di noi: tu ne vestisti
queste misere carni, e tu le spoglia.'

Queta'mi allor per non farli più tristi;   64
lo dì e l'altro stemmo tutti muti;
ahi dura terra, perché non t'apristi?

Poscia che fummo al quarto dì venuti,   67
Gaddo mi si gittò disteso a' piedi,
dicendo: 'Padre mio, ché non m'aiuti?'

from seeing Lucca; and with lean and keen   31
and practiced hounds, he'd sent up front, before him,
Gualandi and Sismondi and Lanfranchi.

But after a brief course, it seemed to me   34
that both the father and the sons were weary;
I seemed to see their flanks torn by sharp fangs.

When I awoke at daybreak, I could hear   37
my sons, who were together with me there,
weeping within their sleep, asking for bread.

You would be cruel indeed if, thinking what   40
my heart foresaw, you don't already grieve;
and if you don't weep now, when would you weep?

They were awake by now; the hour drew near   43
at which our food was usually brought,
and each, because of what he'd dreamed, was anxious;

below, I heard them nailing up the door   46
of that appalling tower; without a word,
I looked into the faces of my sons.

I did not weep; within, I turned to stone.   49
They wept; and my poor little Anselm said:
'Father, you look so . . . What is wrong with you?'

At that I shed no tears and—all day long   52
and through the night that followed—did not answer
until another sun had touched the world.

As soon as a thin ray had made its way   55
into that sorry prison, and I saw,
reflected in four faces, my own gaze,

out of my grief, I bit at both my hands;   58
and they, who thought I'd done that out of hunger,
immediately rose and told me: 'Father,

it would be far less painful for us if   61
you ate of us; for you clothed us in this
sad flesh—it is for you to strip it off.'

Then I grew calm, to keep them from more sadness;   64
through that day and the next, we all were silent;
O hard earth, why did you not open up?

But after we had reached the fourth day, Gaddo,   67
throwing himself, outstretched, down at my feet,
implored me: 'Father, why do you not help me?'

Quivi morì; e come tu mi vedi,   70
vid' io cascar li tre ad uno ad uno
tra 'l quinto dì e 'l sesto; ond' io mi diedi,

  già cieco, a brancolar sovra ciascuno,   73
e due dì li chiamai, poi che fur morti.
Poscia, più che 'l dolor, poté 'l digiuno."

  Quand' ebbe detto ciò, con li occhi torti   76
riprese 'l teschio misero co' denti,
che furo a l'osso, come d'un can, forti.

  Ahi Pisa, vituperio de le genti   79
del bel paese là dove 'l sì suona,
poi che i vicini a te punir son lenti,

  muovasi la Capraia e la Gorgona,   82
e faccian siepe ad Arno in su la foce,
sì ch'elli annieghi in te ogne persona!

  Che se 'l conte Ugolino aveva voce   85
d'aver tradita te de le castella,
non dovei tu i figliuoi porre a tal croce.

  Innocenti facea l'età novella,   88
novella Tebe, Uguiccione e 'l Brigata
e li altri due che 'l canto suso appella.

  Noi passammo oltre, là 've la gelata   91
ruvidamente un'altra gente fascia,
non volta in giù, ma tutta riversata.

  Lo pianto stesso lì pianger non lascia,   94
e 'l duol che truova in su li occhi rintoppo,
si volge in entro a far crescer l'ambascia;

  ché le lagrime prime fanno groppo,   97
e sì come visiere di cristallo,
rïempion sotto 'l ciglio tutto il coppo.

  E avvegna che, sì come d'un callo,   100
per la freddura ciascun sentimento
cessato avesse del mio viso stallo,

  già mi parea sentire alquanto vento;   103
per ch'io: "Maestro mio, questo chi move?
non è qua giù ogne vapore spento?"

  Ond' elli a me: "Avaccio sarai dove   106
di ciò farà l'occhio la risposta,
veggendo la cagion che 'l fiato piove."

And there he died; and just as you see me,   70
I saw the other three fall one by one
between the fifth day and the sixth; at which,

   now blind, I started groping over each;   73
and after they were dead, I called them for
two days; then fasting had more force than grief."

   When he had spoken this, with eyes awry,   76
again he gripped the sad skull in his teeth,
which, like a dog's, were strong down to the bone.

   Ah, Pisa, you the scandal of the peoples   79
of that fair land where *si* is heard, because
your neighbors are so slow to punish you,

   may, then, Caprara and Gorgona move   82
and build a hedge across the Arno's mouth,
so that it may drown every soul in you!

   For if Count Ugolino was reputed   85
to have betrayed your fortresses, there was
no need to have his sons endure such torment.

   O Thebes renewed, their years were innocent   88
and young—Brigata, Uguiccione, and
the other two my song has named above!

   We passed beyond, where frozen water wraps—   91
a rugged covering—still other sinners,
who were not bent, but flat upon their backs.

   Their very weeping there won't let them weep,   94
and grief that finds a barrier in their eyes
turns inward to increase their agony;

   because their first tears freeze into a cluster,   97
and, like a crystal visor, fill up all
the hollow that is underneath the eyebrow.

   And though, because of cold, my every sense   100
had left its dwelling in my face, just as
a callus has no feeling, nonetheless,

   I seemed to feel some wind now, and I said: 103
"My master, who has set this gust in motion?
For isn't every vapor quenched down here?"

   And he to me: "You soon shall be where your   106
own eye will answer that, when you shall see
the reason why this wind blasts from above."

E un de' tristi de la fredda crosta   109
gridò a noi: "O anime crudeli
tanto che data v'è l'ultima posta,

    levatemi dal viso i duri veli,   112
sì ch'ïo sfoghi 'l duol che 'l cor m'impregna,
un poco, pria che 'l pianto si raggeli."

    Per ch'io a lui: "Se vuo' ch'i' ti sovvegna,   115
dimmi chi se', e s'io non ti disbrigo,
al fondo de la ghiaccia ir mi convegna."

    Rispuose adunque: "I' son frate Alberigo;   118
i' son quel da le frutta del mal orto,
che qui riprendo dattero per figo."

"Oh," diss' io lui, "or se' tu ancor morto?"   121
Ed elli a me: "Come 'l mio corpo stea
nel mondo sù, nulla scïenza porto.

    Cotal vantaggio ha questa Tolomea,   124
che spesse volte l'anima ci cade
innanzi ch'Atropòs mossa le dea.

    E perché tu più volontier mi rade   127
le 'nvetrïate lagrime dal volto,
sappie che, tosto che l'anima trade

    come fec' ïo, il corpo suo l' è tolto   130
da un demonio, che poscia il governa
mentre che 'l tempo suo tutto sia vòlto.

    Ella ruina in sì fatta cisterna;   133
e forse pare ancor lo corpo suso
de l'ombra che di qua dietro mi verna.

    Tu 'l dei saper, se tu vien pur mo giuso: 136
elli è ser Branca Doria, e son più anni
poscia passati ch'el fu sì racchiuso."

    "Io credo," diss' io lui, "che tu m'inganni;   139
ché Branca Doria non morì unquanche,
e mangia e bee e dorme e veste panni."

    "Nel fosso sù," diss' el, "de' Malebranche,   142
là dove bolle la tenace pece,
non era ancor giunto Michel Zanche,

    che questi lasciò il diavolo in sua vece   145
nel corpo suo, ed un suo prossimano
che 'l tradimento insieme con lui fece.

And one of those sad sinners in the cold 109
crust, cried to us: "O souls who are so cruel
that this last place has been assigned to you,

take off the hard veils from my face so that 112
I can release the suffering that fills
my heart before lament freezes again."

To which I answered: "If you'd have me help you, 115
then tell me who you are; if I don't free you,
may I go to the bottom of the ice."

He answered then: "I am Fra Alberigo, 118
the one who tended fruits in a bad garden,
and here my figs have been repaid with dates."

"But then," I said, "are you already dead?" 121
And he to me: "I have no knowledge of
my body's fate within the world above.

For Ptolomea has this privilege: 124
quite frequently the soul falls here before
it has been thrust away by Atropos.

And that you may with much more willingness 127
scrape these glazed tears from off my face, know this:
as soon as any soul becomes a traitor,

as I was, then a demon takes its body 130
away—and keeps that body in his power
until its years have run their course completely.

The soul falls headlong, down into this cistern; 133
and up above, perhaps, there still appears
the body of the shade that winters here

behind me; you must know him, if you've just 136
come down; he is Ser Branca Doria;
for many years he has been thus pent up."

I said to him: "I think that you deceive me, 139
for Branca Doria is not yet dead;
he eats and drinks and sleeps and puts on clothes."

"There in the Malebranche's ditch above, 142
where sticky pitch boils up, Michele Zanche
had still not come," he said to me, "when this one—

together with a kinsman, who had done 145
the treachery together with him—left
a devil in his stead inside his body.

Ma distendi oggimai in qua la mano;   148
aprimi li occhi." E io non gliel' apersi;
e cortesia fu lui esser villano.

Ahi Genovesi, uomini diversi   151
d'ogne costume e pien d'ogne magagna,
perché non siete voi del mondo spersi?

Ché col peggiore spirto di Romagna   154
trovai di voi un tal, che per sua opra
in anima in Cocito già si bagna,

e in corpo par vivo ancor di sopra.   157

But now reach out your hand; open my eyes."   148
And yet I did not open them for him;
and it was courtesy to show him rudeness.

     Ah, Genoese, a people strange to every   151
constraint of custom, full of all corruption,
why have you not been driven from the world?

     For with the foulest spirit of Romagna,   154
I found one of you such that, for his acts,
in soul he bathes already in Cocytus

     and up above appears alive, in body.   157

CANTO XXXIV

*V*exilla regis prodeunt inferni
   verso di noi; però dinanzi mira,"
disse 'l maestro mio, "se tu 'l discerni."

   Come quando una grossa nebbia spira,   4
o quando l'emisperio nostro annotta,
par di lungi un molin che 'l vento gira,

   veder mi parve un tal dificio allotta;   7
poi per lo vento mi ristrinsi retro
al duca mio, ché non lì era altra grotta.

   Già era, e con paura il metto in metro,   10
là dove l'ombre tutte eran coperte,
e trasparien come festuca in vetro.

   Altre sono a giacere; altre stanno erte,   13
quella col capo e quella con le piante;
altra, com' arco, il volto a' piè rinverte.

   Quando noi fummo fatti tanto avante,   16
ch'al mio maestro piacque di mostrarmi
la creatura ch'ebbe il bel sembiante,

   d'innanzi mi si tolse e fé restarmi,   19
"Ecco Dite," dicendo, "ed ecco il loco
ove convien che di fortezza t'armi."

   Com' io divenni allor gelato e fioco,   22
nol dimandar, lettor, ch'i' non lo scrivo,
però ch'ogne parlar sarebbe poco.

   Io non mori' e non rimasi vivo;   25
pensa oggimai per te, s'hai fior d'ingegno,
qual io divenni, d'uno e d'altro privo.

   Lo 'mperador del doloroso regno   28
da mezzo 'l petto uscia fuor de la ghiaccia;
e più con un gigante io mi convegno,

The Ninth Circle, Fourth Ring, called Judecca, where Traitors against their Benefactors are fully covered by ice. Dis, or Lucifer, emperor of that kingdom, his three mouths rending Judas, Brutus, and Cassius. Descent of Virgil and Dante down Lucifer's body to the other, southern hemisphere. Their vision of the stars.

*V*exilla regis prodeunt inferni
   toward us; and therefore keep your eyes ahead,"
my master said, "to see if you can spy him."

   Just as, when night falls on our hemisphere   4
or when a heavy fog is blowing thick,
a windmill seems to wheel when seen far off,

   so then I seemed to see that sort of structure.   7
And next, because the wind was strong, I shrank
behind my guide; there was no other shelter.

   And now—with fear I set it down in meter—   10
I was where all the shades were fully covered
but visible as wisps of straw in glass.

   There some lie flat and others stand erect,   13
one on his head, and one upon his soles;
and some bend face to feet, just like a bow.

   But after we had made our way ahead,   16
my master felt he now should have me see
that creature who was once a handsome presence;

   he stepped aside and made me stop, and said: 19
"Look! Here is Dis, and this the place where you
will have to arm yourself with fortitude."

   O reader, do not ask of me how I   22
grew faint and frozen then—I cannot write it:
all words would fall far short of what it was.

   I did not die, and I was not alive;   25
think for yourself, if you have any wit,
what I became, deprived of life and death.

   The emperor of the despondent kingdom   28
so towered from the ice, up from midchest,
that I match better with a giant's breadth

che i giganti non fan con le sue braccia: 31
vedi oggimai quant' esser dee quel tutto
ch'a così fatta parte si confaccia.

S'el fu sì bel com' elli è ora brutto,   34
e contra 'l suo fattore alzò le ciglia,
ben dee da lui procedere ogne lutto.

Oh quanto parve a me gran maraviglia   37
quand' io vidi tre facce a la sua testa!
L'una dinanzi, e quella era vermiglia;

l'altr' eran due, che s'aggiugnieno a questa   40
sovresso 'l mezzo di ciascuna spalla,
e sé giugnieno al loco de la cresta:

e la destra parea tra bianca e gialla;   43
la sinistra a vedere era tal, quali
vegnon di là onde 'l Nilo s'avvalla.

Sotto ciascuna uscivan due grand' ali,   46
quanto si convenia a tanto uccello:
vele di mar non vid' io mai cotali.

Non avean penne, ma di vispistrello   49
era lor modo; e quelle svolazzava,
sì che tre venti si movean da ello:

quindi Cocito tutto s'aggelava.   52
Con sei occhi piangëa, e per tre menti
gocciava 'l pianto e sanguinosa bava.

Da ogne bocca dirompea co' denti   55
un peccatore, a guisa di maciulla,
sì che tre ne facea così dolenti.

A quel dinanzi il mordere era nulla   58
verso 'l graffiar, che tal volta la schiena
rimanea de la pelle tutta brulla.

"Quell' anima là sù c'ha maggior pena,"   61
disse 'l maestro, "è Giuda Scarïotto,
che 'l capo ha dentro e fuor le gambe mena.

De li altri due c'hanno il capo di sotto,   64
quel che pende dal nero ceffo è Bruto:
vedi come si storce, e non fa motto!;

e l'altro è Cassio, che par sì membruto.   67
Ma la notte risurge, e oramai
è da partir, ché tutto avem veduto."

than giants match the measure of his arms;   31
now you can gauge the size of all of him
if it is in proportion to such parts.

If he was once as handsome as he now   34
is ugly and, despite that, raised his brows
against his Maker, one can understand

how every sorrow has its source in him!   37
I marveled when I saw that, on his head,
he had three faces: one—in front—bloodred;

and then another two that, just above   40
the midpoint of each shoulder, joined the first;
and at the crown, all three were reattached;

the right looked somewhat yellow, somewhat white;   43
the left in its appearance was like those
who come from where the Nile, descending, flows.

Beneath each face of his, two wings spread out,   46
as broad as suited so immense a bird:
I've never seen a ship with sails so wide.

They had no feathers, but were fashioned like   49
a bat's; and he was agitating them,
so that three winds made their way out from him—

and all Cocytus froze before those winds.   52
He wept out of six eyes; and down three chins,
tears gushed together with a bloody froth.

Within each mouth—he used it like a grinder—   55
with gnashing teeth he tore to bits a sinner,
so that he brought much pain to three at once.

The forward sinner found that biting nothing   58
when matched against the clawing, for at times
his back was stripped completely of its hide.

"That soul up there who has to suffer most,"   61
my master said: "Judas Iscariot—
his head inside, he jerks his legs without.

Of those two others, with their heads beneath,   64
the one who hangs from that black snout is Brutus—
see how he writhes and does not say a word!

That other, who seems so robust, is Cassius.   67
But night is come again, and it is time
for us to leave; we have seen everything."

Com' a lui piacque, il collo li avvinghiai;   70
ed el prese di tempo e loco poste,
e quando l'ali fuoro aperte assai,

appigliò sé a le vellute coste;   73
di vello in vello giù discese poscia
tra 'l folto pelo e le gelate croste.

Quando noi fummo là dove la coscia   76
si volge, a punto in sul grosso de l'anche,
lo duca, con fatica e con angoscia,

volse la testa ov' elli avea le zanche,   79
e aggrappossi al pel com' om che sale,
sì che 'n inferno i' credea tornar anche.

"Attienti ben, ché per cotali scale,"   82
disse 'l maestro, ansando com' uom lasso,
"conviensi dipartir da tanto male."

Poi uscì fuor per lo fóro d'un sasso   85
e puose me in su l'orlo a sedere;
appresso porse a me l'accorto passo.

Io levai li occhi e credetti vedere   88
Lucifero com' io l'avea lasciato,
e vidili le gambe in sù tenere;

e s'io divenni allora travagliato,   91
la gente grossa il pensi, che non vede
qual è quel punto ch'io avea passato.

"Lèvati sù," disse 'l maestro, "in piede: 94
la via è lunga e 'l cammino è malvagio,
e già il sole a mezza terza riede."

Non era camminata di palagio   97
là 'v' eravam, ma natural burella
ch'avea mal suolo e di lume disagio.

"Prima ch'io de l'abisso mi divella,   100
maestro mio," diss' io quando fui dritto,
"a trarmi d'erro un poco mi favella:

ov' è la ghiaccia? e questi com' è fitto   103
sì sottosopra? e come, in sì poc' ora,
da sera a mane ha fatto il sol tragitto?"

Ed elli a me: "Tu imagini ancora   106
d'esser di là dal centro, ov' io mi presi
al pel del vermo reo che 'l mondo fóra.

Just as he asked, I clasped him round the neck;   70
and he watched for the chance of time and place,
and when the wings were open wide enough,

    he took fast hold upon the shaggy flanks   73
and then descended, down from tuft to tuft,
between the tangled hair and icy crusts.

When we had reached the point at which the thigh   76
revolves, just at the swelling of the hip,
my guide, with heavy strain and rugged work,

    reversed his head to where his legs had been   79
and grappled on the hair, as one who climbs—
I thought that we were going back to Hell.

"Hold tight," my master said—he panted like   82
a man exhausted—"it is by such stairs
that we must take our leave of so much evil."

Then he slipped through a crevice in a rock   85
and placed me on the edge of it, to sit;
that done, he climbed toward me with steady steps.

I raised my eyes, believing I should see   88
the half of Lucifer that I had left;
instead I saw him with his legs turned up;

    and if I then became perplexed, do let   91
the ignorant be judges—those who can
not understand what point I had just crossed.

"Get up," my master said, "be on your feet: 94
the way is long, the path is difficult;
the sun's already back to middle tierce."

It was no palace hall, the place in which   97
we found ourselves, but with its rough-hewn floor
and scanty light, a dungeon built by nature.

"Before I free myself from this abyss,   100
master," I said when I had stood up straight,
"tell me enough to see I don't mistake:

Where is the ice? And how is he so placed   103
head downward? Tell me, too, how has the sun
in so few hours gone from night to morning?"

And he to me: "You still believe you are   106
north of the center, where I grasped the hair
of the damned worm who pierces through the world.

Di là fosti cotanto quant' io scesi;   109
quand' io mi volsi, tu passasti 'l punto
al qual si traggon d'ogne parte i pesi.

E se' or sotto l'emisperio giunto   112
ch'è contraposto a quel che la gran secca
coverchia, e sotto 'l cui colmo consunto

fu l'uom che nacque e visse sanza pecca;   115
tu haï i piedi in su picciola spera
che l'altra faccia fa de la Giudecca.

Qui è da man, quando di là è sera;   118
e questi, che ne fé scala col pelo,
fitto è ancora sì come prim' era.

Da questa parte cadde giù dal cielo;   121
e la terra, che pria di qua si sporse,
per paura di lui fé del mar velo,

e venne a l'emisperio nostro; e forse   124
per fuggir lui lasciò qui loco vòto
quella ch'appar di qua, e sù ricorse."

Luogo è là giù da Balzebù remoto   127
tanto quanto la tomba si distende,
che non per vista, ma per suono è noto

d'un ruscelletto che quivi discende   130
per la buca d'un sasso, ch'elli ha roso,
col corso ch'elli avvolge, e poco pende.

Lo duca e io per quel cammino ascoso   133
intrammo a ritornar nel chiaro mondo;
e sanza cura aver d'alcun riposo,

salimmo sù, el primo e io secondo,   136
tanto ch'i' vidi de le cose belle
che porta 'l ciel, per un pertugio tondo.

E quindi uscimmo a riveder le stelle.   139

And you were there as long as I descended;   109
but when I turned, that's when you passed the point
to which, from every part, all weights are drawn.

And now you stand beneath the hemisphere   112
opposing that which cloaks the great dry lands
and underneath whose zenith died the Man

whose birth and life were sinless in this world.   115
Your feet are placed upon a little sphere
that forms the other face of the Judecca.

Here it is morning when it's evening there;   118
and he whose hair has served us as a ladder
is still fixed, even as he was before.

This was the side on which he fell from Heaven;   121
for fear of him, the land that once loomed here
made of the sea a veil and rose into

our hemisphere; and that land which appears   124
upon this side—perhaps to flee from him—
left here this hollow space and hurried upward."

There is a place below, the limit of   127
that cave, its farthest point from Beelzebub,
a place one cannot see: it is discovered

by ear—there is a sounding stream that flows   130
along the hollow of a rock eroded
by winding waters, and the slope is easy.

My guide and I came on that hidden road   133
to make our way back into the bright world;
and with no care for any rest, we climbed—

he first, I following—until I saw,   136
through a round opening, some of those things
of beauty Heaven bears. It was from there

that we emerged, to see—once more—the stars.   139

DANTE IN HIS AGE

Possessed of every good, Florence has defeated her enemies in war and in great battles. She enjoys her fortune, her victorious pennants, her powerful people. Everywhere she reinforces and augments her power. Ardent, vigorous, she strikes down every enemy. She possesses the sea, possesses the land, possesses all of the world. Under her government, all of Tuscany has become happy. Like Rome, she sits ingathering her victories; she decides everything; she regulates everything with sure laws.

The proud Florentines inscribed this epigraph in stone on the Palazzo del Podestà (now the Bargello) around 1255. It echoed the spirit of the Florentine commune—or commonwealth or republic—during the decade of republican government from 1250 to 1260, the period of the *Primo Popolo,* or First Republic. Florence energetically reaffirmed her economic independence, was jealous of her own political establishment, and was proud of the representative democracy she had constructed. The First Republic was followed by an interval of six years of antirepublican rule, but it was restored in 1266 as the Second Republic *(Secondo Popolo),* which lasted until the fifteenth century.

In 1265, one year before this republican restoration, Dante was born in Florence. And, as he himself lets us know *(Par.* XII, 115–117), his birth fell under the sign of Gemini, between May 14 and June 13. From the *Comedy* we learn that one of his great-grandfathers, Cacciaguida *(Par.* XV–XVII), was knighted by the emperor Conrad III and may have died in the Second Crusade in the Holy Land (1147). Though the Alighieri were certainly not among the most prominent citizens of Florence, some of them were sufficiently active politi-

cally to have suffered exile in 1248 and 1260, years of bitter civil strife. Of Dante's immediate parents not much is known. His father, Alighiero, seems to have been a lender and money changer who accumulated fairly substantial land holdings near Florence. Dante's mother, Donna Bella (Gabriella), died early (between 1270 and 1273). His father remarried quickly and died before 1283.

Florence's network of schools was to become a significant civic achievement in the fourteenth century. But little is known of its schools in the thirteenth century—when Bologna was certainly ahead of Florence in classical training—and nothing of Dante's own early education. But however limited was the formal frame of his early studies, and whether or not he had any formal frame at all, he was clearly an intense self-teacher (with reference to poetry he declares that he had learned "by himself the art of speaking words in rhyme": *Vita Nuova* III, 9); and he surely benefited from the rhetorical and civil teachings he found in the works of Brunetto Latini *(Inf.* XV, 30–124).

Possibly around 1285 (though some date Dante's "effective" marriage later), he married Gemma Donati, to whom he had been betrothed, in accord with the customs of the time, as early as 1277. With Gemma Donati, he had at least three children: Jacopo, Pietro, and Antonia. (Pietro was to become one of the most lucid commentators we have on the *Comedy.)*

Unquestionably, the major event of Dante's youth was, or became, his love for Beatrice. (The historical Beatrice was very probably Bice, daughter of Folco Portinari, a close neighbor of the Alighieri; married to Simone di' Bardi, she died an early death in 1290.) Dante tells us that he first saw Beatrice, and immediately felt the force of love for her, when he was almost nine and she some eight months younger. That first vision was followed, some nine years later, by Beatrice's first spoken greeting to Dante. The Italian for the greeting or salutation she bestowed, *salute,* also means well-being, blessedness, and salvation; and Beatrice, whose name means she-who-blesses, became the essential presence in Dante's mythologizing and theologizing of love.

Dante was a searcher for final meanings; he read the events

that followed his boyhood vision of Beatrice, including the event of her very early death, as an invitation to his spiritual transformation. Dante foreshadowed this transformation in the tale of his love (not least in its title), the *Vita Nuova,* the *New Life,* the autobiographical work in poetry and prose that he compiled in 1293–1294, a few years after the death of his beloved. He fully embodied this transformation in the *Comedy,* where Beatrice is the woman who, in the first canto of the *Inferno,* sends Virgil to rescue the straying Dante from the "shadowed forest" of fear and error, and who will later lead Dante to the vision of Paradise. And when Dante first sees Beatrice—veiled—in the *Comedy,* in the Earthly Paradise at the summit of the Mountain of Purgatory, he exclaims *(Purg.* XXX, 22–39):

> *Within her presence, I had once been used*
> *to feeling—trembling—wonder, dissolution;*
> *but that was long ago. Still, though my soul,*
> *now she was veiled, could not see her directly,*
> *by way of hidden force that she could move,*
> *I felt the mighty power of old love.*

After the death of Beatrice, Dante entered, belatedly but voraciously, a period of philosophic study. His motives were both the need for consolation and the restless, urban, unecclesiastical curiosity that characterized one who was becoming the most complete intellectual of his time. By the 1290s Dante could have drawn on three philosophical-theological schools in Florence: the school of the Dominicans, in Santa Maria Novella; of the Augustinians, in Santo Spirito; and of the Franciscans, in Sante Croce. Dante was also sensitive to many developments in Paris, the place of confluence for philosophic study in the thirteenth century. He was aware of, and may indeed have been tempted by, Aristotelian currents that saw human reason—independent of faith and grace—as having sufficient force to find God; or even by more radical Aristotelian tendencies, which saw human reason as a self-sufficient means of attaining happiness—in essence, a declaration of philosophy's complete independence from theology.

(Cavalcanti, the first among Dante's friends, had probably espoused this radical position—and positions still more unorthodox.) Such philosophic temptations may be one aspect of the forest in Canto I of the *Inferno*.

His philosophic concerns were soon paralleled by his very active political involvement; and certainly the politics of Florence in the years around the turn of the century are an essential part of the *Infern*-al forest.

In 1289 Dante had probably participated in two important Florentine victories, the battle of Campaldino *(Inf.* XXII, 4–5 and *Purg.* V, 91–93) and the taking of Caprona *(Inf.* XXI, 94–95). After the death of Beatrice and his apprenticeship in philosophy, from 1295 on, he occupied a series of public offices on the various councils of Florence, his service culminating in a two-month tenure as one of the six priors, the principal counselors of state, in 1300. During this term of office, Dante was drawn into a conspicuous role in attempting to thwart the ambitions of Pope Boniface VIII. Boniface was the most formidable and determined figure in Italian politics in the years of his pontificate, 1294–1303. And for his attempt to thwart Boniface, Dante was to pay a heavy price. (Boniface, in turn, was to pay a heavy price throughout the *Comedy;* the very last words of Beatrice to Dante in the *Paradiso* are a ferocious condemnation of Boniface—*Par.* XXX, 148.)

Even the briefest view of Dante's political involvement—and much of the political content of the *Comedy*—requires a wider frame: the struggle for power within the Florentine republic and in Italy at large, between forces supporting the Papacy and forces supporting the Holy Roman Empire.

The names designating these forces were Guelph and Ghibelline (Italianizations of the German *Welf,* dukes of Bavaria and opponents of the Swabian/Hohenstaufen emperors, who had an ancestral castle at *Weiblingen).* These names were said to have been imported into Florence in the wake of a family feud that erupted on Easter 1215 between the Buondelmonti and the Amidei *(Inf.* XXVIII, 106–109). But by the third and fourth decades of the century, Guelph and Ghibelline had acquired the larger resonance of pro-Papal and pro-Imperial political parties, respectively, in Florence.

The last Holy Roman Emperor who was a major presence in thirteenth-century Italy was Frederick II. It was his death in 1250 that weakened Imperial factions everywhere and allowed the establishment of the First Republic of Florence. In a city that now had a landed military aristocracy, newer merchant magnates, lower nobility, bankers, and artisans, the Guelph majority banished many Ghibellines and legislated a new balance of power. There were nobles and magnates in *both* parties, but the Guelphs were more sensitive to the pro-Papal sympathies of the guildsmen—artisans and smaller merchants (the *"popolo"* in *Primo Popolo* may mean "people," but it does not quite mean "populace")—and better able to mobilize those sympathies on their own behalf. The Papacy, for its part, had every interest in encouraging city-republics responsive to the Papacy's own temporal interests in Central Italy. An all-embracing emperor or republics with tenaciously pro-Imperial sentiments, like Pisa and Siena, could hardly support any increase in the political power of the pope.

The First Republic ended in 1260, with the defeat of the Florentine Guelphs by regrouped Ghibelline forces at the battle of Montaperti *(Inf.* X, 85–93). The Ghibelline interval lasted until 1266. In that year, Manfred, Frederick II's illegitimate son, was killed at the battle of Benevento (the haunting fate of his unburied body is evoked in *Purg.* III, 112–132). With his death, pro-Imperial partisans were banished from Florence, and the Second Republic restored Guelph power.

Any lingering doubts about that power were eliminated in 1289 by the battle of Campaldino (fought by Florence against Arezzo and the Ghibellines of Tuscany) and by the taking of the Pisan castle of Caprona. These were Guelph victories in which Dante, as noted above, probably took part; they marked the final disappearance from Florence of the Ghibellines.

In place of the divisions between Guelphs and Ghibellines, the 1290s, the decade of Dante's entry into politics, saw the division of the Florentine Guelphs themselves into two new factions: White and Black. The Whites (the party of Dante), led by the Cerchi family, whose considerable wealth was of relatively recent origin, tried—often ineptly—to defend the independence and the freedom of the republic from the ambitions

of the pope and his French allies. The Blacks, led by the Donati, of older, aristocratic origin, appeared more ready to compromise with the ambitions of the pope in order to obtain power over Florence for themselves. Their leader, Corso Donati—distant relative of Dante's wife and brother of Dante's intimate friend, Forese Donati—was arrogant, unscrupulous, and extremely capable (for his violent end, dragged to death at the tail of a horse, see *Purg.* XXIV, 82–87).

It was precisely during the priorate of Dante that the Signoria, the ruling body of Florence, decided to free the city from factious presences, banishing—impartially—leaders of both the Blacks and the Whites. Among those banished was Dante's own friend, fellow poet, and fellow White, Guido Cavalcanti.

Anxious to extend the domain of the Church over Tuscany, Pope Boniface VIII, who had taken office in 1294, profited from the internal discord of Florence. Dante read the aims of Boniface and was among the first to oppose them. He tried to neutralize the secret maneuvers of Cardinal Matteo d'Acquasparta, who had been sent by the pope to Florence in May 1300. The cardinal's apparent aim was to pacify and reconcile factions in the city; in reality he intended to use those very conflicts to affirm Papal influence in Florence with the open support of the Blacks.

The Signoria did not yield, and the pope finally ordered the cardinal to excommunicate all the magistrates of Florence and to confiscate their holdings. At the end of September 1300, when Dante was no longer in office, the cardinal launched an interdict denying the magistrates of Florence sacraments and Christian burial.

In 1301 Boniface decided to send Charles of Valois to Florence, again with the pretext of bringing about peace between the factions, and again with the real aim of helping the Blacks regain power and of destroying the republican constitution.

In October 1301 Dante was sent to Rome with two other representatives of the commune to ask Boniface to clarify his intentions. The pope sent the other two ambassadors back to Florence so that they might persuade the Florentines to yield to

him, but he seems to have kept Dante, from whom he had most to fear, in or near Rome. In the interim Charles of Valois, helped by the Blacks, entered Florence on the first of November without encountering the opposition of the Whites. Once they had power, the Blacks levied penalties and confiscations against the most representative members of the Whites. Among these was Dante, who was asked to appear before the judges in order to defend himself from accusations, formulated without proofs, of barratry, of opposition to the pope and to Charles of Valois, and of having fomented discord and imperiled peace. Dante did not present himself, and on January 27, 1302, he was condemned—in absentia—to two years of exile, to perpetual exclusion from public office, and to the payment of a ruinous fine of five thousand florins within three days. News of the condemnation reached Dante when he had not yet returned to Florence (Leonardi Bruni, Dante's fifteenth-century biographer, places him in Siena then). On the tenth of March, because Dante had not appeared, he was condemned by a new sentence to the confiscation of all his goods and to death by burning should he fall into the hands of the commune.

Thus began the exile that would keep Dante away from Florence until his death.

In exile he wandered through many cities, depended on the generosity of many lords, became aware of how hard it is "to climb and to descend the stairs" of others and how "salt-bitter is the bread" in the houses of others: the arrows of "the bow of exile" *(Par. XVII, 55–60)*.

In 1303 or 1304 Dante was at the court of the Scaligers in Verona, which he refers to as his "first refuge and inn" *(Par. XVII, 70)*. From Verona he probably returned to Tuscany, specifically Arezzo, and then he may have spent time in Treviso, Padua, Venice, Bologna, and Reggio Emilia. In 1306 he was in Lunigiana as the guest of the Malaspina family; they charged him with handling peace negotiations with the bishop of Luni. Early and late in his exile, he was in the Casentino, and in 1308 he was in Lucca. Boccaccio and others also assign to him a stay in Paris. And even this is only a partial list of possibilities. In every way, Osip Mandelstam is justified in wondering "how

many shoe soles, how many ox-hide soles, how many sandals Alighieri wore out in the course of his poetic work, wandering about on the goat-paths of Italy."

Between 1302 and 1304 the exiled Whites, among them Dante, made a considerable number of attempts to reenter Florence, allying themselves with the long-since-exiled Ghibellines. All of their attempts failed, and Dante detached himself definitively from that "wicked, foolish company" and decided to become a party unto himself (see *Par.* XVII, 62–69 and *Inf.* XV, 70–72)—himself and his prophetic-poetic missions.

For wherever Dante went in his exile, he saw an Italy rent by internal wars and encountered other exiles banished from their cities. By Dante's time even southern Italy—once joined under a single monarch, Frederick II—had seen Sicily dissociate itself. Frederick himself, a notorious freethinker, is placed in Canto X of the *Inferno* with "Epicurus and his followers." But in his time Frederick was as formidable an emperor as Boniface, in his time, was a pope. No figure in the thirteenth century gave more flesh to that phantom resurrection of the Roman Empire of the West: the German-based Holy Roman Empire. No figure, after his death, so incited a desire for symbolic return in a successor figure. The true political unity of the Holy Roman Empire was merely a fiction by now, but it was still a fiction that had enormous motivating force as a political idea—especially for Dante.

Meditating on the cause of Italy's afflictions and divisiveness, Dante thought he had found its origin in the lack of a supreme secular head, one who could bring justice and peace among peoples. The Roman Empire was considered by Dante to have been a providential means to meet this need, as he explained in a Latin work of his exile, his *Monarchy* (II, i, 2–3, see below); but since the death of Frederick II, no emperor had come again to Italy to resume the Imperial crown, and thus the throne of the Empire was, to all effects, vacant.

But the years 1308–1312 offered the possibility of the return of a Holy Roman Emperor to Italy. After the death of Boniface in 1303 and the brief pontificate of Benedict XI, which ended in 1305, the archbishop of Bordeaux became

Pope Clement V *(Inf.* XIV, 82–88). In 1309 Clement had established himself in Avignon. Clement was a Frenchman in France, and the French were inveterately anti-Imperial. But despite Clement's affiliations, he announced in 1310 the descent into Italy of the emperor Henry VII, who had been elected in 1308, and invited all to welcome Henry with honors. It was especially this news that kindled Dante's hope for Imperial restoration. The emperor seemed to Dante to be a possible bringer of peace to the Italian communes, and Dante, describing himself as "a humble Italian in unmerited exile," wrote three political epistles in Latin. The first, of October 1310, to the lords and people of Italy, exhorted them to favor the task of the emperor in restoring peace. The second, of March 1311, to the Florentines, rebuked them—"the most empty-headed of all the Tuscans, crazy by nature and crazy by corruption"—for their hostility to the emperor. And the third, of April 1311, written to the emperor himself, asked him to reestablish justice and order in Florence.

Dante's hope was not to be realized. Henry was indeed crowned at Milan in 1311 and at Rome in 1312. But his siege of Florence in 1312 was allowed to lapse quickly (a glorious episode for the Florentines, but for Dante, a disaster). By then Clement, under pressure from the French, had aligned himself against Henry; and Robert of Anjou, the king of Naples, declared the throne of the Empire vacant and transferred all imperial rights to the pope. On August 21, 1313, Henry died suddenly at Buonconvento, and the concrete hope of many exiles for a reconstituted empire faded definitively. (At the next election for emperor, no candidate could command sufficient consensus.)

Whether before or after the destruction of Dante's hope in Henry (somewhere in the period from 1308 to 1317—with conjectures ranging widely), Dante made plain the nature of his political ideas in a passionate pamphlet, the *Monarchia (Monarchy)*. With historical and philosophical arguments, Dante sustained the authority and independence of the emperor. For him the Papacy and the Empire were two suns, not—as some Guelphs contended—a sun and a moon; each derived its own light directly from God and was destined to illuminate

all of humanity. The pope would guide men to eternal happiness, and the emperor would guide them to earthly happiness. Neither of them, however, must usurp the task of the other. The Church must renounce all temporal power, remaining scrupulously within the spiritual realm. (This accounts for Dante's vehemence against the Donation of Constantine: *Inf.* XIX, 115–117, and note.)

The urgency of Dante's political epistles and *Monarchy* was certainly heightened by the fact that the Church, though it had preserved its spiritual prestige until the end of the thirteenth century, had lost the theocratic power that it had enjoyed in preceding centuries. Boniface VIII had attempted in vain to resurrect the ancient universal power of the Church; but after him, and because of his policies, the Church had become, with Clement V's transfer of the Papacy to Avignon, an instrument in the hands of France.

At the death of Clement in 1314, some eight months after the death of Henry VII, Dante wrote another epistle, this time to the Italian cardinals assembled at Carpentras near Avignon to elect a new pope. After denouncing those who are "shepherds only in name," Dante pleads for the return of the Papacy to Rome. This plea, too, proved fruitless. The Italians were expelled from the conclave; and two years later, in 1316, still another French pope, John XXII, was elected. (Much of the hope and the wormwood of Dante's years in exile are condensed in Beatrice's last words to Dante, *Par.* XXX, 133–148. There, in addition to denouncing Boniface, she praises the "lofty" Henry VII and excoriates Clement.)

Perhaps because he had written the epistle to the emperor, Dante was excluded from the amnesty offered to the exiles by Florence in 1311; and when a new amnesty was granted in May of 1315, Dante refused the conditions the Florentines offered as too humiliating for his conscience. In a letter to "a Florentine friend," whom the poet calls "father," Dante declared that he would never reenter Florence except under honorable conditions (Epistle XII, 4). On November 6, 1315—since Dante had not submitted to the conditions required to obtain amnesty—his death sentence was reaffirmed,

but now it included not only Dante but his sons, who had been with him for some time.

Between 1312 and 1321, the year of his death, Dante passed from one court to another. In Verona, at the court of Cangrande della Scala, Dante completed the final stages of his work on the *Inferno* and *Purgatorio* (possibly between 1314 and 1315). There, too, he began work on the *Paradiso,* dedicating his work-in-progress to Cangrande. From Verona he went—possibly in 1318—to Ravenna, to the court of Guido Novella da Polenta, a nephew of Francesca, the woman Dante immortalized in Canto V of the *Inferno.*

In 1319–1320 the scholar Giovanni del Virgilio invited Dante to Bologna to be crowned there as poet. In their correspondence, in Latin hexameters, Dante declined the invitation. He explained that he hoped that with the completion of *Paradiso* he might be crowned on the banks of his "native Arno" if he "should ever return there."

In 1320 Dante did accept an invitation to return to Verona to lecture there on a scientific topic. That lecture is a small treatise in Latin now known as the *Questio de aqua et terra.*

In 1321, possibly on a return voyage from an ambassadorial mission to Venice that he had undertaken at the request of Guido da Polenta, Dante fell ill. He died in Ravenna, probably in the night between the thirteenth and fourteenth of September. The complete *Paradiso* was made public posthumously.

DANTE AS ANCIENT AND MODERN

Dante hoarded experience, then spent his hoard unstintingly. His love for Beatrice, with the grace it announced to him; then, after her death, the consolations and possible temptations of philosophy; the engagement in politics, his violent collision with the force of history; the bitterness and the prophetic hope of exile—all these enter into the making of the *Comedy,* a journey undertaken with all of Dante's "blood" and "bones" *(Purg. XXVI, 57).*

Just as the *Comedy* re-collects the stages and counterstages of a life of passionate fullness and passionate memory, so is it a summa of Dante's long experimentation, his restless wandering as poet, his mastering of many styles. For Dante is a relentless appropriator, a relentless innovator, a relentless tester of limits. Though he does not span tragedy and comedy, as Shakespeare does (Dante's *Comedy* is very seldom comic), he does span poetry and prose (sometimes within the same work), and two languages in his prose, Italian and Latin (with one brief poetic foray, in the later years of his exile, into Latin). And almost all that he spans is absorbed into the *Comedy.*

Some of Dante's appropriations represent a filial love for those who have authority—and can confer it. More often, it is as an equal that he appropriates. For Virgil's moral assurance to him at the threshold of the Earthly Paradise—"Your will is free, intact, and whole—to act / against that will would be to err: therefore / I crown and miter you over yourself" *(Purg. XXVII, 140–142)*—is also Dante's announcement to himself and to us of his artistic autonomy. No poet has been so obsessed with every change to be played on the word "new," from the title of his early *Vita Nuova* to the triple use of "new" at the end of the *Purgatorio:* "As new trees are / renewed when they bring forth new boughs, I was / pure and prepared to climb unto the stars" *(Purg. XXXIII, 143–145).* And no poet has

been so obsessed with the word *"antico,"* "ancient," "old," an obsession most rich when, from the *Aeneid,* he borrows Dido's "I recognize the signs of the old flame" and uses it—precisely before Virgil vanishes from the *Comedy*—to describe his own wonder at reencountering Beatrice *(Purg.* XXX, 43–48):

> *I turned around and to my left—just as*
> *a little child, afraid or in distress,*
> *will hurry to his mother—anxiously,*
> *to say to Virgil: "I am left with less*
> *than one drop of my blood that does not tremble:*
> *I recognize the signs of the old flame."*

Behind these "new" and "old" there lie of course the New and Old Testaments, the newness of Christian as against pagan man, the newness of converted man, who is not what he was before, and many superficial and some profound uses of "new" in the poems of Dante's Romance predecessors. Dante contains and transcends these last, his "modern" antecedents. When he speaks of the vision of the otherworld granted to him as a vision "most unusual for moderns" *(Purg.* XVI, 41–42), Dante is also implying that the craft of the *Comedy* is exceptional among moderns.

At each stage in the growth of his craft Dante is alert to the theoretical dimension of his practice. This is especially so in the *Comedy,* where, within the verse itself, Dante repeatedly calls the reader's attention to the art of making and narrating. And for Dante, theory always involves social and personal memory—history and autobiography. Twice in the *Comedy* he cites emblematic lines from the past of his own poetry; the *Comedy* introduces us directly to ancient and modern predecessors; and Statius, greeting Virgil in Purgatory, may speak for Dante when he says that to "have lived on earth when Virgil lived— / for that I would extend by one more year / the time I owe before my exile's end" *(Purg.* XXI, 100–102). It is as if Dante's Eunoe, the river of recall he invents for *Purgatorio,* the river that restores the memory of the good that we have done, may also be the river of poetic tradition; and drinking from

Eunoe, for which thirst may indeed be "limitless," is a precondition for being "remade."

Dante's Romance antecedents are recapitulated in an incomplete prose work of his exile, *De vulgari eloquentia (On Writing in the Common Tongue)*. There he elaborates on Romance poetic technique, prosody, and word choice, but these technical matters are preceded by a long, ambitious meditation on the nature, origin, and diversities of language after Babel. It is as if he were girding himself with the historical and theoretical supports needed to legitimate the mother tongues and to vie with the poets of Latinity. Dante's encounter with the Provençal poets is much deeper and more personal in the *De vulgari* than it is in his pre-exile years. But it is the *Vita Nuova* (together with the dialogues with his Romance predecessors in Cantos XXIV and XXVI of the *Purgatorio)* that serves most in relating him to his Italian antecedents.

At the court of Frederick II there had flourished, a half-century before Dante, the first poetic literature in Italian, the "vulgar," popular tongue of Italy; and because the court of Frederick was in Sicily, the first poetic school is called "Sicilian." These Italian poets treated the "matter" of love; and their treatment is deeply indebted to Provençal literature, which was the first among literatures in the modern European tongues to affirm itself fully as a complex medium for the poetry of man's love for woman.

Soon after the death of Frederick II in 1250, Tuscany became the new center for Italian poetry. A group of Tuscan poets, and among these principally Guittone d'Arezzo, renewed and refined the themes treated by the Sicilians and made more intricate and dense the poetic craft of the Sicilian school.

Dante had begun to write poetry as a very young man. One of his early sonnets, *"A ciascun'alma presa e gentil core,"* "To every captive soul and gentle heart," was included later as the first sonnet in the *Vita Nuova*. This sonnet, however, already demonstrates substantial apprenticeship, and Dante certainly had exercised himself earlier in poetic *"tenzoni,"* verse correspondence between poets. Dante says that he had sent this sonnet "to many who were famous *trovatori* [poets] of that time," so that they could interpret it and respond to him with other

sonnets. Among the poets who had answered there was one "whom I call the first among my friends," that is, Guido Cavalcanti.

Cavalcanti was already the principal poetic protagonist of a style that derived from Guido Guinizzelli of Bologna, whom Dante in the *Comedy* will call "the father / of me and of the others—those, my betters— / who ever used sweet, gracious rhymes of love" *(Purg. XXVI, 97–99).* Guinizzelli was in effect the precursor of a new mode of poetry, the *"dolce stil nuovo,"* "the sweet (or suasive) new manner," as Dante will call it in *Purgatorio XXIV, 57,* a style more supple and harmonious and often more psychologically and philosophically ambitious than its Tuscan and Sicilian antecedents.

In the 1290s (most probably 1293–1294) Dante reached for the most innovative edge that the "new manner" was to find. In his *"libello,"* or "little book," as he called the *Vita Nuova,* Dante recounts his love and mourning for Beatrice. In this work Dante ingathers a portion of the rhymes of love that he had written before and after Beatrice's death in 1290, commenting on them briefly and inserting them into a continuous prose narrative. The narrative facts belong to his life, but within and into these facts Dante reads the evolution of his life, his love, his poetry, deciphering in a way that is always more spiritual; love ceases to be earthly passion and becomes the thrust of the soul toward virtue itself, virtue incarnate. The *Vita Nuova* is a saint's life, with Beatrice as the saint. It is also Dante's apprenticeship in autobiography, in the use of "I" in narrative, which will grow into that aspect of the *Comedy* that makes it a *Danteid;* and the prose, though less sturdy in its articulations than the later prose of the *Convivio,* does compel Dante toward clarities his poetry might have eluded.

The *Vita Nuova* represents a central stage in the long search, in Provençal and Italian, over two centuries, for poetic language that can chart the passion, nuance, questioning, and celebrations of the mind encountering a force as powerful as love. This search was, of course, indebted to and rivaled by the language of love in theology—that strange discipline of analysis around a center that is unanalyzable or that, insofar as it can

be spoken of, yields only to metaphor. And theologians (witness Bernard of Clairvaux in the century before Dante, Aquinas in the thirteenth century—both will appear in the *Paradiso*—and, almost contemporaneous with Dante, Meister Eckhart) were often metaphorists more masterly than the poets. Dante's indebtedness to the language of theology will be still more ample in the *Comedy*.

In the 1290s—in a mode very different from that of the *Vita Nuova*—Dante also wrote a group of four poems now called the *"petrose,"* around the motif of a woman who resists and incites the poet, a woman hard as *"pietra,"* "stone." These are the most condensed and convincing incarnations of sensuous love to be found in the work of Dante, and with their exacerbated, intricate techniques, they are the poems that link him most to the Provençal Arnaut Daniel—the poet praised in the *Purgatorio* as *"il miglior fabbro,"* "a better / artisan of the mother tongue—surpassing / all those who wrote their poems of love or prose / romances."

Very probably in that same decade (though some say in the 1280s) Dante also composed several railing sonnets against his friend Forese Donati, who responded to him in kind, both of them joining in what might be called realistic-scurrilous play (see *Purg.* XXIII, 115–117). In the poetry of the *Comedy* venom and execration were important sources of poetic energy.

One work dating from the pre-exile years, either the 1280s or 1290s, would add a French predecessor to Dante's Italian and Provençal antecedents. That work is the *Fiore,* now accepted by many as Dante's own: a reduction-translation into 232 Italian sonnets of the more than 22,000 octosyllabic lines of the French *Roman de la Rose.* It is the only work in Italian prior to the *Comedy* that truly foreshadows the linguistic range, exuberance, even boisterousness and verbal inventiveness, of the *Comedy;* that alone is enough to tempt one to assign the work to Dante.

Rime is the name used today for Dante's miscellaneous poems. These include the *petrose* poems and the exchange with Forese, as well as many poems in "the sweet new manner" that

share the mode of the *Vita Nuova* or offer more relaxed examples of the language of love. Still other poems in the *Rime,* some written after the turn of the century, during the early years of Dante's exile, are ambitious, ethical, stately expository *canzoni*. Three of these enter Dante's *Convivio,* and others would probably have been included had Dante completed the *Convivio.* (Both the Italian *Convivio* and the Latin *De vulgari eloquentia* were interrupted in 1307 or thereabouts, when Dante may have begun work on the *Comedy.)*

The *Convivio (Banquet)* is a massive extension of the poetry-and-prose structure of the *Vita Nuova;* the *canzone* at the head of each of three of the four completed books is commented on in prose, in ways that invite us to share in a symbolic banquet of wisdom, a parade of the poet's learning, a distillation of his encounter with philosophy, an arena for allegorical analysis, and—Dante's outpouring of his autobiographical need—a justification of his life by the learned exile. Its prose forges an expository instrument that is an important element in the poetic expositions of the *Comedy.* The work was called by Dante himself "temperate and manly," whereas he saw the *Vita Nuova* as "fervid and passionate." And since the *Comedy* is a summative work, we can expect it to be fervid, passionate, temperate, and manly—and even, at times, three of these at once.

Among the works of exile, the Latin *Monarchy,* the three pro-Imperial epistles, and the epistle to the Italian cardinals have already been mentioned. But their polemical force and, at times, vituperative shrillness are probably contemporary with Dante's writing of the *Comedy,* rather than being way stations toward it. Of the nine other Latin epistles, the most interesting is the one addressed to Cangrande della Scala, bearing the dedication to him of the *Paradiso.* Some have doubted the attribution to Dante of the whole epistle, but—despite doubters—it is now generally accepted as Dante's own.

The *Convivio* had already dealt with problems of allegorical exegesis and offered allegorical commentary on Dante's own three *canzoni* as well as other examples of allegorical treatment. But the Epistle to Cangrande, if authentic, offers a

unique example of brief prose comments on the *Comedy* as a whole and a brief exegesis of a section of the *Paradiso*. There is considerable controversy about the nature of the allegory in the *Comedy*, but no commentator today would see Dante using rigid, abstract allegory as his basic structure, with Virgil as Reason, Beatrice as Theology, etc. All would agree that Dante endows most of his shades with historical individuality. And all would agree that Dante repeatedly insists on his credibility and on the literal reality of his journey. Where exegetes differ is in the weight they give to the way in which the Bible was read as the crucial source for Dante's own way of writing. For most theologians prior to Dante the Bible is the only text that can claim *both* spiritual truth and literal truth. If biblical interpretation is the model for Dante's claims for the literal truth of his voyage, then the Epistle to Cangrande is indeed essential.

Dante's first work in Latin verse is also his last poetic work, except for the *Paradiso*. Between 1319 and 1320, in a probably authentic correspondence reported by Boccaccio, Dante wrote two eclogues in Latin hexameters, imitating the pastorals of Virgil. These were written in response to verse epistles sent to him by Giovanni del Virgilio. Even if by way of the *Eclogues*, rather than the *Aeneid*, these poems are the final emblems of Dante's appropriation of antiquity.

Dante's relation to his Romance predecessors and colleagues is—in addition to being, at times, critical—filial and fraternal. But time after time in the *Comedy* we sense that, however warm Dante's relations to his Romance predecessors, it is antiquity he hopes to join or asserts he has joined. (See especially the scene in Limbo, in Canto IV of the *Inferno*, where Dante joins the poets of antiquity; the poet's vaunts in Canto XXV of the *Inferno;* and, in the *Purgatorio*, Statius' celebration of the *Aeneid:* "the sparks that warmed me, the seeds of my ardor / . . . the holy fire—the same that gave / more than a thousand poets light and flame / . . . When I wrote / verse, it was mother to me, it was nurse *[Purg.* XXI, 94–98].)

Antiquity means—substantially—Virgil, Ovid, Lucan, and Statius. The introduction has already alluded to Dante's Ovidianism, and the poet's indebtedness to Lucan and Statius also merits attention. But Virgil is primary.

In the *Convivio* the increasingly pro-Imperial Dante had come to see Virgil as the poet of Empire, and the Christian Dante had interpreted the piety of Aeneas in a religious vein, as embracing "love, mercy, and other compassionate" feelings. There, too, Dante had continued traditional moral-allegorical readings of the *Aeneid*.

But essentially, it is through Virgil that Dante takes heart; through Virgil's work Dante can confront his own journeying and making. Through Virgil and his itinerant Aeneas, journeying toward a destined end, Dante can realize the *Danteid* aspect of the *Comedy*. Virgil is the man and poet who sang—so amply, so richly—a poem that can embrace both the defeated-then-victorious Trojans and the defeated Latins, a poem that re-presented the whole of a culture even as Dante would embrace as much of the past and present as a poet can. And Virgil is the author of a work that, through descent into the underworld, makes available the past and—prophetically—the future. Finally, in Dante's establishing the right of poetry—of fiction—to share the depth and scope of the discourse of philosophy and theology, Virgil's is the only poem in the available past that can serve him as exemplar for the supremacy of fictions.

Dante's chief appropriation is, thus, the embodied shade of Virgil, from which he draws more life than any living body can provide. From the nearby shades in the otherworld he summons Beatrice; from the distant shades he summons Virgil. In Canto II of the *Inferno,* it is Beatrice herself who calls on Virgil; and for many readers of the *Comedy,* the most present presence will, after all, be Virgil—not least, in the pathos of the chief exemplar of antiquity assessing the destiny of reason deprived of grace, and then, with self-delimiting sadness, enjoining Dante *(Purg.* III, 37–45):

> *"Confine yourselves, o humans, to the* quia;
> *had you been able to see all, there would*
> *have been no need for Mary to give birth.*
> *You saw the fruitless longing of those men*
> *who would—if reason could—have been content,*
> *those whose desire eternally laments:*

I speak of Aristotle and of Plato—
and many others." Here he bent his head,
and said no more, remaining with his sorrow.

Does Dante transform the poet Virgil—the man who wrote
the *Aeneid,* whose body "taken from Brindisi...now belongs
to Naples" *(Purg.* III, 27–28)—when he imports the Latin
shade into his own otherworld? Of course. The "light" and art
of the poet of the *Aeneid* are more equanimous, probably wiser
than Dante's own—but for their shared part of the journey, so
is Dante's Virgil wiser than Dante the journeyman. Yet, then
again, the wisdom of Dante's Virgil is far more didactic and
sententious than the wisdom of the poet of the *Aeneid.* See
them, then, as two lights, two arts, but conversing after "long
silence" *(Inf.* I, 63), with the speech that comes from filial
"long study and intense love" *(Inf.* I, 83), unremitting paternal
care, and final fraternal acknowledgment of autonomy. Dante
the maker may know when to dismiss Virgil, but Virgil knows
when to disappear. (And that knowledge is shared by Dante's
Virgil and the author of the *Aeneid.)* Dante's "light" is the
"new light" that "strikes suddenly against closed eyes" *(Purg.*
XVII, 40–41), more jagged, more abrupt, more darting, more
various than Virgil's, but it is the light of "immense desire"
(Purg. IV, 29), and it, too, can be spacious.

In the century of the *Comedy*'s completion, its supremacy
was immediately recognized. Boccaccio felt its power to the
full, as did Petrarch (however evasively he acknowledged that
power); and lettered and unlettered Italians knew that Dante's
exile in a fragmented Italy had given birth to a work that made
Italy one. For, despite some vicissitudes in the critical fortune
of the *Comedy,* so large is the cultural space it has occupied in
Italy that if a modern Italian poet, mourning the death of Dylan
Thomas, enviously exclaimed that Thomas "had the Bible,"
whereas "we [Italians] do not," it is because the Italians had—
in its stead—the *Comedy.*

In the three centuries that followed Dante's birth, Italy was
mother and nurse of the modern. It was she who made the new.
And the chief of her makings and makers was

that Tuscan who had dug
some hundred cantos up
and down with sharper tercets
than any man has found
to probe the shifting ground

on which our fictions stand.

A.M.

The following annotations are meant to serve as a very basic apparatus; they do not substitute for the three volumes-in-progress, one devoted to each *cantica* of the *Comedy,* of the *California Lectura Dantis.* From its own century until today, the *Comedy* has given rise to many commentaries. Chronologies of Dante's life and works and interpretations of vexed points in the *Comedy* are various and, at times, more conflicting than complementary. Much that is said bears the implicit qualifications, "possibly," "probably," and "perhaps." But some assertions do have more cogency than others, and this modest guide has garnered reasonable, helpful opinion in addition to a fair sum of certainties. In the compilation of these notes, Gabriel Marruzzo, Laury Magnus, and I are grateful indeed for the enlightened collaboration of Ellen E. Martin.

The notes are supplemented by two drawings-diagrams by Barry Moser, showing the moral topology of *Inferno* and the spatial organization of Dante's cosmos. With these, the reader will also find helpful the notes to Canto XI and Canto XXXIV.

In the following notes, the *Aeneid* is cited with the English line numbers of the Bantam Classics edition (that edition carries Latin line numbers at the top of each page). Other works by Virgil carry the Latin line numbers of the Loeb Classical Library editions, as do all works of Ovid, Lucan, and Statius. Ovid's *Metamorphoses* is abbreviated as *Met.;* Lucan's *Pharsalia* as *Phars.;* and the *Thebaid* of Statius as *Theb.*

A.M.

THE UNIVERSE OF DANTE

NOTES

CANTO I

1–3 It is not known exactly when Dante began to write the *Inferno*. But he was surely writing while in exile from Florence; and he was constructing a fiction dated before both his exile and his act of writing began. This predating gives him some advantage in "foreseeing" events that occurred between the date of the tale and the date of the telling.

Dante delays the chief indication of the possible date of his fictive voyage until Canto XXI, 112–114 (see note there for a fuller account). That latter passage allows most commentators to define the night in the dark wood as the night of Maundy Thursday, the night before Good Friday, the evening of April 7 in the year 1300. The day of Good Friday is then spent with the three beasts and Virgil in Canto I, so that the entry into Ante-Hell at the beginning of Canto II takes place on the evening of Good Friday, April 8.

"*Our* life"—with its "possessive of human solidarity" (Spitzer)—links the particularity of Dante the wayfarer to the universality of everyman. In the *Convivio* (IV, xxiii, 6–10), Dante fixes 35 years as the midpoint of man's life, following Psalm 89:10 (90:10 in the King James), which sets 70 years as the length of man's days. Thus, for Dante himself, who was born in 1265, the year 1300 accords well with the cited texts and with the passage in Isaiah (38:10), "In the middle of my days, I shall go to the gates of Hell."

2 The "shadowed" or dark forest is our way station to many images of darkness, blindness, and obscurity that obsess Hell—that realm in which the sun never appears, as it does throughout Purgatory—though Virgil, somewhat clairvoyantly, will refer to the movement of the unseen skies on the earth above "starless" (III, 23) Hell. (While *Inferno* begins at night, *Purgatorio* begins at dawn and *Paradiso* at noon.)

But the forest precedes the journey through Hell. It is the dark wood of life on earth when lived in sin; it is Dante's interior wood; and it is the wood of political darkness, of Florence, of Italy, of papal corruption, of the absence of imperial authority.

5 In accord with most commentators, this translation sees *forte* as "difficult" (that is, difficult to traverse—or, perhaps better, to escape from).

8 The "good discovered there" has a host of probable meanings, but it certainly anticipates Dante's rescue by Virgil and the beginning of the long journey to salvation.

13–18 At this point Dante sees the alternative to the dark forest: the "hill"—that is, the path to virtue, which leads upward. The hill is illuminated

by the sun, which Dante does not see directly but whose rays stand for the light of God's illuminating grace. Dante's access to the hill, however, is blocked by the three beasts he encounters—beasts symbolic of different aspects of human sinfulness (see 31–60).

17 In the Ptolemaic system, the sun is a "planet" revolving around the earth. For the cosmos of Dante see the diagram on p. 343.

21 In terms of the physiology of Dante's time, "the lake of my heart" refers to that inner chamber of the heart thought to be the physical seat of the emotion of fear.

22–25 This first simile of the poem already draws on an important theme of imagery throughout the *Comedy*: the sea. It is not unrelated to the Red Sea of the Exodus (Singleton) and, given Dante's use of *pelago* here for "sea," to the exhausted Trojan survivors of the storm in *Aen.* I, 242; 251–252 (Hollander) or to the landing from the *pelago* that precedes Aeneas's own entry into the underworld *(Aen.* VI, 1–3).

30 The difficulty of interpreting this line has given pause to many commentators. Boccaccio's literal reading was that those who climb always tend to support themselves more on that foot which remains below. This translation is compatible with his reading—and with the view that the firm foot may, alternately, be the left, then the right. Recent allegorists (Freccero, Mazzoni) identify the firm foot as *one* foot, the left—the foot weighed down by appetites, concupiscence, limping will—as against the right—the foot of the intellect. For them, *fermo* means "halting, dragging, inhibiting."

31–60 For most early commentators—and, after many alternate proposals, for many moderns—the leopard represents lust; the lion, pride; the she-wolf, avarice or cupidity. Whatever specific area of sin is assigned to each animal, the Italian certainly links them alliteratively to each other—*lonza—leone—lupa* (Ragonese in the *E.D.*) (which this translation cannot do)—and to Lucifer of Canto XXXIII (Sarolli). The translation's "leopard" keeps the text close, as early commentators do, to Jer. 5:6, which speaks of a lion, a wolf, and a leopard. But *lonza* may be a lynxlike animal (see *Aen.* I, 458) or a strange hybrid.

37–40 The world was believed to have been created in spring, with the sun in the constellation of Aries; and Dante's own voyage takes place in the springtime.

60 Dante's use of synesthesia—the merging of the visual ("the sun") and the auditory ("speechless")—recurs in line 63.

63 This translation's "faint" for *fioco* echoes the auditory and visual connotations of the Italian, though leaning here to the visual: Dante sees Virgil indistinctly—in a shadowed space where the "sun is speechless." This initiates and reinforces Dante's uncertainty, which gives rise to the "whatever you may be" of line 66. But this shadowed space also resonates as time—the long ages in which Virgil did not have the full voice he will now find again through and in Dante.

70–72   Virgil (70–19 B.C.) was born *sub Julio,* in the time of Julius Caesar, though too late to win Caesar's esteem. Though "false and lying gods" is close indeed to Augustine's *"deos falsos fallacesque" (City of God* II, xxix, 2), Dante's own use of pagan gods in the machinery of the *Comedy* would reframe this assertion: the pagan gods were "false and lying" when seen as sufficient ends in themselves, but they carried some truth as prefigurations of the Christian God.

73–75   "The righteous son of Anchises" is Aeneas, hero of the *Aeneid,* to which Dante refers repeatedly in the *Inferno.*

82–87   "The noble style" is the tragic style, the style of epic narrative and of the exalted, spacious, ethically-intellectually committed lyric. Dante can claim to "have been honored" for his achievement in the latter category before 1300, but Virgil was hardly his chief mentor then. This passage seems, rather, to carry wishful meaning, the force and weight of desire, as if Dante were saying, "You, Virgil, using the ancient but ever-living tongue of the Latins, gave full life to the stately tragic style, the noble upper register, in epic; my mixed, comic style, drawing on all three styles—the upper, the middle, the lower—for this my modern, Christian, prophetic epic in the maternal tongue of the Italians, the modern Latins, needs you as exemplary inspiration and would achieve honor comparable to yours."

Boccaccio, glossing "for which I have been honored" with "here he uses the past tense for the future, producing a solecism," senses the same intention.

101   The Greyhound of this prophetic passage, the redeemer who "will restore low-lying Italy" (106), has been identified in very diverse ways: as an ecclesiastic; as a secular political figure; as Christ; as Dante himself; as Cangrande della Scala of Verona, Dante's benefactor and an Imperial viceroy; and as others. Most probably the term connotes a political prophecy; almost as probably it foretells and hopes for a Holy Roman Emperor or his viceroy; and possibly it may refer to Henry VII, who was elected Holy Roman Emperor on November 27, 1308.

103–104   Earthly goods and nourishment are represented by "land or pewter" (which here would stand for "money"); spiritual goods by the attributes of the Trinity—wisdom, the Son; love, the Holy Ghost; virtue, the Father. This is not, however, a necessary argument for reading the Greyhound as a papal or ecclesiastical figure: for Dante elsewhere in his works, temporal authority, too, has its direct source in God.

105   Those who opt for Cangrande della Scala as the Greyhound capitalize the two *Feltros,* referring them to Feltre and Montefeltro, towns that mark the rough limits of Cangrande's domains. But this translation renders a lower-case *feltro* as "felt": the "two felts" would be the two felt-lined urns in which "Yes" and "No" ballots, respectively, were deposited in elections in Dante's time; such urns could call up the image of electing a Holy Roman Emperor. In that case, the "place of birth" would refer, not to the Greyhound's physical birth, but to his birth in and his assumption of office.

106   Virgil's *humilemque videmus Italiam,* "we sight . . . the low coastline of
Italy" *(Aen.* III, 681–682), is a geographic observation: Dante's *umile Italia,*
"low-lying Italy," on the other hand, has moral overtones.

106–107   Those mentioned in these lines are all figures in Virgil's *Aeneid*
who died in the war between the Trojans and the Latins. Camilla was a faithful woman warrior who aided Turnus, King of the Rutulians, in the war of the
Latins against Aeneas *(Aen.* VII, 1055–1072; XI, 854–1126). Nisus and
Euryalus were close friends who died together after a night attack on a
Rutulian camp *(Aen.* IX, 232–597). Turnus was killed in the single combat
with Aeneas that is placed at the end of the *Aeneid* (XII, 928–1271). This is
one point where Dante shares Virgil's overarching compassion, which embraces the victors and the vanquished; Dante alternates Latin, Trojan, Latin,
Trojan—and cites two Trojans who were, themselves, sacrificed in the course
of the Trojans' victorious campaign.

117   This translation sees "the second death" as the state of damned souls
rejoined with their bodies after the Last Judgment, and translates *grida* as
"laments"—a use of this word that presents some difficulty. But as F.
Mazzoni, who is followed here, notes: this line is "more tormented and dis-
puted than, in itself, it deserves to be."

118–120   The souls in Purgatory.

121   "These" are "the blessed people" in Paradise.

122   "A soul more worthy than I am" is Beatrice, born in 1266, the year after Dante's birth, loved by Dante from his boyhood, and celebrated by him—
after her death in 1290—in his *Vita Nuova.* Boccaccio and other 14th-century
commentators, including Dante's son Pietro, identify her as one of the daughters of Folco Portinari; Boccaccio also mentions her marriage to a Simone de'
Bardi. Folco Portinari's will of 1288 confirms this last detail for Beatrice
Portinari. In the *Comedy,* the historical Beatrice is spokeswoman for the divine science of theology.

125–126   Because, as a pagan, Virgil did not worship God, he is not allowed
entry to His city. For a fuller explanation of pagans' status in the Christian
scheme of the afterlife, see Canto IV, 24; 52–61, and notes.

   Virgil's description of Heaven as a city makes explicit the analogy drawn
throughout the *Comedy,* and especially in the *Inferno,* between the Roman
Empire (see II, 13–24, and note) and the heavenly City of God.

134   Since Virgil is to lead Dante through, but not beyond, Purgatory, it is
best to read "the gateway of St. Peter" as the gate of Purgatory, where the
vicar of St. Peter is custodian, rather than the entry to Paradise (which, in any
case, in Dante's account, has no gate).

CANTO II

1–3   These lines echo night scenes in the *Aeneid* (III, 197; IV, 723–730; VIII,
33–34; and IX, 300–302).

7–9   The invocation to the Muses is in the epic tradition, but the invocation

to *alto ingegno,* "high genius" (which may well mean that genius which strives for lofty things), and to *mente* (which here means "memory" rather than "mind" or "spirit") is Dante's innovation.

13–24   Dante draws heavily on Virgil's *Aeneid,* which recounts the wanderings of the defeated Trojans as Aeneas leads them to Italy to found what will become the Roman Empire. In Book VI, Aeneas, who will later become the father of Sylvius, travels to the world of the dead to seek his own father's guidance and to hear his prophecies about Rome. Of course, the pagan city of Rome founded by Aeneas prefigures a greater city—the Holy Seat of the Church in the Christian Era.

28   The "Chosen Vessel" is St. Paul (see Acts 9:15). For St. Paul's ascent to the third heaven, see 2 Cor. 12:2–4.

31   A *topos* ("commonplace") of modesty, emphasized by the rhetorical repetition of the subject, "I" in the following lines. (But see also Introduction, p. xi, for the less modest "I myself alone" of 3–4.)

52   The word "suspended" alludes to the condition of the souls in Limbo. They live without hope of seeing God but with the constant desire to see Him; they are "neither sad nor joyous" (IV, 84).

70   Beatrice is first referred to in Canto I, 122 (see also note).

71   That is, from Paradise.

83   Hell is located at the center of the Earth, farthest from Heaven. For the cosmos of Dante see the diagram on p. 343.

91–92   The blessed in Paradise cannot be touched by compassion for the damned in Limbo or Hell, who died without the grace of God.

94   The "gentle lady" is probably the Virgin Mary. Neither her name nor her Son's is ever explicitly mentioned in the *Inferno.*

96   That is, she softens God's severe sentence.

97   Lucia, the 4th-century martyr saint of Syracuse, is the patron saint of sight and the symbol of illuminating grace.

102   Rachel, the younger sister of Leah, signifies the contemplative life. Jacob was given Leah (symbol of the active life) in marriage before he was allowed to marry Rachel (see Gen. 29:16ff.).

105   In accordance with Dante's theological transmutation of the doctrines of courtly love, the poet has been elevated above common humanity by his love for his lady.

107   "The death he wars against" is the danger of eternal damnation.

CANTO III

1–9   The warning of the speaking door, mouthpiece of Hell, becomes more ominous through the anaphora (verbal repetition) in the first three lines. This inscription is the only text Dante reads in Hell.

1   In Canto I, Paradise had been defined as a "city" (126–128). Now all of Hell is seen as a countercity.

5–6   The "High Artificer" is God in His three attributes: "Divine Authority" is the Father; "Highest Wisdom," the Son; and "Primal Love," the Holy Ghost.

7   The angels, heavens, and primal matter (all "eternal things"—that is, things immortal, which will endure eternally) were created on the first day, and Hell was created shortly afterward to contain the newly created—but fallen—Lucifer and his cohorts. Hell, too, will last eternally.

14   An echo of the Sybil's injunction to Aeneas *(Aen.* VI, 345–346).

18   In the *Convivio* (II, xiii, 6), Dante cites Aristotle's definition of the "gift" or " 'good' of the intellect." This "gift" is truth, and God is the source of truth.

22   Another echo of Virgil *(Aen.* VI, 737).

31   Some editors read *error,* "error," rather than *orror,* "horror." The text and translation choice here follow the latter—traditionally seen as echoing the "savage horror" that took hold of Aeneas *(Aen.* II, 751).

34–42   Those who lived "without disgrace and without praise" are most often called the cowardly, the pusillanimous, the neutrals, or the lukewarm.

52–69   The punishments in the *Inferno* follow the law of *contrapasso*—that is, the punishment is commensurate with the fault (see XXVIII, 142). Here the speedy pace of the banner and the goading by insects for those so ungoadable in life constitute just retribution.

59–60   According to many early commentators, the spirit described here may be Pope Celestine V. Elected Pope in July 1294, he abdicated five months later, making way for the election of Boniface VIII, Pope from 1294 to 1303, the object of bitter references in Cantos XIX, 52–57 and XXVII, 70ff.

71   Acheron is the first of the Infernal rivers, all four of which will be discussed more fully in Canto XIV, 115–129, note.

83   Charon, son of Erebus and Night, is the ferryman who transports the souls across the river, a character taken directly from the *Aeneid* (VI, 394–401). Here he becomes the first of the figures from pagan mythology whom Dante mobilizes as guardians of the circles of Hell.

112–117   The image of autumnal leaves echoes and alters *Aeneid* (VI, 407–408).

117   A simile taken from the moment in hunting when the falcon is called, or lured, down by the hunter.

133   The science of Dante's time explained earthquakes as caused by pent-up underground vapors escaping violently when the earth's hardness resists their escape.

135–136   While the swoon that ends this canto is a somewhat arbitrary device allowing transition, the swoon at the end of Canto V transforms the arbitrary into the necessary.

CANTO IV

24 "Here" is Limbo, where Dante—unlike Aquinas—places virtuous pagans. (The "orthodox" classes of inhabitants of Limbo included children who died before they were baptized, and Old Testament worthies who believed in the coming of Christ and were liberated from Limbo by Him and taken to Paradise—see 52–61.) The pagans' punishment is spiritual—they have a strong desire to see God that will never be satisfied.

45 See Canto II, 52, and note.

52–61 Virgil died in the year 19 B.C.; Christ descended into Limbo after His death in 33 A.D., when Virgil had been in Limbo about 50 years. Christ's descent into Limbo, from which he removed the Old Testament worthies, is known as the Harrowing of Hell. It has its source in the Apocrypha, in a portion of the Gospel of Nicodemus, and was proclaimed as dogma at the Fourth Lateran Council in 1215 and at the Council of Lyon in 1274. (Together with the Old Testament worthies, the Roman Cato of Utica may also, according to Dante, have been delivered from Limbo at that time. Cato will serve as the guardian of Purgatory. For his wife, Marcia, see 127–129, note.)

54 Dante probably had in mind the medieval representation of Christ wearing a halo inscribed with the sign of the cross.

55 The "first father" is Adam.

68 The fire comes from a luminous castle forming a hemisphere of light against the surrounding darkness (see 103).

75 They are "separate" in that they are privileged and distinct from the condition of others in Limbo.

78 Here Dante reaffirms his idea that honor is a reward of virtue and that this reward is recognized in Heaven.

88–90 Like others of his time, Dante did not know the works of Homer directly.

Horace (65–8 B.C.) is the "satirist" (that is, satirist-moralist) cited here especially as the author of the *Satires* and *Epistles*—but Dante probably had direct knowledge only of his *Ars Poetica.*

Ovid (43 B.C.–17 A.D.) died in exile. His *Metamorphoses* is the principal mythographic source for Dante, but Dante also draws in varying degrees on Ovid's *Fasti, Heroides, Art of Love, Amores, Remedies of Love,* and *Tristia.*

Lucan, born in Cordoba in 39 A.D., died in Rome in 65 A.D. (He was a victim of the same unmasking by Nero of the Pisonian conspiracy that led to the forced suicide of Seneca—see 130–141, note.) His incomplete *Pharsalia,* an epic poem on the civil war between Caesar and Pompey, is an important source for Dante.

This first group of dwellers in Limbo, the poets, is supplemented by other groups in this same canto (121–144) and by other names to be found in *Purgatorio* (XXII, 14 and 97–114), where Virgil encounters Statius.

91–92   That is, they share the name of poet with him.

95   Dante considered epic poetry, the "song incomparable," to be the noblest genre.

102   Though highly conscious of writing in a modern language, here Dante places himself among poets of the classical tradition.

103   This is the light of line 68.

106   Though Dante seems to invite an allegorical interpretation of the details concerning the castle and its surroundings, commentators are not in agreement about the intended allegory. Many see the castle as a Castle of Fame, whose seven walls represent the seven liberal arts. The pagans knew reason but not true faith, and they sought immortality by distinguishing themselves in the arts.

121–144   This catalogue of "great-hearted souls" (119) is, on the whole, arranged by groups. The first three tercets celebrate those whose great-heartedness was evidenced in the life of action: the last four, those distinguished by their contemplative lives.

121–123   Electra (not the same person who was the sister of Oretes) was the mother of Dardanus, founder of Troy. Her most illustrious descendants were Hector and Aeneas; just as Aeneas begins the providential history of Rome (see I, 106), so does Julius Caesar begin the imperial chapter of that history.

124–126   This tercet includes figures from, or cited in, the *Aeneid.* Camilla died in her fight against the Trojans when they warred against Latium. The King of Latium was Latinus, and his daughter, who married Aeneas after the Trojan victory, was Lavinia. Penthesilea was the Queen of the Amazons, killed by Achilles. In the *Aeneid,* she is mentioned directly (I, 693–694), and linked in simile with Camilla (XI, 854–856, 871–874).

127–129   Lucius Junius Brutus drove out Tarquin the Proud, the last of the legendary Roman kings, in 510 B.C.; with Lucius Tarquinius Collatinus, he became the first consul of the Roman republic. He is followed by four examples of Roman female virtue:

Lucretia, the wife of Collatinus, was famous for her steadfast goodness. The Roman revolt against Tarquin the Proud was prompted by Tarquin's rape of Lucretia and her consequent suicide.

Julia was the daughter of Caesar and wife of Pompey. Lamenting her death, Lucan *(Phars.* I, 11–120) notes that "she alone" might have reconciled her father and her husband, preventing the bloody civil war between them.

Marcia was the virtuous wife of Cato of Utica (95–46 B.C.). He is referred to in Canto XIV, 15, and becomes central to *Purgatorio* I. Cato had ceded Marcia to Q. Hortensius, after whose death Marcia returned as wife to Cato (see *Phars.* II, 326–391).

Cornelia was either the daughter of Scipio Africanus and exemplary mother of the Gracchi or the Cornelia cited by Marcia in the passage of Lucan's *Pharsalia* noted above. The latter Cornelia was the second wife of Pompey, who married her after the death of Julia.

The tercets of the activist "great-hearted" spirits are completed by a modern infidel, Saladin, Sultan of Egypt from 1171 to 1193. Though he opposed the Crusaders, he was celebrated in the West for his nobility.

130–141 Dante raises his eyes "higher" to see the contemplative "great-hearted" spirits:

First among them, "the master of the men who know," is Aristotle (384–322 B.C.); then come Socrates (470–399 B.C.) and Plato (c427–347 B.C.).

The characterization of Democritus of Abdera (c460–c370 B.C.) is drawn from both Cicero and Aquinas. Diogenes is either the Cynic (400–325 B.C.) or Diogenes of Apollonia (5th century B.C.). In one of Aquinas's commentaries on Aristotle, Diogenes of Apollonia is cited together with four other names in Dante's lines here: Empedocles (5th century B.C.; for whom see XII, 42, note); Thales (6th century B.C.); Anaxagoras (c500–c428 B.C.); and Heraclitus (active around 500 B.C.). Zeno may be Zeno of Elea (active around 460 B.C.) or Zeno of Citium (4th to 3rd century B.C.), founder of the Stoic school of philosophy, or a confusion of the two.

Dioscorides was a Greek physician from Anazarba in Cilicia, active in the 1st century A.D. and the author of a major work, *De materia medica,* on the medicinal qualities of herbs. Orpheus and Linus are mythical Greek poets. Tully is Marcus Tullius Cicero (106–43 B.C.), here considered a moral philospher. Seneca (c4 B.C.–65 A.D.), teacher—and victim—of Nero, may indeed have been known to Dante not only as a philosopher but as the same Seneca who wrote verse tragedies; but here, with the adjective "moral," Dante chooses to emphasize the former aspect of his work. Since Dante may have known that Livy was not only a historian but also a philosopher, some prefer, in line 141, to read "Livy" rather than "Linus," placing three moral philosophers in one line, rather than sandwiching a mythical Greek poet between Cicero and Seneca.

142–144 Euclid, the Alexandrian mathematician, lived around 300 B.C. Ptolemy, the Alexandrian astronomer and geographer, was active in the 2nd century B.C. His geocentric theory lay at the base of medieval astronomy. Hippocrates was the Greek physician of the 5th to 4th centuries B.C. whom Dante celebrates as "great Hippocrates, whom nature made / for those who are her dearest living beings"—that is, humans (*Purg.* XXIX, 137–138). Avicenna (980–1037), of Persian origin, was a notable Arabian physician and philosopher whose works profoundly influenced 13th-century Scholasticism. Dante, placing him between Hippocrates and Galen, seems to remember him here primarily as a physician. Galen was the famous Greek physician from Pergamus, active in the 2nd century A.D. Averroes, the Spanish-Arabian philosopher, was born at Cordoba, Spain, in 1126 and died in Morocco in 1198. He was known in the Middle Ages as "the Commentator" on Aristotle's major works; his commentaries had much influence on Western philosophy.

148 The company "divides in two" as Virgil and Dante take leave of the others. Others see the Italian *"scema in due"* as meaning "has two less [members]" or "is reduced to two."

CANTO V

1–3 The "first enclosure" is Limbo. Each successive enclosure or circle "girdles less space" because Hell funnels downward, as in the diagram on p. 344.

4 In the *Aeneid* (VI, 568–572), Minos is a judge of the underworld. In ancient mythology, Minos, son of Zeus and Europa, and king of Crete, was renowned for the wisdom and severity of his judgments.

6 The place of each sinner in Hell is determined by the number of times Minos' tail twines around his body. Where a circle of Hell has one or more divisions, Minos—at least in XXVII, 124–127—seems to supplement his tail with a more precise spoken indication.

15 They admit their sins and hear their sentence before they are sent down.

20 The emphasis on the width of the gate echoes the Bible (Matt. 7:13) and the *Aeneid* (VI, 175–177).

34–35 This translation of *ruina* as "ruined slope" follows those who see this as a reference to the earthquake that occurred after the death of Christ. For more on that earthquake and its consequences, see Canto XII, 31–41.

58–59 Ninus was the mythical founder of ancient Nineveh; his wife, Semíramis, succeeded him to become Queen of Assyria. Notorious for her licentiousness, she was supposed to have legalized even incest. Because of her reputation, her capital, Babylon, was often confused with the Babylon (Old Cairo) of Egypt and thus her kingdom with that of the Sultans (see 60, note). Dante's source here—"we read," he writes in 58—is the *History against the Pagans* of Paulus Orosius, the 5th-century Christian historian. Legend has Semíramis dying at the hands of an illegitimate son.

60 The Sultan is the ruler of Egypt, at this time El-Melik En-Nasir Muhammed, who reigned from 1299 to 1309.

61–62 "That other spirit" is Dido, wife of Sychaeus, who was murdered by her brother, Pygmalion, King of Tyre. After Sychaeus' shade tells Dido of the murder, she flees Tyre to found a new city in North Africa—Carthage. *Aeneid* I and IV relate her love for Aeneas. He, reminded by the gods of his higher destiny as founder of Rome, departs for Italy; Dido, in despair, commits suicide. Dante mentions her faithlessness to Sychaeus; but it is her violent death for love that places her in these tercets (58–69).

63 Cleopatra, the Queen of Egypt whose beauty was legendary, was mistress first of Julius Caesar and then of Marc Antony. Rather than be taken to Rome as a captive, she killed herself with a poisonous asp. Like Dido, she is placed in a circle higher than the Seventh Circle, Second Ring, the place of the suicides (XIII).

64 Helen, wife of Menelaus, King of Sparta, became the mistress of Paris. Her abduction led to the Trojan War. Legend has her as having died at the

hands of a Grecian woman who avenged her husband, killed in the war against Troy.

65   Achilles was the principal Greek hero in the Trojan War. Homer notes that Achilles was killed under the walls of Troy after killing Hector, the main Trojan hero. Accounts current in the Middle Ages, however, claim that Paris killed Achilles in the temple of Apollo, where he had been lured by promises that he could have Priam's daughter Polyxena if he joined the Trojans. See Servius's commentary on *Aeneid* III, 321 (Latin numbering).

67   Paris was the son of King Priam and Queen Hecuba of Troy, and the abductor of Helen (see 64, note). One tradition has him killed by Philoctetes.

Tristan, hero of medieval French romance, was the lover of Yseult, wife of King Mark of Cornwall, Tristan's uncle, who, in a version cited by Boccaccio, wounds Tristan with a poisoned arrow. In his death throes Tristan embraces Yseult so strongly that both die in that embrace.

97   The "land where I was born" is the territory of Ravenna, and the speaker is Francesca da Rimini, daughter of Guido da Polenta, Lord of Ravenna, who died in 1310. Though married some time after 1275 to Gianciotto Malatesta of Rimini for political reasons, she fell in love with his younger brother, Paolo. When Gianciotto discovered their adulterous love, very possibly in 1285, he killed them.

100–107   These lines recall the 13th-century celebrations of love—not least the *canzone* of Guido Guinizzelli, *Al cor gentile rempaira sempre amore.* Set against such celebrations, these lines become tragically ironic.

101   "him": Paolo Malatesta.

102   For some interpreters the "how" does not refer to the killing of the two lovers by Gianciotto, which left them no time for repentance, but to the ardent passion of Paolo for Francesca, a love that still overwhelms (*offende*) her. This translation does refer the "how" to the killing of the lovers and translates *offende* as "wounds."

103   This doctrine of courtly love was expounded by Andreas Cappellanus in his *De amore* but has religious antecedents as well.

107   Caïna, the first of the four divisions of the Ninth Circle of Hell, is named after Cain, who killed his brother Abel (Gen. 4:8). Caïna is where those who betrayed their kin are punished. It "waits" for Gianciotto because he is still alive in 1300.

121–123   The source of this reflection is Boethius, whose *Consolation of Philosophy* was well known in the Middle Ages (see *Cons. Phil.* II, iv, 2). But "your teacher" is Virgil.

127–138   The book they were reading was one of the French Arthurian romances well known to Dante. It tells of Lancelot, the most famous of the knights of the Round Table at the court of King Arthur. He fell in love with Arthur's queen, Guinevere. Since Gallehault is a character who encouraged the Queen and her lover, the book is "a Gallehault indeed," for it serves Paolo and Francesca as a go-between.

CANTO VI

13–18   Dante takes the brutish figure of Cerberus from Virgil *(Aen.* VI, 550–561, and *Georgics* IV, 483) and Ovid *(Met.* IV, 450–451) and makes him even more grotesque to suit his infernal character.

26   Here Dante departs from the *Aeneid* (VI, 554), where the Sibyl throws a cake, not "earth," into Cerberus' mouth.

42   That is, you were born before I died.

43–45   The pain alters the features of the damned. *Angoscia,* "anguish," also has the meaning of physical pain.

52–54   Ciacco was a Florentine of the 13th century, perhaps well-known for his gluttony—and surely well-known for it in the wake of the *Inferno.*

61–75   Here Dante first explicitly refers to the contemporary political events that ultimately resulted in his exile. After the Guelph's final defeat of the Ghibellines at Campaldino and Caprona in 1289, there was much internal dissension within the Guelph party itself. By the year 1300 the city of Florence had been "divided" between two warring factions—the White Guelphs, led by the Cerchi family, and the Black Guelphs, led by the Donati family—whose civil quarrels emerged in the last years of the century. Ciacco's prophecy that "after long controversy, they'll come to blood" and that "the party of the woods will chase the other out" refers to the bloody fighting of May Day, 1300, after which the "rural" White Guelphs ("the party of the woods," Dante's party) defeated and banished the Blacks from Florence. In less than three years (by April 1302), however, the exiled Blacks regained control of Florence with the help of the hated Boniface VIII. More than 600 Whites were exiled, among them Dante himself. (See note to XXI, 38.)

69   "one who tacks his sails": Dante's first assault on Boniface VIII, here seen as astutely ambiguous in revealing his intentions and preferences. (For Boniface, also see the notes to III, 59–60 and XIX, 52–57 and XXVII, 70ff.)

73   "Two men are just": Candidates for these two unspecified men include Dante himself. Another gloss (Mazzoni) would have not two just men but two kinds of justice, that of natural law and that of codified law, which no one now follows. "Two men" may also mean "few, almost no one" (Bosco-Reggio) with, in that case, no need for specification.

77–84   Dante asks Ciacco about a few famous political Florentines who lived before the division between the Whites and the Blacks. Farinata is found in Hell (Canto X), as are Tegghiaio and Rusticucci (among the sodomites of Canto XVI) and Mosca (among the sowers of scandal and schism in Canto XXVIII). Arrigo is mentioned only here.

96–99   The "hostile Judge" is Christ at the Last Judgment.

106–108   Scholastic doctrine accepted the Aristotelian teaching that the perfection of the spirit and the body lies in their unity. Consequently, only af-

ter the Judgment Day, when all souls are reunited with their bodies, will the dead regain this perfection. With it, the pains of the damned will increase.

115   For some commentators Dante's *Pluto* is the mythological god of the underworld; for others, he is Plutus, the god of wealth. Dante probably made no clear distinction between the two; he transforms the mythological Pluto into a devil, guardian of the circle punishing those who misused their riches through avarice or prodigality.

CANTO VII

1   This first line appears to be the beginning (see 2) of an amazed and angry invocation to Satan; it is understood by Virgil who, "aware of everything" (3), also understands the implicit threat (4–5) along with Plutus' anger and "vindictiveness" (9). *Pape* may be a Latin version of "Oh!" *Aleppe* may derive from aleph, the first letter of the Hebrew alphabet, to designate the first, the ruler, the godly. Thus: "Oh, Satan, oh, Satan the most powerful one." But there are many other possible glosses.

8   According to most early commentators, Plutus is called "wolf" because he is a demon of avarice; thus he recalls the lean and hungry she-wolf (I, 49), symbol of cupidity.

22   The dangers of the Straits of Messina, described by Homer, were familiar to Dante from Virgil *(Aen.* III, 548–564; VII, 399), Ovid *(Met.* VII, 62–65), and Lucan *(Phars.* VII, 459–461).

27   Dante may well have been recalling the myth of Sisyphus (see *Aen.* VI, 818).

28–30   The misers and the prodigal are reproaching each other for their sins when they meet in the middle of the Fourth Circle.

78   This minister is Fortune, whom Dante saw as an Intelligence in charge of administering the world's riches (see 96, note).

86–87   In the *Convivio,* Dante states that these Intelligences, "which are vulgarly called 'Angels,'" were called "gods and goddesses" by the pagans (II, iv, 2–6).

95   These beings are called primal because, with the angels, they were created at the same time as the heavens (see *Purg.* XI, 3, and *Par.* XXIX, 31–48).

96   In setting Fortune as an Intelligence in a heavenly sphere, Dante is creating a variation on the more traditional image of a secular, capricious female turning a wheel at random to determine the fates of humans in this world.

98–99   A complete circle of the starry heavens takes 24 hours. The passage from rising to setting takes 12 hours. Since the Sixth Circle (XI, 113–114) finds the poets at 4 A.M., some commentators believe that the Fifth Circle should find them at a time shortly after midnight of Holy Saturday. If Dante meets the three beasts at dawn of Good Friday, then Virgil may have set out from Limbo and met Dante at noon of Good Friday, with the two of them entering Ante-Hell on the evening of Good Friday (Canto II).

108   In the *Aeneid* (VI, 187, 425) the Styx is one of the rivers surrounding Hades.

110   The "muddied people" punished in this swamp are those quick to anger, who continuously assail each other.

118–124   The commentators followed in the headnotes to this canto see the souls "underneath the water...wedged in the slime" as the sullen. This sullenness may be either a separate sin, *accidia* (which, in *Purgatorio,* is punished as sloth on the fourth terrace)—a view reinforced by the "mist of sluggishness" in line 123 here—or a "bitter" (124), repressed, sad, sullen subclass of anger. The second view accords better with the Aristotelian, rather than purely Christian, categories of sin used for Hell, whereas Purgatory is ordered along more simple and Christian lines.

CANTO VIII

1   Boccaccio—somewhat improbably—saw *"seguitando,"* "continuing," as evidence that Dante resumed the work after it had been interrupted when he was exiled.

19   In Virgil, Phlegyas, a son of Mars by Chryse, king of the Lapithae and father of Ixion, was punished in Tartarus for setting fire to Apollo's temple *(Aen.* VI, 821–823). (Phlegyas had committed this sacrilege because of Apollo's violation of Phlegyas' daughter, Coronis.) Dante transforms him into an infernal boatman, guardian of the damned immersed in the swamp of Styx.

27   An echo of the *Aeneid* (VI, 544–546); like Aeneas, Dante has a real body.

61   Filippo was nicknamed "Argenti" *(argento* means "silver") because he had his horse shod with silver. The ferocity of Dante's anger against this member of the Adimari clan has been accounted for by early commentators as the result of intense political animosity against a factious Black Guelph, retaliation for a slap Dante received from him, and/or retaliation for Filippo's brother having obtained from the Commune of Florence the property of Dante that was confiscated during his exile.

68   Dis is one of the names of Pluto, a classical name for the king of the underworld, whom Dante encounters in Canto XXXIV (and see XXXIV, 20, note). Dis is also the name of the realm.

71   High towers that resemble mosques indicate a city of infidels.

75   Lower Hell lies within the walls of Dis.

83   That is, the rebel angels fallen from Heaven. The neutral "coward" angels are in Ante-Hell (III, 37–39).

97   For "seven," see Introduction, p. xiv.

125–127   These demons—legend has it—tried to stop Christ from entering Limbo after His death. A hymn used on Holy Saturday incorporates the im-

age of shattered doors: "Today our Lord has shattered the doors of death and their locks."

CANTO IX

16–17 "one whose only punishment is crippled hope": that is, a soul from Limbo. Dante is indirectly sounding out Virgil's knowledge of Lower Hell.

23 Erichtho, a legendary sorceress, is probably mentioned by Dante to imply that Virgil's knowledge of Hell is, indeed, extensive and authoritative. In Lucan *(Phars.* VI, 508–827) Erichtho summons a spirit from the dead to reveal to Pompey the outcome of the battle of Pharsalia.

27 "Judas' Circle" is the ninth and last circle of Hell, where Judas is punished.

32 "the city of the sorrowing": the City of Dis.

38–54 In describing the Furies, or Erinyes, Dante draws on Virgil, Ovid, and Statius (see 45, note).

44 That is, Hecate or Proserpina, the wife of Pluto, King of the underworld. Though mentioned periphrastically here and in Canto X, 79–80, she never appears in Hell.

45–48 Dante places three Furies as guardians of the City of Dis. They accord with Statius' description of Tisiphone in the *Thebaid* (I, 103–115); Dante also depends on Virgil *(Aen.* VI, 755–759; VII, 429–437; XII, 1122–1132) and Ovid *(Met.* IV, 451–454; 481–496).

5 Medusa is one of the three Gorgon sisters. The locks of her hair were transformed into serpents by Minerva, making her appearance so fearful that everyone who looked upon her head—even after Perseus severed it—was changed to stone (see Ovid, *Met.* IV, 793–803).

54 This line alludes to the legend of Theseus, who descended to the lower world with his friend Pirithoüs to abduct Proserpina. Both were taken prisoner, but while Pirithoüs was devoured by Cerberus, Theseus was freed by Hercules (see *Aen.* VI, 171–172; 517–524; 820). The Furies lament their failure to have Theseus, too, killed, as a warning for all others.

61–63 Of some 19 or more addresses to the reader in the *Comedy,* only this and *Purgatorio* VIII, 19–21, ask the reader to pay attention to the scene that follows. In both cases, angelic presences are involved (Bosco-Reggio).

63 "verses so obscure": that is, strange, allegorical verses.

76–78 Dante is drawing somewhat on Ovid *(Met.* VI, 370–381) for this simile.

82 "the thick air": the mist of 75, above.

98–99 The rebellion of the devils against God is seen as analogous to the resistance of Cerberus to Hercules, who then chained Cerberus and hauled him away *(Aen.* VI, 520–523).

112 Arles, a town in Provence, is the site of a famous Roman necropolis, later a Christian cemetery.

113 Pola, in northeastern Italy, now in Yugoslavia, was the site of another famous Roman necropolis, which today has disappeared.

132 This is one of only two points in Hell where the poets head to the right, the other being at Canto XVII, 31. Normally the poets head left in Hell and right on the Mountain of Purgatory. The deviation here seems to indicate some special intent, but no commentator has defined it convincingly.

CANTO X

11 According to Biblical tradition, the Last Judgment will take place in the Valley of Jehosaphat, the Kidron Valley, source of the stream that separates Jerusalem from the Mount of Olives.

13–15 The Epicurean doctrine that denied the immortality of the individual soul had many followers in Florence, especially among the Ghibellines. Dante's judgment of Epicurus here seems to differ from his judgment in the *Convivio* (III, xiv, 15; IV, vi, 12; xxii, 15). Epicurus (341–270 B.C.), a Greek philosopher, taught that the soul was not immortal and that the highest human good is pleasure, which consists of the absence of pain. This "pleasure" did not mean sensual enjoyment, but, rather, peace of mind, which results from man's cultivation of the virtues. Such a doctrine would release believers from the fear of gods—whom Epicurus saw as blessedly imperturbable and indifferent to things mortal—and of the eternal punishments that might await an immortal soul.

18 This "longing" is the desire to know whether this circle contains some Florentines, especially Farinata.

32 Farinata was the name used for Manente, son of Jacopo degli Uberti, a famous leader of the Ghibellines of Florence. At the meeting of the victorious Ghibellines at Empoli after the Battle of Montaperti in September 1260, he vehemently opposed the proposal to destroy Florence. He returned to Florence after Montaperti and died in 1264, one year before Dante's birth. In 1283, Farinata and his wife were posthumously excommunicated by the Franciscan inquisitor; their bones were exhumed and dispersed, and the earthly goods of their heirs confiscated.

46–48 Dante's family were Guelphs; the Guelphs had to flee from Florence twice, in 1248 and in 1260.

50 Both times the Guelphs returned to Florence, the second time in 1266, after the defeat of Manfred at Benevento.

51 The Ghibellines were exiled and never returned to Florence. In the peace of 1280 about 60 Ghibelline families were excluded, among them the Uberti.

52–60 This shade is the soul of the Guelph Cavalcante de' Cavalcanti, father of Guido Cavalcanti. Guido, famous Florentine poet and Dante's close friend, married Beatrice, daughter of Farinata, to guarantee the peace between the Blacks and the Whites, the two feuding factions of Guelphs.

62–63 This translation refers *colui* to Virgil, "he who awaits me there"; it allows "one" to refer to either Beatrice or to God; and it interprets "perhaps" as modifying the verb "lead," rather than "disdain." In sum, it closely follows Letterio Cassatta *(Studi Danteschi,* 46, 1969, pp. 5–49), only hedging by not capitalizing "one," which would make the reference to God unequivocal.

77 The "art" here referred to is the skill of returning from exile.

79 Proserpina is identified as goddess of the moon, whose face is fully lighted once a month.

81 Dante himself learned within 50 months how difficult it is to try to return from exile.

83 These "citizens" are the Florentines, who never allowed the Uberti to return to Florence.

86 "The Arbia": On the left bank of this small stream near Siena is the hill of Montaperti, where the Ghibellines defeated the Guelphs in 1260.

88 "in that": that is, in my participation in the battle of Montaperti.

90 That is, without the personal motivation of desiring to return to Florence.

91–93 After the victory of Montaperti, the Ghibellines met at Empoli near Florence. All of them except Farinata proposed the total destruction of Florence.

110–111 "that fallen man": Cavalcante. His son and Dante's friend, the famous poet Guido, was still alive in April 1300. Exiled from Florence in June 1300 (his banishment was decreed when Dante himself was one of the priors of Florence), he returned, ill, to Florence, where he died in August 1300. In 62–63, either seeing "perhaps" as modifying "disdain" (which this translation does not allow) or seeing "did disdain" as referring to a momentary action for which Guido may still make amends before his death (which this translation suggests), one can sense some hope in Dante that Guido, a notorious "Epicurean," may have found a place in the otherworld outside of Hell.

119 Frederick II succeeded his father as King of Sicily and Naples and was Emperor of the Holy Roman Empire from 1215 to 1250.

120 "the Cardinal": Ottaviano degli Ubaldini, a Ghibelline, was Bishop of Bologna in 1240 and was made a cardinal in 1244.

CANTO XI

8–9 Dante may have confused Anastasius II, Pope from 496 to 498, with the Emperor Anastasius I, who subscribed to the Acacian heresy of Photinus, denying the divine origin of Christ. But it is more likely that Dante was correct about the Pope, but was relying on a spurious account of his stance.

50 In the Middle Ages the names of Sodom, a city in Palestine, and Cahors, a city in France, became synonymous with sodomites and usurers respectively.

65 For Dante's Hell and universe, see the diagrams on pages 343 and 344.

79–84 The *Ethics* is the *Nicomachean Ethics* of Aristotle, who was previously cited by Dante (IV, 131) as "the master of the men who know." In 13th-century Europe Aristotle was known in Latin translations made from Greek and Arabic sources and in Latin commentaries and paraphrases, some of them translated from Arabic. For approaching Dante, the most important way stations in this chain of diffusion are Avicenna, Averroes, Albertus Magnus, and Aquinas.

"Incontinence" is the excessive indulgence of, or submission to, passions that in moderation are lawful; it includes the vices of lust, gluttony, avarice (and its paired sin, prodigality), and anger.

"Malice" here means fraud, and "mad bestiality" means violence. Some critics, however, taking into account the "malice" of 22, which has the general meaning of any evil act, ascribe to "malice" alone the two forms of fraud and violence, interpreting "mad bestiality" as heresy, sodomy, or other sins. The sin of heresy, however, does not appear in Aristotle's *Ethics,* which Dante follows here in ordering the sins punished in Hell. As Chimenz notes, the exposition of sins in Canto XI allows no formal place for the cowardly of the Ante-Inferno, those who "lived without disgrace and without praise" (III, 36), who did *not* do; or for the souls in Limbo, on the threshold of upper Hell, who "did *not* [italics mine] worship God in fitting ways" (IV, 38); in parallel fashion, it may allow no place for the heretics who are also on a threshold— this time with respect to lower Hell—and are also punished for *not* doing, for their failure to accept Christian doctrine.

95 Here Dante refers to 50, above, where he implicitly mentioned usury by referring to Cahors.

101 The *Physics* of Aristotle, well known to Dante.

109–110 The usurer earns his living, not through the sweat of his brow (see Gen. 3:19), but through money.

113–114 Virgil indicates the time by the position of the constellations: it is now two hours before sunrise, 4 A.M. The Wain or constellation of Ursa Major is spread out to the north-west in the area of Caurus, another name for the Mistral or northwest wind. Ursa Major is about to set, then; and the Fishes—Pisces—are rising, which do they about two hours before the rising of Aries, the constellation of the rising sun in the season in which Dante sets his poem.

CANTO XII

2 For more on these "broken boulders," see Canto XII, 1–10 and 31–41.

4 Dante compares the "passage down to that ravine" (10) to the "toppled mass of rock," the Slavini di Marco—The Landslides of Marco—on the Adige River, between Trent and Verona. The landslide that produced this formation may have occurred as early as 833 A.D.

11–20 When Pasiphaë, the wife of Minos, King of Crete, conceived an un-

natural passion for a bull, Daedalus, the famous craftsman, built a wooden cow for her to climb into to facilitate intercourse with the bull. From this union Pasiphaë bore the Minotaur—part man, part beast. Minos kept the Minotaur in a labyrinth constructed by Daedalus. When Androgeos, son of Minos, was killed by the Athenians, Minos exacted from Athens an annual tribute of seven young men and seven young women to be devoured by the Minotaur. But Ariadne, Minos' daughter, and half-sister (20) of the Minotaur, fell in love with Theseus, the Duke of Athens (17), and furnished him a ball of thread and a sword. He entered the labyrinth, killed the Minotaur, and, with the help of Ariadne's thread, was able to find his way out again. Dante's principal source is Ovid *(Met.* VIII, 131–137 and *Art of Love* I, 289ff). In an unpublished paper Colin Hardie argues that Dante is following the tradition that the Minotaur had a bull's head and a human body, not the reverse; Barry Moser's illustration follows that tradition.

20 The reference is to Ariadne (see 12–17, note).

22–24 The sources of this simile are Virgil *(Aen.* II, 311–313) and Seneca *(Oed.* 341–342).

34 "The other time": see Canto IX, 22–27.

37–39 I.e., Christ, in His descent into Hell, removed the souls of the just people of the Old Testament, thus robbing Satan of his most "splendid spoils" (see also IV, 52–53, and 52–61, note).

40–41 According to the Gospel (Matt. 27:51), the moment of Christ's death was marked by an earthquake (see XXI, 112–114).

41–43 In his *Metaphysics,* Aristotle refers to Empedocles' explanation of universal order: the principle of Love, which unifies all things, alternates with the principle of Hate, which keeps things discrete and separate. If "the universe felt love" alone, then all things would fly together by mutual attraction, and the result would be chaos.

47 The river is later identified as Phlegethon (XIV, 130; 134–135).

56 Centaurs are mythical beings, half man and half horse.

65 Chiron, the great Centaur, legendary tutor of Achilles and other Greek heroes, is traditionally represented as a wise educator, scientist, and musician. For this reason Virgil singles him out from the other Centaurs. (See especially Statius, *Achilleid* I, 106–118; 195–196; 272–273; 526–527; Ovid, *Fasti* V, 379–414.)

67–69 According to Ovid, Nessus tried to rape Deianira, Hercules' wife, for which Hercules killed him with a poisoned arrow. The dying Nessus gave Deianira his robe dipped in his blood, telling her that it would act as a love charm. Later, finding Hercules in love with Iole, the jealous Deianira, who did not know the robe was poisoned, gave it to Hercules, thinking to win back his love. When he put it on, he died in agony. (See *Met.* IX, 127–133, 152–162, 166–169.)

70–79 These lines list the inhabitants of Upper Hell from the Second to the Fifth Circles, all those punished for sins of incontinence.

72 Pholus, "he who was so frenzied," is mentioned only in passing in Ovid's account of the Centaur's assault on the Lapiths (*Met.* IV, 306). More to the point may be the wrath of Tydeus in Statius (*Theb.* II, 555–562), which is likened to Pholus's action against the Lapiths (563–654); or the "frenzied" Pholus of Virgil's *Georgics* II, 455–456.

84 The "two natures" are of beast and man.

88 "she": Beatrice

107 Alexander may be either Alexander the Great of Macedon (356–323 B.C.) or Alexander of Pherae, the tyrant of Thessaly (c368 B.C.). Dionysius the Elder was tyrant of Syracuse from 405 to 367 B.C.

109 Ezzelino III (1194–1259), a leading Ghibelline, son-in-law of the Emperor Frederick II and Imperial viceroy in the March of Treviso, was notorious for his cruel massacre of the citizens of Padua.

110–111 Obizzo II d'Este (1247–1293), a Guelph noble, fought against Manfred with the army of Charles of Anjou (see XXVIII, 16–18 and note). He was lord of Ferrara and of the region around Ancona. Rumor had it that his own son, Azzo VIII, killed him. Dante seems to accept that rumor and—perhaps—to compound it with Azzo's illegitimacy if *figliastro* is seen not only as an unnaturally fierce or cruel son, but as an illegitimate son.

118–120 In March 1271, Guy, son of Simon de Montfort, viceroy of Charles of Anjou in Tuscany, impiously killed Prince Henry, son of Richard, Duke of Cornwall, during mass at the Cathedral of Viterbo. Villani's *Chronicles* tell how a statue of Henry, holding a golden casket containing his heart, was placed on London Bridge. The image of the heart "that still drips blood" indicates that Henry's murder is still unavenged.

133 Attila, King of the Huns (433–453), was called the Scourge of God because of his cruelties.

135 The Pyrrhus referred to here is probably the son of Achilles and killer of Priam and many other Trojans. Virgil emphasizes his cruelty (*Aen.* II, 628–750). The Pyrrhus cited by other commentators—king of Epirus (319–272 B.C.)—is actually praised by Dante in his *Monarchy* (II, ix, 8). Sextus was the son of Pompey; Dante read of his cruel acts of piracy in Lucan (*Phars.* VI, 420–422).

137 Rinier of Corneto was a famous highwayman in Dante's days. Rinier Pazzo, another highwayman, was excommunicated in 1268 by Pope Clement IV.

CANTO XIII

7–9 The river (and town of) Cécina in Tuscany and the town of Corneto in Lazio mark the boundaries of the Maremma, one of the most desolate places known in Dante's time.

10 The Harpies, again a mixture of human and brute, are monsters in the

shape of birds, with long claws and the heads of women (see *Aen.* III, 278–287).

12 A reference to the prophecy given to the Trojans by a Harpy: that they will have to face hunger and misfortune before they reach Italy.

19 "horrid sand": the Third Ring of this Seventh Circle.

28–51 The episode refers to one of Virgil's own narratives (*Aen.* III, 32–63), in which Aeneas, landing in Thrace, while trying "to tear a green branch from the soil/to serve as leafy cover for [his] altars," is shocked by black blood dripping down from severed roots. The voice that tells him that "the blood you see does not flow from a stem" is the voice of Polydorus, who explains: "Here an iron / harvest of lances covered my pierced body;/for this, sharp javelins have grown above me." Seeing Troy besieged, Priam had sent the young Polydorus to Polymnestor, King of Thrace, who was to have sheltered the youth but murdered him instead and took "his gold by force."

58–78 The speaker is Pier della Vigna (c1190–1249), who was minister, private secretary, and chief counselor to the Emperor Frederick II but fell into disfavor and was jailed and blinded. Soon afterward he committed suicide. The mannered style of Pier's discourse has been seen as a historical characterization of Pier's own chancellery style, of which Pier's epistles are masterly examples (Novati); but Spitzer, noting that this style penetrates Dante's own style in the canto, sees historical characterization as "not the sole, or even the prime, artistic motive behind the use of these rhetorical devices." Instead, he sees "a sort of linguistic, or onomatopoetic rendition of the ideas of torture, schism, estrangement." But it is also true that Dante is given to the same exacerbation of rhetoric in very un-suicidal contexts.

64–68 The "whore" is envy, "Caesar's dwelling" is the imperial court of Frederick II (or any similar court), and "Augustus" is the emperor.

99 Spelt is a type of wheat that grows in thick clumps and very readily.

103–104 At the Last Judgment all souls will be reunited with their bodies.

118–123 "The one in front," identified as Lano (120), is probably Arcolano of Siena, a member of the Maconi family. He belonged to the notorious "Spendthrift Club," a company of youths who agreed to waste money and time on the most fanciful banquets, festivities, and presents they could contrive. Boccaccio says that Lano sought out death in battle—in 1287, against the Aretines—rather than lead a life of poverty (see also XXIX, 125–132 and note). That battle took place at Pieve al Toppo, a town on the river Toppo near Arezzo. The "other shade," named below (133), was a notorious squanderer from Santo Andrea, near Padua. He was killed by Ezzelino III in 1239 (see XII, 109 and note).

130–151 The very uncertainty of the identity of this anonymous suicide would seem to indicate that "Dante intended to underline especially the Florentine-ness of this character rather than his specific identity" (Bosco-Reggio).

143–145 The city is Florence. When the Florentines converted to

Christianity, John the Baptist replaced the pagan god Mars, as patron of the city. Therefore, Mars will forever persecute this city with his art of war—not least, civil war.

147 An original statue of Mars was broken when Totila (here confused with the earlier Attila) destroyed Florence in 542. Popular belief held that the retrieved fragment of this statue set on the Ponte Vecchio had—as a kind of talisman—enabled the people to rebuild their city. This fragment (which was probably not the base of a statue of Mars, but of a Gothic king) was washed away in the flood of 1333.

CANTO XIV

15 The reference is to Cato of Utica, who led the Pompeian troops through the Libyan desert in 47 B.C. (See *Phars.* IX, 378ff.)

28–30 The rain of fire is indebted to Gen. 19:24 and Ezek. 38:22, while "as snow descends on alps when no wind blows" echoes a line of Cavalcanti, *"e bianca neve scender senza venti,"* "and white snow as it falls when no winds blow."

31–36 An apocryphal letter from Alexander of Macedon to Aristotle speaks of a heavy snowfall, with Alexander ordering his men to stamp hard on the fallen snow, and then of a rain of sparks of fire from the sky. Albertus Magnus condenses these two incidents into one in his *De Meteoris* (I, iv, 8), and Dante follows him.

45 The gate of the City of Dis (see VIII, 82–130).

51–75 The speaker is Capaneus, one of the Seven Against Thebes. He was struck with a thunderbolt by Jove when he boasted that not even Jove could stop him. The tale of his daring and death is told by Statius (*Theb.* X, 826–939, and also see III, 598–699).

52 Vulcan, the god of the Forge, and the Cyclopes, his assistants, manufactured the thunderbolts used by Jove. Mongibello, the Sicilian name for Mt. Etna, was thought to be Vulcan's furnace (see *Aen.* VIII, 546–555).

55 The "others" are the Cyclopes.

58 Capaneus refers to the battle of Phlegra, where Jove defeated the rebellious Titans. See Ovid, *Met.* I, 151–162; Statius, *Theb.* X, 909—in the same passages from Statius cited above in the note to 51–75—as well as XI, 7–8.

74 The "slender watercourse" is the Phlegethon (see the "red stream" of 135 and note).

79 The Bulicame was a hot sulphurous spring that supplied water to the houses of prostitutes in the region north of Viterbo.

94–114 Dante's brief tale of the statue of the Old Man of Crete depends, in part, on Daniel 2:31–35 and, in part, on the Ovidian myth of a golden age under Saturn, followed by ages of silver, brass, and iron (*Met.* I, 89–150). Though Dante's sources for individual elements of this passage are evident, the configuration of the statue plus tears plus an otherworldly river seems

unique to Dante. The Old Man has been interpreted as an emblem of the course of degenerating humankind. The statue has its back to the East (Damietta is in Egypt) but faces West to Rome, looking toward that city for regeneration. The leg of iron is the Empire and the leg of clay is the Church—corrupted by its greed for temporal power. (For the role of Crete in Dante's mythical amalgam, also see Virgil, *Aen.* III, 136–152. For more on the golden age, see Virgil, *Aen.* VIII, 418–426, *Eclogues* IV, 6–7 and Juvenal, *Satires* VI, 1–20. For the worst of eras, see *Satires* XIII, 28–30. Pliny's *Natural History* VII, xvi, also mentions the finding of a giant man after an earthquake in Crete; Augustine echoes this in *The City of God* XV, 9.)

100–102   Rhea, or Cybele, wife of Saturn and mother of Jove, hid Jove from Saturn because he was devouring all his children to avert a prophecy that he would be dethroned by one of them. When Jove was about to be born, Rhea fled to Mount Ida in Crete. There she hid the newborn Jove in a cave; and lest Saturn hear his son's cries, she had her followers, the Corybantes, cover his voice with the clamor of their chants and cymbals. Eventually Jove did dethrone Saturn. (In addition to the *Aen.* III passage noted above, see also Ovid, *Fasti* IV, 197–214.)

115–129   Virgil's explanation of the single source of the rivers of Hell seems to support a simple explanation—that they are part of a single stream, which occasionally widens to form a lake before narrowing to a river again. But this simple explanation is contradicted by the syntax of the Italian. *"Lor corso"* (115)—that is, the course of one stream under four names—does not continue as the subject of *"fanno,"* "form," which has instead a plural subject—"they," referring to tears. This fact suggests to some critics (see Pagliaro) that the tears themselves "give rise there to three rivers." What muddies the waters even more is Dante's query in lines 121–123, which implies that Dante has forgotten his own explanation (VII, 101–108), of the Styx as born of a "boiling fountain" (a bit less troubling in this translation, where the term *fonte che bolle* is translated, following Chimenz, as "foaming watercourse"). And there is another difficulty: in Canto VII, 103ff., Dante did indeed already see one of the ringlike ponds or lakes of this river—*if* it is one river. Some commentators have explained the problem in terms of Dante's forgetfulness (Porena), others as a shift in Dante's notions about the rivers of Hell (Chimenz), and Singleton attempts to reconcile the contradiction by referring Dante's question (121–123), not to the *total* course of the river, but only to the passage from Styx to the ringlike lakes or ponds below it. Hence, Virgil's reference to "something new" in line 128 makes sense "because, since encountering the *'ruscello'* (stream) that bubbles up and flows into Styx, they have seen no such canal again until now." But if Virgil is being precise here, he is surely being approximate when he refers to their journey as "always toward the left" (126), for there are two exceptions to this leftward course, in Canto IX and Canto XVII; and the first of these (IX, 132) took place precisely along the downward way from Styx. One forgetfulness may well call up another. Or better, the power of the image of the Old Man of Crete, with its cracks, may have altered Dante's earlier view, leaving a seam in the structure.

119 Cocytus is the last of the infernal rivers (see Canto XXXIV) and forms an icy lake in the last circle of Hell. All four rivers of Hell—Acheron, Styx, Phlegethon, and Cocytus—appear in the *Aeneid*.

135 Dante plays on the etymology of Phlegethon. Servius on *Aeneid* VI, 265 (Latin numbering here), knew that Phlegethon means "fire."

136–138 In classical mythology Lethe is another of the rivers of Avernus, bringing forgetfulness to all who drink its waters. But Dante finds Lethe in the Earthly Paradise (*Purg.* XXVIII, 130) and finds what is probably the run-off from Lethe in XXXIV, 130.

CANTO XV

9 Carentana is probably our modern Carinthia, used by Dante to designate the eastern Carnic Alps of Carinthia, Styria, and Carniola. Once the heat falls on their snows, the melt-off would swell the Brenta.

30 Brunetto Latini (c1220–1294), Florentine and Guelph, famous political figure and writer, was the author, among other works, of a prose encyclopedia in French, *Li Livres dou tresor* (often referred to simply as *Tresor),* and of the *Tesoretto,* a didactic poem in a popular style in Italian. After Manfred's defeat at the Battle of Benevento in 1266, he held official positions in Florence. Though he surely influenced the young Dante, he was not actually his teacher.

44 The "head bent low" is Dante's sign of respect for Brunetto.

61 "that ... people": the Florentines in power at the time of Dante's exile.

62 Tradition reports that when Florence was founded by the Romans after Caesar's successful siege of Fiesole, the hill town north of Florence, Florence was peopled partly by Romans (the nobility) and partly by families from Fiesole ("still keeping something of the rock and mountain"). The troubles in Florence were attributed to the mixture of two different peoples, "the noble, virtuous Romans, and the crude, war-embittered Fiesolans" (Villani, *Chron.* I, 38).

67 The "blindness" of the Florentines was proverbial, though accounts differ as to its origin.

71–72 Though many early commentators interpret "hungry for you" as desirous of having you on their side, it more probably means that each party will be desirous of devouring Dante.

85 Here Dante echoes Brunetto's own words in the *Tresor* (II, cxx, 1).

90 "her": Beatrice.

96 The expression, sounding like a proverb, about letting the "peasant turn his mattock" may be related to an anecdote in Dante's *Convivio* (IV, xi, 8) about a peasant who, by chance, found a treasure while digging on his land.

109–110 Priscian of Cesarea was a famous Latin grammarian (c500 A.D.). His *Institutiones grammaticae* was a work widely used in medieval schools.

Francesco d'Accorso (1225–1293) was a celebrated lawyer and professor of law at the universities of Bologna and Oxford.

112–114 In official acts the Pope is called "Servant of His servants." The use of this term for Boniface VIII is, very possibly, ironic.

Because of his scandalous life, Andrea de' Mozzi, Bishop of Florence (on the Arno), was transferred by Pope Boniface VIII in 1295 to Vicenza (on the river Bacchiglione), where he soon died, the muscles of his body worn out ("strained") by acts of sodomy.

121–123 The race mentioned by Dante was instituted in 1207 and was run in Verona on the first Sunday in Lent; Boccaccio notes that the competitors ran naked. The prize was a banner or a bolt of green cloth; a rooster was, some claim, awarded to the runner who came in last.

CANTO XVI

22–27 These "champions" may be ancient wrestlers or else contenders, in times contemporary with Dante, called on to settle a judicial quarrel—or a hybrid involving both. Dante can use the present tense as he condenses ancient and modern images.

34–45 The good Gualdrada (called "good" because she was a paragon of the "old" virtues of Florence) was mother of Ruggero, father of Guido Guerra VI. Guido, a Guelph, led several actions against the Ghibellines. Tegghiaio Aldobrandi was chief magistrate of Arezzo. Along with Guido, he tried to dissuade the Florentines from undertaking the expedition against Siena in 1260, which resulted in the disastrous defeat at Montaperti and the six-year return to power of the Ghibellines in Florence. Jacopo Rusticucci, also a Guelph, was active in political and diplomatic affairs.

69 Guglielmo Borsiere (Borsiere may be a true patronym or refer to the purse-maker's trade) is spoken of by Boccaccio as "a most courteous man of praiseworthy manners" *(Esposizioni)* and, in the *Decameron* I, 8, as a "worthy, mannerly, well-spoken man."

94–105 Dante compares the roar of the Phlegethon to the roaring waterfall formed by the river Acquacheta near the monastery of San Benedetto dell'Alpe in the Apennines. Beyond the city of Forlì, the Acquacheta changes its name to Montone. Nowadays, because of deviations, channelings, and the like, the Acquacheta joins the Ronco to form the Fiumi Uniti ("Conjoined Rivers"), and the Reno and Lamone are the first to "course eastward from Mount Viso."

106 None of the many glosses on the cord satisfies intellectually. But Dante's invention does tantalize.

CANTO XVII

1–15 The monster Geryon, guardian of the Eighth Circle, is the symbol of fraud. In classical mythology he is represented as a giant having human form with three heads or three bodies (as in the "triple-shaped" Geryon of *Aen.*

VIII, 267–268). Dante's Geryon is a monster of three natures: human, with the face "of a just man"; reptilian, with "the body of a serpent"; and bestial, with "two paws" and the "pointed tail" that is the first detail describing him (see 22–27, note). Son of Crisaore and the ocean-nymph Calliroe, he was king of three Iberian islands. As one of his labors, Hercules killed Geryon in order to take possession of his precious flocks and herds.

16   The Turks and the Tartars were famous in the Middle Ages for their artistry in weaving.

18   Arachne, famous for her weaving, challenged Minerva, goddess of the arts, to a competition. The goddess, angered at Arachne's presumption, changed her into a spider (see Ovid, *Met.* VI, 5–145).

21–27   In Dante's time the beaver was believed to fish by agitating its tail in the water to produce a deceptive liquid similar to oil, which attracted fish. Through this simile Geryon, lying in wait to spear the sinners with his tail, becomes an emblem of craft and deception.

31   Like the movement right in Canto IX, 132, this is one of the only two points in Hell where the poets head to the right. If the earlier deviation has no convincing explanation, this later one may well be explained satisfyingly by the Ottimo: "one cannot move straight [by the normal Hell-ward way, directly left] to fraud."

56–65   The emblems are the coats of arms of families notorious for their usury. The azure lion on a gold field was the emblem of the Florentine Gianfigliazzi family. The red purse with a white goose belonged to the Obriachi family, also of Florence. The white purse with the "azure, pregnant sow" designated the Scrovegni family of Padua.

   The only one of these usurers who speaks is probably the notorious Reginaldo Scrovegni, whose son erected the Scrovegni Chapel in Padova—where Giotto painted his frescoes—as atonement for his father's practices.

68   Early commentators identify this Vitaliano as Vitaliano del Dente of Padua, chief magistrate of Vicenza in 1304 and of Padua in 1307.

72   The "sovereign cavalier" is Giovanni Buiamonte dei Becchi, a prominent Florentine banker. He may have outlived Dante, but just as Dante prophecies Vitaliano's going to Hell for usury, so does he foresee Buiamonte's destiny. The irony of Florence having named a notorious usurer "cavalier" and honoring him with high civic offices is played on heavily by Dante.

107   Phaethon, son of Apollo, pleaded to be allowed to drive the chariot of the sun, normally guided by his father; granted permission, he proved unable to control its horses, and they ran violently off course, threatening to set the earth on fire. Thus Zeus had to kill him with a thunderbolt (Ovid. *Met.* II, 47–328).

109–111   Icarus, son of Daedalus, attempted to fly from the Labyrinth of Crete with wings of wax his father fashioned. Forgetting Daedalus' instructions, Icarus flew too close to the sun. Its heat melted his wings, and he fell into the sea (Ovid. *Met.* VIII, 203–235).

127–132   Unless he sights prey or is called back with a lure by his master, a trained falcon will continue flying until exhaustion compels him to descend.

CANTO XVIII

1   Malebolge ("evil-pouches") is the name given to the Eighth Circle, which is divided into ten *bolge,* or pouches. In its ten valleys, or trenches, the ten types of fraudulence are punished.

4–6   For the "broad and yawning pit" see the final six cantos of *Inferno.* Malebolge slopes down to that pit.

28–33   In the year 1300 Pope Boniface VIII proclaimed a Jubilee or Holy Year that granted indulgences (reductions of the penance set for sins) to those visiting certain Roman churches. Dante may have been in Rome at the time and witnessed the smooth flow of the pilgrims flocking the streets of Rome—the result of impressive traffic controls the authorities adopted on the bridge connecting St. Peter's to the rest of the city. The Castello (Castle) Sant'Angelo would be in the direction of St. Peter's; the Mount would probably be Mount Giordano, in the direction of those heading back from St. Peter's.

46–47   Here the sinner seeks obscurity rather than the renown or notoriety sought by sinners who have thus far confronted Dante.

50   Venèdico Caccianemico dell'Orso (c1228–c1302) was a Bolognese whom Dante places in this *bolgia* because he was said to have acted as a pander to his own sister, Ghisolabella, turning her over to the Marquis of Este. Dante seems to have thought that Caccianemico was already dead by 1300.

61   *Sipa* is a word for "yes" in the dialect spoken in the territory between the two small rivers Sàvena and Reno, which comprise the boundaries of Bologna.

86–96   Jason was the mythical leader of the Argonauts on their expedition to Colchis to get the golden fleece. On their way they stopped at the island of Lemnos, where Jason seduced and abandoned Hypsipyle—who had saved her father's life when the other women of Lemnos killed all their menfolk. Jason's behavior at Lemnos was not uncharacteristic: he also abandoned Medea—daughter of the King of Colchis (87)—who had helped him in gaining the golden fleece; she took her revenge by killing the two children she had borne him. (See Ovid, *Met.* VII, 1–424; *Heroides* VI and XII; Statius, *Theb.* V, 403–485.)

123   Alessio Interminei belonged to a prominent Guelph family of Lucca.

133–135   Thaïs is a courtesan in the *Eunuchus* of Terence, a play commented on by Cicero (*De amicitia* XXVI, 98)—Dante's probable source. Dante's characterization of Thaïs as fulsome flatterer is somewhat misguided, for in Terence's play the flatterer is the intermediary Gnatho (Act III, Scene 1). It is likely that the misconception stems from Cicero's commentary, which does not make clear exactly who gives excessive thanks.

CANTO XIX

1 As reported in the Bible (Acts 8:9–24), Simon Magus tried to buy the spiritual power of conferring the Holy Spirit. The apostle Peter rejected him for even thinking that the gift of God might be bought. The word simony, derived from Simon's name, refers to the sale of spiritual goods or the fraudulent acquisition of ecclesiastical offices. Dante's decision to open the canto with an apostrophe against the simoniacs even before he meets them is unprecedented in the *Inferno*.

16–21 San Giovanni is the Florentine church in which Dante hoped to be crowned as poet *(Par.* XXV, 8–9). His explanation of his motive for breaking the baptismal font (or—some gloss—the stand in which the baptizers, not the baptized, stood) is perhaps intended to dispel any rumors of impiety that may have circulated after such an act—or, more simply, to record the truth.

46–54 The "dejected soul" is Pope Nicholas III, Giovanni Orsini, who was elected in 1277 and died in 1280. Addressed by Dante in lines 46–48, he mistakenly believes that one of his successors (Boniface VIII) has come to take his place in the hole. Like all damned souls, Nicholas has foreknowledge, and, thinking that Boniface would die in 1303, he is somewhat surprised at being addressed in the year 1300—three years too early.

46–47 Hired killers were executed by being placed head-first in a pit that was then filled with dirt, suffocating them.

56–57 The metaphor of the marriage of the Church, the "Lovely Lady," was frequently used by medieval theologians and mystics.

66 The "mighty mantle" is the mantle of the papacy.

67 Nicholas III was of the Orsini family, known as "the cubs of the she-bear."

71 That is, to favor his relatives.

82–88 The "lawless shepherd" is Clement V, of Gascony (in "the west"), pope from 1305 to 1314, whose removal of the Papal See to Avignon in 1309 was the beginning of what is usually referred to as the Babylonian Captivity, which lasted until 1377. Before his election to the papacy Clement was Archbishop of Bordeaux; to become Pope, he negotiated with King Philip the Fair of France, accepting six conditions from him for being elected. Thus he is likened to Jason, who first obtained the office of High Priest of the Jews by bribing King Antiochus of Syria, and then tried to enforce a return to Greek customs and pagan worship.

93 See Matt. 4:19, Mark 1:17, and John 21:19.

95–96 Matthias took the place of Judas Iscariot, "the transgressing soul" (see Acts 1:23–26).

98–99 This barb is directed at Nicholas's intrigue against Charles of Anjou (1226–1285), the King of Naples and Sicily. Dante seems to believe the

charge that Nicholas accepted money in order to assent to the conspiracy against Charles that, two years after Nicholas's death, matured as the Sicilian Vespers, a successful uprising.

106–108 The Evangelist is St. John (see Apocalypse 17:1–3). The whore who "sits upon the waters" was interpreted by the Church Fathers as pagan Rome. Here Dante sees her as the Church corrupted by secular interests.

109–110 The seven heads symbolize the seven sacraments; the ten horns signify the ten commandments.

115–117 Dante alludes here to the medieval legend—supported by a document—of "The Donation of Constantine," thought of as historical fact at the time. Before moving the capital of the Roman Empire to Constantinople in the fourth century, the Emperor Constantine supposedly invested the Church with his temporal power in Rome—with the result that the Church began to acquire the wealth and worldliness it had not had before. For Dante, this marked the beginning of the corruption he denounces in this canto. The Pope who received Constantine's gift was "the first rich father," Sylvester I (see XXVII, 94–96, and note). It was Lorenzo Valla in the 15th century who showed the document to be a forgery, but doubts about it had already been voiced in Dante's time. But Dante's drastic critique of the Church's temporal power would hardly be altered by that philological matter.

CANTO XX

13 The damned in this circle are all diviners and soothsayers, viewed by Dante as practitioners of impious and unlawful arts who attempt to avert God's designs by their predictions. For such impiety, those who have tried to look too far forward now have their heads turned backward on their bodies.

19–24 These lines contain an interesting rhetorical maneuver through which Dante would stimulate the very same emotion in the reader for which he is rebuked by Virgil (27).

28–30 Virgil implies that those who prophesy do so in the belief that their foreknowledge gives them power over the future. Logically, this means they believe that God Himself is "passive" in the face of their attempts to foresee, and possibly change, the future.

31–33 Amphiaraus is one of the seven kings who fought against Thebes (*Theb.* VIII, 690–823; VIII, 1–126; 225–226). Foreseeing his death in the war, he tried to avert it by hiding from battle but soon met his death in an earthquake while attempting to flee his pursuers.

40–45 Tiresias was a famous soothsayer of Thebes. Here Dante mentions an episode from Ovid's *Metamorphoses* (III, 324–331) in which Tiresias came upon two coupling serpents and, striking them with his rod, was transformed into a woman. When, seven years later, an identical encounter provoked the same action, he was changed back to a man.

46–51 Aruns was an Etruscan soothsayer who came from "Luni's hills," near Carrara (famous for its white marbles), and who predicted the civil war and Caesar's victory. (See Lucan, *Phars.* I, 585–638.)

52–93 Manto, famous Theban soothsayer, is mentioned by Virgil, Ovid, and Statius. The latter's account (*Theb.* IV, 463–585; X, 724–725) seems closest to Dante's version of Manto.

59 The city of Thebes was consecrated to Bacchus. The city fell under the tyranny of Creon after the war of the "Seven against Thebes."

67–69 To indicate the exact geographical position of the lake (the present-day Lake of Garda), Dante describes an island in the middle of the lake as a place where the boundaries and jurisdictions of the three dioceses of Trent, Brescia, and Verona meet.

95–96 When Alberto da Casalodi, a Guelph count of Brescia, became lord of Mantua in 1272, he foolishly followed the treacherous advice of Pinamonte dei Buonaccorsi, a native Mantuan, to appease the populace by exiling the nobles who were Alberto's supporters. Alberto soon found himself defenseless, and Pinamonte was able to seize power.

108 The men of Greece were away during the war with Troy.

110–113 Calchas was an augur who indicated the most propitious time for the Greek fleet to depart from Aulis for Troy. Though Dante implies that Eurypylus, another augur, took part in the consultation at Aulis, he is mentioned by Virgil only as advising the Greeks to return home (*Aen.* II, 161–186).

115–117 Michael Scot (c1175–1235), a famous scientist, philosopher, occultist, and astrologer from Scotland, spent many years at the court of Frederick II at Palermo.

118 Guido Bonatti of Forlì, after serving in many places, ended up as an astrologer at the court of Guido da Montefeltro (see XXVII); he wrote prolifically, but all that has survived ia a *Treatise on Astronomy.*

118–120 Asdente (meaning "toothless") was a shoemaker of Parma famous for his prophecies in the latter half of the 13th century.

124–126 Popular belief in Italy holds that God placed Cain in the moon when he attempted to excuse himself for murdering Abel. Thus, the expression "Cain with his thorns" is a circumlocution for the moon with its spots. In short, the moon is now setting at the western edge of the northern hemisphere ("below Seville"). Overhead, in Jerusalem, the time is just after 6 A.M., the dawn of Holy Saturday, April 9.

CANTO XXI

6 While the other pouches of Malebolge ("evil-pouches") are also dark, this one is "wonderfully dark" because of the boiling pitch being prepared for the grafters.

7   The Arsenal at Venice, built in 1104, was one of the most important ship-yards in Europe, enabling the Venetian Republic to remain a great sea power.

37   Malebranche ("evil-claws") is the group name for the devils in this pouch; each of them, however, has his proper name, given in lines 76, and 118–123.

38   The Elders of Saint Zita in Lucca were ten citizens who held executive power along with the chief magistrate. The one punished here is guilty of barratry, the civil equivalent of simony (see XIX, 1, and note). This was a charge leveled against Dante himself by the Black Guelphs who banished him from Florence (see VI, 61–70, note).

Saint Zita (c1208–1278)—not officially canonized until 1690—was widely venerated in Lucca. The anonymous barrator may be Martino Bottaio, a Lucchese who died on April 9, 1300.

41   For Dante, Bonturo Dati was the most notoriously corrupt of the con-spicuously corrupt people of Lucca. He outlived Dante, but Dante reserves a place in Hell for him, just as he did for two usurers (XVII, 68; 72) and even more inventively for Branca Doria (XXXIII, 145–146).

48   The Sacred Face of Lucca was an ancient Byzantine crucifix made of dark wood, said to have been miraculously completed while its carver was sleeping. It was an object of great veneration.

49   The Serchio is a river near Lucca.

76   Malacoda ("evil-tail") leads the other Malebranche here.

95   The castle of Caprona, in the Pisan part of the valley of the Arno, was captured in 1289 by the allied Guelphs of Florence, Lucca, Pisa, and Siena. Dante's words (94) indicate that he himself may have taken part in the siege.

111   Malacoda is lying to them: nearby there is no ridge that forms a path.

112–114   In substance this means that the bridges of Hell crumbled 1266 years ago—at a time five hours later than the present hour yesterday. Dante held that Christ died after having completed 34 years of life on this earth—years counted from the day of the Incarnation. Luke affirms that the hour of His death was the sixth—that is, noon. If this is the case, then Malacoda is re-ferring to a time which is 7 A.M., five hours before noon on Holy Saturday. A credible calculation now falls into place:

In the year 1300 Good Friday fell on April 8 (though some commentators opt for the historical anniversary of Christ's death, March 25). This would place the night in the dark wood at Thursday night, April 7, the night before Good Friday; would allot the day of Good Friday, April 8, to the encounter with the three animals and Virgil; and would assign the entry into Ante-Hell to nightfall (II, 1–3) on Good Friday. Dante is in the Fourth Circle by mid-night (VII, 98), in the Sixth Circle by 4 A.M. (XI, 113–114), in the fourth pouch of Malebolge by 6 A.M. (XX, 124–126), and, here, in the fifth pouch of Malebolge by 7 A.M. of Holy Saturday, April 9.

118–123   The names given to the demons in this pouch are generally fanci-ful coinages of Dante. But Malebranche (37) was a family name in Lucca, as were Graffiacane, Scarmiglione (105), and Cagnasso (here Cagnazzo). Some

possibilities for the derivation of the names are: Alichino comes from *helle-quin*, progenitor of the Italian *arlecchino*, our "harlequin"; Calcabrina is "he who can walk on brine"—that is, the nimble-footed one; Libicocco may condense the names for two winds, the *libeccio* and the *sirocco*; Draghignazzo may be "like a large dragon" or "he who has a smirk"—a *sghignazzo*; Ciriatto could come from the dialect word *ciro*, "hog"; Farfarello relates to *folletto*, a malevolent spirit or phantom (see *Inf.* XXX, 32); and Rubicante may be "he who grows red" (but since the devils are black, a later variant has "Rabicante"—that is, "the furious one"). More simple are: Barbariccia, the "curly-bearded one"; Cagnazzo, "the big dog"; and Graffiacane, "he who scratches dogs." Whatever the mode of their derivation, these devilish names provide a carnival of sounds.

139 The claim of Barbariccia's trumpet to being the most remarkable martial trumpet in Western literature is not lessened by Canto XXII, 1–12.

CANTO XXII

4 "Aretines" refers to the people of Arezzo, whose cavalry Dante may have seen when the Florentine Guelphs defeated the Ghibellines at Campaldino in 1289.

6 "tournaments": a contest involving squadrons. "jousts": single combat.

7–9 These lines enumerate various kinds of battle signals.

19–21 It was a popular belief in Dante's time that dolphins at play foretell a storm. The point of the simile, however, is the raised backs of the dolphins, rather than their benevolence.

44–45 Little more than his name—Ciampolo—is known of this sinner.

53 Thibault, King of Navarre from 1253 to 1270.

81–82 Fra Gomita of Gallura, chancellor of Nino Visconti. Governor of Sardinia—then a possession of Pisa, which had conquered it from the Saracens—was hanged by his lord when Nino learned that he had accepted bribes to let some prisoners escape.

88 Little that is certain is known about the historical Don Michele Zanche, but it is generally supposed that he was much involved in political intrigues and that he was murdered by his son-in-law Branca Doria in 1275 or 1290 (see XXXIII, 137, 143, notes).

121 The "Navarrese" is Cagnzaao (see 106), who was opposed to Ciampolo's proposal and had evidently prepared to be attacked.

125 That is, Alichino (see 112).

CANTO XXIII

4–18 In a fable Dante would have known as attributed to Aesop, a frog promises to help a mouse cross a river by tying the mouse to him and swimming across. Midway the frog dives underwater to try to kill the mouse. A

hawk flying overhead, however, sees them struggling and, depending on the version Dante was familiar with, swoops down and captures either the frog or both the frog and the mouse. In either case, the treacherous frog is punished. The fable's relevance here may be either to the preceding canto's end, where Calcabrina (frog) and Alichino (mouse) fight until both get stuck in the pool of pitch, or to Virgil's (mouse's) discovery, at the end of this canto, that Malacoda (frog) has lied to him about the bridge over the sixth pouch (136–141).

Critics have pointed out that Dante could not have known at the beginning of Canto XXIII that they would find a broken bridge at its end. He is, however, generally anxious and distrustful of their demonic advisors in Hell (13–18). Dante himself seems to see that the fable he recalls at seeing Calcabrina and Alichino may also apply to his and Virgil's situation (10–12).

22 "a leaded mirror": Lead was the normal backing for mirrors in Dante's time.

47 "a land mill"—rather than the more common type of mill that was set on a raft or a boat, its wheels impelled directly by the current, rather than by the water conveyed through canals or sluices that drove land mills.

63 Cluny is a famous Benedictine monastery in Burgundy. Often cited is a letter from St. Bernard to his nephew—who had left the Cistercians to join the Cluniacs—in which he treats with much irony the Cluniacs' elegant robes.

66 It was said that Frederick II punished traitors by dressing them in capes of lead and throwing them into boiling cauldrons.

95 The "great city" is Florence.

103–108 The Knights of St. Mary, or Jovial Friars (initially not a term of reproach), were a religious order of clergy and laymen, originally formed to maintain peace between political factions, to reconcile families, and to protect the weak against oppressors; but members of the order increasingly neglected their duties in favor of their own pleasure. Loderingo degli Andalò, a Ghibelline, in association with others, founded the order around 1260. Loderingo's joint tenure with Catalano, a Guelph, as chief magistrate of Florence failed in its design to establish peace through bipartisan authority; instead, even greater violence resulted. Gardingo was the area of Florence in which the Uberti, an important Ghibelline family, had their houses. These were destroyed in the renewed fighting between Guelphs and Ghibellines during the tenure of Loderingo and Catalano in 1266.

115 "That one" is Caiaphas, the high priest under Pontius Pilate (see John 11:49–50).

117 The "one man" was Jesus.

122 Caiaphas' father-in-law was Annas, before whom Jesus was brought when He was first arrested (see John 18:13).

140–141 For Malacoda's false account, see Canto XXI, 111.

CANTO XXIV

1–2 The sun is in Aquarius from January 21 to February 21.

4–6 The "white sister" of hoarfrost is, of course, snow—but hoarfrost melts down quickly.

51 This image is taken from the Bible (see Wisdom 5:15. The Book of Wisdom is only in the canon of the Catholic Bible).

86–87 This list of serpents is from Lucan (*Phars.* IX, 710ff).

89 The region near the Red Sea is Arabia.

93 The heliotrope was a legendary stone credited with such miraculous virtues as making its wearers invisible. Boccaccio based one of his famous stories on it (see *Decameron* VIII, 3).

107–111 The details concerning the legendary phoenix are derived from Ovid (*Met.* XV, 392–407). After living for a period of 500 years, the phoenix builds a nest that catches fire; the phoenix dies in flames and is reborn from its own ashes.

124–126 "Mule" means "bastard." The speaker is Vanni Fucci, illegitimate son of Fuccio de' Lazzari of Pistoia.

137–139 The sacristy of the Cathedral of Pistoia was the repository of the treasury of San Jacopo. The innocent Rampino Foresi was jailed and almost executed for the crime, but the guilty parties were discovered in time—though Fucci was able to escape from Pistoia.

143–151 Vanni Fucci prophesies the following events: In 1301 the Blacks of Pistoia were expelled and their houses burned. Finding a sympathetic and crafty champion in Charles of Valois, who had come to Florence ostensibly to keep the peace, the Blacks of Pistoia and Florence were able to renew their attacks on the Whites of Florence, whom they expelled in 1302. Vanni continues his prophecy metaphorically: Mars, god of war, is said to draw forth a vapor whose fiery nature will enter into conflict with the watery clouds around it, causing thunder and lightning—a metaphor that accords with the meterology of the time. The vapor from Val di Magra (145) is the Guelph military leader Moroello Malaspina, who will defeat the Whites—here emblemized as mist (150)—just as lightning breaks through clouds. That defeat of the Whites will take place on Campo Piceno, a generic name for the plain of Pistoia that has its source in a passage from Sallust—which was then misapplied. As for the date of that defeat, the prophecy—somewhat indeterminate—may refer to events in 1302 or 1306.

CANTO XXV

2 A fig is an obscene gesture made by thrusting a protruding thumb between the first and second fingers of a closed fist.

12 Pistoia's "seed" is its founder, Catiline, a traitor against the Roman Republic.

15 That is, Capaneus (see XIV, 46–75; 51–75, note).

19 The Maremma was a region infested with snakes (see XIII, 7–9 and note).

25–33 Cacus, monstrous son of Vulcan, lived in a cave beneath Mount Aventine. He stole the cattle of Hercules, tried to deceive him by leading the cattle backward so as to disguise their path, and was killed by him. (See *Aen.* VIII, 255–351; for the detail of his death, see Ovid, *Fasti* I, 575–576.)

43 Cianfa Donati was a noble Florentine whom early commentators speak of as both a cattle thief and a thief who broke into shops.

45 The common gesture urging silence.

58–60 See Ovid, *Met.* IV, 365 for another ivy simile.

61–63 The serpent (50) is Cianfa. He and his victim, Agnello (68), meld together like two pieces of wax being combined, first mixing their colors (a process described by a further simile in lines 64–66), then fusing into a single body (described in 70–78).

68 Agnello de' Bruelleschi, another noble Florentine thief, was said to have disguised himself to steal more safely and, therefore, to be appropriately disguised in fusing with Cianfa.

70–78 For aspects of fusion here, see the tale of Salmacis and Hermaphroditus in Ovid (*Met.* IV, 274–388, especially 373–388).

86 The navel, through which the fetus takes nourishment.

94–102 While Dante's claim may seem unusually arrogant, he is continuing a common literary *topos* of outdoing. But here Dante claims not only that the metamorphosis of the two sinners he witnesses (103ff.) is more remarkable than anything in ancient writers, but also that his ability to describe it—and, implicitly, to invent it—surpasses theirs.

95 Sabellus and Nasidius, both soldiers in Cato's army, were bitten by poisonous snakes in Libya's desert; Sabellus' body turned into a putrefying, formless mass, and Nasidius swelled until he burst. (See *Phars.* IX, 761–804.)

97–99 Dante's source for these transformations is Ovid's *Metamorphoses*. Cadmus (*Met.* IV, 562–603), the mythical founder of Thebes, was transformed into a serpent, and the nymph Arethusa (*Met.* V, 572–641) was changed into a fountain.

140 The "third soul" is Puccio Sciancato (see 148, note). Buoso may be the nephew of the Buoso Donati whom Gianni Schicchi counterfeits (see *Inf.* XXX, 41–44; 32–45, note).

143–144 A strategically—and somewhat hilariously—placed disclaimer, considering the claims made in lines 94–102 and Dante's bravura in this canto.

148–150 This thief, "the only soul who'd not been changed among the three," is Puccio Sciancato, of the noble Ghibelline family of Galigai.

151   The "other one" has been seen above, coming on as "a blazing little serpent" (82–85); with the reference to Gaville—a small town near Florence—he becomes identifiable, for early commentators, as Francesco de' Cavalcanti, known as Guercio ("squinting"). When the people of Gaville murdered him, his family avenged his death so thoroughly that almost no one was, reportedly, left in Gaville.

CANTO XXVI

1–3   Canto XXVI opens with an ironic rendering of the inscription on the facade of the city hall of Florence.

7–9   According to some ancient and much medieval literary tradition, early morning dreams come true.

9   Some say that the city of Prato "craved" misfortune for Florence, for, like other smaller cities, it could not compete with Florentine grandeur. Others say that even Prato, friend of Florence, will turn against her. Still others read "Prato" as Cardinal Niccolò da Prato, who placed Florence under interdict after the failure of his peace-making mission in 1304.

12   Modern commentators have explained this line as follows: Dante's suffering increases the older he grows and the longer he has been anticipating the coming of this just—but painful for him—retribution.

26–28   "The season" is summer; "just when" is dusk.

34–38   "He who was avenged by bears" is Elisha, who is also the witness of Elijah's chariot of fire (II Kings, 2:23–24; 11–12).

52–54   Eteocles and Polynices, twin brothers, were the sons of Oedipus, King of Thebes, and Jocasta. When they forced their father to abdicate, they brought upon themselves his curse—that they would forever be enemies. The curse was realized when their feuding led to the war of the Seven against Thebes. They killed each other and were placed on the same funeral pyre, but the flame from the pyre divided in two as a sign of their undying enmity. (See Statius, *Theb.* XII, 429ff. and Lucan, *Phars.* I, 549–552.)

55–57   Ulysses and Diomedes were two Greek heroes famous for their exploits, combining astuteness and force, during the Trojan War. "To rage" (57) may mean "toward their acts of wrath" or "toward their encounter, through their sin, with God's wrath."

59   The Greeks were enabled to win the war with Troy by building a wooden horse, in which a large military force was concealed. By means of a false prophecy, they persuaded the Trojans to admit the horse through the gates of Troy, and, through this "breach"—of both walls and faith—they gained entry to the city of Troy (*Aen.* II, 18–370).

60   The "noble seed" of Rome is Aeneas and his followers.

62   Deïdamia died of grief when Achilles, the leading warrior of the Greeks, yielding to the persuasion of Ulysses, abandoned her and his son to take part in the war against Troy.

63   The Palladium was a statue of Pallas Athena believed to protect the city of Troy. Ulysses and Diomedes stole it by fraud and violence (see *Aen.* II, 228–240).

73–75   These lines may refer to a popular conception of the Greeks as haughty and disdainful of more "barbaric" cultures than their own; or to the fact that Virgil is an ancient, like Ulysses and Diomedes, whereas Dante is a modern (in the following canto Virgil asks Dante to answer a fellow modern and fellow Italian; see XXVII, 33).

85   The "greater" (or taller) flame is Ulysses.

91–93   The legendary enchantress, Circe, who lived near the Gulf of Gaeta, transformed men into beasts. Ulysses and his companions, encountering her on their way home from Troy, were changed into swine—though Ulysses forced her to change them back. He then stayed with her for another year. (See Ovid, *Met.* XIV, 435–440, for the account—as told to Aeneas—of one of Ulysses' companions who stayed even longer.)

   Aeneas founded Gaeta and named it for his nurse, Caieta, who died there. (See *Aen.* VII, 1–5; *Met.* XIV, 441ff.)

96   Penelope, the wife of Ulysses, remained faithful to him throughout the years of his wandering.

97–99   See Horace, *Ars Poetica,* 141–142, for the translation of the opening lines of the Odyssey that may have echoed for Dante.

106–117   Two promontories, called "The Pillars of Hercules," were formed at the western end of the Mediterranean when Hercules split a mountain in two. These pillars marked the farthest boundary of the world, beyond which no man could sail and hope to remain alive. Ulysses, however, crossed these limits out of his longing to explore the world "which lies beyond the sun."

110   Ceüta was on the African side when one headed westward toward and through the Straits of Gibraltar.

127–129   They had crossed the equator and could see only the stars of the southern hemisphere.

133–135   Most probably, the Mount of Purgatory, the solitary island mountain, scene of Dante's *Purgatorio* and, for him, the only land mass in the southern hemisphere.

141   That is, as God decreed.

CANTO XXVII

7–12   Perillus, the Athenian artisan, constructed a bronze bull to be used as an instrument of torture by Phalaris, the 6th-century tyrant of Agrigentum in Sicily. The screams of the roasting victims echoing in the metal were supposed to sound like the bellowing of the bull. The architect was repaid for his ingenuity by becoming the bull's first victim. (See Ovid, *Tristia,* III, xi, 39–54; and for 7–8, see Ovid's *Art of Love* I, 653–656. Orosius and Valerius Maximus may also have served Dante.)

19–30   The speaker is Guido da Montefeltro (c1220–1298), from the region of Romagna. Guido was a renowned Ghibelline leader whose conversion Dante had praised as exemplary in his *Convivio* (IV, xxviii, 8). Guido quotes the words (21) Virgil used to send away Ulysses and Diomedes (3).

20   In the Middle Ages, Lombardy was the name used to indicate Northern Italy. Since Virgil was born in Mantua, he was, geographically speaking, a Lombard. And since Dante believed that the Italian dialects went back to not-too dissimilar dialects used in the time of Virgil, he has Virgil speaking the local dialect of Italian used in Lombardy.

41–42   The "eagle of Polenta" was the coat of arms of the Polenta family. This noble family ruled Ravenna and the small city of Cervia after 1275, when Guido da Polenta the Elder, father of Francesca da Rimini, took power.

43–45   Forlì, besieged by both French and Guelph troops sent by Pope Martin IV in 1282, broke the siege and decimated the French troops under the leadership of Guido da Montefeltro. The "green paws" were the coat of arms of the Ordelaffi family, new tyrants who ruled Forlì in 1300.

46   The mastiffs were Malatesta and Malatestino da Verrucchio, lords of Rimini. Both were cruel tyrants who killed Montagna de' Parcitati, head of the Ghibelline party in Rimini.

49–51   The cities of Faenza and Imola, on the Lamone and Santerno rivers respectively, were under the rule of Maghinardo Pagani da Susinana, whose coat of arms displayed the figure of a lion on a white ground. He was a Ghibelline by birth, but with respect to Florence acted as a Guelph.

52–54   Cesena, the city on the Savio, existed as a free municipality during this period, although its politics were dominated by Galasso da Montefeltro, Guido's cousin. Thus it enjoyed considerably more freedom than most cities.

61–66   T.S. Eliot brought these lines into prominence for English readers by using them (in Italian) as an epigraph to "The Love Song of J. Alfred Prufrock."

67   Guido began as a leader of the Ghibellines in Boniface's struggle against rebellious cardinals; later, toward the end of his life, in 1296, he made peace with the Pope and entered the Franciscan order, whose members wore robes belted with rope cords; he died in the monastery of Assisi in 1298.

70   "the Highest Priest": Pope Boniface VIII.

85   "The prince of the new Pharisees" is Boniface.

86   The Lateran Palace was the papal residence. Dante is here alluding to the feud between Pope Boniface—who belonged to the Caetani family—and the Colonna family and faction, who were contesting the legitimacy of Celestine V's abdication and, thus, of the election of Boniface as Pope.

89   The city of Acre, the last Christian possession in the Holy Land, was taken by the Saracens in 1291.

90   All Christians were prohibited from trading with the Saracens.

94–96   According to legend, the Emperor Constantine, having been af-

flicted with leprosy for his persecution of Christians, had a dream one night in which St. Peter and St. Paul advised him to seek out Pope Sylvester on Mount Soracte, where Sylvester had fled for refuge. Acting on this vision, Constantine was baptized by Sylvester, and his leprosy was immediately cured. Guido's "counsel" (98) suggested a considerably more sinister cure for Boniface's "fever" (97)—the Colonna family (see 100–111, note).

100–111 Pope Boniface wished to crush the Colonna family, whose stronghold was the castle at Penestrino or Palestrina, a town southeast of Rome. He persuaded Guido to give him ruthless advice in this affair by assuring him of an official—but in fact unholy and invalid—papal absolution, no matter how evil his counsel. Acting on Guido's advice, Boniface offered the Colonnas unconditional amnesty if they surrendered; but when they did so, he razed Palestrina to the ground.

103–104 The "two keys" are the keys of condemnation and absolution (see Matt. 16:19).

105 The "predecessor" was the ascetic Pope Celestine V, who was frightened into abdicating when Boniface depicted the sins invariably connected with holding public office. (See III, 59–60, note.)

113 "black cherubim": ironically, devils.

120 The law of contradiction is a basic principle of Aristotelian logic: to repent of one's sin and to want to commit it at the same time is a self-contradiction.

CANTO XXVIII

8 Puglia—the Latin "Apulia" in the Middle Ages—designated, not only the present-day region, but the whole of southern Italy. All the battles mentioned in subsequent lines took place in that area.

9 Lazio, scene of the Trojans' wars in Italy, seems too far north even for an extended concept of Apulia. Dante may be using the term "Trojans" to mean their Roman descendants and referring to the Samnite wars of 343–290 B.C. and the Tarentine wars of 280–274 B.C.

11–12 According to Livy's *History* (XXXIII, xii, 1–2), during the Second Punic War (219–202 B.C.). Hannibal brought to Carthage a pile of gold rings taken from the fingers of slaughtered Romans.

14 Robert Guiscard (1015–1085), a Norman adventurer, fought the Greeks and Saracens in southern Italy.

16 Ceperano was a small town in southeastern Lazio, located at a strategic pass on the border between the Papal States and the Kingdom of Naples and Sicily, which the barons of Apulia were pledged to defend for Manfred, the natural son of Frederick II. Despite this pledge, they betrayed Manfred and allowed free passage into Naples to the troops of Charles of Anjou, who subsequently killed Manfred in the battle of Benevento (1266), a crucial defeat for the Ghibelline cause.

17–18 In 1268, at Tagliacozzo, Manfred's nephew Conradin was defeated by Charles of Anjou, who was following the advice of his general, Erard ("Alardo") de Valery. "Old Alardo"'s strategy involved the surprise use of reserve troops.

31 In Dante's time Mohammed (570–632), founder of Islam, was believed by some to be an apostate Christian. Whether or not Dante held this belief, he certainly thought of Mohammed as a "sower of dissension" (35)—that is, of religious disunity.

32 Alì, Mohammed's nephew, was one of the first followers of Mohammed and married his daughter, Fatima. His claim to succession to the caliphate was contested; the argument divided Islam into two sects, the Sunnites and the Shiites.

55–60 In 1300 Fra Dolcino was head of a reformist order known as the Apostolic Brothers—a sect pronounced heretical and condemned to extirpation by Clement V for its beliefs in the communality of goods and women. Fra Dolcino and his followers took to the hills between Vercelli and Novara but were forced by starvation to surrender. Many, including Dolcino and his mistress, were burned alive at Vercelli in 1307.

73 Nothing is known of the historical Pier da Medicina. According to early commentators, he was a habitual sower of discord, especially between the Polenta and Malatesta families.

75 The town of Medicina lies in the Po Valley between Vercelli and Marcabò.

76–90 The "foul tyrant" (81) who "sees only with one eye" (85) is Malatestino (see XXVII, 46, and note). He called Guido del Cassero and Angiolello di Carignano, two nobles of Fano, to a parley at the coastal town of La Cattolica, and then had them thrown overboard on their way—probably to facilitate his take-over of their city.

82 Cyprus, at the eastern end of the Mediterranean, and Majorca, at the western end, together signify the whole of the Mediterranean.

83 Neptune is the god of the sea.

84 The Argives are, literally, natives of Argos; the name is given to all Greeks.

89–90 Their drowning abrogated the need to pray for safety while navigating the treacherously windy headlands of Focara between La Cattolica and Pesaro.

96–102 Caius Curio was bribed by Caesar to leave Pompey's party and betray his former friends. Dante follows Lucan's account (*Phars.* I, 279–281), making Curio responsible for having "quenched the doubt in Caesar" about crossing the Rubicon and invading the Roman Republic.

106–109 In 1215 the Ghibelline Mosca de' Lamberti renewed feuding with the Guelphs when he urged the Amidei family to kill the Guelph Buondelmonte dei Buondelmonti for breaking his engagement to one of their daughters. Some 60 years later the Ghibelline Lamberti family was ex-

iled from Florence. For Dante's earlier query concerning Mosca, see note to Canto VI, 77–84.

134–38 Bertran de Born (c1140–c1215), nobleman, soldier, and finally monk, is best known as one of the earliest troubadour poets. A Provençal biography notes that King Henry II believed Bertran had instigated the rebellion of his son, Prince Henry, "the fledgling king," much as King David's counsellor Achitophel incited Absalom, David's son, to rebel against his father (see II *Samuel* 15–17:23).

142 See Canto III, 52–69, and note.

CANTO XXIX

8–9 Dante's reason for specifying 22 miles for the circuit of this pouch and 11 miles for the next (XXX, 86) is not known with certainty. But the figures certainly reinforce the credibility of Dante's narrative.

10–11 Since the moon is below them, the sun—at the zenith of Jerusalem, which lies directly above Hell—is directly overhead when the moon is full. The moon was at the full two days earlier, however (see XX, 127); and since the moon loses about 50 minutes per day on the sun, the sun is now at a point close to 2 P.M. The journey to the center of Hell lasts 24 hours; a little over 4 hours are therefore left.

20–36 Geri del Bello, son of Bello di Alighiero I, was first cousin to Dante's father and a notorious troublemaker. It would seem that he was killed by a member of the Sacchetti family; that his death was avenged by the Alighieri in 1310; and that the Alighieri and the Sacchetti families feuded until 1342, when they signed an act of reconciliation in Florence.

28–29 Dante was talking with Bertran de Born, Lord of Hautefort Castle (see XXVIII, 134).

31–33 In Dante's time, vengeance by relatives—"anyone who shares his name"—was permitted by law.

41 "Lay brothers" is a bitter metaphor for the damned souls associated with the "cloister" of the previous line.

47 The river valley of Val di Chiana, the region of Maremma, and the island of Sardinia, were all plagued by malaria.

58–64 Ovid (*Met.* VII, 523–660) tells the story of Aegina, a nymph ravished by Jupiter, and the island their son Aeacus named for her. The jealous Juno infested the island with a pestilence that killed all its inhabitants except for Aeacus. Jupiter—answering the prayers of Aeacus—repopulated the island by turning ants into men; the islanders were then called Myrmidons, after the Greek for ant.

109–120 The "one" who answers is Griffolino of Arezzo, who cheated the gullible Albero of Siena of a large sum of money by promising to teach him the art of Daedalus—flying. (For Daedalus, see XVII, 109–111 and note.) Griffolino seems to have selected the wrong dupe, however, for Albero was a

favorite—and may have been the illegitimate son—of the Bishop of Siena, who had Griffolino burned at the stake on a charge of heresy. But it is for alchemy that Griffolino is now in this pouch of Hell.

125–132   Dante lists a group of young people from Siena who were living examples of vanity and profligacy. They were members of the "Spendthrift Club" (see XIII, 118, note), a group of young noblemen who reveled in squandering their estates. Several of them were soon reduced to poverty and ridicule.

136–137   Capocchio, a Florentine or Sienese, was burned at the stake as an alchemist in 1293. Early anecdotes celebrate his inventiveness in every kind of imitation.

CANTO XXX

1–12   Semele was the daughter of Cadmus, King of Thebes. Juno was incensed with her because she had been loved by Jupiter and had borne him Bacchus, patron of Thebes. Juno took vengeance on Thebes by driving Athamas, husband of Semele's sister Ino, to madness. Insane, Athamas thought Ino and their two sons were a lioness and two cubs; he killed his son Learchus, and Ino drowned herself and her other son, Melicertes. (See Ovid, *Met.* IV, 512–530.)

16–21   After the fall of Troy, Queen Hecuba went insane when, enslaved by the victorious Greeks, she saw her daughter Polyxena sacrificed on Achilles' tomb and later saw the unburied body of her son Polydorus, murdered by his uncle, Polymnestor, King of Thrace. Ovid tells that, in her madness, Hecuba howled like a dog and leaped into the sea (*Met.* XIII, 404–575).

28   Capocchio is mentioned in Canto XXIX (136–139; see 136, note).

31   The Aretine is Griffolino d'Arezzo, mentioned above (see XXIX, 109–120 and note).

32–45   Gianni Schicchi (who died before 1280) of the Cavalcanti family of Florence, was renowned—and here punished—for impersonation. At the request of Simone Donati, Gianni impersonated Simone's uncle, Buoso Donati, who had just died, and dictated a new will in Simone's favor. Gianni took the opportunity to bequeath to himself Buoso's best mare or she-mule ("the lady of the herd")—or so Dante would have it.

37–41   Myrrha was the daughter of Cinyras, king of Cyprus. Overpowered by an incestuous passion for her father, she impersonated another woman and slept with him. When he discovered her deception, the King was going to kill her, but she fled, and the gods transformed her into a myrrh tree. From this incestuous union Adonis was born (see Ovid, *Met.* X, 298–502).

52–57   Dante's description follows closely the medical science of his time.

61–90   Master Adam was possibly an Englishman who came to Bologna after a stay in Brescia. He counterfeited the gold coin of Florence for the Guidi, counts of Romena, a town in the Casentino region near Florence. Like the Florentine coins, his were stamped with the image of the city's patron saint,

John the Baptist; but unlike them, they contained 21, rather than 24, carats of gold. He was burned at the stake, the penalty for falsifiers, in 1281 (75).

78 Since part of his punishment is thirst, drinking from the Fonte ("fountain") Branda, possibly the famous fountain of Siena, would indeed be welcome to Master Adam.

79 "One of them" is Guido II of Romena, who had died as early as 1292.

86 Half the circumference of the Ninth Pouch in the preceding canto (see XXIX, 8–9, and note).

97 The wife of Potiphar falsely accused Joseph of trying to seduce her after Joseph had, in fact, rejected her advances (Gen. 39:7–19).

98 Sinon convinced the Trojans to bring the wooden horse into Troy (see XXVI, 59, and note).

129 The mirror of Narcissus is water. According to Ovid (*Met.* III, 407–510), Narcissus fell in love with his own image reflected in a pool and, consumed by this futile passion, faded away until he was transformed into the narcissus flower.

CANTO XXXI

4 Achilles' father, Peleus, gave him a lance that had the power to heal any wound it inflicted simply by being placed on the wound again. (See Ovid, *Met.* XIII, 171–172.) Poets from the 13th century through to Petrarch used this lance as metaphor for the kiss and gaze of the beloved.

16–18 Dante refers to the episode in the French epic *La Chanson de Roland* that describes the annihilation of Charlemagne's rear guard at Roncesvalles. Although too late, Roland blew his horn so loudly that Charlemagne returned to avenge his men.

40–41 Montereggioni, a fortress surrounded by a wall with 14 towers, was built by the Sienese in 1213 to defend Siena against the attacks of Florence.

43–45 When the Giants tried to attack the gods' home on Mount Olympus, Jove struck them down with lightning bolts. His thundering still frightens the Giants in Hell. For the battle of Phlegra, see XIV, 58.

59 This bronze pine cone, over four meters high, stood outside St. Peter's in Dante's time; today it is in the Vatican.

63 Frieslanders, inhabitants of the northernmost province of the Netherlands, were reputed to be the tallest men of the time.

67–81 Though many attempts have been made to explain Nimrod's words, early commentators regard them as meaningless, and Dante himself states that these are incomprehensible words from a language "no one knows" (81). Whatever may be the case, Nimrod's inability to make himself understood is fitting punishment for his having brought about the confusion of tongues. According to the Bible, it was in Babylon, which Nimrod ruled (Gen. 10:8–10), that the Tower of Babel was built to reach the sky. To thwart such

presumption, God decreed that men would henceforth speak in many languages (Gen. 11:1–9).

71 Nimrod is given a horn here because the Bible describes him as a "mighty hunter before the Lord" (Gen. 10:9).

94–96 The giant Ephialtes and his twin brother Otus were born of Neptune and Iphimedia, wife of the giant Aloeus, who raised the twins as if they were his own sons. The brothers tried to attack Mount Olympus by piling Mount Ossa onto Mount Pelion (though others say they piled Pelion onto Ossa, or both onto Olympus). Virgil had placed both brothers—the "twin sons of Aloeus"—in Tartarus (*Aen.* VI, 771–774).

99 Briareus was another giant who fought against the Olympian gods. Dante follows Statius (*Theb.* II, 596) in describing him rather than following Virgil (*Aen.* VI, 379, and X, 778–781—in the latter he is to be identified with Aegaeon) who represents him with 100 arms and 50 heads.

100–132 Antaeus was a giant who was not born in time to participate in the war against Olympus and is therefore "unfettered." He lived in a cave near the valley of the Bagradas River (see 115–118, note) and ate lions that he captured. Hercules, who once wrestled with him, defeated him by lifting and keeping him off the Earth—the mother of the Giants and the source of their strength (see Lucan, *Phars.* IV, 593–660).

115–118 The valley of the Bagradas River in Tunisia was the site of the decisive battle in the war between Rome and Carthage, where the Roman Scipio defeated Hannibal in 202 B.C.

121 "The sons of earth" are the Giants.

123 The frozen lake of Cocytus is in the Ninth, and last, Circle of Hell.

124 Tityus and Typhon are two more Giants. Tityus was cast into Tartarus for trying to rape Latona, mother of Apollo and Diana (see *Aen.* VI, 789–796; Ovid, *Met.* IV, 456–458). Typhon was punished for attacking the Olympian gods at the urging of his mother, Earth. (See Lucan, *Phars.* IV, 593–97.)

136–138 Garisenda is one of the leaning towers of Bologna. When a cloud passes over the tower, moving opposite the direction of the tower's slant, an observer from below receives the illusion that the tower is falling away from the sky.

CANTO XXXII

1–9 To suit the matter he is about to treat, Dante declares the need for a "mixed" style, making use of harsh, cacophonous sounds that he would consider inappropriate for loftier subject matters. (Such topics would be treated in the "high style" of decorous words and harmonious sounds.) But in, and after, declaring his inability to meet the need for ruder sounds, Dante proceeds to fulfill it.

2 The "melancholy hole" is the Ninth Circle, the frozen lake formed by the River Cocytus, a lake that serves as the bottom of Hell.

10–11 The ladies are the Muses, who inspired Amphion to so charm the stones of Mount Cithaeron by playing a lyre that those stones came down and arranged themselves into walls around Thebes. (See Horace, *Ars poetica* 394ff.)

28–29 Mt. Tambernic is possibly Mt. Tambura, close to Mt. Pietrapana in the Apuan Alps.

34–35 "the place where shame can show itself": the face.

36 The harsh, clacking sound of the stork exemplifies the "mixed style" Dante has adopted here (see 1–9, note).

56–57 The Bisenzio River falls into the Arno about 10 miles above Florence. The noble Florentine family of Alberti owned castles in the Bisenzio Valley. When Count Alberto degli Alberti died, his sons Napoleone (a Ghibelline) and Alessandro (a Guelph) killed each other over politics and their inheritance at some time between 1282 and 1286.

59 Caïna, the first of four subdivisions of Cocytus, takes its name from Cain, who murdered his brother Abel. Those who betrayed their relatives are punished here.

61–62 Dante is referring to Mordred, nephew of King Arthur, who tried to kill his uncle and take over England. When Arthur pierced Mordred's body with a lance, a ray of sunlight, passing through the large wound, was seen in Mordred's shadow. Both the French *Histoire de Lancelot du lac* and the Italian version record this legend.

62 Vanni de' Cancellieri, nicknamed Focaccia, a particularly violent noble White Guelph of Pistoia, treacherously killed his cousin, Detto de' Cancellieri.

65 Sassol Mascheroni, of the noble Florentine family of Toschi, murdered a relative.

68–69 Camiscion de' Pazzi, a Ghibelline, murdered Ubertino, a relative, to gain control of some fortresses they held in common. Carlino, of the same family and still living in 1300, later betrayed the Whites by giving the Castle of Piantravigne into the hands of the Blacks. As a traitor to his party, he is punished more harshly than Camiscion, whose fault, by comparison, appears less grave; thus Camiscion's expectation that Carlino will "absolve him."

78 This "one" is identified as Bocca degli Abati in line 106 (see note).

88 Antenora is the second subdivision of Cocytus, named after Antenor, the Trojan warrior who betrayed his city to the Greeks. In this section those who committed acts of treachery against their country, city, or political party are punished.

106 Bocca degli Abati, a noble Guelph of Florence, is said to have betrayed his party, cutting off the hand of the Guelph standard bearer during the battle against Manfred's troops at Montaperti in 1260. At the loss of their rallying banner, the Guelphs panicked and were defeated by the Ghibellines.

115–117 Buoso da Duera, a Ghibelline, lord of Soncino and later of Cremona, betrayed Manfred, King of Naples, whom other Ghibelline lords had agreed to protect from the French. In 1265 Charles of Anjou—or possibly his wife—bribed Buoso to allow the French troops free passage into Parma on their way to Naples.

119–120 Tesauro dei Beccheria, a Ghibelline of Pavia, was Abbot of Vallombrosa and Pope Alexander IV's legate in Florence. He was accused of treason by the Florentine Guelphs and was beheaded in 1258.

121 Gianni de' Soldanieri, a noble Ghibelline of Florence, was a traitor to his own party, joining the Guelphs after Manfred's death in 1266 occasioned a popular rebellion against the Ghibellines.

122 Ganelon betrayed the rear guard of Charlemagne at Roncesvalles (see XXXI, 16–18, and note).

122–123 Tebaldello, of the Zambrasi family of Faenza, was a Ghibelline, but to avenge himself against the Lambertazzi—the exiled Ghibelline family of Bologna who had taken refuge in Faenza—he opened the gates of Faenza to Guelph enemies from Bologna. The date of his treachery was November 13, 1280.

130–131 Tydeus, one of the Seven against Thebes, was mortally wounded by Menalippus but killed him before he himself died; in a fit of madness he gnawed at his enemy's scalp. (See Statius, *Theb.* VIII, 716ff.)

CANTO XXXIII

13–75 Ugolino della Gherardesca (born in the first decades of the 13th century), Count of Donoratico, a Ghibelline, was exiled from the Ghibelline city of Pisa in 1275 for plotting. He returned a year later with the help of the Florentine Guelphs and regained his wealth and position. In 1284 he became chief magistrate of Pisa after its defeat in the war against Genoa. To save Pisa from Guelph threats, he negotiated with the cities of Florence and Lucca and ceded three castles to them, a politic action that his enemies regarded as a betrayal.

In 1285 Ugolino's grandson, the Guelph Nino Visconti, was called to share the office of chief magistrate with his Ghibelline grandfather. But the two men fell to feuding and were forced out of office in 1288. At this point Dante seems to follow a version of events that would have Ugolino, who then was outside Pisa, returning to the city in response to the invitation of the Ghibelline Archbishop Ruggieri, who promised Ugolino reconciliation with those who had forced him out of office. But the Archbishop betrayed Ugolino, imprisoning him together with his sons Gaddo and Uguiccione and his grandsons Nino (nicknamed "Brigata"—and not to be confused with the other Nino above) and Anselm. For nine months they were kept in the tower of the Gualandi, and in March 1289 the Archbishop ordered the tower locked up and the keys thrown into the river.

22 The tower of the Gualandi, which served as a prison through 1318, was

called the Eagles' Tower because the commune kept its eagles there when they were changing plumage.

28–36 In Ugolino's dream, "this man" is Archbishop Ruggieri, who, with the Ghibelline families named in line 33, hunts down and kills Ugolino and his sons—the "wolf" and the "whelps" of line 29.

30 Mount San Giuliano lies between Pisa and Lucca.

69 See Matt. 27:46, "My God, my God, why hast Thou forsaken me?"

75 Both the Italian and this translation of line 75 allow the possibility that Ugolino cannibalized his children; but neither decides unequivocally for that as against the less horrifying reading.

79–80 Just as northern France was the land of *oïl* and Provence the land of *oc,* Italy is "that fair land where *sì*"—its word for "yes"—"is heard."

82 Caprara and Gorgona, which belonged to Pisa, are two islands northeast of Corsica along a horizontal sight line extending from the mouth of the Arno.

91 They passed into the third subdivision of Cocytus: Ptolomea (124), most probably named after Ptolemy, governor of Jericho, who killed Simon, his father-in-law and high priest, and two of his sons while they were dining with him (see I Maccabees 16:11–17, in the Catholic Bible). In Ptolomea, those who have betrayed their guests are punished. It is less likely that Ptolomea is named for Ptolemy XII of Egypt (51–47 B.C.), who was probably responsible for the murder of Pompey.

103–105 Since the sun's heat was thought to cause wind, Dante wonders why he feels wind in this cold place.

118–120 Fra Alberigo was a member of the Guelph Manfredi family of Faenza. In 1267 he joined the Jovial Friars (see XXIII, 103–108, and note). He killed his relative Manfredo and Manfredo's son during a banquet in his house, signaling his assassins with an order to bring the fruit. Fra Alberigo is saying that he was punished more severely than he deserved (a date is more valuable than a fig).

124 See 91, note.

126 Atropos, one of the three Fates, cut the thread at the moment of someone's death.

137 Branca Doria, member of the famous Ghibelline family of Genoa, murdered his father-in-law, Michele Zanche—whom Dante encountered among the barrators in Canto XXIII—during a banquet (see XXII, 88, and note). His cohort in this assassination was "a kinsman" of his (145–146).

142–146 Even before the murdered Michele Zanche reached his place among those damned in the Fifth Pouch of Malebolge, a demon entered the body of his murderer, Branca Doria. The demon expelled Doria's soul, flinging it down to Cocytus. Thus, Doria's soulless body still lives on earth; but, in a piece of mordant comic invention, his soul is already in Hell. What is true

of his body and soul is also true of his "kinsman, who had done the treachery together with him," and of others in Ptolomea (124–126).

154   That is, Fra Alberigo.

155   That is, Branca Doria.

CANTO XXXIV

1   "The banners of the king of Hell draw closer." The first three Latin words are the opening lines of a famous hymn written by Venantius Fortunatus, Bishop of Poitiers, in the 6th century. The hymn is sung at Vespers on September 14, the feast of the Exaltation of the Holy Cross, and—more to the purpose—on the Saturday before Passion Sunday through to Maundy Thursday.

18   That is, Lucifer, meaning "light bearer," the most beautiful of all the angels before he rebelled against God and was renamed Satan.

20   Dis, a name for Pluto in the *Aeneid* (VI, 358 and 524—though translated in 524 as "Pluto") is given by Dante to Lucifer (see note to VIII, 68).

39   Satan's three faces are a grotesque counterversion of the three Persons of the Trinity.

58–63   The "forward" or foremost sinner is Judas Iscariot, the Apostle who betrayed Christ.

64–67   Marcus Junius Brutus conspired with Gaius Cassius Longus to assassinate Julius Caesar in 44 B.C. Both were suicides in 42 B.C. after the defeat at Philippi. Dante's description of Cassius as "robust" troubles some commentators.

78–93   Virgil and Dante are passing through the earth's center by climbing halfway down Satan's body and then making a 180-degree turn in order to climb up the other half. Their turning marks the passage from the northern hemisphere (thought of as the hemisphere of land) to the southern hemisphere (considered the hemisphere of water). As Dante sees it, the top half of Lucifer's body is in the northern hemisphere. Therefore, when Virgil, with Dante on his back, turns himself around into the other hemisphere, Dante becomes confused, completely losing his sense of direction.

Where this translation has "his legs" in line 79 as Virgil's, some commentators see those legs as Lucifer's.

95   "The way is long"—that is, it takes between 21 and 22 hours to ascend through the southern half of the earth's interior before they can reach the shore of the Mountain of Purgatory before dawn of the following day, Easter Sunday. Thus this portion of their journey is almost as long as their 24-hour journey through Hell. (But remember that, in their passage to the southern hemisphere, Dante and Virgil will have regained 12 hours of the 21 to 22 hours their journey from earth's center to Purgatory took.) Dante stays on the Mountain of Purgatory until noon of Wednesday, April 13, when he crosses into Paradise.

96   About 7:30 A.M. In Hell the sun is never referred to in telling the time of the journey. But now that Dante and Virgil have left Hell, the sun is used for that purpose. Because night has begun in the northern hemisphere, the sun has risen in the southern hemisphere, where the poets now find themselves.

109–120   Virgil tells Dante that they have passed through the center of the universe and of gravity from the northern hemisphere of land to the southern hemisphere of water. The sun, which had just been leaving the upper half of the world, is now appearing in the lower half, so that Virgil and Dante have moved from a place where "night is come again" (68) to a place of morning: they have come back to the time of Holy Saturday morning.

112–115   That is, they are directly opposite Jerusalem, where Christ was born and died; Jerusalem was believed to be exactly under the zenith and in the center of the northern hemisphere.

116–117   The last subdivision of the Ninth Circle, where traitors are punished, was named Judecca by Dante, after Judas Iscariot, who committed the greatest betrayal of all.

121–126   When Lucifer was thrown down from Heaven, he fell into the southern hemisphere, whose land, frightened by the falling of Lucifer, drew away to the north. Lucifer crashed through the water into the center of the earth and remained fixed there. But in order to avoid contact with him, the land that formed part of the ball of the earth through which Lucifer crashed recoiled back into the southern hemisphere. There it formed the only land mass in the waters, the island mountain crowned by the Earthly Paradise. Its lower slopes were later made to serve as the terraces of Purgatory, Dante's next destination.

128   Beelzebub is the name given in the Gospels to the chief of all devils. (See Matt. 10:25; 12:24; 27; Mark 3:22; Luke 11:15; 18.)

130   The stream is probably Lethe, whose run-off descends from Purgatory, carrying down to Hell the sins that have been washed away (*Purg.* XXVIII, 130).

139   As he does in *Purgatorio* and *Paradiso,* Dante ends the *Inferno* with the word "stars." Since Homer's "stars shining clear in the windless air, around the gleaming moon...when all the stars are visible, and glad, the shepherd's heart" (and, some scrutinists claim, long before Homer), stars have been a staple of the "natural" sublime; but they can also bequeath their light to the transnatural sublime, pointing to their Maker.

The foregoing translation and brief annotations are much indebted to the exegetes cited in the Introduction to this volume, as well as to many earlier commentators. Recent publications that have been consulted throughout are:

The *Enciclopedia Dantesca,* the six-volume work directed by Umberto Bosco, with Giorgio Petrocchi and (from Vol. IV on) Ignazio Baldelli as general editors, Rome, 1970–1978. The first five volumes are ordered alphabetically. The sixth volume includes: Petrocchi's biography of Dante; a unique

collective series of essays on the language and style of Dante; a bibliography; and the texts of all of Dante's works—and works that may be Dante's. The *E.D.* is one of the finest examples of a collective scholarly-critical enterprise that our times have produced, but the special bibliographical section in Vol. VI is much less cogent and complete than many of the separate bibliographies at the end of the alphabetically-ordered entries.

Francesco Mazzoni's edition of the commentaries of Tommasso Casini-Silvio Adrasto Barbi (the latter revising the former after Casini's death in 1917) and of Attilio Momigliano: Dante Alighieri, *La Divina Commedia: Inferno,* Florence, 1972. Mazzoni has careful bibliographical indications and brief but precious exegetical updates on each canto of the *Inferno.*

Essays on the individual cantos of the *Inferno* are to be found far beyond the range of the principal collective volumes—or pamphlet collections—of *Inferno* readings. But the following compilations (with their separate essays on each canto, in the Lectura Dantis format that the *California Lectura Dantis* volumes, now in progress, will follow) have been both convenient and particularly helpful:

Letture dantesche: Inferno, ed. Giovanni Getto, Florence, 1955 (now in the 1965 single-volume edition of the three *cantiche*(; *Lectura Dantis Scaligera: Inferno,* ed. Mario Marcazzan, Florence, 1967; the separate pamphlets of the *Lectura Dantis Romana,* ed. Giovanni Fallani, Turin, 1959–1967; the first three volumes of the *Nuove letture dantesche* of the Casa di Dante di Roma, Florence, 1966–1969; *Inferno,* ed. Silvio Zennaro, Rome, 1977; *Letture dell'Inferno,* ed. Vittorio Vettori, Milan, 1963; and readings of *Inferno* cantos scattered through Vols. II–VII of the eight volumes of the *Letture Classensi,* Ravenna, 1969–1979.

The notes themselves make abbreviated references to several exegetes. These references are here expanded to include the work referred to and, where the reference is not *ad locum* (to the same place in the *Inferno* at which the exegete is cited in these notes), page numbers:

Boccaccio: Giovanni Boccaccio, *Esposizioni sopra la Comedia di Dante,* ed. Giorgio Padoan, Vol. VI of *Tutte le opere di Giovanni Boccaccio,* ed. Vittorio Branca, Milan, 1965. References to Boccaccio are *ad loc.*

Bosco-Reggio: Umberto Bosco and Giovanni Reggio, eds., Dante Alighieri, *La Divina Commedia: Inferno.* Florence, 1979. References to Bosco-Reggio are *ad loc.*

Chimenz: Siro A. Chimenz, ed., Dante Alighieri, *La Divina Commedia: Inferno,* Turin, 1963. References to Chimenz are *ad loc.*

Freccero: John Freccero, "Dante's Firm Foot and the Journey without a Guide," *The Harvard Theological Review,* 52 (1959), pp. 254–281.

Hollander: Robert Hollander, *Allegory in Dante's "Commedia,"* Princeton, 1969, pp. 84–86.

Mazzoni: Francesco Mazzoni, *Saggio di un nuovo commento alla*

"Divina Commedia": Inferno, Canti I–III, Florence, 1967. References to Mazzoni are *ad loc.*

Pagliaro: Antonio Pagliaro, *Ulisse: Ricerche semantiche sulla "Divina Commedia,"* 2 vols., Messina-Florence, 1969, Vol. II, pp. 516–519.

Porena: Manfredi Porena, ed., *La Divina Commedia di Dante Alighieri: Inferno,* Bologna, 1966. The reference is *ad loc.*

Ragonese: Gaetano Ragonese, in the entry on *"fiera,"* in *E.D.,* the *Enciclopedia Dantesca* (see above), Vol. II, p. 860.

Sarolli: Gian-Roberto Sarolli in an unpublished manuscript.

Singleton: Charles S. Singleton, "In exitu Israel de Aegypto," in *Dante: A Collection of Critical Essays,* ed. John Freccero, Englewood Cliffs, 1965; pp. 102–121, for the reference in the note to Canto I, 22–25.

                 Charles S. Singleton, translator and commentator, Dante Alighieri, *The Divine Comedy: Inferno.2. Commentary,* Princeton, 1970, pp. 244–248 (but it is *ad loc.),* for the reference in the note to Canto XIV, 115–129.

ALLEN MANDELBAUM's five verse volumes are: *Chelmaxions; The Savantasse of Montparnasse; Journeyman; Leaves of Absence;* and *A Lied of Letterpress.* His volumes of verse translation include *The Aeneid of Virgil,* a University of California Press volume (now available from Bantam) for which he won a National Book Award; the *Inferno, Purgatorio,* and *Paradiso* volumes of the California Dante (now available from Bantam); *The Odyssey of Homer* (now available from Bantam); *The Metamorphoses of Ovid,* a finalist for the Pulitzer Prize in poetry; *Ovid in Sicily; Selected Poems of Giuseppe Ungaretti; Selected Writings of Salvatore Quasimodo;* and *David Maria Turoldo.* Mandelbaum is co-editor with Robert Richardson Jr. of *Three Centuries of American Poetry* (Bantam Books) and, with Yehuda Amichai, of the eight volumes of the JPS Jewish Poetry Series. After receiving his Ph.D. from Columbia, he was in the Society of Fellows at Harvard. While chairman of the Ph.D. program in English at the Graduate Center of CUNY, he was a visiting profesor at Washington University in St. Louis, and at the universities of Houston, Denver, Colorado, and Purdue. His honorary degrees are from Notre Dame University, Purdue Unversity, the University of Assino, and the University of Torino. He received the Gold Medal of Honor from the city of Florence in 2000, celebrating the 735th anniversary of Dante's birth, the only translator to be so honored; and in 2003 he received the President of Italy's award for translation. He is now Professor of the History of Literary Criticism at the University of Turin and the W. R. Kenan Professor of Humanities at Wake Forest University.

Born in Chattanooga in 1940, **BARRY MOSER** was educated at Auburn University, the University of Tennessee at Chattanooga, and the University of Massachusetts, where he did his graduate studies. His work as illustrator, designer, and printer, which includes the books of Pennyroyal Press, is represented in numerous collections, museums, and libraries in the United States and abroad, among them, the British Museum, the Library of Congress, the New York Public Library, the National Library of Australia, the London College of Printing, the Houghton Library at Harvard University, the Bienecke Library at Yale University, and the Firestone Library at Princeton University. Mr. Moser's illustrated books form a list of over sixty titles, including the Arion Press *Moby Dick,* the University of California Press edition of this translation of *The Divine Comedy*, and the Limited Editions Club of New York edition of Homer's *Odyssey*. The Pennyroyal *Alice's Adventures in Wonderland* was awarded the American Book Award for design/pictorial excellence. An associate of the National Academy of Design, Mr. Moser frequently lectures and acts as visiting artist at universities and institutions across the country. His most ambitious work, the heralded Pennyroyal Caxton Bible in two volumes, with 231 engravings, appeared in October 1999.

ASK YOUR BOOKSELLER FOR THESE BANTAM CLASSICS

BABBITT, Sinclair Lewis, 0-553-21486-1

MAIN STREET, Sinclair Lewis, 0-553-21451-9

THE CALL OF THE WILD and WHITE FANG, Jack London, 0-553-21233-8

THE SEA WOLF, Jack London, 0-553-21225-7

TO BUILD A FIRE AND OTHER STORIES, Jack London, 0-553-21335-0

THE PRINCE, Niccolo Machiavelli, 0-553-21278-8

DEATH IN VENICE AND OTHER STORIES, Thomas Mann, 0-553-21333-4

THE COMMUNIST MANIFESTO, Karl Marx & Friedrich Engels,
     0-553-21406-3

OF HUMAN BONDAGE, W. Somerset Maugham, 0-553-21392-X

THE BALLAD OF THE SAD CAFE AND OTHER STORIES, Carson
     McCullers, 0-553-27254-3

THE HEART IS A LONELY HUNTER, Carson McCullers, 0-553-26963-1

THE MEMBER OF THE WEDDING, Carson McCullers, 0-553-25051-5

BILLY BUDD, SAILOR AND OTHER STORIES, Herman Melville,
     0-553-21274-5

MOBY-DICK, Herman Melville, 0-553-21311-3

ON LIBERTY and UTILITARIANISM, John Stuart Mill, 0-553-21414-4

THE ANNOTATED MILTON, John Milton, 0-553-58110-4

THE SCARLET PIMPERNEL, Baroness Emmuska Orczy, 0-553-21402-0

COMMON SENSE, Thomas Paine, 0-553-21465-9

THE DIALOGUES OF PLATO, Plato, 0-553-21371-7

THE TELL-TALE HEART AND OTHER WRITINGS, Edgar Allan Poe,
     0-553-21228-1

CYRANO DE BERGERAC, Edmond Rostand, 0-553-21360-1

IVANHOE, Sir Walter Scott, 0-553-21326-1

THE COMPLETE WORKS OF SHAKESPEARE (25 vols.), William Shakespeare

PYGMALION and MAJOR BARBARA, George Bernard Shaw,
     0-553-21408-X

FRANKENSTEIN, Mary Shelley, 0-553-21247-8

THE JUNGLE, Upton Sinclair, 0-553-21245-1

THE WEALTH OF NATIONS, Adam Smith, 0-553-58597-5

ONE DAY IN THE LIFE OF IVAN DENISOVICH, Alexander Solzhenitsyn,
     0-553-24777-8

THE COMPLETE PLAYS OF SOPHOCLES, Sophocles, 0-553-21354-7

DR. JEKYLL AND MR. HYDE, Robert Louis Stevenson, 0-553-21277-X

KIDNAPPED, Robert Louis Stevenson, 0-553-21260-5

TREASURE ISLAND, Robert Louis Stevenson, 0-553-21249-4

DRACULA, Bram Stoker, 0-553-21271-0

UNCLE TOM'S CABIN, Harriet Beecher Stowe, 0-553-21218-4